Shroud of Doom

Shroud of Doom

Book 2

Tarizon Saga

by

William Manchee

Top Publications, Ltd.

Dedication

The Tarizon Saga is dedicated to my grandchildren, Joshua, Alex, Isabella, Andrew and Travis.

Tarizon: Shroud of Doom
Book 2
Tarizon Saga

Cover Design by Dan Silverman

Top Publications, Ltd.
Dallas, Texas

ISBN 978-1-929976-86-7

NORTHLAND
North Sea
Rigimol
LEMAINE
SHANE
Tributon
Lecton
Serie
Tuht
Synclare
Merria
Emerald Ocean
AZOLLO
TURVIN
Straits of Tributon
TARIZON
Lyon
Quori
Dark Land
Allso
Coral Sea
Lower
Serie
POGO
Tunisu Island
DALO
MUHL
CHALLA
VENTE
OCK MEZAN
N
RENNA
VENTE
W
E
Duci
Talo
Morissee
Beet Islands
LOWER
AZOLLO
Ledium
LORTEC
S
Dark Sea
Queenland
Southern Sea
GLACIER DOME

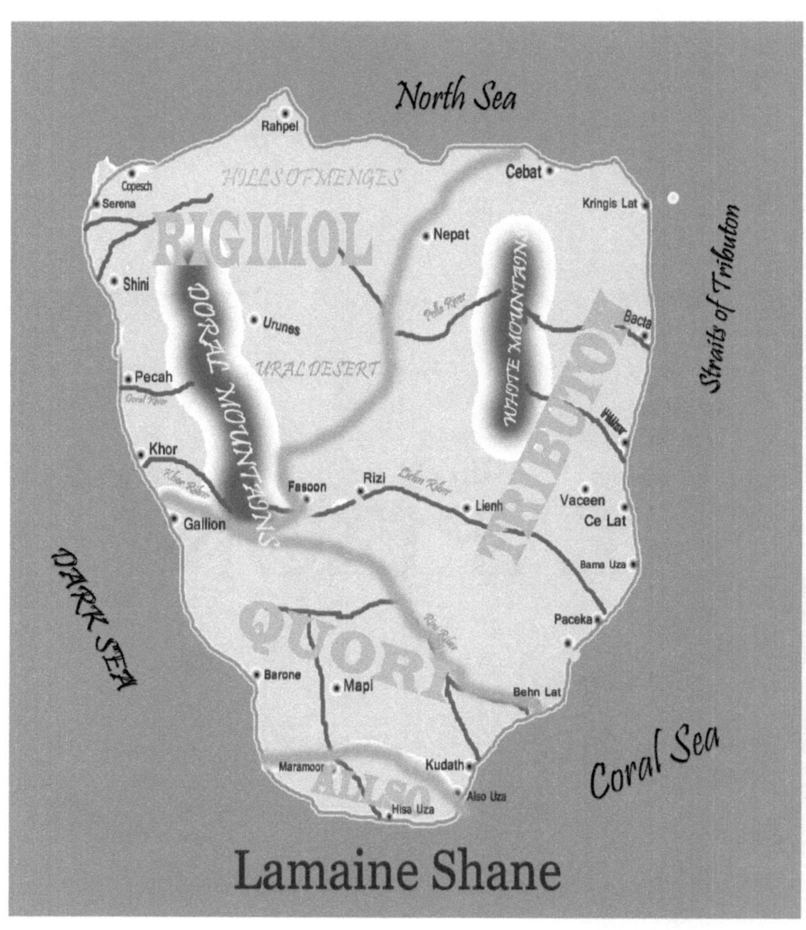

Lamaine Shane

NORTHLAND
North Sea
Straits of Tributon
Pali Bat
Drasha
Solamana
Tuht Uza
Rappadat
Dingus
Sint River
TUHT
POHL
Quito Uza
Kinomba River
Zillan
Gohi
Mt.Pohl
Elish
Palazaba
Renda River
Kinomba
SYNCLARE
Shahla
Mt.Rumbla
Duesi Desert
Rendi Mountains
Roshaunda
MERRIA
Rendi River
Keba
Rallis
Artis Cul
Tazi Strip
Vinaverde
Golden Hills
Sarie
Guth River
Calamar
Lilial
ROUR
Bramapour
SONI
Dengali
Rour River
Mana
Mt.Pakuta
Mt.Soni
Mt.Drala
Cana Uza
Shisk
Dingus River
Pakuta River
Jedeva
Tuppazak
Dromma Dal
Coral Sea
Emerald Ocean
Palma Uza
Tol Uza
Crysta Uza
Mt.Bambi
TUNISU ISLANDS
Barabara

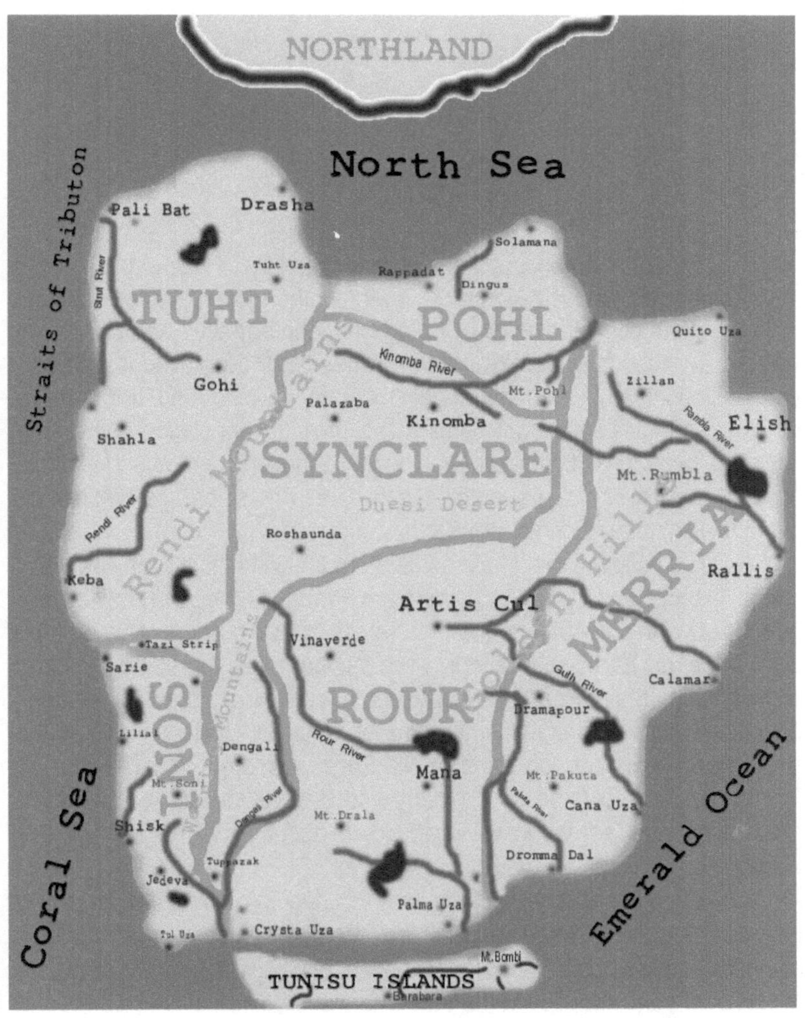

TURVIN

Prelude

Tarizon's historical manuscripts claimed there was a much larger and greater human civilization far away in another galaxy. It was said that these humans occupied a planet called Pharidon and that their civilization was so advanced that people there sometimes lived nearly a thousand Earth years. Consequently, Pharidon became overcrowded and the planet's natural resources could not support the growing population. When the situation became critical explorers began searching for other habitable planets where their citizens could relocate. One of these groups of explorers came to Tarizon and another to Earth.

It is believed that these settlers brought with them many animals, plants, insects, and other organisms from Pharidon. They were raised and nurtured by the first settlers and then released to live and evolve on their own. Although Earth and Tarizon were settled about the same time and brought with them Pharidon's advanced technology, their civilizations developed quite differently. At the time of Tarizon's Unification it was the early twentieth century on Earth. While Earth was about to experience its first World War, Tarizon had already endured seven and was about to embark on one last world war that would destroy 80% of the planet's population.

During this time Tarizon was divided into thirty-one separate nations. These nations had been fighting amongst themselves for thousands of cycles, a cycle being Tarizon's equivalent of an Earth year. In the twenty cycles before the adoption of the Supreme Mandate millions of soldiers and civilians had lost their lives and much of the infrastructure of the planet had been destroyed. From out of the rubble a peace movement was born led by a charismatic holy man named Sandee Branh. Sandee had been elected Chief Minister of Lyon, the largest nation of Tarizon. Sandee claimed as a child that God had chosen him to save Tarizon from self-destruction.

When Sandee was a boy he lived with his parents in Lecton which is situated on the continent of Azollo. They were poor farmers who barely survived in the barren land that is characteristic of that part of the world. Sandee was eleven years old and had no brothers or sisters. He had to hike many kylods, Tarizon's equivalent of an Earth mile, every day to go to school and when he returned home in the afternoon there were many chores to be done before he could have dinner and go to bed.

It was a time of near anarchy. Lecton was at war with its neighbor, Serie. Soldiers from both sides often raided each other's territory and plundered and pillaged everything in their path. One day the Branh farm was overrun and Sandee's parents were murdered. Sandee himself would have been killed except that he was on an errand for his father when the soldiers came. When he returned home, he was devastated to find that he'd lost everything that was precious to him.

Unknown to Sandee the soldiers had left two men behind to be sure they'd taken everything of value. When these men saw Sandee they vowed to kill the last witness to their murderous venture, but God had other plans. Upon seeing the men Sandee fled along the river trying to outrun them, but they were stronger and faster and soon overtook him. This is when the rhutz appeared.

A rhutz, to an Earth human, would look similar to a wolf. But besides being ferocious hunters, they also had strong telepathic and telekinetic abilities which made them formidable adversaries. Fortunately, the rhutz had always been peaceful and kept to themselves, but they were proud and had strong survival instincts. If they were pushed they would not only stand their ground but punish those who challenged them.

The rhutz came out of the brush and nearly ripped off one of the soldier's legs. The other soldier tried to shoot the rhutz but couldn't get a clear shot. He finally decided to flee while he had the chance, but after the rhutz finished off the first soldier he went for the second. The second soldier never had a chance.

This is when God appeared to Sandee who was lying on the bank of the river in great shock and sorrow over the death of his parents. God told Sandee that he'd been one of many victims of the evil that was choking Tarizon. He told him He wanted him to bring peace and justice to Tarizon and that He would give him the strength and power to do it. Of course, this eleven-year-old boy was shocked and confused at this and nobody believed him at first when he told them God had spoken to him, but the rhutz stayed with him and became a constant companion. This odd and wondrous sight of a small boy protected by the savage rhutz gave many pause. There were other miracles too and within a few years it was clear that God was indeed with this boy and he quickly became renowned for his intelligence and wisdom.

From the day He first appeared to him, Sandee devoted his life to spreading God's message of peace and unity. Sandee told his followers that the petty national governments should be scrapped in favor of one worldwide authority. Since so many were weary of war and feared the destruction of civilization on the planet if something wasn't done, Sandee's movement gathered momentum until there was enough support to call a World Council.

At the World Council, representatives from all of the thirty-one nations hammered out the Supreme Mandate and then called for a worldwide referendum to ratify it. All of the nations agreed to abide by the decision of the people. If the Supreme Mandate was ratified by a majority of its citizens, each nation agreed to subject itself to the World Council and abide by the Supreme Mandate. The World Council set the referendum date off six cycles to allow plenty of time for debate. On the day of the referendum nearly seventy percent of the population voted and the Supreme Mandate was ratified by sixty-one percent of the popular vote.

The government was called Central Authority and it ruled in accordance with the Supreme Mandate which guaranteed the right to assemble, to speak freely, to vote, and a fair trial for those accused of crimes against the public. It abolished slavery and provided many other civil liberties as well.

Unfortunately, Central Authority was initially only able to maintain order in the major cities of Tarizon. Huge domes had been constructed over these large cities so water and air could be filtered and purified. A controlled environment allowed the urban population to go about their daily lives without protective clothing and fear of radiation poisoning. Some areas outside of the domes were governed by local town councils or regional governments who were pledged to uphold the Supreme Mandate but only loosely controlled by Central Authority. Much of the rural area had no government and a state of anarchy persisted.

The dominant populations of these rural areas were mutants who hadn't enjoyed the protection from radiation that the domes provided and suffered the consequences. Whereas there were some mutants in the domed cities, the vast majority were unspoiled humans. Two political parties emerged during this time, the Purists and the Loyalists. The Purists represented the unspoiled humans who believed they were superior to the mutants and all other life-forms on Tarizon and should rule over them. Their opponents, the Loyalists, considered themselves loyal to the intentions of those who had written the Supreme Mandate. They believed all life-forms, tainted or not, were protected by the Supreme Mandate and should be treated equally.

It's now 25 A.U. (after unification) in the City of Vaceen, State of Tributon, on the continent of Lemaine Shane. Vaceen is a small city ruled by its Town Council.

1

Rhutz Hunt

Shadow and Shimmer, two young rhutz, were frolicking in a lush green meadow after finishing off a range deer they'd killed for breakfast. They had recently mated and were enjoying a beautiful spring morning in the lush hills of the White Mountains of Tributon. A creek ran through the meadow and when Shimmer felt an urge to drink, she took off toward it. Shadow raced after her and nearly beat her to the cool water. They waded in knee-deep and began to drink deeply when the ground began to move beneath their feet. They repositioned themselves to keep from losing their footing and looked around. Tremors were not unusual as the White Mountains were the home of three active volcanos. A loud crack pierced the morning tranquility. Shadow looked toward the sound wondering if the tremor had caused a tree to fall. He looked over at Shimmer wanting to get her take on the noise. Then he felt a stab of pain—not his pain but Shimmer's as Rhutz were telepathic and could feel each other's thoughts and emotions as if they were their own. He looked over at her curiously. She stumbled, let out a mournful howl, and then collapsed into the water. Blood began gushing out of her chest turning the water red. Two more shots rang out in quick succession forcing Shadow to abandon his mate and take cover behind a large boulder.

Shadow looked in the direction of the shots and spotted three humans, one with a long rifle. They were laughing and congratulating the shooter for his good shot. Anger welled in Shadow. He was torn between pursuing the men and rushing to his mate to see if she were still alive. The men were scrambling to their feet and taking flight. His concern for his mate left him no choice but to go to her side, but not before he summoned help from the rest of his pack.

"Stop the three humans running north from Flat Meadow. They've shot my mate," Shadow demanded as he rushed over to Shimmer. When he reached her, she lay on the bank of the creek barely breathing. He licked her face tenderly. *"Oh, my love. Why are they stealing your life? What is their purpose?"*

"Humans need no purpose," Shimmer replied. *"They are greedy. They want God's gifts all for themselves."*

"But surely that was not God's intent?"

"No. Tarizon is rich. There is plenty for all, if they could only see it."

"I will make them pay, my love. I will steal their lives and the lives of their families to bring back balance in the world."

"No, it will only lead to more slaughter. Let it go."

Anger consumed Shadow as he watched Shimmer's life slowly bleed away. He didn't understand the humans. They didn't need rhutz for food. When they stole a life, they just left it to spoil in the hot sun. What was most disturbing was the apparent joy they felt after each theft. Their cheers and laughter when Shimmer fell in mortal pain echoed in his mind. To Shadow this meant only one thing. Those who stole for pleasure were evil, sent by Gorgas himself, to destroy all that God had created.

Shimmer, who knew what Shadow was thinking, pleaded to her mate, *"No. Not all humans are bad. You must not judge all of them for the evil of only a few."*

Shimmer's thoughts were growing weaker and weaker. Shadow looked at her with growing fear and anxiety. He knew her life was almost over. Great sadness fell over him. If only there were something he could do. The humans had casualty centers and doctors who tried to heal their sick and wounded, but Rhutz believed when God came to get them they should go without resistance. Shadow didn't share this view. He believed, as many other Rhutz did, that God had made a mistake when he gave a four-legged creature a powerful mind but no hands with which to build or create. It was true that the rhutz' telekinetic gifts were useful in building structures, moving objects, and defending themselves in battle, but they lacked the fine motor skills of the humans that gave them dominance over all other life-forms.

Shadow felt another stab of horrific pain and then a feeling of complete and utter emptiness. He looked down at Shimmer and felt a cold wave permeate his body. He shook involuntarily. *"Don't leave me! You are too young to go to God. What could be the purpose of your summons?"*

Shimmer did not answer. Shadow howled a long agonizing lament and then tuned his mind into the pack's collective consciousness to find out what had become of the humans. Three rhutz were in pursuit, but the humans were on jet cycles making overtaking them difficult. He looked mournfully at Shimmer one last time and then took off to join the chase.

Rupra Bruda eased the trigger of his Ruggi 7 smart shot rife. The two rhutz were dancing around the water making it difficult to get a bead on them. Then the ground began to move beneath his feet. He cursed under his breath and waited for the tremor to stop. Bruda's two companions looked around nervously knowing a tremor could fell a tree or open a crack in the soil and swallow them up. When they felt safe again, they turned their attention back to the rhutz. This was the first time Rupra had fired this experimental weapon. The manufacturer of this new class of rifles claimed the bullets would bend slightly toward a warm object. This they promised would increase accuracy by up to 10%. Heat-seeking bullets had long been in the design stage and this was the first actual product that had finally been manufactured. Rupra's father, the townhead of Vaceen, had acquired the rifle direct from the manufacturer and he'd given it to Rupra and told him to go try it out. Rupra loved to hunt, so he had gathered two of his teenage friends and organized this rhutz hunt.

The two rhutz finally stopped to drink from the stream. Bruda pulled the trigger as the smaller of the two rhutz came into focus. A loud, angry crack broke the silence of the morning. Bruda held his breath, waiting to see if he'd hit his target. The smaller rhutz stumbled and then collapsed. Bruda raised his hand triumphantly. His companions let out a collective cheer.

"Let me try," his friend Callus said.

Bruda smiled and handed him the rifle. Callus put it to his shoulder, aimed and fired. The shot missed, so he quickly fired a second round. The second shot also missed and by then the second rhutz had found cover behind a rock.

"You've got to wait until the target comes into focus, you dirkbird!" Rupra said angrily. "Weren't you watching me?"

Callus shrugged and handed Bruda the rifle.

"Let me try," his other friend Romas said.

"No. We've got to get out of here. The pack will be all over us in a loon. If they catch us, they'll tear us to threads."

The three men picked up their gear and began to run back to where they'd left their jet bikes. They had lay in wait on a ridge overlooking the meadow and had to run five thousand strides to their Tempest 2000 Jet Bikes. They knew once they were on the bikes they'd be safe, at least they hoped so. As they came down the hill, they spotted a rhutz between them and their bikes. Bruda stopped and aimed his rifle. The rhutz took flight when he saw the rifle pointed his way and the shot missed.

"Come on! We've got to get to the bikes," Bruda yelled.

The three hunters began running again and finally made it to the bikes. They quickly secured their gear, gunned their engines, and took off. Three rhutz suddenly appeared in front of them. Bruda pulled out his rifle again but before he could aim it flew out of his hand.

He glared angrily at the rhutz knowing he'd be in serious trouble if he came home without the rifle. "Go!" he exclaimed as his bike shot forward toward a gap between the rhutz. His two companions followed and Rupra and Romas made it through, but the gap had been closed by the time Callus got there and one of the rhutz sunk his teeth into his leg as he went by. Callus was jerked off his bike and dragged to the ground. He screamed in pain and horror as the rhutz attacked. Bruda and Romas stopped and looked back in horror as Callus was ruthlessly attacked by the three rhutz and ripped to pieces.

"Get out of here!" Bruda ordered. "I've got to get that rifle." Romas gave him a look but took off without objection. Bruda took advantage of the fact that the three rhutz were concentrating on their kill. He shot forward and then circled back to where the rifle lay on the ground. One of the rhutz looked up when he heard the jet bike returning but Bruda was coming fast and got to the gun before the rhutz could react. He scooped up the rifle and then took off trying to evade the now charging rhutz. Just as he thought he was in the clear he felt the sharp pain of a claw slicing through his leg. A sudden dizziness almost made him lose his balance and fall off his bike, but he willed his mind to clear and regained his balance.

Romas was waiting for him at the clearing where they'd left the jet copter. He looked at Rupra's blood-soaked pants and rushed over to him. "You'd better get a healing wrap on that or you're going to bleed to death."

"I know. Get one for me while I load the bikes," Bruda said.

Romas nodded and climbed aboard the jet copter. A tik later he returned with a roll of healing wrap and a cleansing pack. Bruda waved him off. "We've got to get out of here. I'll put the strip on while we're airborne."

"What about Callus?"

"Callus is dead. There's nothing we can do for him."

"Oh, my God! What will his parents say?"

"It's not our fault. It's those soulless beasts, the rhutz, who killed him. My father will send out a hunting party to rid the area of them."

As they were climbing into the copter a dozen rhutz, led by Shadow, surrounded them. Romas started the engine and the lifters began to spin. The jet copter rose quickly. Shadow concentrated on the lifters, causing them to sputter. The copter dipped, wobbled, and spun around. Bruda buckled himself in, picked up his rifle, aimed and fired down at Shadow through an open door. The jerky motion of the jet copter caused the bullet to go harmlessly over Shadow's head, but it was enough to distract the rhutz and make him release the copter from his mind's grip. The copter shot forward and soon disappeared over the treetops.

Shadow and his pack returned to Flat Meadow and went straight to Shimmer's body. Shadow dragged the lifeless body a hundred strides to a grassy area in the center of the meadow. Then members of the pack, now twenty-seven-strong, milled around trying to understand why Shimmer had been taken from them. They howled mournfully all during the night protecting the body from the scavengers who would have otherwise fed on the carcass had it been left unattended. The rhutz honored their ancestors and believed their souls went to God upon their passing. Each pack disposed of bodies in an honorable and respectful manner depending on where they lived. Usually they were burned or buried, but in the forests of Tributon fire was too dangerous and the ground too rocky for digging. So, Shadow's pack had come up with something different. At first light, the pack stood watching the body expectantly. Suddenly thousands of black spidery creatures called sligots swarmed out of their nest, onto Shimmer's body and began consuming her. In just a few loons she had disappeared and the sligots retreated into their nest. Shadow took one last sorrowful look at the place where Shimmer once lay, then turned and trotted away with the rest of the pack at his heels.

Rupra Bruda and Romas Lantra carefully went over their story as they flew back to Vaceen. They knew they would be interrogated separately by their parents and the authorities after they informed them of Callus' death. Unfortunately, Callus's brother Idra was there to meet them when they landed.

Not seeing Callus after Rupra and Romas had disembarked, Idra frowned. "Where's my brother?"

Rupra took a deep breath. Romas swallowed hard. "I've got bad news for you, Idra. I'm so sorry," Romas said.

"What's happened?" Idra pressed.

"We ran into a pack of rhutz while we were hunting and they attacked us. We tried to get away on our jet cycles and almost made it, but one of the rhutz caught Callus' leg and pulled him off his bike. I shot at them trying to scare them away, but one of them pulled the rifle away with his will. By the time I retrieved the rifle, Callus was dead."

"No!" Idra wailed. "You're lying. This couldn't have happened. This is some kind of cruel joke, right? My brother is hiding somewhere, isn't he?"

Rupra shook his head slowly. "No. It's the truth. We should go to your parents and tell them."

Idra began crying. "No. my brother is not dead. He cannot be dead!"

Romas grabbed Idra and pulled him into an embrace. "I'm sorry, Idra, but he's gone. You've got to be strong."

After they'd packed all their gear into Idra's ATV, Idra drove them to his home. Rupra had planned to tell his father what had happened first, but since Idra had picked them up they had no choice but to go home with him. Callus' mother came out when she heard the ATV pull up. Rupra looked at Romas and grimaced.

Icelia scanned the ATV for her son and when she didn't see him asked, "Where's Callus?"

Romas looked at Rupra and was about to explain what had happened when Idra blurted out, "He was murdered by a rhutz!"

Icelia's face paled and she fainted. Rupra rushed over and caught her before she hit the ground. They carried her inside and laid her on a recliner. Callus' father, Rubbias, stood up when he saw his wife being carried inside.

"What happened?" he asked worriedly.

Rupra told him about Callus' death and what had happened. Rubbias collapsed in a chair in dismay.

"I'm going to call my father," Rupra advised. "I'm sure he'll want to organize a hunting party to kill the rhutz responsible for Callus' death."

Rubbias looked up. "I don't understand it. Rhutz never attack humans. They only kill what they need to eat and they have no taste for human flesh. I can't understand why they attacked you."

"I don't know," Rupra said. "Maybe they were infected by a spinal tick. They acted like they were mad. Either way, they must all be killed. We can't let a pack of mad rhutz roam around the country killing people indiscriminately."

"No, you're right," Rubbias agreed. "Go ahead and call your father. I want to recover Callus' body at the very least."

"If any of it is still there," Romas said dejectedly. "When we left they were ripping it apart."

Rubbias paled at the image. Romas shrugged. "Sorry, Father, but that's the truth."

Rubbias' sorrow turned to rage. "Call your father, Rupra! We must track down the beasts before they kill others."

A faint smile came over Bruda's face. "Yes, sir. Right away."

Rupra went outside and pushed a number on his wrist array. His father, Progasis, responded quickly. "Rupra. You're back. How was your trip?"

"Not so good, Father," Rupra said wondering how to break the news to him.

"The Ruggi 7 didn't perform well?" Progasis asked. "The manufacturer assured me they'd worked the kinks out of it."

"No. It's a great rifle. That wasn't the problem. We were attacked by a pack of rhutz."

"What? Rhutz attacked you?"

"Yes," he lied. "We were just hunting for range deer when they surrounded us. If I hadn't had my jet cycle close at hand, I wouldn't have escaped them. As it is, they slashed my leg."

"Oh, no! Is it bad?"

"No. Romas bound it right away in healing wrap. I'll be fine."

"Oh, thank God you're safe," Progasis gasped.

"Unfortunately, Callus wasn't so lucky."

"What do you mean? Is he okay?"

"No. The rhutz pulled him off his bike and ripped him to pieces. They acted like they were mad."

"He's dead?" Progasis asked in shock. He hadn't considered the hunting trip to be the least bit dangerous. He'd taken his boys camping in those woods many times and the rhutz had always ignored them.

"Yes. Rubbias thinks they must be infected by the spinal tick."

"The spinal tick? But that virus was eradicated twenty cycles ago."

"He thinks it may have survived somehow and infected some of the rhutz. You know how quickly it spreads."

"But you might be infected then, if you were cut by the rhutz."

Rupra immediately realized he'd gone too far. He didn't want anyone thinking he had been infected by a spinal tick. "Ah, well it was just a shallow wound. I'm sure the healing wrap killed any virus that might have been present."

"We should have you tested, just to be sure."

"Right," Rupra groaned.

"So, how did you get away?"

"I shot at them with my rifle, trying to get them off Callus, but it was too late. He couldn't have been alive, but it did drive them away, so we could make our escape while we could."

"Where are you?" Progasis asked.

"I'm at Callus' house. His father asked me to report what happened to you. He wants you to organize a hunting party to go after the mad pack. He says they must pay for killing Callus."

"Indeed, they must! I can't believe they'd attack humans that way. I must bring this to the attention of the town council at once. The hills are full of rhutz and if one pack is infected others may be as well."

Medical science on Tarizon was highly advanced and most viruses had been eradicated long ago, but the eripititis virus, carried by the spinal tick, was one of the last strains to be eliminated. It had become resistant to all antibiotics and only became contained when medical researchers figured out how to attack it on a molecular level. Modern day treatment was long, painful, and expensive. Also, since its carrier, the spinal tick, infested most forests on Tarizon, it wasn't feasible to eliminate that insect without killing thousands of other species that were vital to Tarizon's natural ecological balance.

Shadow paced back and forth in front of the pack's cave. His sadness had now turned to anger at what the humans had done. Vengeance for Shimmer's murder was on his mind, but the pack had killed one of the humans. Was that death enough, he wondered? Shimmer's thoughts came to him. *"Not all humans are bad. You must not judge all of them for the evil of only a few."* Shimmer was right, he knew, but he still felt like the humans should pay for what they had done.

He'd never communicated with a human, although he knew it was possible, since some humans were telepathic. The human spiritual leader, Sandee, had talked to the rhutz. One of them, Whisper, had become his friend and companion. Shadow longed to link his mind to a human and find out more about them. He wanted to know why some were evil and others full of love and joy. *The wise one might have the answer. Perhaps he'll know of a human who will link with me.*

The oldest member of the pack was called *the wise one* and was always consulted before any major decisions affecting the pack were made. Shadow entered the cave and went to him.

"Wise one. I need your counsel."

The old rhutz who'd been sleeping, as he did most of the time since his age was more than a hundred cycles, looked up and focused on his visitor. He shook his head trying to clear his mind. "Yes, how can I help you, Shadow?"

"I know it is the policy of the rhutz to stay out of human affairs, but the attack on my mate has filled me with a desire for vengeance."

"That is understandable, my brother, but you must control those urges for they can only lead you along a dark path."

"True. I can see that, but I want to understand why a human would murder a rhutz for no apparent reason. Perhaps if I could find out the answer to that question I might find some peace."

"That is one of the enigmas about the human race that we have struggled with since the beginning of the world. Perhaps that was God's purpose in calling Shimmer."

"What do you mean?" Shadow asked.

"Perhaps he wants you to seek greater understanding of the humans."

"Could that be?" Shadow asked, incredulous.

"Yes. Everything God does has a purpose."

Shadow thought about that a moment and then said, "I have heard of rhutz linking with humans. Perhaps if I could do that I'd find some answers."

"That is possible. You'd have to find a human who is pure in heart, for many are afflicted with fear and mistrust. Those will be of no help because they will lie and try to deceive you."

"Do you know an honest human who is pure in heart?" Shadow asked.

The old rhutz considered the question for a moment and then replied, "There is one I have heard stories about. His name is Tobin Sandista and he's a councilor in Urunes."

"Urunes?" Shadow thought. "That is across the White Mountains in the Ural Desert, isn't it?"

"Just north of the Ural Desert, but you must cross the desert to get there or travel an extra thousand kylods to go around it."

Shadow sighed. "Such a long journey with no guarantee he will even link to me."

"It's a good idea, though, Shadow. Understanding is always the beginning of the end of a problem."

Shadow nodded. "Then I shall travel to Urunes and link with Councilor Sandista."

"I wish I could travel with you, but I haven't the strength," the old one mused.

"It's all right. There is no need. I will open my mind to you so you can join the link."

"I look forward to it with great anticipation. May the spirit of Whisper be with you."

"Thank you, Wise one."

Shadow left the old rhutz and rejoined the main pack. He told them of his decision to go to Urunes. Several rhutz offered to travel with him, but he declined the offers as he knew he could travel much faster alone. Besides, there were packs of rhutz along the way he could link with for information and guidance. His only worry was the fifty kylods across the Ural Desert. There was no water, but he told himself he could travel at night and probably make it without too much difficulty.

The next morning before the sun had risen, Shadow began his long trek to Urunes planning to travel to the Hilor River and then follow it west to its closest point from Urunes. From there he'd cross the perilous desert. If he made it, he wondered how he'd be received by Councilor Sandista, and what it would be like to link to a human. A horrible thought crossed his mind. What if Councilor Sandista wasn't even telepathic? He'd have risked his life for nothing. *Surely that could not be, for if it were, that would mean Shimmer died for no purpose, but everything God does has a purpose.*

2

Flat Meadow Massacre

Rupra Bruda turned on the video communicator and sat back in a chair to watch his father in action. The emergency meeting of the town council was just beginning. Progasis Bruda called the meeting to order.

"I've called this emergency meeting to inform you of some disturbing events in the hills of the White Mountains. My son Rupra and his two companions, Callus Tripolis and Romas Lantra went on a hunting trip two days ago to try out the new Ruggi 7 smart rifle currently in final development by Ruggi Manufacturing. While they were staking out a meadow for range deer, they were attacked by a pack of rhutz. One of the boys, Callus Tripolis, was murdered by the pack."

The members broke out in excited chatter. Progasis waited for the members to quiet. "I believe it is imperative that we authorize a hunting party to go out, find this pack of rhutz and kill them all."

A councilman raised his hand.

"Councilman Garciah, what say you?"

Councilman Rammel Garciah was a staunch supporter of the Supreme Mandate as his father had been a signatory on the historic document that had brought peace to Tarizon and unified it under one world government. Under the Supreme Mandate all life-forms were guaranteed freedom to speak freely, to assemble and debate the issues, to vote, if accused of a crime, the right to a just advocate, and to live freely. Unfortunately, the document itself only mentioned humans, Seafolken and mutants. Since the adoption of the Supreme Mandate by the people, scholars came to realize that the Rhutz and the Nanomites might also be sentient life-forms and thus entitled to the protection of the Supreme Mandate. Unfortunately, this issue was yet unsettled and there were many who opposed recognizing them as sentient life-forms. Progasis Bruda was one of them.

"I know this is an unsettled issue, but I believe, as do other members, that the rhutz is a sentient life-form and they cannot simply be gunned down because they are suspected of a crime. If one or more of them participated in a murder then they should be tried and given an opportunity to defend themselves."

"You know there is no precedent for that," Bruda spat. "Nowhere in the Supreme Mandate is the word Rhutz even mentioned. Only humans enjoy the rights guaranteed by the Supreme Mandate. I question whether they are really a sentient life-form, anyway."

"Nevertheless, until the issue is settled by the Council of Interpreters, can we disregard the possibility they are sentient beings and risk sanctioning a murderous hunt?"

Another councilman raised his hand.

"Councilman Quaris, what say you?" Progasis asked.

"It could be many cycles before the Council of Interpreters makes a final determination on this matter. We must act now before this pack kills more innocent people or infect other packs."

"Your point is well taken, Councilman Quaris," Progasis said. "I have been told the rhutz in question acted as if they were mad. At this moment my son is being tested for the eripititis virus which you all know is a super virus carried by the spinal tick."

There were gasps of shock from the audience.

Councilman Garciah raised his hand.

"Councilman Garciah, what say you?"

"Should we not wait for the results of these tests before we vote on this matter? I fear a vote now will be tainted by unfounded fears."

"There is some logic in that," Progasis said, "but the results of the tests won't be known for twenty kyloons, I'm told. Can we afford to do nothing and perhaps allow other packs to be infected?"

Councilman Garciah sighed. "Then we should find them and isolate them until the test results come back. If they are infected, there are treatments available."

"The rhutz won't submit to treatment," a man from the audience spat. "Kill the beasts now before there are other victims!"

Progasis smiled. Other members of the audience cheered their agreement.

"That's a good point," Progasis said. "Getting the rhutz to cooperate in a judicial proceeding may not be possible."

Councilman Quaris stood. "I move the Public Enforcer organize a volunteer hunting party to hunt down the pack of rhutz who killed Callus Tripolis and kill every last one of them."

"Aye," another councilman said.

Progasis nodded. "There is a motion on the table. Is there any objection?"

Rammel stood.

"State your objection," Progasis said begrudgingly.

"I must point out that the Town of Vaceen lacks legal authority to commit murder or even execute criminals, once there has been a lawful adjudication of their crime."

Councilman Quaris stood.

"Your response, Councilman Quaris," Progasis said.

"The Animal Control Act authorizes the city to cause the eradication of infected pets, rodents, or wild beasts that imperil the population."

"That is correct," Progasis said, "and since there is no legal authority for the proposition that the rhutz is anything other than a wild beast, I find that the Town of Vaceen does have the right and authority to eradicate these beasts that have clearly imperiled this population. If there is no further objection, we shall vote on the matter."

Rammel started to stand again but then thought better of it.

"Hearing no more objections, we shall put the matter to a vote." He nodded to the council secretary and a big screen lit up behind them with the twenty-one names of the Vaceen town council members on it. Red and green lights began popping up alongside each councilman's name. Green for "aye" and red for "nay."

Progasis looked at the results and said, "The 'ayes' have it. The resolution is passed twelve to nine. There being no further business, this meeting is adjourned."

Shroud of Doom

Rupra Bruda smiled and turned off the VC. *Now all I have to do is convince Father to let me volunteer for the hunt. The only problem is that damn test. He's not going to let me go until the results of the test come back. Skutz!*

That night Rupra tried to convince his father to let him go on the hunt but both his mother and father were adamant he stays home, in case any symptoms of the infection manifested themselves. Rupra was disappointed but resigned himself to having to stay home. He vowed to be more careful in crafting his lies in the future.

That night Veda Kulchz, the Public Enforcer deputized forty-one citizens to be part of the hunting party including Progasis Bruda and Rubbias Tripolis. At first light the next morning the hunting party set out in seven jet copters to track down the rhutz. They found them without any trouble as they hadn't moved from their den. Shadow never saw the jet copters as he'd been gone for over a kyloon when they showed up.

The copters landed at strategic locations around Flat Meadow and the hunters took up positions ready to ambush any rhutz who tried to escape. When the trap had been set, eleven hunters including Bruda and Tripolis, moved on the pack. The rhutz had heard the copters landing but didn't know what to do since they were a peace-loving species and had never before been confronted by a hostile force bent on killing them.

With Shadow gone, a rhutz named Splash had taken charge of the pack. He was strong and intelligent but lacked experience. The attack baffled him as he'd never heard of humans attacking a pack of rhutz before. His initial instinct was to run as he knew the pack was no match for the humans with their flying machines and guns, but his scouts quickly informed him that all paths from the meadow were covered by the humans. Since he had no option but to fight, he linked his mind to all the packs of rhutz in the area.

"Brothers. We are under attack by many humans with copters and guns. They will kill us all unless you come to our aid. Come quickly. Time is short."

Seven pack leaders within five kylods of Flat Meadow responded to the call promising immediate help. Splash then turned to his immediate problem, eleven humans with guns walking straight at them. With nowhere else to go, Splash ordered all twenty rhutz to attack the eleven at once in three columns. His thinking was that such an assault would be difficult to defend. Whereas the first few rhutz might be killed the remainder would get through to attack the humans.

His strategy worked perfectly. When the rhutz came at them the forward hunters easily picked off the first two in each column, but they quickly felt the steel teeth of the third and fourth rhutz as they viciously attacked. The other hunters stood and watched the melee, unable to use their weapons without endangering their fellow hunters now in mortal combat with the rhutz. Suddenly, the other eleven humans, including Bruda and Tripolis, found themselves in close combat with the rhutz. Many dropped their rifles, that were now useless, and pulled their knives and pistols. The men fought desperately but in close proximity the rhutz were able to use their telekinetic powers to rip these weapons out of their hands before they could be of any use. Soon all eleven of the hunters were dead and their bodies left lifeless on the blood-soaked ground.

The Public Enforcer was shocked and appalled by the loss of eleven of his deputies. Panic-stricken he ordered his men to retreat to the copters. Unfortunately, the remaining rhutz were in his path, so he had no choice but to confront them again. His men marched across the meadow firing at any rhutz along the way. Seeing their retreat Splash pondered whether to order the remainder of the pack to retreat or take another suicide run at the human intruders. Looking over the meadow and seeing his slain brothers everywhere, he decided he had no choice but to attack the cowardly humans with one more suicide attack. He had to make them pay for what they had done.

Unfortunately, this time the Public Enforcer had anticipated the attack formation and stationed four snipers on both sides, just out of view of the main party. When the rhutz came at them in single file they were easily picked off by the snipers. When the last rhutz fell the fifteen remaining hunters let out a triumphant cheer.

Shadow reached the Hilor River late that night. He was exhausted so he killed a young range deer that had strayed from its herd and picked it clean. Then he found a hollowed-out tree and slept for the night. All the next day he followed the Hilor River west toward Rigimol. He'd never been to Rigimol, as rhutz had no need to travel long distances. They had all they needed in the vast forests their ancestors had left them. After Shadow had crossed the White Mountains, however, the scenery changed dramatically. There were fewer trees and bushes and more open grasslands. This bothered him as he felt alone and more vulnerable out in the open. But what lie ahead was even worse—the Ural Desert—devoid of all life except scrub brush and hideous looking vultures who circled overhead.

As long as he followed the river he wasn't in any danger. He found a few lizards and rodents to sustain him and the river provided all the water he could drink. After a few days he realized he needed to cross the river and go north, but he didn't know precisely where to do that, so he opened his mind to see if he could link with any local rhutz who might be able to help him. It took a while but he finally made contact with a pack several kylods to the south. They agreed to come to him and show him the path to Urunes.

The pack leader was a female rhutz named Moonlight. She was saddened by Shadow's tale of the loss of Shimmer, his mate. "I don't understand why the humans killed her."

"Nor do I," Shadow said. "That is why I must go to Urunes and talk to Councilor Sandista. Perhaps he will have the answer I seek."

"The trail to Urunes is long and harsh. You cannot make it without water. There are snakes and scorpions, too. They will smell your water a kylod away and come after it."

"But I must get there. Can't I travel at night?"

"Yes, the snakes and scorpions sleep at night, but you will still need water. Even at night it is hot in the desert."

"So, what should I do?"

"We can strap an ox skin full of water on your back."

"An ox skin?"

"Yes, it's the stomach of a river ox. It's watertight. If you find yourself traveling during the day, just be alert and keep moving. As long as you can see the desert scorpions and lizard snakes, you should be able to keep your distance. It's when you slow down or stop that you'll likely be attacked. If you get bitten you'll likely die, so keep moving."

"Do you think I will make it?" Shadow asked worriedly.

"You'll be all right the first day because you'll have water. After that it will depend on your speed, strength, and the will of God."

Shadow nodded. "I believe God has sent me on this quest, so I trust He will send Whisper's spirit to guide me and give me the strength to make it."

"I pray that be the case. Be sure and link with me on your way back as I too would like to know the answers you seek."

That night Moonlight used her telekinetic skills to fasten the ox skin on Shadow's back. The water was heavy and made travel more difficult, but having his own supply of water relieved a lot of Shadow's concerns about traveling across the desert. He felt sure he could make it now. The only things that still worried him were the desert scorpions and lizard snakes. He wondered if they'd be easy to spot or they'd show up unexpectedly. As he began his trek across the desert, he was glad it was night and he didn't have to worry about them.

The first surprise when he crossed into the desert was how big the sky was. In the hills of the White Mountains it seemed much smaller, but here it looked huge. The stars were much bigger and brighter here as well. He'd never paid a lot of attention to stars before but now he marveled at how beautiful they were and how they illuminated his path across the desert.

Even traveling at night, it was very hot and he found himself wanting to drink. Moonlight had inserted a long narrow sponge into the ox skin which hung down near Shadow's mouth where he could suck out water as he needed it. The water came out very slowly, but even so he soon realized he'd drank half of his supply. Rhutz had difficulty determining the time at night. During the day it was easy with the sun racing across the sky. He thought the night was about half over, so at that rate he'd be out of water by daylight.

Moonlight had told him he should get to Urunes by noon. That meant he'd be without water for four kyloons during the worst heat of the day. He wished somehow he could shed his fur as it would make the heat even worse. As he walked, he wondered how he was going to approach Sandista. A rhutz just couldn't walk into a building like a human could. He could prowl the streets as rhutz often did looking for rodents. The humans hated rodents and gave the rhutz free reign to rid the cities of them. But a rhutz could not enter a building, particularly a public building, without having someone summon the Public Enforcer.

He finally decided he'd have to observe Sandista for a day or two to see where best to stage an encounter. It wouldn't be an easy task as Sandista would have to be alone and the contact would have to be telepathic. As he thought about it he had misgivings. What if he'd come all this way and couldn't talk to the councilor? *Am I being foolish to even try to make contact with the humans?*

When the sun began to rise in the sky, the heat became unbearable. Shadow's water ran out about an hour after sunrise. To lighten his load, he shook his torso violently causing the ox skin to tumble to the ground. He considered stopping to lick up the last few drops of water leaking out of the jug, but quickly moved on when a desert scorpion came out of nowhere and scampered over to it. He quickened his pace and looked around warily.

Time seemed to drag on in the hot morning sun. It seemed like he should have already reached Urunes. The sun was up high in the sky but, even so, he could only see endless desert ahead. Weariness overcame him. He had an overwhelming urge to lie down and sleep, but he knew if he did he'd never get back up. He trotted on, thinking about Shimmer to get his mind off his discomfort and urgent need for water. She had been a good mate and he thought of all the things they'd done together in the three cycles since they'd been mated. He missed her terribly and dreaded the thought of living the rest of his life without her. That gave him comfort, for if he died in the desert this day at least he'd soon be with Shimmer in the afterlife.

3

A Delicate Situation

The Public Enforcer shook his head as he surveyed the carnage at Flat Meadow. He'd underestimated the fighting ability of the rhutz. He'd assumed forty men with high powered rifles would easily overcome them, but he'd failed to consider two things. His deputies were not trained enforcers but mere recreational hunters and the rhutz were not wild beasts but an intelligent life-form equal in intellect to human beings. Now he was scared. When the town council found out he'd lost fifteen men he'd be forced to resign in disgrace. There might even be criminal prosecution. But as it turned out that was the least of his worries as two more packs of rhutz arrived and encircled the meadow. When the rhutz saw their slaughtered brothers at the hands of the humans they were outraged and wanted revenge.

The rhutz came at the stunned hunters from every direction catching them completely by surprise. They hadn't taken into account the rhutz collective consciousness and paid dearly for their error. In just a few loons they were overrun and ripped apart by the angry rhutz and the Flat Meadow Massacre was history. Forty-one men and twenty-nine rhutz had been brutally slain for no apparent reason. When the fight was over the survivors dragged the slain rhutz, one by one, over to the sligot nests and watched solemnly as each carcass was quickly consumed. They didn't bother to dispose of the human bodies knowing the humans had their own burial rituals.

When the hunting party failed to report in that night a local news crew flew out in a chopper to find out what had happened to them. When they saw the carnage at Flat Meadow from the air they reported it to Tarizon's Global Army, usually referred to as the TGA. Within minutes a heavily armed search and rescue team, led by Lt. Rule Diviil of the TGA Regional Command Center at Rini, was flown out to investigate. They landed in the same clearing young Rupra Bruda and his friends had landed two days earlier. Several news crews and local officials were there to meet them. One of the local officials was Councilman Rammel Garciah. He knew Lt. Diviil so he walked with him through the battle scene. Mutilated bodies were everywhere. The stench of death was heavy in the air. Rammel pulled a handkerchief out of his pocket and held it over his nose.

"What do you think happened here, councilman?" Lt. Diviil asked.

"The rhutz were attacked so they defended themselves. You can't really blame them."

"Perhaps not, but I understand they killed a human first without provocation."

"That's what Rupra Bruda and his companion say, but I'm not sure I believe it. I've never heard of a rhutz attacking a human."

"So, you think the boy is lying?"

The councilman shrugged. "That would be my guess, but I have no proof of it."

"I guess it doesn't really matter now," Lt. Diviil mused. "With forty-one dead citizens the outcry for vengeance will be deafening."

Rammel sighed. "I knew it was a mistake to try to kill them. I tried to talk the council out of it."

"They should have listened to you," Lt. Diviil said. "I wonder what happened here. There are no slain rhutz. Surely your hunters must have killed some of them."

"From what I have read about the rhutz, they dispose of their dead bodies much like we do. They wouldn't have left them behind."

"So, you think we'll find them buried somewhere?"

"Probably. They may have a cave around here somewhere."

As they were talking a soldier walked up. "Sir, there are no rhutz in the area now but it appears from their tracks that there were three groups of them. One occupied this area, another came in from the north and a third from the east."

"Any idea where they are now?" Lt. Diviil asked.

"It appears they went back the same way they came."

"So, we can track them then?"

"Yes, sir. It shouldn't be hard at all."

Lt. Diviil looked at Rammel. "You know, it almost appears that the local pack here called for help when they came under attack. Do you think that is possible?"

"Yes. They communicate telepathically. I don't know how it works exactly or the range over which they can communicate, but I'd say you're right. They called for reinforcements and the neighboring packs responded."

Lt. Diviil frowned. "So, that means if we go after them the same thing is going to happen again."

Rammel nodded. "Yes, if you keep attacking them you'll soon find yourself at war with every rhutz in Lemaine Shane."

Lt. Diviil swallowed hard. "How many are there, you think?" Lt. Diviil asked.

"Hundreds of thousands, I'm sure. I doubt there's ever been a census, so I don't know for sure."

"Damn, I guess I better call my commanding officer and let him decide whether we want to go down that path."

"Yes. That would be prudent," Rammel agreed. "There are rhutz everywhere and if they all start attacking humans, untold numbers will die."

Lt. Diviil got on his global communicator and called his commanding officer. They talked a long time as Lt. Diviil wanted to be sure Central Command understood the serious situation they faced. Finally, he hung up and shook his head.

"What did they say?" Rammel asked.

"They've instructed me to secure the area and stay put. They don't want to provoke the rhutz into more killing. Central Command needs more time to evaluate its options."

"Good," Councilman Garciah said. "I think this situation was an aberration. Somehow the rhutz felt they had no choice but to fight. I'd suggest you interrogate Rupra Bruda and his friend. The story they are telling may be a lie."

"Why do you say that?" Lt. Diviil asked.

"Because Bruda was testing the new experimental Ruggi 7 rifle for his father. He says they were hunting range deer, but you don't need a heat-seeking rifle for that. No, I think young Bruda wanted to try the rifle out on something more challenging."

"Like a rhutz?"

"Exactly. Hunting a rhutz would be like hunting a human target and that is what this rifle has been designed to do."

"Alright. I'll be sure to talk to them."

"Well, I think I'm going to go back and report to the town council," Rammel advised. "I promised I'd be back right away. There are many families who will have to be notified as to what happened here today."

"I don't envy you," Lt. Diviil said solemnly.

Rammel shook his head and walked away. He took one last look at Flat Meadow and then walked briskly back to the staging area where the copters and ATVs were parked. When he got there a mob of reporters swarmed around him.

"Councilman Garciah. Are there any survivors?" a reporter asked.

Rammel shook his head. "I didn't see any, but you should check with the medical response team to be sure."

"Do you know why the rhutz did this?"

Rammel looked at the reporter incredulously. "They did it because they were under attack, obviously. If someone is trying to kill you it's a natural instinct to fight back, don't you think?"

"Are you defending them?" a reporter asked.

"No. I was simply stating the obvious," Rammel said angrily. "What's important is that we find out exactly what happened here before we draw any conclusions. I asked the town council to do that before they sent a bunch of amateur hunters up here to kill the rhutz, but they didn't listen."

"Did you suspect the men would be slaughtered?" the reporter asked.

"No. I thought they'd slaughter the rhutz and that would be a tragedy. Obviously, something went terribly wrong, and we'd better find out what it was before we act blindly again."

"Councilor!" another reporter yelled.

"No more questions," Rammel said as he strode away. "I've got to report back to the town council."

As Rammel's plane took off he couldn't shake the image of forty-one blood-soaked bodies strewn across Flat Meadow. He wished there was some way he could find out what had happened out there. There was obviously something going on with the rhutz that nobody understood. He knew that the citizens of Vaceen would soon be demanding vengeance and the Town Council would probably be forced to do something—but what? Kill more rhutz? That simplistic approach had already backfired once, he couldn't let it happen again.

Shadow was ready to collapse from dehydration and heat exhaustion when he caught the scent of water in the air. The sweet smell gave him the incentive he needed to go on. On the outskirts of Urunes he found a well with an open pool of water surrounding it. There were several people drawing water as he approached. When they saw him, they got up quickly and ran off. He drank deeply and then just sat there and rested for a while looking around wondering why it was so quiet. A gunshot rang out and dust flew up beside him. He looked at the spot where the bullet had hit curiously. *What was that?* Another near miss got him to his feet. He looked in the direction of fire and saw a man with a rifle pointed at him. He was confused. *Has the human population gone mad?* Finally, he ran between two buildings to get out of the line of fire. The man started to chase him but Shadow easily escaped into the back alleys of Urunes.

He walked for a long time staying away from humans. He needed time to think. *What is going on?* He reached out with his mind to see if there were any rhutz in the area. He found one quickly.

"I was just shot at! Is that how they treat rhutz in Urunes?"

"Sorry, my brother, apparently you didn't hear about the Massacre at Flat Meadow."

"What? I just left Flat Meadow."

"You must be Shadow, then. I am Starlight. We wondered why you were not killed with the others."

"What others?" Shadow asked warily.

"Your entire pack was murdered by the humans."

"No! That cannot be. They were fine when I left them."

"Sadly, it is true but you will be pleased to hear all of the humans responsible for the massacre have also been killed."

"Oh, Whisper save us. So, that's why the humans are shooting at me?"

"Yes, as soon as word of the massacre got out, the humans here

in Urunes have taken up arms against us. I'm afraid we've all been driven away. You should leave immediately. You're welcome to join our pack since yours is no more."

"Thank you for your generous offer, but it is now more important than ever that I make contact with the humans and try to put a stop to this madness."

"But is that even possible? The humans and the rhutz have never communicated."

"Yes, they have. Sandee and Whisper communicated telepathically and I have heard of others who have managed it. I must try."

"Who will you seek among the humans for this communication?"

"I'm told councilor Tobin Sandista is a wise man with a fair and open mind. I'm hoping to make contact with him."

"Yes. His name is familiar to me. He does have a reputation for being fair to the humans, but I'm sure he has never talked to a rhutz."

"Surely, he will understand the need to do so now."

"Do you even know if he is telepathic?"

"No. I pray he is, though, as time is short. I don't have time to seek another."

"Even if he is you don't know his language. You may only be able to communicate by sharing your memories."

"But that is not good enough. We must be able to exchange ideas clearly and quickly."

"Our Old one knows how to read the human language. Perhaps he will teach it to you if you ask him."

"How did he learn it?"

"He's been studying it a little at a time over many cycles. He likes to know what the humans are up to."

"If I come to you now, will you take me to him?"

"Yes, I'm only a kyloon east of town. Where are you?"

"Near the well as you enter the town from the south."

"Wait there. I will come to you."

Shadow sat down and waited. He hadn't thought about the human language. He assumed if he linked to a human they would understand each other, but now he realized how stupid he'd been. Depression overcame him as his task seemed more and more impossible. After a while a beautiful silver rhutz stepped into his vision. He stood up and walked toward her. They sniffed each other as rhutz did to memorize their scent, then looked into each other's eyes to enhance their link. It was much easier for rhutz to connect when they were looking in each other's eyes. In this fashion they could not only share thoughts but exchange memories as well.

Starlight growled as she felt the memories of Shimmer's death. *"The human murdered her for no reason."*

"That's why we followed them and tried to kill them. Unfortunately, two got away and brought back more murderers."

"God, save us," Starlight thought.

"That's why I must talk to the humans. There can't be a war between the rhutz and the humans. It would be the end of us."

"Or, the end of humans," Starlight disagreed.

"No, it would be the end of the rhutz. The humans have many weapons and armies trained to kill. We'd be no match for them."

"Perhaps, but it would be a costly fight."

"Take me to your old one," Shadow said, *"We have little time to lose."*

Starlight turned and trotted away with Shadow at her side. Starlight picked up the pace and soon they were racing through the grassy plains east of Urunes toward the Drogal Mountains. When they got close to Starlight's pack she stopped and howled to the sky. Before she was done six rhutz stepped into view.

"Come on. The old one is waiting," Starlight advised and took off after the other rhutz.

After a loon, roughly the Earth equivalent of a minute, they came upon a pile of logs that turned out to be the roof of a makeshift cave. Starlight entered the cave with Shadow right behind. The six rhutz took up positions behind the Old one. Shadow looked into the Old one's eyes. They both opened their minds and shared their recent memories.

"So, you think you can stop the war?" the old one asked.

"I must. Such a war would be unthinkable."

"True, but I fear it is too late. A lot of blood has already been shed and the humans have an unquenchable thirst for vengeance."

"But if I can explain what happened. If they know that a human murdered my mate, perhaps they will understand why the rhutz killed one

of theirs."

"I fear it won't work, but I hope I'm wrong. What can I do to help you?"

"Starlight tells me you know the human language?"

"Yes, as a pup I was befriended by a human child. Neither of us knew humans and rhutz were not supposed to be friends. We spent time together alone and shared our thoughts. At first it was just memories and mental pictures, but in time the human taught me to read and think in Tari. This allowed us to communicate as well as any two humans."

"Can you teach me?" Shadow asked.

"Not the entire language. There's not enough time, but I can teach you enough to get your message across to the human you are seeking out."

"Thank you. How shall we begin?"

The old one ran everybody off and spent seven days with Shadow teaching him the human language and how humans wrote it down with symbols. Shadow was highly intelligent and keenly interested in the topic, so he learned quickly. At the end of the seventh day the old one wished him good luck and retreated back into the den. While Shadow had been learning Tari, Starlight had been hunting and sharing her kill with Shadow. He accepted it appreciably as he didn't have time to hunt. While they were eating Starlight offered to accompany Shadow back to Urunes to meet Councilor Sandista. Shadow accepted the offer as he liked Starlight's company and knew it would be good to have another set of eyes with the humans being out for blood.

"Of course, I would love your company, but it will be dangerous," Shadow thought.

"I believe in what you are doing, so I don't mind taking the risk."

"Don't you have a mate who will miss you?"

"No. My mate was run down by truck a cycle ago."

"Oh, no. How did that happen?"

"He'd just killed a ringlet in an alley and was enjoying his lunch when a human driving a truck recklessly turned the corner and struck him. The human didn't even bother to stop."

"So, you must have the same questions about the humans as I do."

"Yes, and I enjoy your company as well, so come to my bed and we can rest. Dawn will soon be upon us."

Shadow didn't argue but immediately followed Starlight deep into the den. They cuddled up together and went to sleep. During the night Shadow went over his meeting with the Councilor in his mind over and over again. Each time the encounter became clearer and more focused until communicating in Tari seemed almost natural. When he woke up at first light he felt excited and confident he'd be able to communicate effectively with Councilor Sandista. Now the only problem was finding him and cornering him somewhere so he'd have to listen.

When Rammel got back to his office, he called the governor. The situation was no longer a local matter and he wanted to explain everything to the governor before the media or one of the other councilmen got to him. Although Rammel didn't know Governor Wilfin Errius all that well, they were both Loyalists so they were on good terms. After some difficulty, he got the governor on his global communicator or GC and explained the situation.

"That *is* disturbing news. I agree we need to do whatever it takes to avoid further bloodshed."

"The TGA will be under a lot of pressure to move against the Rhutz," Rammel reasoned, "both from the Town Council and the General Assembly."

Not only was Progasis Bruda a Vaceen town councilman but he was also the son of Cornelias Bruda, the Chairman of Tributon's General Assembly.

"Yes, this is a most difficult situation."

"You'll have to move quickly to head them off."

"Indeed, I will," the Governor agreed. "I'll get right on it."

Rammel left his office and went straight to the Bruda compound. He assumed Progasis Bruda's widow would already know her husband had been killed since it had been the feature story on the news, but he wanted to give her his personal condolence. He also wanted to talk to Rupra Bruda to see if his suspicions were true about Rupra's testing the new rifle on the rhutz. When he got there several news reporters were milling outside. When they saw him, they swarmed around him.

"Councilman. Are you here to inform the family of Councilman Bruda's death?" a reporter asked.

"Well, I'm sure she already has heard about it. I'm here to give her more details and see if there is anything she needs."

"Is the TGA going to track down the rhutz responsible for this atrocity?" another reporter asked.

"Central Command and the Governor are studying the matter as we speak. No decisions have been made."

"What's there to study? Surely, they have no choice but to eliminate the two packs that are responsible?"

Rammel sighed. "They want to understand exactly what happened before more lives are lost. The town council acted hastily and look what happened. The public enforcer has already underestimated the rhutz, the TGA won't make the same mistake."

Rammel moved through the crowd to the front door. Mistress Bruda, who had heard the commotion outside and opened the door, let him in. She closed the door behind them.

Rammel turned and shook his head. "I'm so sorry, Mella," Rammel said.

She shrugged. "It's not your fault. I heard you were against the hunt."

"Yes, I feared it was a bad idea to send out an angry mob to deal with them, but I must admit I didn't expect the mob to be massacred."

She wiped a tear from her eye. "Yes. That baffles me as well? Progasis was sure it would be no problem dealing with them. In fact, Rupra almost went with them. Thank God he had been slightly injured in the previous encounter, otherwise he'd be dead too."

"Speaking of your son. I need to speak with him a moment. I want to get more details of that first encounter. It would be good to understand why the rhutz attacked the boys."

Mella nodded. "Of course. I'll go find him for you."

"Thanks."

Rammel knew if his suspicions were correct it would further complicate an already delicate situation. Rupra's father had been well liked and respected as a town councilman and Rupra's grandfather was the most powerful man in Tributon, being the Chairman of the General Assembly. If Rammel accused Rupra of murdering the rhutz and then lying about it, he knew he'd have to have irrefutable evidence to prove the accusation. Even with this proof Rammel would become an enemy of one of the most powerful families on the planet. Rammel's thoughts were interrupted when young Rupra Bruda appeared, not looking too pleased about the summons.

"What do you want?" he spat. "You here to gloat over my father's death?"

"Rupra!" Mella exclaimed, "Watch your tongue."

"No," Rammel replied. "Your father's death is very tragic. I feel horrible about it. My opposition to the hunt was out of respect for the rhutz. I thought it important we know all the facts before we scheduled an execution."

"I told you the facts. They attacked us for no reason and murdered Callus."

"That's what I understand. I just wanted to ask you a few more questions."

"Like what?"

"You say you were riding your jet cycles when they attacked you?"

"Yes, we were on our way back to the copter to go home."

"So, where were you coming from? Had you been to Flat Meadow?"

"No. We followed a herd of range deer and tested the new Ruggi 7 on strays and stragglers. We never saw a rhutz until they attacked us."

"So, why do you think they attacked you?"

"I don't know," Rupra said irritably. "Like I said, they acted mad."

"Were they foaming at the mouth?"

Rupra shrugged. "I don't know. We were running for our lives. I didn't have time to look at their mouths."

"Oh, by the way. How did your test results come out? Were you infected?"

"No," Mella said. "Thank God the test came out negative."

"So, if the rhutz weren't mad, I wonder why they attacked you. I've searched all our databases and I can't find a single report of an unprovoked attack by a rhutz in Tributon in the past 10 cycles. It's very perplexing."

"You calling me a liar?" Bruda challenged.

"No. No. Like I said. I'm just perplexed. There must be an explanation. I just can't figure it out."

Mella looked suspiciously at her son and then turned to Rammel.

"Thank you for coming by Rammel. "If you don't mind, I'm rather tired. I think I'll retire."

Rammel nodded. "Of course. Let me know if you need anything. I'm so sorry about Progasis."

From the Bruda home Councilman Garciah went to the Tripolis home to give his condolences to his widow over the death of Callus and Rubbias Tripolis, however, Mistress Tripolis was under sedation so he was unable to talk to her. Finally, he went to the home of Romas Lantra to verify Rupra Bruda's account of the first rhutz attack. Romas wasn't pleased to see him and seemed quite nervous. Rammel figured Bruda had warned him of the likely visit and they'd worked out any discrepancies in their stories, but he also knew it wasn't easy to lie and that liars could be tripped up. He pushed the record button on his wrist array so he'd have a recording of the conversation to play back later.

"So, I guess you heard Rupra's tests came out negative?" Rammel noted.

He nodded. "Yes. That's great."

"So, if the rhutz weren't mad, what do you think caused them to attack you?"

Romas looked away and shrugged. "How should I know why a rhutz does something?"

"I don't know. You were there. I wasn't. I just thought maybe you observed something that might shed some light on what happened."

Romas shook his head. "No. It's just like I told the PE, we were on our way back to our plane when we were attacked for no reason."

"On your way back from Flat Meadow?"

Romas looked at Rammel warily. "Ah, I guess."

"So, the range deer were feeding in Flat Meadow and you were taking random shots at the herd?"

"Ah. Right."

"How many did you kill?"

"Just a couple."

"So, what did you do with your kill?"

"Ah, well. We just left them for any scavengers that wanted them."

Rammel knew somebody was lying since Bruda had claimed they hadn't been to Flat Meadow. He also knew range deer were a prized catch and nobody would shoot one and just leave it laying around.

"But range deer are pretty tasty. I can't believe you didn't tie them on the back of your bikes and bring them home."

Romas shrugged. "I hate skinning them. It's a lot of work."

"You could have taken them to the meat plant. They would have paid a good price for them."

"I guess. I never thought of that."

"You didn't think of it because you didn't kill any range deer," Rammel challenged. "The only thing you shot with the new Ruggi 7 was a rhutz, isn't that right?"

"No," Romas protested. "We shot two range deer."

"Well, I spent a lot of time searching Flat Meadow and I guarantee you there was no evidence of any recently killed range deer. There would have been a fresh carcass even if scavengers had eaten the meat. In fact, since a pack of rhutz live on the edge of Flat Meadow I doubt many range deer venture near the place."

Romas paled. "Well, I—"

"I won't tell anyone about this conversation. I just need to know the truth."

"Rupra will know that I told you. He's telepathic."

Rammel let out a frustrated sigh trying to restrain his anger. "I think you should come with me to the PE's office. Perhaps a dose of truth serum will refresh your memory. Of course, if you lie to the Public Enforcer and he finds out you'll go to prison."

Romas swallowed hard, tears welling in his eyes.

"If I make sure the enforcers interrogate Rupra first, he'll have no reason to ask you if you gave him up."

Romas shrugged dejectedly. "Okay, you're right. Rupra shot a rhutz. He said he needed to test the rifle on a more difficult target. The thing is the rhutz was just walking through the meadow unaware that he was about to be killed. Hardly a challenge, huh? As soon as the rhutz fell the rest of the pack came after us. We almost got away, but Callus got scared and stopped to look back to see how far away they were. That was a big mistake. It was just enough time for the rhutz to catch up with him before he could get on his bike and take off. He didn't have a chance. If we'd have gone back after him, we'd have all been killed."

Rammel sighed. "Okay. That's what I figured. Rupra didn't consult you about whether to shoot the rhutz or not, right?"

"No. He did it on his own. Callus and I didn't think it was a good idea and told him so."

"Good. You were smart to tell the truth. Did you take any shots at the rhutz?"

"No," he lied. "We only had one Ruggi."

"Good. You did the right thing. I'd stay away from Rupra for a few days. Can you go visit a relative or something?"

Romas took a deep breath and exhaled slowly. "My grandmother lives in Ce Lat. She's been asking me to come visit her."

"Excellent. I'd leave immediately. Tell your parents that you need to get away because of the shock of seeing Callus die. Tell them you don't want to be disturbed so not to tell anyone where you are."

"Okay."

Rammel was elated that he'd managed to dig the truth out of Romas and had a recording of his confession. As soon as he left the house he called Governor Errius.

"Governor, I just wanted to inform you I've confirmed that Rupra Bruda is responsible for the Flat Meadow Massacre. His friend Romas just admitted to me that Bruda killed a rhutz without provocation."

"Oh, Sandee! What was he thinking?"

"I suspect he wasn't thinking. His father made a mistake giving the Ruggi 7 to a teenager to test."

"Yes, and it cost him his life," the Governor noted. "So, now I'm duty bound to have Master Bruda arrested."

"His grandfather will not take so kindly to his incarceration," Rammel warned.

"I know. But we need to stop this insane war before it gets out of hand and the only way to do that is to expose Rupra Bruda's crime."

Rammel sighed. "I fear the Chairman will not believe it."

"No. He won't. He's grooming Rupra for a career in politics. This will devastate him. He'll have no choice but to defend him," the Governor said.

"So, what should we do?" Rammel asked.

"I don't know. I just got off the GC with General Seelor. He's ready to declare war against the entire population of Rhutz."

"Oh, my God. You can't let that happen."

"I know, but many support his position," the Governor said. "There's an emergency meeting of Tributon's General Assembly set for tomorrow morning to consider the matter. Only they can authorize a campaign against the Rhutz. You should be there to play your tape of Master Romas' confession."

"I promised not to involve him. If I played the tape or called him as a witness against Bruda it would be his death sentence. The Purists don't tolerate disloyalty."

"Then, you better come up with a new strategy or, I fear, thousands more will die," the Governor warned.

Rammel ended the call and considered his few remaining options. He could get one of his allies in the General Assembly to insist on Rupra Bruda's testimony. Then if they could catch him in a lie, he could be compelled to take the truth serum. It was a longshot but the only other option would be to argue that each Rhutz had a right to a trial before any of them could be executed. Unfortunately, that hadn't worked with the town council and he thought it even less likely he'd be able to convince the full General Assembly that the Rhutz were a protected life-form under the Supreme Mandate. He decided that he had no choice but to confront Master Bruda.

4

The Connection

Shadow and Starlight were up and running hard toward Urunes by dawn's first light. As they ran they contemplated their strategy in cornering Councilor Sandista. They knew where he lived and the government hall where he worked, so they decided to follow him and hope for an opportunity to confront him alone. He lived in a single story crushed-stone home with a tile roof. This type of structure was common in central Rigimol as it was an arid terrain with few trees. They watched the house from the hill behind the structure. About a kyloon after they'd taken up their position, the councilor came out his front door and got into his personal transporter or PT as the humans called them.

Shadow and Starlight jumped up and ran to catch up with the PT. It wasn't traveling too fast as traffic was heavy, so the two rhutz were able to keep up with it, although it wasn't easy. The humans weren't used to having rhutz running along the roadway, and the rhutz had no idea what the signs and signals along the road meant. Several times they nearly collided with vehicles coming at them seemingly out of nowhere. They were much relieved when the PT slowed and turned into the parking lot across the street from the government center. Now their only problem was where they could conceal themselves while they waited for Councilor Sandista to make his next move.

They finally settled on an alley across the street from the parking lot. From that vantage point they could see the Councilor's PT, so if they kept a close eye on it they wouldn't miss him when he left. While they were watching and waiting Starlight offered to hunt for food. Since they'd traveled many kyloons since their last meal, Shadow didn't object.

"Be careful. Don't let the humans see you." Shadow cautioned.

"Don't worry. The humans are usually preoccupied and don't pay attention to rhutz."

Shadow knew she was right. Humans always seemed to have a lot on their minds and didn't pay much attention to what was going on around them. It was a shame since they were missing many wondrous things that occurred every day.

"But things have changed now since Flat Meadow."

"I know. I'll stay out of sight."

Starlight roamed through the back alleys looking for anything edible. She could smell many aromas coming from restaurants and bakeries but she didn't dare go close to any human habitats. Finally, she honed in on the smell of a zoot, a large scavenger often found in the cities. The zoot looted trash cans and garbage pits and grew quite large in the cities. Starlight thought zoot a tasty meal and began to salivate with the thought of it. She stopped abruptly, feeling the spirit of the animal close at hand. She reached out and felt the fear in the zoot's mind. It had sensed danger but didn't know the nature of it. Suddenly it panicked and began to run. It was no contest as Starlight leaped forward and snatched the zoot in midair. The zoot whined in horror at being the silver rhutz' lunch. Starlight felt exhilarated as she trotted back to where Shadow was waiting.

Shadow was impressed and gratified at how quickly Starlight had produced lunch. Back in the hills of the White Mountains he often hunted for kyloons for a meal. The two rhutz ate heartily and nearly forgot about Councilor Sandista. The hum of an engine coming to life grabbed their attention. The Councilor was on the move. Shadow looked at the half-eaten zoot and told Starlight to finish it off while he followed Sandista's PT. Starlight never looked up.

The PT traveled west several kyloons and then pulled into a public park. A stream ran through the middle of the park providing water for a large grove of trees and lush bushes. Shadow wondered why the Councilor would come to such a place in the middle of the day, but he was gratified as it resembled his home in Flat Meadow. The PT finally stopped and the Councilor got out. Shadow then saw why he'd come to the park. His family was already there preparing to eat the noon meal. Shadow ran behind a tree and watched the Councilor and his family enjoying their time together in the pleasant surroundings. A sense of relief came over Shadow. Surely this man full of love for his family will understand the importance of peace between human and rhutz.

A few loons later Starlight walked up and lay down next to Shadow. He looked at her gratified that she had finished off the zoot and not let it go to waste. Food and water were precious, he knew, and mustn't be wasted. Finally, Councilor Sandista stood up and appeared to be going somewhere. Shadow became alert, sensing his moment might have come.

"Excuse me a moment, my love," the Councilor said to his wife. "I need to freshen up."

His wife nodded and turned her attention to her children who had begun to taunt each other. Shadow looked around wondering where the Councilor would be going. He saw a building in the distance and decided that must be the destination. To get there the Councilor would have to go through a cluster of trees and shrubs that would provide the cover they needed to make contact. The two rhutz raced into position. When the Councilor walked through the trees Shadow stepped out in front of him. The Councilor froze. Shadow could feel his fear. The Councilor slowly turned around to return the way he came, but Starlight stepped out blocking his path.

"Fear not, Councilor Sandista," Shadow thought. *"We mean you no harm."*

Councilor Sandista turned back around, swallowed hard, and looked intensely at Shadow.

"Are you speaking to me, or is it my imagination?"

"I am speaking to you through my thoughts. This is how the rhutz communicate. I'm glad to know you can do the same."

"Yes, I'm fortunate to have the gift, but I didn't know the rhutz could talk telepathically as well."

"Yes, that is a gift God has given us."

"So, it is true. You are a sentient life-form. I've often wondered if that were the case."

"I don't know the meaning of your word, but if it means we appreciate God's gifts, then it is true."

"So, what is your name?"

"Those in my pack call me Shadow. My companion is Starlight."

"Such delightful names. So, Shadow, why have you made contact with me?"

"To explain the Massacre at Flat Meadow. It was not the rhutz'

doing."

Shadow shared his thought about Flat Meadow with the Councilor and how he was afraid the killing would escalate if something weren't done.

"I fear you are right. They have called a special meeting of the General Assembly to authorize the killing of the two packs responsible for the death of the forty-one humans."

"If those two packs are killed four more packs will join in the fight. There'll be no end to it."

"So you can communicate over long distances?"

"Each rhutz can link over a few kyloons, but there are many rhutz and minds can be joined to make a solid link from the Dark Sea to the Straits of Tributon."

The Councilor turned and looked at Starlight. "I must bring you two to Rizi to talk to the leaders of the General Assembly before they act."

"But that is a long way and we won't have time to get there."

"We can go in my jet copter. It will only take a few kyloons. Hopefully we can get to Rizi before the General Assembly declares war on the rhutz."

"Good, then. Let us make haste."

Councilor Sandista opened a link on his wrist array to his pilot and ordered his jet copter brought to him immediately. Shadow had never flown before and felt a little uneasy at the thought of getting in a machine that flew through the air like a dirkbird. He looked at Starlight apprehensively.

"Don't worry, my brother," Starlight thought *"I see these machines flying everywhere. They seem to be quite reliable."*

"But it is unnatural to fly through the skies. If God had wanted us to fly He would have given us wings."

Councilor Sandista smiled. *"I was a little reluctant to get in a jet copter the first time, myself, but they rarely crash."*

"Crash?" Shadow said.

"Ah. Fall from the sky."

"No. I understand crash," Shadow thought. *"What I don't understand is **rarely**."*

"Oh. That means, not often."

Before the Councilor could respond the familiar sound of a jet copter could be heard in the distance. The Councilor excused himself to tell his wife what was going on. When he returned the big blue copter was landing and Councilor Sandista ran over and climbed aboard. Shadow and Starlight looked at each other and then warily trotted over to the copter and jumped aboard. As the copter quickly lifted off the ground, Shadow looked down through the big transparent bubble that encircled them. He was alarmed as the people below were getting smaller with every tik. Suddenly he felt like he was going to vomit up his zoot, but the feeling went away as the jet copter leveled and accelerated toward Rizi.

5

The Eighth World War

When Councilman Garciah got home it was late and he was exhausted. He hadn't eaten so his wife, Petrina, warmed up some pribbett with ocles for him and then sat and kept him company as he ate. A pribbett is a large bird native to Lower Azollo that is quite tasty and so popular that pribbett ranching had sprung up in almost every province. Ocles are white vegetables that are very nutritious and a staple on Tarizon. While he was eating he filled her in on the tragic events of the day. When he was done eating they retired to the study where his two young children were playing. When they saw him, they jumped up excitedly and rushed over.

"Papa. You're home," Eroh, his eight-cycle-old son said. "Just in time to tell us a story before bed."

"Your father is too tired to be telling you stories," Petrina scolded.

"But Papa we've been waiting all day to see you," Ellah, his eleven-cycle-old daughter complained. "We've missed you."

Petrina gave her daughter a scathing look but it didn't faze her. "Please! One story. Tell us about Grandpa's escape to Earth."

"Yes!" Eroh agreed. "Tell us about Earth."

Rammel sighed. "But, I've told you that story a hundred times."

"I don't care," Ellah replied. "I love that story."

Rammel rolled his eyes and then smiled. "Okay, but I'm going to give you the short version. It's nearly time for you to go to bed."

Eroh and Ellah clapped their hands approvingly and then sat at their father's feet to listen.

Petrina took a deep breath and walked over to the relaxation chair across from them and sat. There was a swishing sound as the fabric formed around her body and began to massage her. She sighed in delight. Rammel smiled at her.

"Alright," Rammel said. "Nearly a hundred cycles ago the Eighth World War broke out. It started as a dispute between Synclare and Soni over a thin corridor of land between Soni and Tuht called the Tazi Strip. For over a hundred cycles the Tazi Strip had provided Synclare unrestricted access to the Straits of Tributon. It was needed so Synclare could maintain its own merchant fleet and navy. Without it Synclare would be forced to pay high tariffs to Merria and Soni and lose its competitive advantage over the rest of the nations of Turvin.

It all came to a head when a military dictator, Rhust Gorda, seized power in Soni. He'd been backed by wealthy industrialists who supported the restoration of the Tazi Strip to Soni, so one of Gorda's first actions when he took control of the government was to launch a surprise attack on Synclare's navy and send troops in to the strip and seize Synclare's merchant fleet.

"Of course, Synclare couldn't allow this, so they mobilized and declared war against Soni. Tuht, Rour and Merria joined in on Soni's side hoping to divide up the country between themselves. Tributon, however, being a strong trading partner of Synclare joined the war on their side. After that the war spread everywhere.

"Unfortunately, by this time most nations had nuclear weapons and weren't afraid to use them. It was total insanity. Before long every major city in Lemaine Shane, Azollo and Turvin had sustained at least one nuclear attack. Millions died of radiation poisoning, cities lay in ruins, most of Tarizon's beautiful forests had burned, and once rich farmlands were laid barren. Soon there was nothing but chaos and anarchy on Tarizon. Tarizon had become barely habitable.

"In anticipation of the war a group of twenty wealthy merchants had bought a spaceship and outfitted it in case of this type of emergency. Your grandfather was one of them. They put themselves in indefinite hibernation and set their ships on autopilot to orbit Tarizon. The ships' computers were programmed to monitor Tarizon's atmosphere and when it was again habitable, it would wake its passengers who then could return to the surface of the planet. The big advantage of going into hibernation was that a person didn't age much.

"When the computers finally woke up the passengers fifty-one cycles later your grandfather was seventy-seven cycles old but looked to be in his twenties. Soon after he returned he was mated with your grandmother who was twenty-eight and a cycle later I was born."

Eroh and Ellah laughed in delight.

"The end. Now it's time for you two to go to bed."

The children stood up with big smiles on their faces. They hugged Rammel and then followed their mother out of the room. When they were gone Rammel leaned back in his chair and closed his eyes. He wondered how he was going to prevent the General Assembly from acting foolishly and trying to exact some kind of punishment against the rhutz. He was worried about Romas too. He was afraid Rupra Bruda might hurt Romas if he found out he'd talked. He felt a little guilty going to him and forcing him to betray a friend, but he had to know the truth. He didn't want to protect the Rhutz if they didn't deserve it. Depression swept over him like a hot summer wind. He loosened his collar and twisted in his chair trying to get comfortable.

Petrina walked in and immediately felt his distress. They weren't telepathic but they knew each other well enough to know when the other was in pain.

"Don't worry, Rammel. It will all work out. I know you'll figure a way to make the assemblymen listen to reason."

Rammel opened his eyes and sat up. "Listen to reason? I wish it were that simple. They respond to emotion or self-interest more readily than reason. My only hope is that I can make them understand how costly a war with the rhutz will be. If I can get them to understand that, then maybe they'll be reasonable."

"Well, if anyone can do it, you can," Petrina assured him.

"Thank you for your words of encouragement, my dearest, but I fear I have run out of miracles. Only God and Sandee can save us now."

Rupra Bruda was upset that his friend Romas hadn't attended his father's funeral. It was very unusual because they always went everywhere together. He didn't know what to make of it. Surely Romas couldn't have had anything more important to do. Was he so shaken and distraught that he couldn't deal with a funeral? No. He didn't think that was it. Romas was a tough kid. That's why Rupra liked him so much. They had made plans to join the TGA when they were old enough and to go into politics once their tour of duty was over. *Where are you my friend?* A horrible thought came to Bruda. *Have the enforcers got to you? Did they force you to betray me?* Bruda groaned at the thought, but knew that was a distinct possibility. Romas wasn't as good a liar as him.

He knew if the inquisitor had questioned Romas and found any discrepancy in their stories he might have taken him to headquarters and forced him to take truth serum. That would be a disaster. He went over to where his grandfather was talking to some mourners.

"Grandfather?"

Cornelius turned quickly, annoyed by the interruption. "Yes, Rupra. What do you want? Can't you see I'm busy?"

"Yes. Sorry, grandfather, but I have a matter of great urgency to discuss with you."

Cornelius sighed and smiled at the mourners. "Sorry for the interruption, but you know children, everything is an emergency. Thank you for coming." He turned to Rupra. "What is it?"

"Romas is missing. I'm afraid the public enforcers might have taken him to headquarters."

"So what? They'll let him go once they are through questioning him."

"Maybe. Maybe not."

Cornelius frowned. "What are you talking about?"

"I wasn't entirely truthful to the PE."

"Oh, God save us. What lie did you tell them?"

"I may have accidentally killed a rhutz before they attacked us."

"What?"

"There was a rhutz stalking the range deer and I didn't see him. There was a tremor about the time I pulled the trigger and I hit the rhutz by mistake."

"Why didn't you just say that in the first place?" Cornelius asked angrily.

"Because I didn't come up with that story quickly enough?"

Cornelius closed his eyes and took a deep breath trying to contain his anger. "So, what really happened? No more lies."

"Remember the stories you used to tell us about rhutz hunting when you were a teenager? Your father owned a ranch and the rhutz would kill his livestock, so you and your father would go hunting for rhutz."

Cornelius moaned. "Yes, but it was nearly impossible to get close enough to kill them. Usually we were just trying to drive them off our land. They were trespassers."

"Well, dad gave me this new rifle to try out and it had much longer range than anything I'd ever seen. I wondered if I could actually kill a rhutz with it. It turns out I can."

"Didn't you consider what would happen if you killed a rhutz?"

"Yes, I thought we'd get on our jet cycles and easily outrun the rest of the rhutz. I didn't expect Callus to be such a dirkbird."

"Did you tell your father this?"

"No. I just thought the hunting party would kill all the rhutz easily and that would be the end of it."

Cornelius shook his head and began to pace. "Now what are we going to do? The General Assembly is going to meet tomorrow to decide whether or not to kill the two packs of rhutz. Many think if such an order is issued it will mean general war with the Rhutz. Do you know how many people could die because of you!"

Mourners looked up when they heard Cornelius yelling at Rupra. He took Rupra by the arm and escorted him several strides away. "You need to find your friend and see what he's told the PE. If he has confessed then you may have to go with your accident story. I'll back you up and if you apologize and show remorse, the public enforcers may not present your case for prosecution. It will hurt me politically to have such an idiot for a grandson, but I'll survive. If the inquisitors haven't talked to your friend, then we will stick with your story. If it wasn't for your father's death, I would have been thrilled to have an excuse to kill a rhutz. If every last one of them were dead, Tarizon would be a better place."

Rupra smiled. "So, let's hope Romas hasn't betrayed me."

"Yes, pray that is the case," Cornelius said.

"Who's sponsoring the bill tomorrow?" Rupra asked.

"Assemblyman Sealey."

Rupra nodded. "He's a good man."

"Yes, he is. Now locate your friend quickly and let me know what you find out."

Rupra nodded and went off looking for Romas' parents whom he'd seen earlier. They were at the bar drinking and talking to some other mourners. He went over to them.

"Hello, Mistress Lantra . . . Mister Lantra. Thank you for coming. Where's Romas?"

Mistress Lantra gave Rupra a guilty look and then turned away. "Ah. He hasn't taken this whole affair very well, I'm afraid," Mr. Lantra said. "Callus' death really shook him up. He's gone away for a while."

"Where is he? I'd like to talk to him. Maybe talking with someone, particularly a friend, might help."

Mistress Lantra smiled faintly. "You are very kind, Rupra, but Romas just needs some time alone to reflect on things."

Rupra knew they were lying and suspected now more than ever that Romas had betrayed him. At an early age Rupra learned that he had strong telepathic abilities. This was common in the Bruda family, but Rupra's gift was stronger than his parents and even his grandfather's. The Bruda family was proud of this ability and considered it a gift from God, and a sign that they were destined to do God's work. This was one reason Rupra didn't feel badly about many of the strange things he did like killing animals with his invisible arm, as he liked to call it. He killed the rhutz, however, out of hatred—a hatred passed on by his grandfather, to his father, and then to him. He figured since God had placed him in the Bruda family and given him so much wealth, power and extraordinary abilities, that whatever he did was God's will. So, he decided to use his telepathic ability to find out where Romas was hiding. After all, God would want him to escape any repercussions from the Flat Meadow Massacre.

He smiled back at Mistress Lantra and peered deep into her eyes. A flood of her thoughts rushed into his mind. In just a few tiks he knew the answer to his question. Romas was with his grandmother in Ce Lat. With the purpose of his conversation achieved he nodded and took his leave. As he walked away he wondered what he should do about Romas. If he hadn't talked to the PE, everything might be okay, but he knew he must have talked to someone or he wouldn't have slithered away and hid. He sighed. Rupra knew what he had to do. Romas had betrayed him and could never be trusted again. There was no choice in the matter—he must die!

Rupra went home and waited until everyone was asleep. Then he climbed out of his bedroom window and went to the roadway where he'd left his jet cycle earlier. He didn't want to start it near the house where it might be heard. It was a two-hour drive to Ce Lat so he had plenty of time to go there, take care of Romas, and return before daybreak. After programming in Romas' grandmother's address, he got on and took off. There was no traffic so he rode fast, anxious to put this threat behind him.

On the way he wondered what he could do to the rhutz to make them pay for killing his father. The hatred he'd had for them had turned to rage. He'd underestimated their abilities, obviously, and would have to be more careful the next time he confronted them or he might end up like his father. But, he knew some day he'd get his revenge. He'd just have to wait for the right opportunity.

When he arrived at his destination he hid his bike and surveyed the two-story whitewood structure. Ce Lat was surrounded by forests of tall whitewood trees which were strong and durable, so most of the local housing was built from it. He'd have to find Romas' room and gain entry without waking anyone up. Opening his mind, he searched for Romas' thoughts. It wasn't hard to find them as they were filled with fear and trepidation. He walked until he found the spot where the thoughts were the strongest and then deduced the room Romas must be occupying. A drain pipe running vertically up to the roof made the climb to Romas' window quite easy. The window was latched from the inside, so Rupra used his invisible hand to turn the latch and pull the window up slowly.

Once inside he wondered if he should wake Romas and question him, but after careful thought he decided that was too risky. He couldn't be linked in any way to the murder, so he simply reached into Romas' mind and searched his memories. It didn't take him long to find out what he was looking for. It was the skutz Garciah who had forced him to talk. Anger welled in Rupra. Rammel Garciah had always been a troublemaker, but his father and grandfather had never done anything about it. *It's time Garciah pays.*

Knowing now that Romas had betrayed him, Rupra focused his invisible hand on Romas' lungs and squeezed them with all the force he could muster. Romas squirmed and jerked around trying to breathe, then fell limp. Rupra relaxed and smiled at his handiwork. There would be no evidence left behind for the inquisitors to find since he'd worn gloves, hat and mask when he climbed to the roof and entered the house. Leaving as stealthily as he'd come, he rode back to Vaceen and was in his bed when the maid came in to wake him.

6

General Assembly

The next day Rammel Garciah got up early and took his jet copter to Rizi. Since he'd arrived well in advance of the time set for the General Assembly to convene, he had arranged to have breakfast with the Governor to discuss last minute strategy. The Governor brought along Assemblyman Tobick Doban who would be presenting the case for those who believed the Rhutz should be afforded legal protections under the Supreme Mandate. They met in front of an Allso restaurant called Café Maramoor. Allso was a small country at the very tip of Lemaine Shane that was known for its fine cuisine and beautiful women which was attributed to the tropical climate and laid-back lifestyle of the inhabitants. They shook hands, went inside and were seated immediately. A waiter came over and took their orders.

"My staff has been polling the delegates," Doban advised, "and the sentiment is strongly against the Rhutz. Chairman Bruda has called in a lot of favors to ensure the Assembly takes strong action against them."

"That is not surprising since his son was one of their victims," the Governor noted.

"Yes, but if he cared at all for justice he'd recuse himself. There is no way he can be impartial."

"It was suggested to him," Doban said, "but he ignored the suggestion."

"So, how are you going to play it?" Rammel asked.

"We've ordered the public enforcers to bring in both witnesses, Rupra Bruda and Romas Lantra."

"What?" Rammel said. "I promised Romas he'd be left out of it."

"You had no authority to do that?" Doban replied. "Besides, it would look like Romas had struck a deal if he wasn't brought in to testify. If we put both of them under the truth serum it will be assumed both refused to talk."

Rammel sighed. "I just pray you are right."

Doban's wrist array vibrated. He looked at it and pushed a button to allow the incoming call to come in. His face turned grim. "Oh, God and Sandee help us," Doban exclaimed.

"What happened?" the Governor asked.

Doban swallowed hard. "That was the PE's office. When they went to pick up Romas in Ce Lat to bring him to Rizi they found him dead."

Rammel shook his head in despair. "This was all my fault. I should have left Romas alone."

"Nonsense," Doban replied. "You weren't the one who crushed his lungs."

"Crushed his lungs?" the Governor repeated. "He was killed by telekinesis?"

"Yes, a very clever way to kill someone. There's never any evidence left behind."

"Rupra Bruda has strong telepathic abilities, I'm told. I wonder if he also has the gift of telekinesis," Rammel said.

"I don't know, but even if someone witnessed his death and testified that Rupra was there at his side, you still couldn't prove he was responsible."

"Nevertheless, it does give us more reason to put Master Bruda under the truth serum."

Doban sighed. "I guess that's all we can do. The chairman will be angry, but hopefully the members will see the necessity of what we seek."

"Hopefully," the Governor said and stood up. "We must leave if we are to get to the Capitol Building on time. Rammel and Doban got up and they all left the restaurant and got in a Grinden PTV waiting for them outside.

Shadow was glad to get off the jet copter. Although the ride had been uneventful, it was unnerving to look down and see a bed of clouds beneath him. Not that it wasn't a wondrous and beautiful sight, but he preferred to have his paws on Mother Tarizon. Starlight, however, seemed quite at ease in the copter and ran from portal to portal so she wouldn't miss any of the sights. Councilor Sandista sat thoughtfully as he pondered how to present the two rhutz to the General Assembly. Finally, he called a friend in Rizi and asked him who was spearheading the opposition to Chairman Bruda's bill to have the two packs of rhutz killed. His friend told him the only opposition he'd heard about was from Assemblyman Doban who had requested time to speak against the bill. Sandista gave him a call.

"You have what?" Doban exclaimed.

"I have two rhutz with me. One of them wants to testify as a witness to the Flat Meadow Massacre."

"And you can communicate with them?"

"Of course. We talk telepathically and we can share memories."

"Holy Sandee! That's amazing. I'd heard it was possible, but you're the first person I've known who has actually talked to a rhutz."

"Well, I'm just a translator. They sought me out to help them get on the agenda for the special session."

Doban laughed. "Oh, the Chairman is going to be livid. I can't wait to see his face."

"Good. So, where should we go?"

"I'll send a Grinden to pick you and your friends up. I think it would be best to keep them out of sight until it's time for them to testify."

"You're probably right, but how can we do that?"

"They can wait in my office. I'll put them on the agenda. What are their names?"

"Shadow and Starlight."

"Hmm," Doban groaned. "That won't do. I'll put your name down instead and you can defer to Shadow when they call you."

"That will be fine."

"Now you were saying he wants to testify about the Flat Meadow Massacre?"

"That's right."

"Was he there?" Doban asked.

"Yes, it was his mate who was shot by Master Bruda."

"Well, that's good news. Our other witness appears to have been murdered to shut him up."

"Oh, my God. Who would do that?"

"I think you can probably guess."

"Oh, of course. Master Bruda."

"Unfortunately, we'll never be able to prove it. It was a telekinetic kill—severe lung trauma with no apparent source."

"Really. I didn't realize Master Bruda had that gift."

"Yes. He and his grandfather are formidable adversaries. We'll have to be very careful."

"Indeed. Can you requisition some security from the PE's office?"

"No. We can't risk anyone knowing about your witnesses. I don't think they will be in danger as long as no one knows about them in advance."

"Alright then. I'll see you at your office."

Sandista told Doban where they would be landing and he got the suite number for Doban's office in the Capitol Building. The news about a witness already being killed upset him. He wished he'd thought of picking up some security before he took off from Urunes, but it was too late now.

Shadow felt his distress. *"Don't worry about us,"* Shadow thought. *"We can take care of ourselves. We too have the gift of telekinesis. No one will be able to hurt us in that manner."*

"Yes, but we know a bullet can kill you. I'm more worried about that," Sandista replied.

"As long as we know of the danger we will be alert and it will be difficult for anyone to hurt us."

Sandista smiled and noticed they were approaching Rizi. When they arrived at the heliport the Grinden was waiting for them. Shadow and Starlight had never ridden in a PTV so they were a little hesitant to get in what appeared to be a cave on wheels. But the Councilor assured them it would be safe, so they jumped aboard and soon were darting through Rizi at an alarming speed. As they approached the capitol the Councilor had them lay low in their seats so nobody would see them. When they got to the office building, one of Doban's aides came out and brought them into the building through the freight elevator to be sure they made it to his suite without being spotted.

The Assembly Hall occupied the south side of the Capitol Building with the governor and council of interpreters sharing the north side. It was a magnificent structure built just after unification some twenty cycles earlier.

The gallery was filling up quickly and most of the members of the General Assembly were already in their seats waiting for what would, no doubt, be a historic session. Although the issue of the legal standing of the rhutz had been the subject of much debate, it had never been finally determined by any legislature or judicial authority on Tarizon. Due to the worldwide outrage over the Flat Meadow Massacre that issue would now have to be addressed.

Chairman Bruda went up to the podium and looked out over the crowd. He was an imposing figure standing over six feet tall with a grim face and dark brown, penetrating eyes. The bailiff stood up and three chimes announced the session was about to begin. The great assembly hall became quiet. Bruda, dressed in the Chairman's lavender robe, cleared his throat.

"Governor, fellow assemblymen, and citizens of Tributon, I commence this 23rd session of the General Assembly with a heavy heart. As you know 41 of our brothers and sisters, including my own son, were recently killed by two packs of rhutz at a place called Flat Meadow. The purpose of this session is to finally deal with the long-standing issue as to whether or not the Rhutz is an "animal" and thus subject to the Animal Control Act of 12 A.U. or a sentient "life-form" and thereby protected by the civil rights provisions of the Supreme Mandate. The importance of this determination is obvious. If the Rhutz are animals the public enforcer can deal with the two packs of rhutz as he deems prudent. If the Rhutz is a sentient life-form then the matter of the Flat Meadow Massacre would have to be turned over to the Public Prosecutor and each rhutz found to be responsible for any of the forty-one human deaths would be assigned advocates and tried in the public courts.

A yellow light began blinking on a transparent display above the Chairman's head. The Chairman glanced at it and said, "The chair recognizes Assemblyman Rendh Sealey who will introduce the resolution.

Assemblyman Sealey stood up and took the podium. He was thin with long gray hair and walked with a limp. "Governor, Chairman Bruda, fellow assemblymen. You have each been provided a revised version of the Animal Control Act of 12 A.U. The changes in the text of the law have been highlighted. The main change in the law is to specifically include the Rhutz by name as a common animal and thereby subject them to the provisions of the Act. The practical effect of this amendment will be to bring clarity to the law such that the recent events at Flat Meadow can be dealt with by the Public Enforcer in a swift and expeditious manner.

"Now I know that a few scientists have written articles claiming the Rhutz are an intelligent life-form. They claim that they can communicate with each other and have gifts such as telepathy and telekinesis. Well, for every scientist who believes that, there are ten who scoff at such nonsense. In your packet of materials are several articles by renowned zoologists who have studied the Rhutz for many cycles. While they do show a greater intelligence than other animals they are still just animals. They hunt, eat, sleep, mate, and that's about it. They don't do anything more than what is necessary for survival. They do build fairly intricate dens and caves in which to live, but everything for them is about survival. There is no evidence that they love, create, invent, or are capable of any of the advanced functions of a sentient life-form. So, I urge you to vote for the changes to the Animal Control Act so that each rhutz responsible for this atrocity can be put down before they kill more innocent citizens."

Assemblyman Sealey limped off the podium and sat down. Another yellow light began blinking.

"The chair recognizes Assemblyman Doban."

The robust assemblyman stood up and slowly walked to the podium. After carefully laying out his notes he began. "Governor, Chairman Bruda, and citizens of Tributon. Amending the Animal Control Act is no way to deal with the tragic events at Flat Meadow. In fact it's an outrage to even suggest it. Not only did forty-one humans lose their lives but twenty-four rhutz also died at Flat Meadow. What we should be worrying about right now is what caused this terrible tragedy and not rush to judgment. In our history there have been very few instances of a rhutz attacking a human. It is so rare I had trouble finding any cases of it in the history books. So, what we need to be focusing on is what happened at Flat Meadow and what can we do to prevent it from happening again. Unfortunately, there were only three witnesses to the original encounter—Callus Tripolis, Romas Lantra, and Rupra Bruda. I'm sure you know Callus was killed by one of the rhutz, but I doubt you know Romas Lantra is also dead having recently been found with his lungs crushed without any apparent cause."

There were gasps of shock. Doban wanted to say that Romas

Lantra was obviously murdered to keep him quiet, but everyone would know he was accusing Rupra Bruda or the Chairman of murder. Without rock-solid proof he could not even suggest such a thing.

"So, this leaves us with one witness, Rupra Bruda. We've all read the PE's report of his interrogation of Master Bruda. He claims the rhutz attacked him without provocation yet that is contrary to the historical nature of the rhutz. The fact that two of the three witnesses are dead further makes his account of the events suspect. And since this amendment will fundamentally diminish the rights of the Rhutz life-form, I think it is imperative that Master Bruda be administered a dose of truth serum and be interrogated before this body."

Chairman Bruda gasped and stood up angrily. "This is an outrage!" There were many other screams of outrage from members of the Assembly as well, but also many who came to their feet in support of the demand. Yellow lights began flashing on the screen above the Chairman's head indicated assemblymen who wanted to be heard. The Chairman was so shaken by the demand he seemed paralyzed. Finally, he said, "There's been a demand that Master Bruda be compelled to take the truth serum. Is there a second?"

Several members stood up and gave their second to the motion. "Very well, at the conclusion of the debate, I'll put the matter to a vote, if the demand has not been retracted."

Everyone knew that was a thinly veiled threat. The chairman wanted those who had questioned the integrity of a member of the Bruda family to reassess their position and see if they really wanted to be his enemy. Assemblyman Doban, however, already knew the gamble he was taking, particularly since Romas Lantra had already been killed to prevent the truth from being revealed. But he also knew that if the Supreme Mandate meant anything the people had the right to know the truth, and he as an assemblyman had an obligation to provide it to them.

The assembly debated the issue for another kyloon and then the Chairman asked Veda Kulchz, the Chief Public Enforcer, to explain to the members how he would proceed should they pass the amendment to the Animal Control Act.

"Chairman Bruda. Although under the Animal Control Act it would be my responsibility to track down the two packs responsible for the Flat

Meadow Massacre, I have arranged with Lt. Diviil, commander of the Regional TGA Command to provide a highly trained platoon to accompany my men when they commence this mission. As we know the rhutz are extremely dangerous beasts and we have to be sure there is no repeat of Flat Meadow."

"Have you considered the possibility that other packs will show up to defend the two packs you've targeted?"

"Yes, of course. Lt. Diviil has agreed to provide air reconnaissance of the area to detect any other threat to our extermination team."

There were boos and angry protests from the gallery at the use of the term *extermination*. The Governor, who was watching from the floor of the hall, shook his head in disgust. Chairman Bruda smiled briefly then typed some commands into his wrist array. Finally, the Chief Enforcer answered one last question and sat down. The chairman looked up at a name blinking on the tally board over his head.

"Alright. It's getting late and we need to vote, but apparently, we have one more person who would like to be heard. I'm not sure what relevant testimony Councilor Sandista from Urunes will have, but since he has traveled so far, I suppose we should let him speak."

Councilor Sandista came in from a side entrance, took the podium and looked out over the huge hall. "Governor, Chairman Bruda, citizens of Tributon. I'm not here to testify myself but to act as an interpreter. Today you will witness a historic event for this General Assembly, for the State of Tributon and for Tarizon."

The Chairman frowned and looked around nervously. The audience became deadly quiet curious as to what the Councilor was talking about.

"I know it is generally believed that there were only three witnesses to the Flat Meadow Massacre, but I am here to tell you there was one other and he is here today to testify."

Conversation broke out in the gallery, the chairman paled, and Assemblyman Babor's face lit up in anticipation of a surprise witness. The Governor said something to Councilman Garciah, but he just shrugged.

"Shadow, please come forward."

Shadow came bounding in and jumped up on a chair next to Sandista at the podium. There were gasps and screams from the gallery. Many assemblymen backed away from Shadow.

"Don't be alarmed. Shadow is here to testify, not maul anyone."

There were several tentative laughs from the crowd.

"As you may know the rhutz communicate telepathically between themselves. This is why I will be able to communicate with him. He has learned Tari from another rhutz who learned it from a boy that he befriended cycles ago. I have also linked with Shadow's memories and have seen what actually happened at Flat Meadow. After Shadow testifies I will invite a few of you with telepathic abilities to link with Shadow so you can verify the veracity of his testimony. Now, I present Shadow."

Shadow nodded and looked at the Councilor. Sandista closed his eyes and began speaking. "Governor, Chairman Bruda, and citizens of Tributon. I am honored to be here today and to be able to talk to the human race at last. Since the beginning of time the rhutz have lived at peace with humans. Although the rhutz and humans have had little or no communication, they have respected each other's territory and tried not to interfere with each other's lives. This is why I was so shocked when a human shot and killed my mate, Shimmer, as we were enjoying a beautiful summer day in Flat Meadow just a few days ago. It was so unexpected and so unnecessary that I was beside myself.

"After the first shot there was another, so the pack did what our instincts demanded and what, I am sure humans would also do under the same circumstances. They acted to defend themselves from further attacks. When the murderers had been driven away and my mate had been sent back to God, I yearned to find out why these humans had attacked us for no reason. So, I traveled to Urunes to find a man I had heard had a good and just heart, Councilor Sandista. It was my hope I could communicate with him and find out why these humans had so brutally attacked my pack.

"When I got to Urunes I met Starlight, and she told me about the Flat Meadow Massacre. I was stunned and saddened by this escalation of hostilities for no apparent reason. I knew that if the human attacks continued there would soon be all out war between man and the rhutz, for an attack on one rhutz is an attack on all of us. I knew then my quest had now become even more important.

"Starlight told me about their pack's Old one who had been friends with a human and learned Tari from him. Gladdened to hear this, I went to the old one and learned enough Tari to talk to Councilor Sandista. So, I am here today to ask you, why my mate was killed and why does this General Assembly want to kill more rhutz?"

There was a stir in the gallery. Someone yelled, "This is a fraud! How do we know it's the rhutz talking? You could be making this up."

Councilor Sandista stiffened. "Perhaps it is time for two or three of you with telepathic abilities to come forward and talk to Shadow yourselves. Perhaps you will be able to convince the others that today we really are communicating with a sentient life-form. Do I have any volunteers?"

A man stood up and raised his hand. "Come forward, please."

Another assemblyman stood up and came up to the podium. Shadow looked in the first man's eyes. He gasped. "It is true. The rhutz speaks!"

The other man stepped in front of Shadow and peered into his eyes. "Oh, God and Sandee. I have seen Rupra Bruda murder the rhutz, Shimmer."

The Chairman stood up and banged his gavel. "That's enough. Alright, Councilor Sandista. Your time is up. Let's move on."

"Chairman Bruda," Assemblyman Doban said. "In light of Shadow's testimony, it's time to vote on whether to compel Rupra Bruda to take the truth serum."

"No, there's no time for that," the Chairman spat. "It's time to vote on the matter at hand, the Amendment to the Animal Control Act is on the floor. Please cast your vote. You'll have two loons."

The big screen lit up as two columns appeared to record the voting. Green blocks were affirmative and red negative. Everyone stared at the screen as the votes started coming in. Almost immediately a large number of green votes popped up. The Governor frowned. Then a red block appeared, another and then several more. Soon the board looked fairly even with about two-thirds having voted.

"One loon left to cast your ballots," the Chairman warned.

Suddenly, the tide turned as red block after red block popped up. A bell rang when the final vote had been taken. The final tally read: 121 green, 179 red.

The Chairman looked at the big screen and grimaced. "The reds have it, the Amendment is defeated."

There was applause and cheers of triumph from the gallery. The

Governor stood up and shook Rammel's hand. The Chairman quickly disappeared. Shadow and Starlight came back out to the podium and many assemblymen crowded around to see them and welcome them to Rizi. It was a historic day and a new beginning for the relationship between man and rhutz. Although Shadow still grieved the loss of his mate, he felt a little better now knowing she hadn't died in vain.

That night the Governor invited Shadow and Starlight to dine at the Governor's Palace along with Councilor Sandista, Rammel Garciah and Tobick Doban. The Governor was interested in learning more about the Rhutz and establishing some kind of reliable communication link between them and the Tributon government. After they talked long into the night the Governor offered them a room to sleep in but they declined, choosing to sleep outside in the garden instead. After the two rhutz were gone they talked about Chairman Bruda and Rupra.

"The Chairman was humiliated today. He's going to be very angry and someone will pay dearly on account of it," Rammel said.

The Governor nodded. "I wouldn't want to be in Rupra's shoes tonight."

"He's lucky his grandfather protected him and didn't allow a vote on the demand for him to take the truth serum. Had he taken it and his lies uncovered in that manner the public enforcers would have had no choice but to arrest him."

"So, what do you think the Chairman will do to quench his anger?" Doban asked.

"I'm not sure," Rammel admitted. "But I'd suggest we all double our security. I'm sure we are all on the list of persons he'd like to see dead."

7

The Plight of the Masses

In the aftermath of the nuclear holocaust of World War 8, while the rich and powerful were living on Earth or orbiting around Tarizon in their incubation ships, seventy percent of those less fortunate died. If it wasn't from the bombs themselves, they died of radiation poisoning, disease, respiratory issues, starvation or as casualties of the general anarchy and civil unrest that plagued Tarizon for nearly fifty cycles.

Because of the rampant spread of diseases, air and water pollution, and radiation poisoning most women became infertile and those who did give birth found their children to be mutated in one form or another. The mutations often were minor—an extra or missing finger or toe, the lack of body hair, or an unusual complexion. But there were more grotesque children born with extra or missing limbs, and occasionally multiple heads. This fact of life on Tarizon deterred many from having children. Few parents wanted their children to have to face the horrors of the postwar era. Accordingly, the birthrate on Tarizon plummeted and the population of the planet began to shrink.

These toxic conditions on Tarizon often caused mental aberrations both negative and positive. Most affected by the toxins had mental deficiencies but there were those with extraordinary mental abilities as well, including telepathy, telekinesis, and genius. One of the most extraordinary of these mutants with enhanced abilities was a teenager named Tribius Nocteris, called "Trib" by his family. He lived in the City of Liehn, Tributon with his mother and three siblings, all with severe mutations. Trib's father had recently died of respiratory failure leaving his mother, Cirrus, to support the family. Cirrus was in poor health herself and struggled to keep the family fed and pay the rent. Trib wanted to help his mother but his appearance was so grotesque that nobody would give him a job. He had a wide head with three little chins each with a thick black beard. Along with the wide head came an abnormally large brain–triple the size of a normal human one.

Although discouraged and depressed over his appearance, Trib soon realized he had many talents and abilities that others didn't possess. For one he could read people's minds. He learned this early on when he was playing with his siblings or the kids in the neighborhood. He found that if he watched them carefully as they played a game he could reach into their minds and learn what they were thinking. Consequently, he rarely lost a game, giving him great satisfaction and frustrating his opponents to no end. Unfortunately, in time, nobody would play with him as they knew defeat was inevitable.

Trib also found he was very intelligent and a quick learner. Perhaps because he wasn't allowed to go to school, he developed an insatiable thirst for knowledge and read everything he could get his hands on. Although he wasn't allowed in Liehn's public library, he made a deal with the janitor, another less deformed mutant, to do part of his work in exchange for time on his computer terminal. This gave him access to the full wealth of knowledge contained in the library which he swallowed up with alacrity.

Once he'd read all the volumes in Liehn's library he began to turn his attention to the internal workings of the computer wondering how it was built and why it did the marvelous things that it did. This is when he realized just how intelligent he was as he quickly picked up the fundamental principles and complexities of math involved in computer engineering and design. Soon he yearned to go beyond the library's system and on to Tarizon's Global Network or TGN. Unfortunately, about the time he was ready to tap into the network, his life was turned upside down.

When he got home late one night after working on his new program at the library, he found a note that his mother was sick and had been taken to the casualty unit. Frantic, he ran the two kylods to the CU and rushed inside. His ten-cycle-old-brother, Nicirius, was sitting in the crowded waiting room with a worried look on his face.

"Nic. What happened?" Trib asked rushing over to him.

"Mother had a coughing attack and couldn't breathe. Murl called for an ET to take her to the hospital but there weren't any available, so we brought her on the subtram."

Murl was a neighbor and friend who often watched the children if Cirrus had errands to run or had to go to the doctor. There was a shortage of Emergency Transporters, or ET's as they were called, as the mutant population was generally unhealthy. Only the rich or politically connected could actually get one in a hurry. The subtram, if it was working properly, was actually just as fast as an ET, so if the patient was ambulatory the subtram was the way to go. Luckily, that had been the case with Cirrus.

"Where is she? How's she doing?" Trib asked frantically.

"I don't know. She had to wait two kyloons to be seen."

"Oh, Sandee!" Trib said looking around the room worriedly. "Where's your sister and Murl?"

"They went in with Mother. There was a two-limit visitor rule, so I had to wait here."

"Skutz! I want to know what's going on. How bad was she?"

"Pretty bad," Nic replied holding back his tears. "She was coughing terribly and gasping for air."

"And they made her wait two kyloons!" Trib spat. "That's unconscionable."

"That's what?" Nic asked.

"Ah. Inexcusable."

"Right. They need more doctors and nurses."

Finally, Trib sat down next to his brother. Sensing his fear, Trib put an arm around him. "Sorry, I wasn't home when this happened."

Nic shrugged. "What were you doing?"

"Trying to figure out how to tap into the TGN."

"The what?"

"Tarizon's Global Network."

"Why would you want to do that?"

"To see what is out there. I'm sure there's some fabulous stuff."

"Like what?"

"Like the whole world. Once I get hooked up I'll be able to set up a VC for us so you can watch things going on all over Tarizon."

"Why would you want to do that?"

Trib frowned. "Aren't you curious as to what is happening around the world?"

Nic thought about that a moment and then said, "Not really."

Trib laughed. "Well, I am. I want to know everything about the everything."

"Why?"

"Why? So, I can figure out how to make life better for Mom and all of us. There has to be a better way to run things—a way where everyone will have whatever they need."

"That's a good idea, but if things could be run better wouldn't someone have already figured it out?"

Trib smiled. "Well, you'd think that would be the case, but it seems a lot of people care only for themselves and want to hoard everything."

Nic nodded as a door opened and a medical aide stepped out holding a chart. "Nic?"

Nic jumped up and rushed over to the aide with Trib on his heels. She reeled at Trib's grotesque face. "Who are you?"

Trib smiled. People's repulsion to him didn't bother him anymore. In fact, he thought it amusing. "I'm Nic's older brother. How's my mom?"

"Not too well, I'm afraid. She's calling for you."

Trib's heart sank. *What did that mean? Was she dying?* The aide did an about-face and led them to an examination room. Sick people, many coughing and sneezing, were lined up along the way waiting to get into a room. Nic looked at them warily as they went by. Cirrus was sitting up in her bed and smiled when they walked in. Murl and Artisural, or Artis for short, the youngest member of the family, looked solemn. Trib rushed over to her.

"Mom? Are you okay? I've been so worried."

Cirrus smiled faintly. "I know. I'd like to say I'm fine, but I'm afraid I'm not. The doctors say I don't have much more time."

Tears began to well in Trib's eyes. He'd feared his mother was dying but couldn't quite believe it was true. "No. You can't die. Surely they can do something."

"My lungs are shot. I need a transplant but there are no healthy lungs on this planet, so I'm told."

The aide nodded. "Yes, there are thousands waiting for lungs but only rarely does one become available and the cost of a lung is staggering."

Trib swallowed hard. He wracked his brain trying to think of a solution, but he knew deep down there wasn't any. Cirrus coughed and gasped for air. "Trib," his mother said with much difficulty. "You are the eldest. You must take care of the family. I'm sorry to thrust this burden upon you, but I have no choice. It's God's will, I guess, but I can't say why He'd want such a burden placed on someone so young."

Trib began to cry. "Don't worry, mother. I'll take care of Nic and Artis."

"I don't know how, but Murl will help you figure it out. She's a very resourceful woman," Cirrus said smiling at Murl. "You've been a great friend. I don't know how I would have made it these last few cycles without you."

Murl knelt down and took Cirrus' hand. "It's been my pleasure to be your friend. You're a good woman and there will be a hole in my heart when God takes you away."

"Don't die, Mom," Nic moaned, tears running down his cheeks. "We need you."

Cirrus smiled faintly and uttered her final words, "I'm sorry."

The aide looked at all the monitors, manually checked for a pulse, and then shook her head. "She's gone. I'm sorry."

Artis began to cry and Murl took him in her arms. Trib put his arm on Nic's shoulder and pulled him into a comforting embrace. "It's alright. Mom's going to be with Dad. He'll take care of her now."

Trib had mixed feelings about God. He understood the concept of evolution but it was still hard to believe all the wonders of the universe were here by accident. It seemed there must be an omniscient being out there somewhere responsible for everything, but if there was why hadn't He done a better job? Tarizon was certainly not a model world. In just the recent history that he had studied it had been ravaged by eight world wars and its ecology had nearly been destroyed.

It was said that God had sent Sandee to unify the world and stop the bloodshed, but little had been done since then to rebuild the planet's infrastructure and improve conditions for the inhabitants who had survived the nuclear holocaust. Then it occurred to him, maybe that's why he had been given so many gifts. Maybe God wanted him to use those talents and powers to make Tarizon a better place to live. Perhaps that is why he had a third eye and an invisible hand. If he used all his talents he certainly could help change things for the better. He just wished God would talk to him like He had Sandee. If he could talk to God or even get a sign from Him, then he'd know he was doing God's work and would work tirelessly to make

Tarizon a better planet, not only for he and his family, but for everyone.

But Trib had more immediate problems as he suddenly found himself the head of the family and responsible for his younger brother and sister. They had a house they rented, food for a few days, but rent would be due soon and their food would be running out before he knew it. *What am I going to do? I have no money—no job—but worst of all, nobody can stand to look at me, let alone give me a job.*

That night depression came over him like a winter fog chilling him to the bone. God had given him all those wonderful gifts, but how could he use them? He decided to go out for a walk so he could clear his mind and think. He'd go to the library and see if his friend had any suggestions on how to get a job. On the way he heard the familiar music of the Mighty Jolly, a local pub. He'd never been in the place as he had been too young, but he suddenly realized as the head of his family he now had the legal right to frequent such places. Unfortunately, to go into a pub you needed credits and he didn't have any. Nevertheless, he decided to go there and take a look inside, even if he couldn't go in.

As he approached the Mighty Jolly he could feel the excitement and joy of the patrons inside. He wondered what was going on inside that was making everyone so happy. Just as he was about to go through the swinging front door two drunken men came out and collided with him. There was a clatter as something fell out of one of the men's hand.

"Watch where you're going you little dirkbird," one of them spat as he staggered down the street. The other one gave Trib a hard shove knocking him flat on the ground.

As Trib got up and started to brush off his clothes he noticed two silver coins on the ground. He realized one of the men had dropped the money—probably their change when they settled up their tab. "Hey, mister! You dropped something!" he yelled.

One of the men turned and gave him a vulgar gesture. Trib sighed and then picked up the money. They were silver coins worth twenty-five credits, enough to pay the rent and feed his family for a week. He toyed with the coins for a moment wondering if he should take the coins home or go inside and see why everyone was having such a good time. Then he remembered his wish. *If God would only give me a sign I'd know what He wanted me to do. Was this a sign? What else could it be? What are the odds of this happening randomly?* He made a mental calculation of the odds and they were staggering. *Yes, this definitely is a sign.*

Taking in a deep breath, he pushed the door open and stepped inside. The music was so loud it was almost deafening and the smoke so thick he wished he'd brought along his breather. He'd been afraid that the moment he went inside and everyone saw his hideous face that they'd throw him out, but he was shocked as nobody seemed to even notice him. A smile came over his face. He liked this place and it was a comfort to think there was a place he could go whenever he wanted and find music and laughter and nobody would look at him in disgust. The thought of it almost made him cry.

Someone tapped him on the shoulder. He turned quickly and saw a beautiful young lady with purple hair. "What can I get you, Triple-chin?" the girl teased.

"Ah," Trib said embarrassed by the nickname and not being prepared for the question. He knew nothing of bars and what he should order to drink. An article he'd read about a tekari distillery came to mind. He'd never had tekari as it was a very strong drink and his mother wouldn't allow it, but it was all he could think of.

"Tekari, please," he finally said, "and please don't call me Triple-chin."

The girl nodded and gave him a big smile. "Alright, Threebeard."

Trip frowned but the waitress was gone before he could object. He sighed and took a look around. There was a seat at the bar so he went and sat down. The first thing he noticed was that almost everyone in the bar was a mutant. He realized that was why nobody paid any attention to him. Then he noticed a naked lady dancing in a cage and his long mouth dropped. While he was gawking at the dancer the waitress returned with his drink.

"Okay, Threebeard. Here you go," the waitress said.

Trib frowned but didn't bother to complain about the nickname for fear of what the next one she selected might be. "What's your name?" he asked.

"Rigella," she replied. "I haven't seen you in here before."

"That's because he's underage," a deep voice said behind him.

Trib turned cautiously and looked up at the seven-foot giant with arms the size of tree trunks.

"Yes. I'm underage but I'm head of household. My mother died today and left me to take care of my sister and brother. So, under Article 22.13 of the Tributon Domestic Code I am now considered an adult."

The giant gave Trib a hard look. "How do you know so much about the law?" the giant asked skeptically. "I bet you just made that up."

"No. I read the Domestic Code not too long ago and now I seem to remember it verbatim."

"You have a photographic memory?" the giant asked.

Trib shrugged. "I don't know. This is the first time I realized I'd memorized something like that."

The giant grunted.

"Oh, leave him alone," Rigella said. "Didn't you hear? Threebeard's mother died today for the sake of Sandee."

The giant sighed, then turned and walked away.

"Sorry about your mother," Rigella said sincerely. "What about your father?"

"He's dead too."

"Well, I know how you feel. My parents died cycles ago. It's tough being left all on your own. At least you have a brother and sister. I don't have anybody."

"Well, I'll share my brother and sister with you," Trib said playfully.

Rigella sighed. "Oh. You've got a kind heart, Threebeard. I may have to take you up on that."

Trib shrugged. "Anytime."

"So, what's your pleasure—a little gambling, a good woman to cuddle up to, or what?"

Trib thought about that for a moment before he replied. "I've never gambled before. Would you show me how?"

Rigella sighed. "Well, I'm off in an hour. Why don't you go take your tekari and go watch Meldina dance over there until I'm done? Then I'll show you how to play tin tan."

Trib looked at the naked lady swinging around the pole and smiled. Sure, I can do that. Do I have to pay her anything?" he asked.

"No, unless you want to take her home with you after her shift."

Trib blushed. "Ah. No. Probably not."

"Then just keep buying drinks and you can watch as long as you want."

Trib nodded and took his drink over to a table near the stage. Meldina winked at him as he sat down. He took a long drink and nearly died as the pungent brew went down his throat. "Holy Sandee!" he said giving the tekari a hard look. Meldina laughed as she danced around the poll and gave Trib a seductive look. After a few tiks Trib took another drink of tekari. This time it went down easier as his throat was numb and he had a little buzz. By the time Rigella got off work he was feeling pretty good.

"So, you ready to gamble?" Rigella asked as she sat down.

Trip nodded. "Absolutely."

"How many credits do you have?" she asked.

"Fifty," Trib replied.

Rigella grimaced. "Hmm. That's not a lot. We may not be playing long."

"What do you mean?" Trib asked.

"Well, the first thing you should know is the odds favor the establishment. That means unless you're really good, you'll probably lose."

"So, how do you know I won't be good?"

Rigella laughed. "It takes cycles to become a good tin tan player. You're going to lose your money, so if you can't afford to lose it, you shouldn't play."

"Show me how to play and then I'll decide," Trib said.

"Okay," Rigella replied taking Trib's hand and escorting him to the tin tan table where eight people were playing the game.

They watched for a while as Rigella explained the rules of the game. Trib watched fascinated by their play. After a while he looked at Rigella and said, "Well, I understand the game now. Let's play."

Rigella studied him warily. "It took me a week to learn the rules. Are you telling me you already understand them?"

Trib nodded. "I think so. Let's give us a try and we'll see soon enough."

Rigella laughed. "Okay. Give me your money and I'll go get you some chips."

Trib pulled the two coins from his pocket and handed them to her. She left and returned a few tiks later with a stack of twenty chips. "Okay, Mr. Genius. Let's see if you're as smart as you think you are."

Trib took the chips and went over to an empty seat at the table. Rigella stood behind him so she wouldn't miss anything. The dealer passed out the cards and then asked for bets. Trib placed two chips on the square and the game was on. Two kyloons later Trib stood up and started to collect his take of some two hundred and twenty chips. One of the losing players stood up.

"Do I understand this was the first time you've ever played this game?" the man asked angrily.

Trib nodded. "Yes. It was. I'm a fast learner."

"Well, I don't see how you could play so well. I think your little lady friend helped you cheat!"

Trib looked around nervously. Rigella glared at the man. "He didn't cheat you stupid dirkbird. Everybody knows you can't cheat in this game. He's just a hell of a lot smarter than you."

The man took a step toward Rigella but Giant suddenly grabbed the man and picked him up off the ground. "I think it's time for you to go home. You're drunk."

The man wriggled around trying to get loose. "Let me go! Let me go!"

"Are you going to behave yourself?" the giant asked.

"Yes. Just let me go."

The giant released the man and he fell hard onto the ground. Scrambling quickly to his feet he gave Trib a scathing look and left the tavern. Rigella took Trib's arm and escorted him to the cashier to collect his winnings.

"Well, that was fun. You *are* a fast learner. I'll give you that."

"Thanks for your help. I couldn't have done it without you."

As Trib was about to leave Giant showed up and blocked his path. "The boss wants to see you before you leave."

"Really? Why?" Trib asked warily.

"Don't know. He just said to invite you back to his office."

A horrible feeling came over Trib. He couldn't figure out why the boss would want to see him, but he didn't figure it could be anything good. Had he won too much money? Did the boss think he'd cheated too? Reluctantly, he followed the giant to the back room.

Pazillo Lerhrie was a huge mutant with a big bald head, mustache, and penetrating eyes. He smiled amicably at Trib when he walked in. "Come in, Threebeard. Sit down," he said gesturing to a wooden stool. "Call me Paz." Trib nodded and took a seat warily. "So, you were a big winner tonight."

Trib shrugged. "Yeah. Rigella's a good teacher."

"Yes, but I doubt she had much to do with your success."

Trib wriggled around in his chair. He didn't like where the conversation was going. He forced a smile. "Well, I've always done well at games."

"I don't doubt it. You have the gift."

Trib looked up startled by the statement.

"What do you mean?"

"Don't worry. I won't tell anyone about your secret. I have also been blessed. I could feel your mind boring into your opponents all the way in here. I don't know that I've ever felt such a strong presence."

Trib stifled a smile. "Well, I guess I shouldn't have done that, but I was desperate. My mother died and left me a brother and sister to provide for, but no money."

"It's alright. But you can't gamble at this establishment ever again."

Trib's head dropped. He'd had high hopes that the Mighty Jolly was the answer to his prayers. There had to be a way he could make a living.

"But, I do have a job for you, if you're interested?"

"A job," Trib repeated.

"Yes, I'm getting old and I need an apprentice so someday I can retire. Hopefully sooner than later."

"But I have no experience," Trib protested.

"That's why you'll be my apprentice. I'll teach you the business and then you can buy me out. I know you have the head for it. Anyone who can master tin tan in a couple of kyloons has to be super intelligent, plus I noticed that third eye in the back of your head. Does it work?"

Trib nodded. "Yes, but I have to close my front eyes to use it."

"Good. That will come in handy in this business. People will steal you blind if you let them."

"So, what will I be doing?" Trib asked.

"First. Your name is Threebeard from now on. Don't ever tell anybody your real name. Everything is close to the vest in this business.

The less people know the better. Be here at 700 kyloons tomorrow morning. You'll start at the bottom and work your way to the top. As soon as I think you have mastered each job I assign you, I'll move up to the next one. How fast it takes you to get to the top will depend on you."

Trib was excited about his new job and went straight home to tell Murl and his siblings, although he wasn't sure how Murl would take the news. Being a tavern keeper wasn't exactly his mother's dream for him, but it would bring in good money and keep them from being tossed out on the street. When he got home, however, his fears turned out to be unfounded as Murl was only mildly concerned about the propriety of his new profession. In fact, she seemed incredibly relieved that she wouldn't be burdened with three more hungry children.

"Oh, but I'm going to have to change my name."

"What?" Murl said.

"You deal with a lot of shady characters in this business so it's best nobody knows your true identity. So, from now on everyone should call me Threebeard."

Murl shrugged. "Well, at least the name fits."

8

Deep Sea Defense League

Jox Senna and his wife Ariela, lived in a small shack in the Seafolken village of Copesch on the northern tip of Rigimol. Seafolken were a race of amphibious humans who lived in or near the sea. They had been enslaved and persecuted for hundreds of cycles by the humans who considered them an inferior race. When the Supreme Mandate was signed slavery was abolished and supposedly all Seafolken became free. Unfortunately, not everyone complied with the dictates of Tarizon's new law.

Ariela had inherited their abode from her father three cycles earlier. Like much of the population he'd suffered from respiratory problems that eventually led to lung cancer and his early demise. Jox and Ariela were fortunate to have given birth to two beautiful children, a daughter, Lenira, and a son, Ulith. Fortunate, because to have two normal children on Tarizon, considering the toxic atmosphere and dismal living conditions, was a blessing from God and Sandee.

Jox made a living as a fisherman. He had a small fishing boat that he took out into the North Sea each day searching for the schools of tripett that frequented those waters. A tripett was a large fish, which at maturity measured over three feet in length. It was quite tasty and in high demand. While many species of fish had been adversely impacted by high levels of radiation in the world's oceans, the tripett seemed immune and hadn't diminished in numbers over the cycles since the 8th World War.

Every night the family would wait for Jox to come home from his daily journey to wherever the tripett were schooling before they would have their evening meal. It was a tradition among the Seafolken that the entire family eat at least the evening meal together in order to maintain a strong family bond. On this particular evening, however, Jox was a kyloon late and Ariela was worried.

She knew that sometimes the tripett would school farther out to sea than usual and that would make the journey back and forth to the fish take longer. She told herself that this had to be the reason Jox wasn't home yet, but that didn't stop her from worrying. She was only too aware of the many dangers that fishermen faced in the North Sea. It was cold and dotted with icebergs that sometimes were hidden just below the surface of the ocean. If a fishing boat hit an iceberg it was almost certain doom as few hulls could withstand such a collision. Fortunately, they had radar and sonar that was supposed to detect icebergs in time to avoid them, but they didn't always work the way they were advertised. Then there was the unreliability of the ships' engines and equipment.

Most of the fishing boats that the Seafolken used were old relics. New ships were in short supply and very expensive, so they had lots of maintenance issues and frequently broke down. Ariela wondered if that was the problem. She went to the front window and looked out over the harbor hoping to see her mate on his way home from the docks.

Just as she was about to turn and go back into the kitchen he came over the hill. She smiled as relief washed over her. She loved Jox so much and cherished each loon they were together. He was a wonderful mate and a loving father. The thought of losing him was incomprehensible. She couldn't imagine life without him.

Ariela blinked as she saw three men come into view behind her husband. She wondered who they could be. She knew they weren't fisherman because the town was the other way and their shack was the last one in this direction. She waved her hands and pointed with her finger to warn Jox of the men behind him, but he didn't seem to understand.

She cringed when the three men began to run toward her husband until they overtook him. She screamed as the three men fought with Jox until they had subdued him. Lenira, her daughter and Ulith, her son came running to the front door.

"What's wrong, momma?" Lenira asked as she reached the door. She looked out toward the docks at her father who was struggling with the men. She screamed in fear and horror at seeing her father's plight.

Ulith, without hesitation, ran toward his father in a vain attempt to help him. One of the assailants grabbed Ulith and held him from behind by both his arms as he desperately struggled to get free. "Let me go, you scutz!" he screamed as he tried to wriggle out of the man's grasp.

Ariela grabbed her daughter's hand and pulled her away from the door. "Go find a place to hide. I'm going to call for help."

Lenira protested, but finally ran off. Ariela closed her eyes and tried to make a connection with her sister. *"Talla, it's the slavers! They've come back and they have Jox and Ulith. Send help! Please send help!"*

"We're coming!" Talla replied. *"Hold them off. Don't let them take you away!"*

Ariela went to the closet and pulled out a rifle. She grabbed a handful of bullets and stuck them in her pocket. Then she put a bullet in the chamber of the rifle. But when she got to the front door she saw it was too late. An ugly bearded man had a knife to Ulith's throat. Her heart sank.

"Drop the rifle or I'll slit your son's throat," the bearded man promised.

Lenira sighed and then dropped the rifle. "Who are you and what do you want?" she demanded.

"My name is Pratt and we are here to claim your body and soul into servitude."

"But slavery has been abolished by the Supreme Mandate."

Pratt spit on the ground. "The Supreme Mandate carries no weight here, mistress."

"Yes it does. It's the law all over Tarizon."

Pratt laughed. "Well, there's no one here to enforce it, so I'm afraid you are out of luck. Who else lives here with you?"

"No one," Lenira lied. "It's just the three of us."

Pratt looked at his shipmate. "Let's see if she be lying. Burn it down!"

Guliah nodded and rushed inside the shack. Jox elbowed the man holding him, trying desperately to escape but to no avail. The man hit him hard across the face with the barrel of his pistol causing his nose to bleed. Jox winced in pain. Smoke started billowing out the front door as Guliah emerged.

Ariela screamed, "My daughter! My daughter's in there."

The bearded man shook his head in disgust. "Go back in a get her," he ordered.

Guliah rushed back inside and returned a second later with Lenira in his arms. Ariela took her daughter away from the man and held her tightly.

"You lied to me," the bearded man scolded as he grabbed her by her hair and yanked her head back. She stumbled and fell to the ground. Ariela grabbed his arm and bit it.

Pratt slapped Ariela across the face and shook himself free. "All right," he said angrily. "That's enough."

"Let's get back to the ship before someone comes," Guliah suggested. "I'm sure they've called for help."

Pratt nodded and pushed Ariela forward. Jox resisted and tried again to free himself, but Guliah grabbed him by the collar and hit him hard in the stomach causing him to double over in pain.

"If you give us any more trouble, I'll put a bullet in your daughter's head," Pratt said coldly.

"No! No!" Ariela replied. "They'll be no more trouble. Will there, Jox?"

Jox took a deep breath and then nodded.

The three slavers took them to a cove half a kylod from the harbor. An old freighter was anchored in the middle of it. Three long boats were ferrying captured Seafolken out to the ship. Jox recognized two of his friends who had been loaded into one of the long boats that was getting ready to launch. He shook his head in utter despair. *How can this be happening? Slavery has been abolished. This isn't right. God and Sandee save us.*

After they were transported to the freighter they were put in a cargo hold with dozens of other Seafolken who, by the smell of the place, had been there for some time. When the door to the hold was closed it was black as night save a few shafts of light that slipped between the wooden planks above them.

Grenz Lozich, a Seafolken, lived with his wife and three children in a shack on the north shore of Pogo Island. There were few inhabitants on this part of the Island and that was one reason Grenz chose to live there. He'd been separated from his family at an early age when the slave traders captured his father and mother and transported them to the city of Shisk on the continent of Turvin, to be sold at auction. His elder brother and sister, who'd been away when the traders raided their Seafolken village, provided him some comfort and protection while he was growing up, but Grenz pretty much raised himself.

At age fourteen Grenz joined the TGA and served on a battleship for six cycles. During that time, he became a master seaman and soldier. When his tour of duty was up he went to Shisk to try to find his mother and father. He searched there for half a cycle before he finally faced the reality that he'd never see his parents again. Although they'd been taken to Shisk to be sold at the slave markets, he realized their buyers could have taken them anywhere on Tarizon after the purchase.

To honor his parents, he decided to devote his life to combating the growing slave trade business. To accomplish this Grenz formed the Dark Sea Defense League and enlisted Seafolken from lands adjoining the Dark Sea. He trained his recruits to attack slave ships, free the Seafolken slaves aboard, and kill the slavers. The captured slave ships were either sunk or refitted for use by the Defense League to pursue slave traders.

In the fall of 23 A.U. Grenz was commanding a ship patrolling in the Dark Sea just south of Allso on the southern tip of Lamaine Shane. They were looking for slavers on their way to Shisk to sell their Seafolken cargo. Although slavery had been abolished by the Supreme Mandate many ignored the law and few were prosecuted for disobeying it. Since Central Authority did nothing to stop slave traders, the Dark Sea Defense League, took it upon themselves to put as many slave traders out of commission as possible and free their sisters and brothers from a lifetime of hard labor and misery.

Grenz was at the helm of a light cruiser called *Revenge* that had been captured several cycles earlier from the docks of Gallion. The slavers had stopped to restock and while they were out at the local taverns, Captain Lozich and his Seafolken crew overtook the seamen left aboard and set sail. Since slave trading was illegal they couldn't complain to the TGA or the local authorities about their loss of their ship. Of course, the slavers vowed to avenge the theft of their valuable ship and cargo, but trying to locate a Dark Sea Defense League cruiser that could be anywhere on the vast oceans of Tarizon was a daunting task to say the least.

"Captain. There's a ship twenty kylods northwest of us traveling fast," his executive officer, Lt. Ullum Yels, advised.

"Time to intercept?" Grenz asked.

"Eighteen kyloons."

"Send out a drone to check it out."

"Will do, Captain."

The captain looked up at the weapons pad above the upper deck and watched a missile take off toward the oncoming ship. The missile would take the location drone to a position near the ship. The missile and drone would then separate and the drone would fly over the ship and take a full set of reconnaissance photos. Five kyloons later pictures of the approaching ship were displaying on the ship's main monitor.

"It's a Hinderbrat Cargo Cruiser out of Ock Mezan," Lt. Yels reported. "They call it *Chaser*."

"Cargo?"

"Slaves, Sir."

"Defenses?"

"Machine guns, torpedoes, and two small cannons, Sir."

"Alright. Ready the Ionic Interrupter."

"Yes, Sir."

The Ionic Interrupter was a bomb that let out an intense ionic pulse when detonated. It could be dropped on a target or delivered via a missile. In this case it would be attached to a missile. The Ionic Interrupter would do little damage to its target but would knock out all of its electronics rendering it defenseless.

"Interrupter ready for launch," Lt. Yels reported.

Captain Lozich watched his monitor waiting for the right moment. "Launch now!"

A missile shot out from the weapons pad and sped toward its target. Everyone turned to the monitors and watched *Chaser* in anticipation of the strike. A few loons later there was a flash and the Chaser's engine failed causing it to sink into the water and come to a stop.

"Full speed ahead! Boarding party, prepare to drop your boats," Grenz ordered.

The ship took off with a lurch as the thrusters were engaged. Wings began to extend out of each side of the boat lifting eighty-five percent of its bulk out of the water. This decreased the ocean's resistance to the hull dramatically allowing the craft to triple its previous speed. Since the crew of *Chaser* would be working frantically to restart the engines and get defenses back on line it was imperative to overtake the ship quickly and board her before that could happen.

A few loons later the disabled transport ship could be seen ahead, dead in the water. The boarding crews took up positions next to their boats and were ready to launch just as soon as they were close enough. Snipers took positions on each mast ready to take out anyone who posed a threat to the boarding party.

Revenge's thrusters stopped and the ship slowed down as it approached the slave vessel head on. Two machine guns began firing at them as they approached. The machine guns were mechanical rather than electronic so the ionic interrupter had no effect on them. In response to the machine gun fire the snipers quickly took out the two machine gun crews and their guns went quiet.

A thousand strides from the slaver *Revenge* swung around starboard and the boarding ships were dropped with their crews already aboard. Their engines immediately came to life on impact and the two ships sped away toward *Chaser*. As they were approaching the ship the captain eased *Revenge* in closer so the snipers would be in range to provide support for the two boarding parties.

A few shots rang out as the boarding parties began to climb up onto the ship, but the snipers silenced those in short order. Soon the ship surrendered, the crew was taken into custody, and the boarding party secured the vessel. Once the captured crew had been moved to *Revenge's* brig, Captain Lozich went aboard the captured ship to explain to all the slaves that they were now free.

His men opened *Chaser's* cargo hold allowing sunlight to come flooding in. Hundreds of weak and frightened Seafolken raised their hands to ward off the bright sunlight.

"Come forth my brothers and sisters," Grenz said cheerily. "We have come to set you free."

The crew rushed in and cut the ropes that bound the slaves. Slowly they crawled out of the cramped hold and onto the deck of the ship warily, fearing this was but a cruel joke by their captors.

"My name is Captain Grenz Lozich. My crew and I are here to tell you that you are no longer slaves. Under the Supreme Mandate slavery is abolished on Tarizon and each of you can now live your life as you see fit."

The stunned Seafolken looked around at each other in dismay. Finally, one of them raised his fist and exclaimed. "Praise God and Sandee! We're free."

The others, now finally beginning to understand what was happening, started laughing and talking excitedly. One of the Seafolken women stepped forward. "Captain. We are pleased that you have rescued us, but now what's going to happen to us?"

Grenz smiled at the attractive young woman. "What is your name, mistress?"

"Ariela."

"Are you alone or do you have family with you?"

"Jox, my mate, and two children are with me," Ariela said and motioned to her husband to come forward. A tall muscular man stepped up and took Ariel's hand. Two children joined them on each side.

"Where are all of you from?" Grenz asked.

"From Copesch in the far north, but the slavers burned our house. We have nothing to go back to."

"Don't worry. We're going to help you relocate, find jobs and start over. Right now, just take a deep breath and enjoy your first day of freedom. We'll sit down with each and every one of you soon to discuss your future. In the meantime, I'm sure you are all very hungry, so our chefs are in the process of preparing you a fine meal to celebrate the beginning of your new lives."

A Seafolken woman named Serie raised her hand. "Captain. Where will you be taking us once we get underway?"

"Our plan is to sail up the coast of Lemaine Shane and stop at each port for a few days. There is usually work available at each port and if you can find a job there, then you can stay. If not you can look for work at the next port. This has worked well in the past as Seafolken are known to be capable workers."

"What about work for women?" Serie asked skeptically.

"Ah. Don't worry. Seafolken women are in high demand in the hotels and taverns."

It was common knowledge that Seafolken women were very alluring and possessed an uncanny ability to seduce human males. This made them very valuable to tavern or hotel owners who exploited their talents for profit. One of the weapons the Seafolken women possessed was a small stinger on the tip of their tongues called a tortiac. The tortiac's natural function was to paralyze fish so that they wouldn't thrash around in the Seafolken's mouth during feeding, but it was also used on males during mating for intense sexual stimulation.

"Or, if that doesn't suit your fancy, factory work is always available—not to mention there'll be men looking for mates."

Everyone laughed. Serie smiled feeling somewhat relieved. She was very happy to be free but still apprehensive about what it meant. Soon, however, she forgot about her misgivings about the future as she was ushered into the ship's galley and saw plate after plate of luscious meats, vegetables, breads, desserts and fine spirits that had been prepared for the feast. Tears of joy welled in her eyes at the sight. She couldn't remember how long it had been since she'd eaten more than a crust of stale bread or a hunk of dried fish. That night for the first time in many cycles she went to sleep with a full stomach and had pleasant dreams rather than nightmares.

Threebeard mastered the tavern business quickly and he and Paz struck a deal whereby Threebeard would take over operation of the business and pay Paz a ten percent royalty on gross sales. Threebeard made it clear, however, that only revenue from liquor, food, entertainment, and lodging generated from the existing location would be considered as sales. Thus Threebeard didn't have to worry about giving Paz a cut of any revenue from new taverns he might set up or new ventures he might undertake in the future.

One of the first changes Threebeard made to the Mighty Jolly was to turn Paz's cluttered office into a state of the art computer center. Now with plenty of money Threebeard bought extensive computer equipment and soon figured out how to hack into the TGN. This gave him full access to all government and military computers but also those private ones tied into the network. Although most computer systems tied into the TGN had sophisticated security, understanding computer technology perhaps better than anyone on Tarizon, Threebeard quickly learned how to get around this security without detection. So, now Threebeard had access to just about every bit of information available to anyone on Tarizon and he spent kyloon after kyloon searching through this vast sea of information soaking up knowledge like no human had ever done before.

Threebeard even learned a lot about Earth through the TGN. Cycles earlier regular Earth shuttles were sent to Earth to study the planet as a possible place to settle should Tarizon become uninhabitable. While the shuttles orbited Earth, they monitored TV and radio stations and recorded most of the programming coming from them. Threebeard liked to watch American movies and listen to popular American music. He even learned to speak English and became familiar with the American political system. There probably wasn't anyone on Tarizon who knew more about Earth than Threebeard.

Over the next few cycles Threebeard expanded his tavern business to other parts of Tributon and Quori to the south. Soon every major city in those regions had at least one Mighty Jolly. This, of course, caused a myriad of logistical problems which often frustrated Threebeard. It was hard to find enough good talent to provide entertainment to all his customers at so many locations. This is why he was drawn to a news report about the Dark Sea Defense League's capture of a slave ship traveling from Copesch to Shisk and the release of 211 slaves held in defiance of the Supreme Mandate's abolishment of slavery. What particularly interested him were the 130 Seafolken women who were in need of employment.

The article indicated the ship *Revenge* would be sailing up the west coast of Lemaine Shane stopping at each port hoping to find homes and jobs for the newly freed slaves. Threebeard noted the expected arrival date of the ship at the first port, Allso Uza, and vowed to be there to see if any of the men or women would be suitable for employment. He was excited about the prospect of meeting the Seafolken because he had read extensively about them, the women for their allure and sexuality and the men for their strength, courage, and unusually strong telepathic and telekinetic abilities.

On the day *Revenge* was to arrive at Allso Uza, Threebeard was at the docks with Rigella who he had promoted to personnel manager as a reward for helping him acquire the Mighty Jolly from Paz. A large crowd of spectators, media, and prospective employers were also at the dock patiently waiting for *Revenge's* appearance. To ensure that he would have the first opportunity to talk to Captain Lozich and the Seafolken aboard *Revenge*, Threebeard had agreed to house all of them for free at his two local taverns. Threebeard enjoyed a further bit of good luck as the ship didn't arrive until after dark, thus depriving many of his competitors from talking to the captain or the Seafolken that first evening.

After the guests were all assigned rooms, Threebeard invited them all down for a dinner and entertainment. While they were eating and enjoying his entertainment he went around and talked individually to as many as possible. As he was mingling he realized how incredibly intelligent and talented the Seafolken were and knew he could use almost all of them in one fashion or another. Before they retired for the evening he gathered them together and made a proposal.

"Captain Lozich, my Seafolken friends, I am honored to have you as my guest for the evening. It is such an injustice for anyone to have to live in slavery today and I celebrate your release and honor Captain Lozich and his crew for freeing you."

There were cheers from the audience.

"Now I know starting over with nothing is difficult with no money, no family, or friends to turn to for help. So, I want to ease that burden for you if I can. I don't know if you know it or not, but I have many Mighty Jolly taverns all over Quori and southern Tributon. One day I will have one in every city in Lemaine Shane. So, there are many employment opportunities at the Mighty Jolly and I invite each and every one of you to apply for employment. My good friend and our personnel manager, Rigella, is here to tell you about these opportunities and take your applications if you are interested. And let me just say that we have one of the highest pay structures in the tavern industry and when you come to work at a Mighty Jolly you are joining not a business but a family. Just ask any of our employees here tonight what that means. I'm sure they will be happy to tell you. Finally, since none of you have a place to live right now, anyone who comes to work at the Mighty Jolly will be given free room and board for a reasonable time to allow you to accumulate some earnings and find adequate housing."

The room broke out in appreciative applause. Captain Lozich shook his head in amazement and turned to Threebeard. "That is a most generous offer."

"Well, it's nothing compared to what you have done. I salute your efforts to rid Tarizon of slavery. Before you go, I want to make a generous contribution to the Deep-Sea Defense League. I know it must be expensive to operate a fleet of ships as you do."

"Yes, our crews serve without pay fortunately and we have acquired our fleet without cost."

Threebeard scratched his middle beard. "So, how did you manage that?"

"The Chief Public Enforcer here in Allso Uza is a Seafolken, so when we bring in ships we have captured and their crews, he prosecutes them for slave trading and their property is forfeited to the state. The forfeiture statutes allow for the payment of a reasonable bounty to those who bring in slavers or their property. We have an arrangement with the Chief Public Enforcer to split any revenue generated by the sale of the seized property. This provides us funding for our operations and, if a ship doesn't sell at auction, we can take possession of it in lieu of our bounty."

Threebeard nodded. "Excellent. I'd like to meet this PE. He sounds like a fine prosecutor."

"Yes, he is. I'll invite him over to meet you before I leave."

"Good. I shall look forward to it."

Before the evening was over nearly two-thirds of the Seafolken guests had signed up to work for the Mighty Jolly taverns. Threebeard was pleased and anxious to put his new employees to work. It took time to train them and put each in the right job, but in time his efforts paid off. The most immediate success was the Seafolken women who were hired as barmaids and dancers. Men flocked to the taverns to see them and were not disappointed. Once they'd had time to recover from their imprisonment, put on a little weight, and learn their jobs they became quite intoxicating and the human males who frequented the taverns couldn't keep their eyes or hands off them. Fortunately, Giant and other bouncers were always there to protect them if a customer got out of control.

Another news report that intrigued Threebeard one night was the story out of Vaceen in Tributon about the Flat Meadow Massacre. He was appalled by the butchering of rhutz and knew there must be more to the story than what was being reported. He followed the story each day and hacked into both the TGA and the Vaceen PE's computer system. He learned that there were accusations that a teenager named Rupra Bruda had actually killed a rhutz without provocation thus causing the rhutz to kill one of the humans. His interest in the story was further heightened when he read the transcript of the session of Tributon's General Assembly where an amendment to the Animal Control Act was debated. He couldn't believe the government was seriously considering committing genocide of the Rhutz and was shocked and delighted when two rhutz appeared to testify as to what actually happened at Flat Meadow.

Shocked and fascinated that the rhutz had actually been able to communicate with humans, he contacted Councilor Sandista to see if he could arrange a meeting.

"I believe Shadow is staying with Starlight's pack for a while. I could contact them and try to arrange a meeting."

"Excellent. I can't wait to meet them."

"May I ask why you want to make contact?"

"I believe strongly that the Supreme Mandate was meant to protect all sentient life-forms and I want to do whatever I can to force Central Authority to accept that truth. I recently have gotten involved in helping to free Seafolken who are still being held as slaves all over Tarizon. I believe the plight of the rhutz is something equally important. If I can establish a line of communication with the Rhutz I think it will be advantageous for us both."

"Then I will do what I can to help you make contact. Shadow's agenda is very similar to yours. He wants to open up communication between humans and the Rhutz to avoid senseless killings in the future."

Several days later Threebeard and his brother Nic traveled to Urunes to meet with Shadow and Starlight at Councilor Sandista's government office. Both Threebeard and Nic were ecstatic over the prospect of actually talking to a rhutz. Nic loved animals and demanded Threebeard take him to the meeting. They both shook the Councilor's hand and then turned to Shadow and Starlight.

"How does this work?" Threebeard asked. "I understand they communicate telepathically. I have the gift, but I'm not sure how to reach out to them."

"It works the same way as with humans. Just look into their eyes and share your thoughts."

Threebeard nodded and smiled at Shadow. *"I'm so sorry about your mate, Shimmer."*

Shadow dipped his head slightly. *"Yes, there isn't a day that I don't think about her. She was a wonderful mate and I loved her dearly."*

"I read with great fascination the transcript of your appearance at the General Assembly. I hadn't realized humans and rhutz could communicate. I guess I should have realized it since the great Master, Sandee, and Whisper must have communicated with each other."

"Humans assumed the Rhutz were just another forest animal and treated them as such. Of course, many of us knew better but didn't realize the importance of establishing communication. I only thought about it when my mate was needlessly murdered."

"I want to do whatever it takes to make Central Authority recognize the Rhutz as a sentient life-form and recognize that it is entitled to all the protections of the Supreme Mandate."

"Yes. That is my dream. Do you have any idea how that can be accomplished?"

"Of course. We must organize the rhutz in every state on Tarizon and establish a means of communication that legislators can use to start a dialogue with the rhutz. Once we get enough dialogue going Tarizon's General Assembly will have to deal with the matter."

"That won't be an easy task," Shadow replied. *"The rhutz are organized by packs and do not have any political structure."*

"But you can communicate with other packs, can't you?"

"Yes, each rhutz has two levels of consciousness—an individual consciousness in which they live their daily lives independent of each other—and above that primary consciousness there is also a collective consciousness that is common with every other living rhutz on Tarizon. The collective consciousness is rarely invoked but when it is, it interrupts the rhutz' primary consciousness and puts him in direct communication with every other rhutz in the region."

"How does a rhutz know when to invoke the collective consciousness," Threebeard asked.

"It's instinctive," Shadow replied. *"When the hunting party came to my pack, the first one who saw them knew instinctively to invoke the collective consciousness. He didn't even have to think about it."*

"So, what you are saying is we will not be able to use the collective consciousness whenever it suits us."

"No. It can't be invoked at will. We'd have to communicate on a much more restrictive basis—with one pack at a time."

Threebeard shrugged. *"Well, nobody said it would be easy, but I think it is worth the effort, don't you?"*

"Yes," Shadow agreed.

"Shadow and I can travel from pack to pack and talk to our brothers and sisters about this project. I'm sure they will go along with the idea. What you could do is set up a network of contact persons throughout Lemaine Shane and then we can assign packs to each contact."

"Yes, Nic will do that and we can link the contacts over the TGN so these communications can be done quickly."

"What's the TGN?" Shadow asked.

"It's a computer network that stretches all across Tarizon and facilitates the sharing of information."

"But what is a computer?"

Threebeard chuckled. He realized for the first time that the rhutz knew nothing about human technology. *"Think of it as an artificial brain that can store and process unlimited amounts of information."*

"Does such a thing exist?"

"Oh, yes. It's a wonderful invention and has opened up the Universe to the people of Tarizon."

"The Universe?"

"Yes, the worlds you see when you look up at the stars."

"Humans can travel to the stars?" Starlight questioned.

"Yes, Tarizon has a sister planet million of kylods away called Earth and we send ships there all the time. It's the only planet that we know of like Tarizon."

"That is truly amazing. We have so much to learn," Starlight thought.

"Don't worry," Threebeard replied. *"I shall enjoy teaching you about the human world and look forward to you telling me more about the life of a rhutz."*

After kyloons of conversations Threebeard and Nic finally tore themselves away from Shadow and Starlight and returned to Liehn. Before they left, however, they all agreed to begin work on the network that would one day link the humans and rhutz together so that there'd never be a tragedy like the Flat Meadow Massacre again.

Rendh Sealey walked into Cornelius Bruda's office and took a seat across from him. The Chairman looked up. "So, what is so urgent that you had to see me immediately?"

"There's a petition circulating calling for your resignation."

"My resignation! Whatever for?"

"They say you are protecting a murderer."

"You mean Rupra?"

"Yes. By protecting him from the public enforcers you have abused your office, they say," Sealey explained.

"I'm not going to let my grandson be tried for killing a rhutz. That's like prosecuting me for stepping on an ant!"

"Well, technically what they intend to charge you with is obstruction of the assembly. A motion had been made to have Rupra take the truth serum, but you failed to call it to a vote. That, they say, was an abuse of your power and grounds for removal from office—particularly since you were protecting a family member."

Cornelius sighed. "Oh, what next. I lose my son. My grandson is a lunatic and now I must resign from office. How did this happen?"

Sealey swallowed hard. "Perhaps your grandson needs help. If you swore out a lunacy indictment, you could blame everything on his mental instability. If you apologized and explained you were under a lot of stress with your son's death and all, maybe a majority of the members would forgive you."

"You want me to have my own grandson thrown into a lunatic asylum for the rest of his life?"

"Well, he did kill the rhutz without provocation, didn't he?"

"Yes, but that's my fault. Don't tell anyone, but I've killed a rhutz or two in my day. I'm afraid I may have bragged about it to Rupra. The rhutz have no respect for private property. They used to come by my father's ranch and help themselves to the horthogs and launas. Usually I just shot over their heads to scare them off, but if they lingered I shot straight at them."

"Oh, my God!" Sealey exclaimed. "But—"

"But what? They were stealing my property for the sake of Sandee."

"So, what are you going to do?"

"I have no choice but to resign. Go to whomever is circulating this petition and tell them I'll resign if Rupra is not prosecuted and no action is taken against me or anyone in my family."

Sealey nodded sadly. "Yes, Mr. Chairman. I'll go make that deal at once."

"Thank you, Rendh. You've been a good friend. I'm sorry it turned out this way."

"Yes, Mr. Chairman. Oh, I was just wondering, when you were a rancher, why it was the rhutz didn't attack you after you killed one of them."

Cornelius thought about that a moment. "I wondered that myself and incorrectly concluded that they were just dumb animals and were afraid of me. I know differently now."

"How's that?" Sealey asked seeming confused.

"After the Flat Meadow Massacre, I realized there had to be another reason why they never attacked me."

"What was it, you think?"

"The only conclusion that I can make is that when I attacked them I was defending my home. They knew they were taking my food so they expected me to fight back and didn't blame me for it. In Rupra's case there was no reason for the attack. He didn't need the rhutz for food, nothing had been taken from him, and he wasn't under attack. What the rhutz wouldn't tolerate was someone just randomly killing them for sport."

Sealey raised his eyebrows. "If you are right, then the rhutz are truly sentient beings."

Cornelius shrugged. "Yes, which makes this whole affair even more tragic."

When reports began to circulate that his grandfather had announced his resignation as Chairman of Tributon's General Assembly and was resigning his seat in that body, Rupra Bruda was aghast. He couldn't believe shooting one dumb animal could have such far-reaching consequences. He was angry that so many people had come out in support of the rhutz. What was this world coming to when human beings were bowing down to common animals? *Is everyone on Tarizon insane? How can I face my mother and my grandfather after this? Don't they understand I was doing God's will, that it was my destiny? He wants me to put the rhutz in their place or kill them if they are not happy with what God has given them.*

He began pacing back and forth in his room wondering how long it would be before his mother knocked on his door and confronted him. Fear and outrage welled within him. *What am I going to do? More importantly, what will my grandfather and mother do? Will they forgive me or cut me off? What's more important to them, their own flesh and blood or what others think? He wished he would be the most important thing to them, but if they blamed his father's death and grandfather's disgrace on him, then they may not have much love left for him.*

There was a knock on the door. He wondered what he should do. Should be accept his fate or move on to make his own destiny without the support of his family? Finally, his pride won out. He couldn't accept the ridicule and humiliation of his family and friends. There was no choice but to disappear for a while until things quieted down. He grabbed his bag and stepped out his window onto the roof. He'd go to Shisk, he decided. It was the world capitol where people who believed as he did were in the majority. No one there worshiped the rhutz or any of the other lesser life-forms like the Seafolken or the nanomites. They wouldn't care if he'd killed a rhutz. They'd probably applaud him for what he'd done.

9

Nanomites

On their way home to Liehn, Threebeard mentioned there was still another life-form on Tarizon that no one had communicated with, the nanomites.

"Who are the nanomites?" Nic asked.

"They are a microscopic life-form that usually live inside solid objects."

"So, what do they do?"

"We don't know exactly, but they build magnificent cities that are very strong and durable."

"Really? But how can something so small build anything significant?"

"One molecule at time, I guess. We don't know much about them. Scientists believe they live in swarms. Each swarm has millions of nanomites who somehow work together. They think each swarm is controlled by a swarmmaster who controls all of the individual nanomites."

"Hmm. That's fascinating. How does the swarmmaster communicate with them?"

"I'm not sure. It's probably similar to the way our human brain controls the cells of our body, except nanomites don't have to be connected. They only have to be in the swarm field to be under the control of the swarmmaster. This gives them the ability to avoid barriers and slip through cracks and voids in the objects they are penetrating."

"So, what is it about them that interests you?" Nic asked.

"Some people believe they are a sentient life-form."

"Really? Why?"

"Because they build such incredible structures in their desert homelands. It just doesn't seem possible for them to build the kind of things they do without someone quite intelligent guiding them."

"How did you find out about them?"

"While I was surfing the TGN I intercepted a report from Berne Baldrige to the Commerce Secretary. Baldrige is a scientist for Central Authority who has studied the nanomites for many cycles. The government has been looking for alternative methods of construction due to the labor shortage. Baldrige's latest report suggested it might be possible to enlist the nanomites to do some inexpensive construction for them."

"Of course, any way to make coin," Nic said.

"Exactly. Although most people don't consider the nanomites to be an intelligent life-form, Baldrige believes the nanomites have to be highly intelligent because of their building and engineering skills. He also was sure they had some means of rapid communication because to build these structures took considerable coordinated effort."

"I wonder if communication with them is possible?" Nic mused.

"I don't know, but that's what he wants us to find out. If they communicate like the Rhutz, then making contact would be possible."

"So, you've talked to him?"

"Yes. He wants my help in establishing communications with them."

"How many nanomites are there?"

"In his report Baldrige estimated there were about five million swarms in each of the nanomite cities he studied. They need a dry environment to build. Moisture slows them down and makes it impossible for them to work efficiently. They also need a chemical called bacuum that is naturally produced in the deserts where they live."

"That's mind boggling," Nic said. "To think that millions of little nanomites can work in a coordinated fashion on a construction project."

"I know. It's amazing."

"So, how are you going to find the time for this?"

Threebeard laughed. "I doubt I could, so I thought it might be a nice project for your sister. She was upset when I took you to visit with the rhutz and didn't bring her along."

"Good idea. I prefer making friends with something I can see. Trying to talk to a microscopic life-form is a bit hard to grasp."

"Yes. It is, but if we can do it, think of the possibilities."

"So, how will you proceed?"

"I think your sister and I are going to be taking a little trip to the Ural

Desert. Baldrige mentioned a city he'd found about midway between Guhl and Urunes."

"Well, Artis will be excited."

"Yes, while I'm busy with her you can get started lining up people to act as liaisons between the rhutz and the humans."

"That will be fun. I can't wait to start."

When they got back to the Mighty Jolly they found it rocking as usual with its loud music, dancing, gambling and rowdy customers. Ever since the Seafolken women had been introduced into the taverns business had been booming. Rigella saw them come in and went over to greet Threebeard.

"You're back. How did it go?"

"Excellent. We talked to both Shadow and Starlight and they agreed to work with us on a project to open communications between the two life-forms."

"That's amazing. I can't believe it's possible."

"Oh, that's nothing. Wait until Father tells you about his next project."

"What's that?" Rigella asked warily.

"Where's Artis? I'll tell you both at the same time."

Artis was in the corner of the tavern talking to a group of young men. She came over immediately when Nic summoned her. Threebeard filled her in on their successful trip and then asked her if she wanted to work on a project for him.

"Yes, of course. It's about time you gave me something to do more challenging than clearing tables."

"You have heard me talk about the nanomites before, right?"

"Un huh."

"How would you like to go search for them in the Ural Desert?"

Artis swallowed hard. "The Ural Desert— like where they have lizard snakes and scorpions?"

Threebeard smiled. "Yes. That's the place."

Artis rolled her eyes. "I prefer the city, actually."

"Well, you were mad when I didn't take you to see the Rhutz. I'm just trying to give you an opportunity. Besides, I'll be needing your telepathic skills."

Artis' eyes widened. She had inherited strong telepathic abilities but rarely had occasion to use them. "So, you think we can establish a link with them like you did with the rhutz?"

"Yes, but it will be much more difficult. Shadow and Starlight had already learned Tari and linking to them was simple. The nanomites are another story. Their language, if they even have one, will not be easy to learn. We'll probably only be able to see a few visual images and work from there. It will take a lot of hard work and discipline to make it happen. Obviously, I don't have much time to devote to it, so I thought you might want to take on the project. If you are successful it could be very important to Tarizon's future."

Artis was astonished that her brother would give her such an important task. She didn't know if she could do it, if it were even possible, but she could hardly turn it down. "When do we leave?" she asked excitedly.

"In a week or two. I'll get you the Baldrige study to read in the meantime. That will give you some time to think about the project and then we'll make the trip."

Artis ran off to tell Murl about her new assignment and Nic wandered over to where the Seafolken dancers were performing before a large crowd of mesmerized men. They were so beautiful and let off an aroma that he couldn't resist. If Threebeard hadn't made them promise not to seduce any of the staff, he'd have long ago given his soul to them.

Three weeks later, after Threebeard had checked on all his taverns and other business interests and felt they were running smoothly, Artis and he took off for the Ural Desert. Figuring it would take some time to make contact, he'd set aside ten days to help Artis set up her laboratory and then leave her there until they were successful or decided it was a hopeless task.

The desert was not a hospitable place for humans, so they had to bring plenty of food and water and a camcube shelter in which to do their research. Camocubes were portable structures easily put together like tents but much stronger and more durable. Not knowing the area Threebeard hired a local guide, Faruk, and brought their cook, Poldra with them. Giant also came along to provide protection as the Ural Desert was infested with many venomous spiders, snakes and lizards.

They traveled in three ATVs through the Liehn River Tube to Guhl. Tubes were superhighways enclosed within a gigantic cylinder so they would be protected from the weather and the contaminated environment. The Liehn River Tube had been built during the 7th World War when the atmosphere was so toxic that people couldn't live outside of protective shelters. The atmosphere had since cleared but tubes were still popular because without weather, cross traffic or pedestrians to worry about you could travel at maximum speed without worry.

They stayed overnight in Guhl at the Mighty Jolly and then left at the crack of dawn for the Ural Desert. There were only two paved roads through the desert, one from Guhl to Urunes and another from Rizi to Urunes. They had chosen the Guhl route because it came closest to where some of the nanomite structures had been spotted. The structures themselves, of course, were many kylods off the highway and nowhere near any human habitation.

The Ural Desert lay east of the Doral Mountains. Since all weather patterns on Tarizon went from west to east almost all of the moisture that rolled in from the Dark Sea was spent as it was lifted over the high Doral Mountain peaks. The highest mountain was Mt. Survius towering to 14,737 feet and being located fifty kylods northwest of Guhl. Although general rain was rare, isolated thunderstorms did occur and usually caused flash flooding because of the sparse foliage and sandy terrain.

Threebeard loved the Ural Desert. He found it inspiring to see life struggle defiantly to survive under such hostile conditions. It reminded him of the human struggle on Tarizon during the world wars when the planet nearly became uninhabitable. The desert had a unique and powerful beauty with its rocky hills, ragged cliffs, exotic plants, and sandy washes spattered with scrub brush and an occasional desert flower.

When they turned off the main road in the direction of the nanomite formations Artis felt a wave of apprehension come over her. She'd never been to the desert and although it was beautiful, it was a bit scary as well, particularly since they were traveling off-road.

"So, aren't you afraid we'll get stuck in all this sand?" Artis asked.

"Possibly, but since we have three vehicles we should be okay. If one of us gets stuck the other two should be able to pull the other one out."

"How do we navigate out here without a map?" she asked.

"I've hacked into the TGA's G.P.S. system. I'll show you how it works when we get to our location. You'll be able to do as much traveling as you like without fear of getting lost, however, I doubt you'll have to do much traveling as the nanomites are pretty sedentary from what I've read about them."

"So, how are we going to do this?" Artis asked. "I've thought a lot about making contact with them, but I don't have any idea how to start."

"I know. It's going to be a lot of trial and error. Obviously the human and nanomite minds are going to be very different, but they both must radiate some sort of energy waves from their minds. The trick is going to be how to make those energy waves meaningful to each other. It's going to be more difficult than it was between rhutz and humans because nanomites may not see things the way humans do."

"Then how could it even be possible?" Artis asked.

"Well, they must have some sort of sight, otherwise how could they build these huge structures?"

Artis pondered this wondering if she had made a mistake taking on such a seemingly futile venture. "What if the nanomites don't want to make contact with us?"

Threebeard shrugged. "They may not in which case we won't be able to make contact with them."

"Maybe we shouldn't contact them," Artis said worriedly. "It might be a mistake introducing them to the human population. You know how some people try to exploit others."

Threebeard looked at her thoughtfully. "You're right, of course. It could backfire on us. But just because we make contact with them doesn't mean we have to tell anyone about it. We'll let them decide if they want to meet others."

"Of course, but how could they make a rational decision having had no previous experience with humans? They might think all humans were like us."

"That's a good point, but everyone faces that dilemma when they meet someone. If they decide to meet with others we'll be there to guide them and give them the benefit of our experience."

Artis didn't press the issue as she didn't want to disappoint her brother particularly after he'd finally given her something important to do.

They plodded on for kyloons over the rocky terrain until they came to a gorgeous red rock canyon. It was a bit scary; giant red boulders were so precariously perched on the canyon walls, that it seemed a slight breeze could send them plummeting down upon them.

At the end of the canyon a wide valley emerged, its floor made of hard white rock and gravel. After they'd traveled about a kyloon into the valley strange imposing objects appeared in the distance.

Artis blinked not believing what she was seeing. Out here in the middle of nowhere there appeared to be a city—a magnificent crystal city, complete with skyscrapers, domed buildings, and some sort of interconnecting highways that almost looked like veins in the human body. She looked over at Threebeard who was smiling.

"Now, you understand why I think the nanomites are a sentient life-form. Only an intelligent being could build something so magnificent."

As they got closer to the city the sky suddenly darkened. They looked up and saw that a storm was quickly brewing.

"Skutz! We better look for cover. If we get caught out in the open in a flash flood our ATVs will be carried away and we'll all end up being drowned."

"Where can we go?"

Threebeard looked around. He spotted a pile of large boulders in the distance. "Let's park behind those boulders. They don't look like they'll be going anywhere. Fasten your seat restraints."

They altered their course and headed for the boulders. Just as they reached them the skies opened up and the rain came down in a torrent. Within a few loons, water began rushing past them through the valley like it was a river bottom. At first it was just a foot or two but soon the water was up to the tops of the wheels. Artis looked apprehensively at her brother.

"Don't worry. The boulders will divide the water and keep the current from sweeping us away. We should be okay. Deploy the anchors."

Giant nodded and pushed a sequence of commands into the ATVs computer. The ATV vibrated as anchor holes were drilled into the ground beneath them. When their vibration stopped the ATV rocked as anchors were secured in place. The water continued to rise until it was up to their windows but the boulders didn't budge and the anchors seemed to be holding them. Then there was a thunderous crash in the distance.

Threebeard looked toward the sound nervously.

"Okay, hang on and pray to Sandee!" Threebeard exclaimed as a huge wall of water came crashing over the boulders. Although the ATV's were heavy they were watertight and quite buoyant. If dropped into water they'd float by design so the occupants wouldn't drown. So, when the wave hit them the tremendous lift ripped the anchors out of the ground and threw the ATVs into the surging flood waters. Giant gave Threebeard a horrified look.

"What should I do?" he asked worriedly.

"Nothing. We'll just have to ride it out. These ATVs are tough. Hopeful, they'll hold together."

Just as Threebeard said that their ATV hit a boulder and bounced away violently. "Ah!" Artis screamed.

They watched through their front windshield as they bobbed up and down in the flood, sometimes riding on top of the waters and other times being totally submerged But just as suddenly as it had hit them, the wave dissipated and left them upright ten kylods away.

"Is it over?" Artis asked hopefully.

"Yes," Threebeard replied. "I'm glad I bought first quality ATV's. They saved our lives."

"Yes, I can't believe they weren't shredded to pieces when we hit those boulders."

"They have a limbidium shell like they use on the shuttles that go to Earth. It's nearly indestructible."

"Thank God and Sandee," Artis said.

After the three ATV's regrouped they drove back to the nanomite city. Remarkably the flash flood hadn't seemed to damage the nanomite structures in the least. Artis was shocked at this. "How can they build such strong structures?"

"I don't know. You need to ask them that when you make contact."

That night they set up camp on a ridge overlooking the crystal city. They wanted to make sure if there was another flash flood that they wouldn't be in the waters' path this time. The next morning while Giant and the others were putting the laboratory together Threebeard and Artis began to inspect the city.

They climbed back down into the valley and entered the city from the west. The light from the rising sun flowed through the white crystal structures and seemed to power it up. Threebeard counted about seventy-five distinct structures from twelve feet to fifty feet in height. Artis ran her hand over the surface of one of the edifices and marveled at how smooth and hard it was. They continued on, searching for an entry of some sort but finally decided it was a solid structure. That made sense since nanomites were a microscopic life-form and had no need for individual rooms or compartments.

"Do you think each nanomite has its own room?" Artis asked.

Threebeard laughed. "I doubt it. I think each swarm probably has a room or space to occupy while they are not working."

"I wonder how many swarms are in this city?"

"Millions, I'm sure," Threebeard replied.

"Do you think they know we're here?"

"I don't know. It depends on how they perceive the world. If they have sight then they know we are here. If they don't I'm sure they can feel our presence."

"If they feel our presence, do you think they will feel threatened?"

"I'm sure they will be on their guard. That is why we must not do anything threatening."

"What would be threatening to a nanomite?" Artis asked.

Threebeard shrugged. "Well, don't carry a pick ax with you when you're examining the city."

Artis nodded.

After they'd traversed the entire circumference of the city and found no doors or streets through it, they went back to their camp. Their crew had been working hard while they were gone and had erected a nice camocube structure which included a lab, kitchen, lounge, bedrooms and restroom facilities.

"So, now what?" Artis asked.

"Now we have to come up with a technique to teach the nanomites Tari."

"How do we do that?"

"Well what I'm hoping will work is to conjure up images in your head and then, in your mind, describe them with the appropriate words in Tari. That way the nanomites, if they are linked in, will see an image and then relate to the spoken word referring to the image."

"Assuming we see things the same way they do," Artis noted.

"Right," Threebeard agreed. "But, I suspect they do otherwise they wouldn't be able to survive in our world."

"So, each day I'll plan a lesson and then deliver it to them and hope they are listening."

"Exactly."

"So, how will I know if they are listening?"

"I'm hoping they'll talk back to you and you'll sense their presence. It will probably be something very faint but quite exotic, so you'll know it when you hear it."

"So, when do we start?" Artis asked.

Before Threebeard could answer there was a scream and the sound of crashing tin cans. They got up and rushed outside to see Giant fighting off three large lizard snakes and two scorpions who were trying desperately to get at their water supply. When Threebeard saw the melee, he tossed the snakes and spiders away with his invisible hand. Unfortunately, this didn't deter them. Each time he tossed them away they came crawling back. Finally, he began inflicting a little pain on them when he tossed them away and eventually they gave up. When they were gone Giant relaxed and nodded at Threebeard gratefully.

"You'll have to seal the food and water in an airtight cooler so they can't be smelled by the local wildlife. Food and water are precious commodities out here."

Artis looked at Threebeard skeptically. "What if they decide we might taste good?" she asked.

Threebeard laughed. "No. They're more afraid of you than you are of them. Just keep your distance and they won't bother you. The medical kit has antivenom if you need it."

Later that afternoon Threebeard and Artis began their attempts to link with the nanomites. They started with simple images and words and gradually made them more complex each day. Without feedback it was a difficult process, but they stuck with their plan hoping they would feel the presence of the hives at some point. Unfortunately, by the time Threebeard had to leave, they had no indication if their plan was working. Nevertheless, Artis stayed on as they had agreed it might take several phases or even a full cycle to teach the nanomites enough Tari to communicate.

The Speaker for the nanomite city asked for silence. The swarmmasters wanted to watch and listen to the humans who were circling their desert city. Sentinels had warned them of the presence of humans. This was not unusual as humans and other beasts often sniffed around their city trying to gain entrance, but rarely did anyone try very hard. The buildings nanomites built were solid crystal and as hard as any metal found on Tarizon. They had to be in order to protect the fragile nanomites from wind, water, and weaponry.

Frustrated humans often took shots at the city's exterior to see if their weaponry would pierce it. Of course, the destruction of any of the structures would mean the death of millions of nanomites. The desert winds could be powerful too and a lesser structure might easily be ripped apart. But water was the biggest threat to nanomites as its presence destroyed their ability to move freely and quickly and deprived them of oxygen and nutrients that they needed to live.

The swarmmasters could see a cloudy image of the two humans walking slowly around the perimeter of the city. Their Sentinel swarms providing the view moved through the city keeping their receptors focused on the two intruders. The swarmmasters weren't usually concerned by the presence of visitors but there was something odd about these two humans. Not only could they see them but they could feel their presence. The feeling was strange and didn't mean anything to them, but they knew these weren't ordinary humans and that bothered them.

"Make sure our visitors leave the area," the Speaker said.

The Sentinel swarmmasters were surprised by this order as leaving the protection of the city was rare and quite dangerous. Nanomites could easily travel through any solid object, that wasn't the problem. The problem was their frail physique. If they encountered water, a strong gust of wind while they were traveling through loose soil, or if an animal or human inadvertently stepped on them, millions of nanomites would die. But the sentinel swarmmaster didn't hesitate despite his surprise. Commands from the Speaker had to be obeyed instantaneously without question. In fact, nanomites didn't know how to disobey such orders. Obedience was ingrained in the very fabric of their being.

The Sentinel swarm followed Threebeard and Artis just below the surface of the ground as they slowly walked up the hill to their camp. The swarmmasters watched their progress warily. The Swarmmasters wondered what had caused them to make this visit and whether their intentions were hostile. The nanomites were no threat to the humans but they had observed humans act cruelly to animals and other life-forms for no apparent reason. They knew that some humans seemed to enjoy killing and destroying things just to prove they could do it.

When Threebeard and Artis reached their camp, the Speaker gasped. "The humans have set up a camp!"

"Yes. That appears to be the case," the Sentinel swarmmaster confirmed.

"Why do you suppose that is?"

"I assume they are going to stay a while and study our city."

"Do you sense their thoughts?" the Speaker asked.

"Yes, I am feeling faint signals. I can't get any meaning from them, but they definitely are communicating without vibrations."

Nanomites had no ears but they could feel vibrations from human speech. They knew this was how the humans communicated so the realization that Threebeard and Artis were communicating differently confused them.

"I'm sending out more Sentinel swarms to help you. We have to keep a close eye on these humans until we know what they are up to. I'm going on with my daily tasks. Alert me if anything unusual happens."

"Yes, Speaker."

The first Sentinel swarmmaster watched the humans from the perimeter of their camp. When a second and third sentinel swarm arrived, they spread out to cover all the entrances while the first Sentinel swarmmaster took his swarm inside the camp to take a closer look at what was going on. He noted that there were three more humans at the camp who appeared to be servants. He felt vibrations from them but no discernible thoughts. The other oddity was the lack of equipment. In the past when visitors came and set up camp they brought with them all sorts of equipment which they spent an inordinate amount of time watching closely. But there were only a few pieces of equipment with these visitors. He decided to report this to his master.

"Speaker."

"Yes," the Speaker replied.

"There are a total of five visitors in the camp. The other three appear to be servants with no detectible mental transmissions. Also, these humans have very little equipment—only a VC and a few global communicators."

Nanomite swarmmasters had observed many humans over the cycles and knew they almost always carried video and global communicators. They knew this equipment was used to communicate with other humans, which they thought odd as nanomites didn't need mechanical devices for communications.

"Thank you for the update. Keep us informed."

"Yes, Speaker."

The sentinel swarms maintained their vigil during the night and were relieved as soon as the sun rose the next morning. The Sentinel swarmmaster took over command of the human surveillance and noted little activity with the exception of an increase in mental images, and static coming from the two odd looking humans which they now identified as Intruder 1 and Intruder 2.

"Speaker, Sentinel reporting."

"Yes. Give me your report."

"Both Intruder 1 and Intruder 2 are emitting mental images and unintelligible noise."

"Really?"

"Are they communicating with each other?"

"It doesn't appear so. It seems they are trying to communicate with us since they are here next to our city."

"So, what kind of images are they showing us?"

"Common things. Pictures of people doing different things, common objects like rocks or trees. Each image is followed by a distinct bit of noise."

"So, what do you make of it?" the Speaker asked.

"The only conclusion I can draw is that they are trying to teach us their language so we can communicate."

"That would be my conclusion as well. I wonder if we should try to learn their language or ignore them."

"A good question, Speaker. One that I am not qualified to answer."

"Of course. We'll consider this gesture. In the meantime, just ignore them."

"Yes, Speaker."

The Speaker immediately directed his thoughts to all the swarmmasters who inhabited the crystal city. Within a few tiks a serious debate erupted between the thousands of swarmmasters.

Humans are evil.... We should avoid any contact with them. We've never talked with the humans before and we shouldn't start now.... They may have something important to tell us. We can't hide from the rest of the world forever....Why not?...Perhaps we could help each other out and make the lives of all nanomites better....Contact with the humans will lead to the extinction of all nanomites....They want something from us and after they get it we won't hear from them for another hundred cycles....Many humans are good....The humans almost destroyed Tarizon in the last world war....That is why we need to communicate with them, to try to keep that from happening again.

When the debate was over the consensus was that communication was in the best interest of the nanomites. The humans had tremendous power over their lives and if there was a way for the nanomites to help prevent future wars or other intrusions into the nanomite worlds those avenues should be explored.

The next day when Threebeard and Artis began sending out images and descriptions in Tari hundreds of nanomite scholars were listening. They carefully noted each image and the corresponding noise that was associated with each image. After a few kyloons they slowly began to recognize distinct noises and associate them with mental images. It was a tedious process but these humans and nanomites were highly intelligent and greatly motivated, so it was just a matter of time before meaningful progress would be made.

10

Shisk

Shisk had been reduced to rubble during the 8th World War. It had sustained six nuclear strikes and those who were not killed in the explosions died shortly thereafter from the radiation. Twenty-five cycles later when Tarizon regained its sanity and adopted the Supreme Mandate, the rebuilding of Shisk began. It took nearly five cycles just to clear the rubble before construction of the new world capital could begin. Starting from scratch, however, had its advantages. The scientists and urban designers had plenty of time to create the most spectacular and extraordinary city Tarizon had ever known.

Sitting between majestic Mt. Soni to the east and the vast Coral Sea to the west, Shisk was located in one of the most beautiful parcels of real estate on Tarizon. Although Mt. Soni was an active volcano, soaring to 11, 221 feet, it hadn't erupted in over a hundred cycles and was far enough away not to be a threat to the city.

Besides beautiful sky scrapers that seemed to reach the stars, Shisk had no streets and thus no noise or pollution from transport vehicles. There was no need for PTVs as the city was interlaced with an elaborate subtram system which could take its citizens anywhere at lightning speed. There was also an independent subtram system for bringing in goods and supplies to the city and disposing of refuse. For those who didn't like the confines of the subtram there were sky cabs available to whisk you off to wherever you wanted to go traveling high above the city. The elimination of streets allowed for the city planners to create more green belts, parks, and spectacular expositions of artwork and sculpture.

Of course, the diamond shining brightly in the center of the city was the Hall of the World Assembly. A huge building of unprecedented beauty and architectural splendor. It rose five hundred feet from the ground to the top of its main dome and was surrounded by five three-hundred-foot sub-domes representing the five continents of Tarizon. Inside the mammoth structure the greatest artists of Tarizon had created murals, paintings, and sculpture depicting Tarizon's long and tragic history. It was hoped these works of art would remind people of the price Tarizon had paid for peace and freedom.

Enclosed in a transparent dome to filter air and water going into the city, Shisk was a wonder to behold and the destination of thousands of tourists each day from all over Tarizon. With an abundance of tourists, the entertainment industry had flourished and Shisk was known for its outstanding nightlife and was the playground of the rich and famous.

Rupra Bruda booked a freighter in Bama Uza headed for Shisk where he knew his political philosophy would be more appreciated. His family had friends there too, so he felt certain they would help him out for a while until he was able to get a job and sink some roots. He thought after running off rather than facing his mother and grandfather he'd miss them, but all he'd felt was relief. He rationalized his indifference to his family as simply an indication it was time for him to move on. He knew he had important work to do and it couldn't be done under his mother and grandfather's thumb.

The freighter carried a cargo of rinzee which was the main commodity shipped out of the Liehn River delta. It was a staple in most Tarizonian's diet and had been in short supply until recently when production levels had finally recovered from the effects of the war. Freighters weren't supposed to carry passengers but greedy ship captains often bent the rules and allowed a few aboard if they were willing to pay handsomely for their passage. Usually passengers seeking passage on a freighter were hiding from the authorities or, for some other reason, didn't want anyone to know where they were going. Bruda didn't want his mother or grandfather to know his whereabouts as he feared they would try to stop him from leaving Tributon.

Young Bruda wasn't too thrilled with his accommodations on the freighter as he was shown to a small storeroom that he was expected to share with two other passengers—a Seafolken named Twyst who'd just escaped from a slaver and Rugga, a mutant going to Shisk to join his brother who had just opened a new restaurant and needed help getting it established.

Bruda was afraid of the big Seafolken as he was a good foot taller than he, had a powerful physique, and seemed to harbor a lot of animosity toward humans. Rugga's grotesque appearance, on the other hand, revolted Bruda so much he spent most of the trip across the Straits of Tributon miserably on a bench outside the ship's bridge.

By the time the freighter made it to Shisk, Bruda had developed a bad upper respiratory infection and was feeling badly. He hadn't been able to contact his friend to tell him he was coming to Shisk, so there was nobody to meet him when the ship docked. Feeling weak he stopped at the first tavern he came to and booked a room. After he was settled in he went to the front desk and asked where he could get medical attention. The attendant directed him down the street to a clinic where a pretty nurse gave him an injection and a course of drugs to take for the infection. When he returned to his room he felt so poorly, he went straight to bed and slept for two days. While he slept he dreamt about the nurse who had given him the shot and the drugs. She was so beautiful and gave him so much comfort. *Was she an angel sent by God to take care of me?*

When he finally woke up he was shocked to see the nurse standing over him. "You're real," he muttered.

She smiled. "Well, I hope so."

"Why are you here?" Rupra asked struggling to sit up. He swung his feet around and sat on the edge of his bed feeling a little dizzy. The nurse stepped back and took a seat in a bedside chair.

"You were so sick when you came to the clinic I asked you where you were staying. You told me you had just arrived and were staying here at the tavern, so I decided to check up on you."

"How did you get in my room?"

"I knocked on the door and you let me in."

"Holy Sandee. I don't remember anything," Rupra said shaking his head.

"You were delirious. It's a good thing I came. Your fever was very high and I don't think you would have taken your medicine had I not been here."

Rupra studied the pretty brunette. He couldn't believe she had taken it upon herself to take care of him. No one other than his mother had ever shown any concern for him. Did she like him or was she after something? She was definitely a looker, tall and slim, and someone he could see himself falling for.

"What's your name?"

"Essyria. Essyria Tomaso."

"So, what did your mate say when he found out you were here with me?"

"Oh, I don't have a mate yet. I don't have to apply until next cycle."

Due to the population crisis on Tarizon, Central Authority had enacted the Population Stabilization Act essentially taking over the task of mating men and women. Love had taken a back seat to the practical necessity of making sure men and women were always in a relationship so they could conceive as many children as possible and help stabilize Tarizon's declining population. So many had died during the war that the number of widows and widowers was staggering. This caused great hardship to children and hampered the growth of the population, so mandatory mating was adopted as an emergency measure to deal with the problem. Under the law, by age twenty-one every man and woman had to enroll into the mating selection process. Once enrolled Central Authority computers would compare data on the enrollees and assign mates who supposedly were the most highly compatible. If a mate died each widow or widower had one cycle to apply for a new mate.

"I don't either. I have another eighteen phases."

"I'm not thrilled about letting Central Authority pick my mate."

Bruda shrugged. "Back in Tributon, where I come from, you can get around that."

"How?" Essyria asked curiously.

"Central Authority isn't always in control outside the domed cities. For the right price in Vaceen you can pick your own mate."

"Why did you leave then?"

"Well, I had a little run in with a rhutz?"

Essyria frowned.

Rupra explained what had happened but claimed he'd killed the rhutz by accident.

"What rotten luck. I can't believe you went through all that for a stupid rhutz."

Rupra smiled at the remark again marveling at how lucky he'd been to find Essyria. He wanted to find out more about this woman who had suddenly thrust herself into his life.

"So, do you still live with your family or are you on your own?"

"I still live at home although it's getting a bit tedious these days."

Rupra smiled thinly. "Yes, I know what you mean. I thought I'd miss my family when I left, but I scarcely think of them now that I'm out on my own."

"It's only natural at our age to be independent."

"What does your mother and father do?"

"My father is a merchant trader and my mother is a seamstress."

"What type of merchant trader? Commodities, finished goods–"

"Medical supplies and equipment."

"Ah. A very lucrative business these days."

"Yes. He does quite well."

Rupra laughed. "My father was an arms dealer. Not such a great profession when the world is at peace."

"So, why didn't he sell something else? Any decent salesman can sell just about anything."

"He didn't think the peace would last. He said it was human nature to fight and eventually there'd be another world war. His company was gearing up for that eventuality."

"Right, but how did he expect to survive until that happened?"

"Oh, just because the world is at peace doesn't mean the arms business is bad. There are a lot of people who are stockpiling weapons just to be prepared if another war comes. If that happens nobody can afford to be caught with a bunch of obsolete weapons. That could be a disaster."

"Hmm. So, everything isn't as peaceful as it seems," Essyria mused.

"No. Just look how close we came to having a war with the rhutz."

"So, your skirmish with the rhutz wasn't altogether accidental."

Essyria's observation startled Rupra. He gazed into her hazel eyes and tried to read her mind but she was guarding it closely. He suddenly realized there was much more to this woman than he had first thought. She was very perceptive and obviously she had the gift of telepathy.

"So, does that change your opinion of me?" Rupra asked.

She shook her head. "No. My father taught me that part of the job of being a salesman was to help create a market for your products. So, hell, if you're an arms dealer and you can provoke a war, I must congratulate you."

Rupra laughed, not believing this woman. "So, are you teasing me or are you serious? I can't read your mind."

"No. What would be the fun of that? A woman is supposed to be a mystery."

"You are definitely a mystery. I'm not used to having to guess what someone is thinking."

She smiled. "Me either. That's what makes our relationship interesting."

"Our relationship? We've only known each other a few kyloons."

She stood up and put her hands on his shoulders. He leaned back and looked up at her. "I know it hasn't been much of a relationship with you being so sick, but I was hoping that would change."

She leaned over and their faces inched toward each other until their lips brushed together lightly. Rupra felt a surge of sexual delight at the touch. He put his hands around her neck and pulled her down to him. They kissed passionately until she broke away abruptly.

"Okay, you're still sick. Let's take it slow. How about you take me to dinner tonight. I know a good restaurant, the Gohi Dodi. You'll probably be feeling a lot better by then."

Rupra shook his head still feeling like it was full of cobwebs. He realized Essyria was right. He wasn't entirely well yet. He took a deep breath.

"Sure. But I ride a jet cycle. I don't know how you feel about that."

"That's okay. Nobody drives in Shisk. We'll take the subtram. It will get us where we want to go as quick as a lick."

With that Essyria turned, walked to the door and disappeared leaving Rupra feeling like he'd been run over by a freight transporter. He couldn't help smiling, though, as he thought about it. He'd never known a girl could be so assertive. Maybe it was because she was a nurse and she was used to telling her patients what to do. But, whatever it was, it was refreshing to meet someone his equal.

For several weeks Artis continued her crude attempt to teach the nanomites the Tari language. She spent kyloons each day lying on a cot or sitting in a hard chair concentrating on images and corresponding words. It wasn't an easy task as her mind desperately wanted to stray to other topics and concerns. It required great discipline and concentration to stay focused on displaying images and their corresponding meaning in Tari. Depression often swept over her as she questioned if she'd ever make contact. *Are they listening? Do they have any idea that I'm trying to talk to them? Oh, Sandee! This is such a waste of time.*

The thought occurred to her that perhaps she should move around the perimeter of the city and establish links at different locations. Before she altered her plan, however, she decided to run it by Threebeard.

"Brother." She thought.

"Artis?" Threebeard responded.

"Yes."

"How goes your work?"

"Not well. I have no idea if I'm getting through. It's so frustrating."

"I knew it would be."

"It's so hard to keep my concentration. I often find myself daydreaming about something else or falling asleep."

"Yes. The mind gets bored with tedious work. It's too bad we can't figure out a way to let your subconscious mind do the work while your conscious mind finds more entertaining things to think about."

"Yes, wouldn't that be nice? I've been thinking that perhaps I should move around the perimeter and try different locations."

"No. You'd have to start over each time. It wouldn't be feasible. I'm certain the nanomites can hear you from any location around the city. Just stay where you are."

"Okay. But I don't know how much longer I can do this without going crazy."

"Listen. You say you're having trouble staying awake."

"Yes."

"Well, that may be the answer. Go ahead and fall asleep. Don't fight it. Perhaps your subconscious mind is trying to take over but you're not letting it."

"So, I should just go to sleep?"

"Yes, I often do that. At night if I want to figure something out that has eluded me while I'm awake I think about it just before going to bed. Then, during the night, I dream about it and quite often solve the problem."

"Really. So, you think my subconscious mind might do a better job than my conscious mind."

"Exactly. Give it a try for a few days and see what happens."

"Alright,"

Artis went over to her cot and lied down. She looked over her lesson plan and, in her mind's eye, resumed sending out her thoughts. Soon an incredible weariness came over her, but this time she didn't fight it and fell asleep.

The nanomite scholar swarmmasters reeled at the sudden rush of images and human words that spilled out of Artis' mind. They worked frantically trying to absorb the information. Soon they were overwhelmed and had to call for more scholar swarms to help keep up.

"Speaker."

"Yes."

"The human has increased her rate of emissions. We can't keep up with them without more help."

"Interesting. I wonder why this is?"

"Perhaps, she is growing weary of the task and is uncertain if she is getting through to us."

"You're probably right. We don't want her to stop and leave before we can establish a link. What do you think we should do?"

"Give her a sign, so she knows we are listening to her," the Scholar swarmmaster advised. *"That should ease her mind and allow her to relax a bit."*

"Alright. Do it then," the Speaker said.

"What kind of sign?" the scholar swarmmaster asked.

"I'll leave that up to you. Just be sure it is something that will leave her no doubt that she's made contact with us."

"Very well. It shall be done."

Rupra Bruda and Essyria became inseparable after Rupra recovered from his illness. They spent every daylight hour exploring the wonders of Shisk and each night exploring each other's bodies. They talked a lot during this time and traded many secrets, but neither would allow the other to see into their minds directly. Both feared that revelation would be their undoing. They were having dinner one night when Essyria brought up the inevitable question of their future.

"So, I want you to meet my mother and father."

"Do you think that is wise? They may have heard of my troubles in Tributon."

"So, they are practical parents. I don't think they'll hold that against you."

"Well, I don't know."

Rupra was pretty certain when Essyria's father did a background check on him that their relationship would be over. No father with any political clout would allow his daughter to be mated with someone who'd been disgraced the way he had. He might even contact his grandfather who would then send someone to Shisk to bring him home. That thought horrified him.

"You need a job, too. He could use someone like you in his business. Once he gets to know you he'll realize how valuable you'll be to him and forget about the blemishes on your record."

"I don't know."

"It can't hurt. Besides, if we are to be mated—" Her voice trailed off as she realized she may have made a mistake bringing up mating.

Bruda let out an audible sigh. *Maybe that is the answer? If we're already mated and you're with child—they'll be nothing he can do but accept me into the family. That will also give me an excuse to stay in Shisk. Even my grandfather couldn't argue with that.*

"You're right. Now that we've met, I couldn't imagine spending a lifetime with anyone else but you."

Essyria's eyes lit up. She took his hands and pulled him to her. They kissed.

"So, why don't we leave the dome and find someone to mate us?" Bruda suggested.

"My parents will be upset if we do it in secret."

"It's the only way it will work. Central Authority won't allow us to be mated. They will insist on their computers making the match."

She nodded. "Okay. If that's what we have to do, then I'll do it."

Rupra smiled. "Good. I'll check around and find out where we can go to get it done."

They kissed again and then Bruda broke away. "I've got to go. I'm meeting my friend, Peeta Escabus, at Capitol Square."

"Oh, you finally made contact with him?"

"Yes. I had to be careful. His father and my father were friends. I had to make sure I met Peeta alone."

"Okay," Essyria said not thrilled that Rupra was leaving her for the rest of the evening. "Have a good time. Let me know how it goes."

"I will," Bruda said giving her one last kiss.

Rupra left the restaurant and hailed a sky cab. "Capitol Square," he said. There was no driver but a receiver picked up his destination and repeated it back.

"Capitol Square?"

"That's correct," he said.

The sky cab lifted quickly and shot off toward the center of Shisk. Rupra felt good. For the first time since he'd arrived in the capital city his life was starting to come together again. He loved Essyria, knew she'd be a great mate and once he was a part of her family he'd be in a position to get into politics—his ultimate goal in life. He loved power and everything that flowed from it. He'd seen how it had empowered his grandfather and he longed to have people love and respect him like they did his grandfather before he had been forced to resign. It made him sick to think of his grandfather's resignation and disgrace.

He pondered how his grandfather had so quickly fell out of grace. He had been weak and had let his opponents get the better of him. Rupra vowed never to let that happen to him. Once he was in a position of power, he wouldn't let anyone take it away from him. His grandfather had been a fool to resign. Had he not been a coward and fought to retain his seat, Rupra was sure he would have prevailed. *No rhutz could ever defeat a Bruda in a fair fight!*

The sky cab dropped suddenly startling Bruda and forcing him to grab onto the handrail. Looking down he saw Capitol Square coming into view. The sky cab stopped, hovering a foot above the landing pad. Bruda got out and ran his hand above the scanner.

When he got to Shisk he had feared his sensor chip would give him away and ultimately lead to his grandfather finding him. But his fears had not materialized as the citizens of Vaceen, not being in a domed city, had not been added to Central Authorities' database. When he was scanned at the clinic in Shisk it was the first time Central Authority knew he existed. Fortunately, there were so many tourists and migrants seeking refuge in the domed city his name was soon buried with millions of others.

He'd brought gold and paper money with him from Vaceen which he converted to Sony credits once he'd been accepted as a citizen of Shisk, as coin and paper currency were not accepted by the local merchants in this ultra-modern city. A citizen wanting to pay for something simply waved his wrist over a scanner and the charges were taken from his account. Similarly, each worker's wrist was scanned at the beginning of each day's work and his wages were deposited into his account instantaneously. The downside of this system was that Central Authority always knew where a citizen was if they needed to find him, how much money he had, and collected taxes due on a daily basis.

It also eliminated most crime since it was impossible to hide anywhere in the city. Of course, serious criminals soon learned how to remove their tracking chips so they could move about the city without notice. But if they were ever caught without a tracking chip they'd be given the truth serum and soon would be blurting out all of their criminal history like a child telling his mother about a trip to the zoo.

Rupra looked around for his friend but didn't see him. It had been five cycles since he'd seen Peeta Escabus, so he wasn't sure he'd recognize him. They had spent a lot of time together as children when their families got together and were very close. Rupra had grown at least a foot since then so he assumed they both would look quite different. Finally, he saw a man strolling toward him. He recognized Peeta's slim face and distinctive chin. Rupra started walking toward the man and they embraced.

"Hello, my friend," Rupra said giving Peeta a once over.

"Rupra Bruda. I couldn't believe it when you called. How have you been?”

“Oh, good and bad. You know how that goes.”

“What brings you to Shisk?”

“Fate, I’m afraid.”

Peeta gave him a curious look. “Does that mean you’re staying for a while?”

“Yes. I’ve left Tributon. I’ve had enough of that place.”

“Really. What happened?”

“It’s a long story.”

“Well, there’s a new Tavern in town you’ll love. Why don’t we go there and I’ll buy you a tekari?”

Rupra nodded. “Sure. I could use a drink.”

“Good, and when we’re done they have Seafolken women there who can make you forget your troubles.”

“Seafolken women?” Rupra questioned.

“Yes. You’ve heard about Seafolken women, surely.”

“Of course. But I didn’t expect to find any in Shisk.”

“This new tavern, the Mighty Jolly, is the only place you can find them in the city.”

“The Mighty Jolly? I’ve heard of it.”

“Yes, I bet you have. They began in Tributon. I’m surprised you haven’t been to one.”

Rupra laughed. “My mother kept me on a pretty tight leash when it came to bars and women, I’m afraid. The family reputation, you know.”

“Well, your mother is no longer a factor, so tonight you will experience your most erotic fantasies.”

Rupra smiled wryly. “Sounds good to me.”

Peeta led Rupra to a tram station and they caught the next tram going to their destination. After a quick smooth ride, they got off the tram just two blocks from the Mighty Jolly. Rupra frowned as they walked toward the establishment noticing many mutants, sickly humans, and derelicts lurking about.

“I didn’t know they allowed mutants in Shisk,” Rupra said.

Peeta shrugged. “Since Shisk is the capital city we can’t keep any humans out of the city, although most of us would like to.”

“Hmm. That’s a shame. Look how they’ve run down this part of the city already. It's a disgrace."

"I know. Just don't make eye contact and they'll leave us alone."

As they approached the Mighty Jolly a rhutz suddenly strolled out of an alleyway. Rupra froze and Peeta looked on in horror.

"What the—!" Rupra exclaimed.

The rhutz growled showing its sharp fangs. People around looked on in shock. The rhutz circled Rupra looking like he was going to attack him at any moment. Then the door to the Tavern swung open and a huge one-eyed mutant strolled out. Eyeball, the security chief, glared at the rhutz.

"Get out of here, Misty," Eyeball said. "You're scaring away my customers."

The rhutz growled one more time at Rupra and then disappeared down the alleyway from where he'd come. Rupra let out a sigh of relief.

"Sorry about that," Eyeball said. "I don't know what got into that rhutz. He's never caused us any trouble before."

"Why do you tolerate such beasts?" Rupra spat.

"They keep the rodent population down and they provide security at night."

"Provide security?" Peeta questioned.

"Yes. They are very smart and quite reliable," Eyeball replied. "Come on in. The first drink is on the house."

Rupra nodded and stepped inside. Eyeball put his big hand on Peeta's shoulder and guided him in."

"Shellee, give these boys a drink, on the house," he yelled. "They've had an unpleasant run in with a rhutz."

A girl with bright yellow hair and an orange metallic body suit nodded. "Okay, over here boys."

Rupra and Peeta walked over to the bar and took a stool.

"What can I get you, boys?" Shellee asked.

Rupra looked a Peeta. "Two tezaries," Peeta replied.

"Coming right up," Shellee said.

A loon later she brought them their drinks and smiled brightly. "So, what did you do to piss off the rhutz?" she asked.

Peeta shrugged. "You've got me. That was the first rhutz I've ever seen."

"Hmm. So it must have been you he didn't like," Shellee said giving

Rupra a suspicious stare.

Rupra shrugged, turned and proceeded to look at the naked girls dancing in the corner of the tavern. Seeing the rhutz had brought back a lot of unpleasant memories. Peeta smiled, grabbed his drink, and started to move toward the dancing Seafolken.

"Come on. Let's get a little closer so we don't have to strain our eyes to see these wonders of the sea."

Rupra nodded to Shellee, picked up his drink and followed Peeta.

"You won't believe how good these girls smell," Peeta said. "They're more intoxicating than these tezaries."

"Come on," Rupra said laughing. "They're just women."

As they got closer Rupra began to sniff the air. Something did smell good he admitted to himself. Peeta looked at the expression on his face and smiled.

"See. What did I tell you?"

"It must be a perfume they are wearing," Rupra objected.

"No. It's their natural scent. Wait until they lure you into their bed. Then you'll have no doubt."

"Bed? I don't plan to sleep with them?"

"It's too late my friend. They are irresistible. Don't fight it. Just enjoy yourself."

Suddenly Rupra felt a hand on his shoulder. It felt warm and tender so he didn't resist. He turned around slowly and saw before his eyes a goddess of unfathomable beauty. She began to dance before him, circling around and brushing her naked breasts against his cheeks. His pulse quickened and he became so aroused he had difficulty breathing. Suddenly, she moved in and wrapped her arms around him. He put his arms around her and jerked her hard into his body. The woman laughed then leaned over and kissed him on the neck. He felt a slight prickling sensation and then experienced the most wonderful feeling he'd ever known. His vision blurred and he felt weak. Now, in a fog, he felt a tug on his arm and found himself being led through the bar to a back room. Peeta looked on with great amusement when he suddenly felt a woman dancing close to him as well. He smiled broadly in anticipation of the pleasures that would soon be his.

11

Replica

Shellee escorted Rupra and Peeta to a lounge where customers could recover from their encounters with the Seafolken women. She handed them each a cup of sankee and two pills.

"Take these pills and then drink a couple of cups of sankee. The pills will help clear your head and the sankee will wake you up."

"I don't remember anything," Rupra complained.

"Yes, that's one of the properties of tortiac's sting. If you remembered all the pleasures you've experienced you would become addicted to it and then we couldn't get rid of you."

"But that's not fair."

"Don't fret about it," Peeta said. "It's true your conscious mind doesn't remember anything, but your subconscious mind certainly does. I promise you for several weeks you will be dreaming about your Seafolken goddess and wake up more relaxed and content than you've ever been in your life. The experience is definitely worth the money."

Rupra took the pills and washed them down with the sankee. "So, how much did this little adventure cost me?"

"You were scanned for four thousand credits," Shellee replied.

"Four thousand credits!" Rupra exclaimed.

"Yes, our rates are posted by the door. Didn't you read them before you came in?"

Peeta laughed. "It's okay, Rupra. If you're short on credits I'll lend you some until you get a job."

Rupra sighed. "It's not that. I have plenty of credits. It's just that I've never paid for sex before. If my family found out—"

"They won't. Every man has to experience a Seafolken woman at least once in his life. It's an unwritten law."

Rupra smiled. "I guess you're right. Let's get out of here. I need to call Essyria. She's probably wondering where I am."

They got up and staggered out of the side door to the Mighty Jolly and headed toward the subtram station.

"I'd stay away from her for a day or two. If you see her today she'll smell the Seafolken scent on you."

"What?" Rupra said. "You mean even if I take a shower, she'll still be able to smell it."

Peeta smiled broadly barely able to contain his glee. "I told you this was an experience of a lifetime."

"Scutz! How am I going to stay away from her for two days?"

"Well, you need a few days to arrange your mating. Just call her and tell her you're leaving the dome to make arrangements for the mating ceremony."

Rupra considered that, then nodded. "Okay. That's a good idea."

As they turned the corner they ran into the huge, one-eyed mutant they'd met the previous day.

"So, gentlemen. Did you have a memorable weekend?" Eyeball asked.

Peeta smiled. "Oh, yes. Quite memorable. Thank you."

"Good. Now, don't ever come back here again. You're not welcome here."

Rupra and Peeta frowned. "Why not?" Peeta asked angrily.

"I've been told your friend here has killed a rhutz and is responsible for many more dying."

"What?" Rupra spat. "Who told you that?"

"That rhutz you ran into last night. While you were enjoying your evening I linked up with him to find out why he was so hostile to you. He says you murdered a rhutz in Tributon and sparked a small war between the town's people and several packs of rhutz."

"How could he possibly know that?" Rupra asked.

"Don't you know the rhutz can communicate with each other telepathically? The word got out about you, apparently. I'd watch my back if I were you and stay away from the Mighty Jolly. We don't need any trouble."

Rupra stepped past Eyeball and walked off angrily. Peeta looked at Eyeball and shrugged. "I don't know anything about it," he said as he ran to catch up with Rupra.

"Can you believe the rhutz recognized you?" Peeta said.

"No. I didn't anticipate that," Rupra said thoughtfully.

"What are you going to do?"

Rupra stopped and looked Peeta in the eyes. "What would you say to a rhutz hunt?" Rupra asked.

Peeta smiled. "I'd like that," he replied, "and I have some friends who might want to join the hunt, too."

"Good. Why don't you talk to your friends and when I get back to the dome we'll find that rhutz and let him know he's not welcome in Shisk!"

Peeta nodded. "Leave it to me. I'll find us some weapons and do some research on the rhutz population in Shisk too. I hadn't realized there were rhutz in the city. My family will be quite distraught when they learn of it."

"Really. They're not rhutz lovers?"

"No. Shisk was built to be a model city. A lot of people were upset when they started letting mutants in. You can see how their neighborhoods have deteriorated. It's a disgrace."

As he stepped into his sky cab, Rupra was feeling very good. Peeta had been right. He could still smell the Seafolken woman on his skin and clothing and it was quite intoxicating. Getting reacquainted with Peeta had gone very well too—better than he could have ever hoped. It gave him great satisfaction to know others felt the same way about the mutants and the rhutz as he did and were prepared to do something about it.

Artis fell into a deep sleep and began to dream. She was walking through a thick fog and could barely see anything around her. It was deadly quiet and the path beneath her feet was hard but smooth. As she walked the fog began to lift and she beheld a magnificent white crystal city all around her. As she walked through the city she felt the warmth of the sun filtering down upon her. She looked up but saw nothing but bright white light overhead. Suddenly an insect-looking creature appeared before her. It had four legs beneath a half-shell body but also a torso with two hands like a human. Its head was divided into three distinct parts held together by a thick membrane.

"Welcome, Artis of the humans!" the Speaker said. *"I speak for all the nanomite swarmmasters in our colony."*

"Hello, Speaker," Artis said. *"Are you real or am I dreaming?"*

"You are dreaming but we are real. Thank you for teaching us your language. We have long wondered about humans and are anxious to learn more about them."

"That is our wish about the nanomites, as well," Artis replied excitedly. *"Your city is magnificent."*

"Thank you. It suits us well and protects us from the elements."

"How are you able to construct such a strong and durable structure? It's amazing to us humans and is what drew us to you."

"Our building techniques have evolved over time. We are a fragile life-form and must be protected from wind and water. Either of these common elements can kill billions of our brothers and sisters if they are not protected from them."

Artis had so many questions she didn't know where to begin. She feared she'd wake up at any moment and lose the opportunity to find out the answers to them.

"So, will we be able to communicate in this manner in the future?" she asked hopefully.

"No. Once we have mastered your language we hope to establish a direct link between our swarmmasters and your mind. You may not remember this dream, so we have left you a sign that you will discover when you awake. Hopefully that sign will help you recall our conversation so you will not lose heart and abandon your efforts to communicate with us."

"Oh. I see. Well thank you for contacting me. I was getting discouraged."

"Yes, we knew you must be and therefore constructed this dream and left you this sign to give you hope. Goodbye for now. Don't give up."

Artis woke up with a start. Sitting up, she looked at her wrist array and was shocked at how long she'd been asleep. She stretched and then rubbed her temples as bits and pieces of a dream danced in her head. She wondered if her subconscious mind had indeed taken over her task of teaching the nanomites the Tari language. It was a stretch to think that it would ever be possible. Feeling a hunger pain, she went outside to find Poldra and ask her to fix her something. When she stepped outside she saw Poldra staring at something with her mouth open. She walked over curiously to see what had captivated her attention. Poldra looked over at her with wonder in her eyes. Artis looked down at the spot that had captivated Poldra's attention and gasped.

A miniature model of the nanomite city had been constructed on their front doorstep. It depicted the city in precise detail and sparkled in the bright sunlight. Memories of the previous night's dream came flooding into Artis' mind. She gasped in delight. Tears began flowing down her cheeks.

"Oh, God and Sandee. We have done it!"

Artis grabbed Poldra and began dancing around with joy.

"It's a miracle," Poldra said now also crying.

Faruk and Giant rushed over to see what all the excitement was about. They stopped when they saw the model city and stared at it in wonder. They looked at Artis.

"You've done it," Faruk said smiling broadly. "I can't believe it. I thought you were wasting your time. This is quite amazing."

"Have you told Threebeard?" Giant asked.

"No," Artis said and then closed her eyes to establish a link with her brother.

"Threebeard! Come to me."

Threebeard was working diligently on the computer in the back room of the Mighty Jolly when he felt Artis' call

"What is it, Artis?" he thought.

"We've done it! The nanomites contacted me in my dreams and they have constructed us a beautiful monument of their city so there can be no mistake that we've made contact."

A rush of joy and excitement came over Threebeard. He struggled to keep his composure.

"Wonderful! That is spectacular news! I knew you could do it. I will come at once to see this marvel."

"Yes. Come now. The nanomites want to establish a direct link and they are anxious to talk."

"Alright. I'll be there in a few kyloons. Excellent work, Artis!

Excellent work!"

Just as Threebeard was about to break the link, the ground began to shake violently knocking Artis and Faruk to the ground. Giant staggered but managed to stay on his feet.

"What happened?" Threebeard asked feeling Artis' distress.

"There has been a tremor. A small one luckily. We're okay?"

"I've been reading reports of tremors all over Tarizon. Hundreds of them in the last 54 kyloons. There's been a couple in Tributon too."

"Really? What do you think is causing it?" Artis asked.

"I'm not sure. They all seem to be volcanic in origin," Threebeard noted, *"which isn't unusual except for the large number of them."*

"And this is happening all over Tarizon?"

"Yes, I've been monitoring seismic activity on the global web. There's activity on every continent."

"So, what should we do?" Artis asked.

"Take some pictures of the model city in case there are more earthquakes. If it gets swallowed in a fissure I want to be able to prove we've made contact. Check the ground around you too. If you see any cracks you may want to relocate the camp."

"I wonder what the nanomites are thinking? I bet they are worried about the quake," Artis said.

"Well, hopefully you'll be able to talk to them soon and find out."

"I know. Won't that be wonderful?"

"Yes. I'll see you soon. Be careful."

Artis broke the link with Threebeard and then looked at Giant. "You need to check the camp for cracks. If a fissure opens up around here we don't want to be in the middle of it."

Giant nodded and started walking around the camp examining the ground carefully. "Faruk," Artis said. "How far away is the nearest volcano?"

Faruk looked off to the west. "Mt. Alabash is about a hundred kylods from here, I believe."

"Good. It shouldn't be a direct threat then. I wonder if there is any way we can secure this model of the city. I'd hate to lose it if there is another tremor."

Faruk looked at the magnificent replica. He noticed a notch etched all around it so he went over to inspect it. A smile came over his face. "It's solid rock but the ground beneath it is lose gravel. All we have to do is dig around it and we should be able to remove it and mount it on a flat surface for transport.

"Really? The nanomites must have done that on purpose, knowing we would want to preserve it. That's wonderful. Go ahead and secure it for me, would you?"

"Of course," Faruk said motioning for Poldra to come and help him.

Artis ran down to the nanomite city to see if it had sustained any damage. She noted several cracks but nothing that looked too serious. As she walked the perimeter there was another tremor. It felt much longer and stronger than the first. When it was over she looked up at the city and saw that the cracks had widened and deepened. Shaking her head in dismay she ran back to camp and saw that some of the camocubes had torn apart and were sagging. She saw Giant and rushed over to him.

"We should go. I don't think it is safe here on the bluff and I want to get the replica back home where it will be safe. We can come back later and talk to the nanomites. I think they are going to be occupied for a while, anyway, repairing their city."

Giant nodded. "I think you are right. There is a long fissure that starts two hundred feet to the north and it looks like, if it widens, it will run right through our camp."

"Okay. Hurry and get everything packed up."

A kyloon later they had the camp packed up and loaded in their transport vehicles. Artis took one last look at the nanomite city and then got in and told Faruk to move out. As they started to move the earth began shaking again, more violently than before.

"Get us out of here quick," Artis ordered.

Faruk looked back worriedly and then took control of the vehicle manually. He pushed the throttle causing a cloud of dust and gravel to spit out from under the wheels. The ATV lunged forward just as the ground beneath it gave way. The back end of the ATV dropped into the fissure but the momentum from the forward lunge pulled them out onto solid ground. Artis looked back and gave an audible sigh of relief. Then he saw Giant racing away from the fissure, trying desperately not to be sucked in. Just as it looked like the fissure would consume the ATV, Giant swerved it to the right and out of danger.

"Holy Sandee! That was close," Artis exclaimed taking a long breath.

"Yes," Faruk said. "It's a good thing we left when we did."

"Thank God and Sandee. I wonder what is happening? I've never heard of so many tremors happening at the same time on every continent."

Before Faruk could reply there was a tremendous explosion coming from behind and to their west. Faruk stopped the ATV and looked back in the direction of the sound. Large billowing clouds of smoke were rising out of the Doral Mountains.

"It looks like someone dropped a nuclear bomb," Artis said.

"No. It's Mt. Alabash! It's erupting."

"Holy Sandee! I've never seen a volcano erupt. It's so beautiful."

"It won't be so beautiful when the ash starts falling from the sky," Faruk warned. "In a few kyloons the ground will be a foot thick with ash, the engines will get clogged up and stop running, and we won't be able to breath. We need to keep moving away from it."

Artis' mouth dropped. "Then get us out of here, Faruk. We can't afford to get stranded out here in the Ural Desert."

Faruk started the ATV and increased their speed. Giant, who had finally caught up with them in the other ATV, followed close behind. The sky around them began to turn white as they drove and big flakes of volcanic ash started to rain down upon them. Faruk turned on the wipers as it was getting difficult to see. Soon the ash was so thick the sky began to darken and Faruk had to turn on the rolling lights so they could see the ground ahead.

"I hope we find the highway soon," Faruk said. "We've got to make better time if we're going to outrun the ash."

"How far is it?" Artis asked.

"My global tracker says it should be just two kylods ahead, but I can't see a thing."

"Just keep following its settings. I'm sure it's accurate," Artis said praying that she was right.

A day after his encounter with the Seafolken, Rupra Bruda left Shisk and traveled on his jet cycle south to the town of Jedeva. His friend

Peeta had given him the name of the townhead there who was a friend of his father. It was a beautiful ride through the thick tropical forests of southern Soni. Mt. Soni was to his left and he couldn't help but glance up at it from time to time as he drove.

He had called ahead and was told to meet Silbus Ghant at his office in the government building late that afternoon. Jedeva was a small town that reminded Rupra of his hometown of Vaceen except here the buildings were primarily wooden because of the abundance of timber, whereas in Vaceen everything was built of stone or brick. Rupra parked his bike and then walked into the main lobby of the building. After consulting a directory, he took the lift to the third floor.

The receptionist took his name and told him to take a seat. A few moments later a middle-aged man appeared and greeted him.

"So, you're a friend of Peeta Escabus?" Ghant said.

Rupra stood up and nodded. "Yes, that's right."

"How long have you known him?"

"Since we were children."

"Hmm. Come with me. We can talk in my office."

Rupra followed Ghant down the hall and into his cluttered office. Ghant cleared a section of a plush sofa so Rupra had a place to sit. Rupra looked at the walls adorned with many paintings and photographs. He noticed a plaque indicating Ghant had been awarded the Medal of Merit while serving in the TGA.

"Can I get you a drink?"

"Sure," Bruda replied feeling a little parched from being on the bike for so long.

Ghant went to a bar in the corner of his office and grabbed them both a tekari. He handed one to Rupra. "So, how was your drive from the city?" Ghant asked as he sat in the chair behind his knotwood desk.

"Actually, quite pleasant. The scenery around here is quite spectacular," Rupra replied.

"Yes, it is. It's recovered nicely since the last war. Not quite like it once was. The trees still look a bit sickly from the pollution, but give it another ten or twenty cycles and everything will be back to normal."

Bruda nodded. "That would be nice."

"So, I understand you have found someone you'd like to mate."

Rupra smiled. "Yes, I have. We are quite compatible and know we'll be good together."

"How long have you known this girl?" Ghant asked.

"Not too long, but we have a lot in common and are quite happy in each other's company."

Ghant nodded knowingly. "I'm sure you feel that way, but you may only be infatuated. You think you are in love and you'll always be happy, but one day you will wake up and wonder why you ever wanted to be mated. Believe me, the computers are much better at picking a durable mate than the human heart."

"We are both telepathic and share similar political ambitions and beliefs," Rupra noted. "I've never met a woman my equal, but Essyria has truly been sent to me by God."

Ghant raised his eyebrows. "Well, who am I to interfere with a match made by the Almighty. To be honest with you, I personally believe every man and woman should have the right to pick their own mate. Unfortunately, Central Authority doesn't share my viewpoint."

"But I understood Central Authority didn't monitor mating outside the dome."

"True enough, but from time to time they send out auditors, so we have to be careful. A paper trail will have to be created showing that you were both residents of our town and that your circumstances fell within one of the exceptions to mandatory computer mating."

"What are the exceptions?"

"Pregnancy is the easiest. One of the primary objectives of computer mating is to encourage childbearing, so if you've already got that taken care of it makes it easier."

"Well, she's not pregnant. At least I don't think she is. I suppose I could try to get her pregnant but I'm not sure we want children immediately."

"It's no matter. For the right price we can find you a doctor who will certify that she is pregnant. Later on, if Central Authority checks up on you and your mate and wants to know what happened to your child, the doctor will certify that you had a miscarriage. With the miscarriage rate currently at 62% his word will not be questioned."

"What about the residency requirement?"

"You can stay a few nights at the local inn to establish your residency. There's been no census in many cycles and the auditors don't have the resources to conduct investigations of those sorts of things."

"Good. Then what do I need to do?"

"You'll both have to come and visit the doctor. He'll need ten thousand credits in Soni gold coin."

"But that's not legal tender anymore?"

"Central Authority doesn't accept it, but it's still good on the black market."

"Okay."

"Then you and your mate will have to come over here and fill out the proper paperwork and I'll sign off on it."

"So, how much cash will I need to bring *you*?"

"Nothing. I'm doing this as a favor."

Rupra nodded warily. He didn't like owing people favors, but he didn't have a lot of extra credits to be throwing around so he didn't object. "Thank you. Someday I'll repay you for your kindness."

"I'm counting on that," Ghant replied wryly.

Rupra stood up. "Well, thank you for your hospitality. I'll call you in a few days to arrange a time to conclude this matter."

Ghant nodded and started to rise when the building began to shake violently. Photos and pictures fell from the walls and the lights blinked on and off. Rupra sat back on the sofa and covered his head to protect it from falling debris.

"What the hell?" Ghant said with one hand on his desk to steady him.

"It's a tremor," Rupra advised. "We get them a lot in Tributon."

"Really. I can't remember ever having one around here."

"It's nothing to worry about," Rupra assured him as the room stilled. They both looked around warily. "Thanks, again," Rupra said as he stood up and left hurriedly. He preferred being outdoors during a tremor, particularly when he didn't know how sturdy the building was.

When he got to his jet cycle he looked east at Mt. Soni. What he saw startled him. On his way here, the mountain had been quiet and the sky above it clear, but now white smoke was billowing out of the big volcano. Although the sight was surprising it didn't upset Rupra because he knew volcanos often let off steam just to relieve pressure. He'd seen it many times before back home. Still, on his ride back to Shisk he kept a watchful eye on the big volcano.

The next morning Rupra took a long bath with lots of scented soaps. He wanted to be sure any trace of the Seafolken woman was off him when he went to see Essyria. He'd called her when he got to his hotel and filled her in on his meeting with Ghant. She was excited by the news and anxious to talk more about it. They agreed to meet for lunch at the Soni Isle restaurant on the boardwalk along the Coral Sea. The boardwalk had only recently been built outside the dome when environmentalists determined the air was safe.

They arrived at the restaurant a little early so the hostess seated them in the bar until a table was ready. The news was playing on the VC. Rupra looked up and saw a volcano erupting. He pointed to it.

"Look. That's Mt. Alabash in Rigimol. I climbed to the top of it one time."

"Really? That must have been quite a hike."

"Yes. It was but the view from up there is unbelievable."

Rupra looked over at the bartender and tried to get his attention.

"Yes, sir. What can I get you?"

"We'd like a couple of tezaries and could you turn the volume up on the VC?"

"Yes, sir," the bartender said reaching over to the VC and hitting the volume control.

"The only warnings of the eruption were a few tremors early this morning," the reporter advised. *"Then at 1403 kyloons a quantum eight quake struck the area toppling buildings, bridges and severing highways leading to the big volcano. Moments later steam and ash began shooting into the sky followed by a river of molten lava that began flowing down the east side of the mountain.*

"All residents within a hundred kylod radius from Mt. Alabash have been evacuated as the smoke, ash, and lava are expected to kill all life and vegetation within that zone. In addition, all air traffic has been diverted within a 250 kylod radius as the thick ash will clog the engines of most aircraft.

"Although, Mt. Alabash is the only volcano currently erupting, scientists are watching several other volcanoes around the globe as seismic

activity around them has been unusually high in the past 54 kyloons. This includes Mt. Soni which experienced a quantum four tremor yesterday. Mt. Soni has not erupted in over 100 cycles, so scientists don't expect it to now, but the increased seismic activity around the globe has many scientists on edge."

The hostess came over and told them their table was ready. Rupra and Essyria got up and followed the hostess to the other side of the restaurant where they were seated in a booth and given menus.

"You know, I felt that tremor yesterday. I was talking to Mr. Ghant when it hit. It knocked a bunch of pictures off his walls."

"Really? I didn't feel anything here. Were you scared?"

"No. Tremors are pretty common in Tributon."

"Hmm. I hope that doesn't mean Mt. Soni is going to erupt."

"Me too."

"So, Mr. Ghant said all we have to do is pay off a doctor and sign some paperwork to be mated in Jedeva?" Essyria asked to be sure she had it right.

"And we have to stay in town a few days to establish our residency beforehand."

"So, that's nothing. Let's go do it tomorrow."

Rupra smiled. "What will you tell your parents?"

"I don't know. I'll tell them I'm going to visit one of my friends. Silla will cover me."

"Silla? I've never met her."

"She's one of my best friends. She lives on the other side of the city, so I often stay overnight with her. I can invent some reason I need to be away for a few days."

"Well, I've got something to do this afternoon, but tomorrow I'll call Ghant and arrange everything for next week. Will that be soon enough?"

"Next week?" Essyria moaned.

"That's not far off," Rupra said.

"I know. I'll just feel better when we're mated. I'm afraid my parents will find out what we're doing and try to stop us."

"Just don't act suspiciously and there is no reason for them to find out."

"Okay. Next week then."

That afternoon Rupra was to meet up with Peeta and the friends he'd recruited for their rhutz hunt at the subtram station near the Mighty Jolly. He dropped off Essyria at the clinic on the way. When they kissed Essyria gave Rupra a questioning look.

"Did you change your cologne? You smell different."

Rupra held his breath as he wondered if the scent of the Seafolken woman was still on him. "Ah, well . . . I was so grimy from my trip I threw a bunch of bath scents in my tub this morning."

Essyria looked at Rupra warily. "Bath scents? Just when I think I know you, you do something out of character."

Rupra shrugged. "I didn't want to smell like a stinker rat when I met up with you."

She laughed. "Well, thank you for that."

"I've got to run or I'll be late."

"Have a good time."

Rupra nodded and made a hasty exit. A few moments later he was boarding the subtram to the Silver Park Station. When he arrived Peeta and three of his friends were milling around. Peeta introduced Rupra to Allie Chalke, Tibor Raseen, and Blinh Bligh and then pointed to a park bench where they could discuss strategy.

"This won't be like killing a dirkbird," Rupra said. "The rhutz is fast and if he sees that you have a gun he'll try to wrestle it out of your hand with his invisible hand."

"So, how do we kill it?" Peeta asked.

"We'll have to find it and then lure it into a trap. He can't disarm all of us," Rupra said pulling a map out of his pocket and spreading it out on the park bench. "This is a map of this precinct. Our best bet is to lure the rhutz into this warehouse district just south of the Mighty Jolly. Once we get him to go down one of those walkways between the warehouses we can ambush him."

"So how do we lure him into the trap?" Chalke asked.

"I'll have to do that. He knows my scent and will come after me the moment he smells it. What we'll do is walk around the precinct until he makes his appearance. Once we see him three of you will go here," Rupra said pointing to a spot on the map.

"How are we going to kill it once we lure it into the trap?" Raseen asked.

Peeta put a bag on the table. "I've got lasers for everyone. We don't want to make a lot of noise and attract anyone's attention."

"Where did you get so many lasers?" Rupra asked appreciatively.

"My father is somewhat of a gun collector. In fact, he's got so many guns I didn't figure he'd notice if I borrowed a few for the afternoon."

"Alright," Rupra said. "Let's synchronize our communicators so we can talk to each other when we split up. Who's going to stick with me?"

"What if he just attacks you the moment he sees you?" Bligh asked.

"I don't think he will. He didn't the last time. He'll probably just stalk us for a while deciding what to do. If we move quickly we should be able to lure in between the warehouses where no one is likely to see us kill him. But if he forces our hands we'll just have to shoot him when he attacks. If someone witnesses the kill, we'll justifiably claim self-defense. That's why I need some backup. He could disarm me, but not both of us."

"I'll back you up then," Bligh said. "I'm pretty good with a laser. I've trained a bit with the TGA."

"Oh really?"

"Yes. I'm in the peace reserves, actually."

"Good. The rest of you find some cover so the rhutz doesn't see you when he enters the walkway. Once he's passed you then someone needs to cover the flank so he'll have no place to run when Bligh and I turn around and confront him."

Bligh grinned. "He's not gonna know what hit him."

Bruda nodded. "That's the idea."

"What if he's got friends?" Chalke asked.

Bruda shrugged. "We didn't see any the other night, but it's a possibility. Either way we should have plenty of fire power to eliminate any further threat."

"Alright. Let's do this!" Peeta said raising his fist.

They all got up ready to start the hunt. Bruda and Bligh led the way with Peeta, Chalke and Raseen fifty strides behind. They walked casually toward the Mighty Jolly and by the alleyway where Bruda and Peeta had run into the rhutz a few days earlier. They passed many mutants and a few Seafolken who gave them hard looks as they went by but there was no sign of the rhutz. After they'd walked a few kylods, Bruda stopped and looked around.

"He may be off somewhere else in the city today," Bruda surmised.

Peeta shook his head. "Or, he might be watching us waiting for the right opportunity to strike."

Rupra turned around and scanned the area. "Let's walk back to the tram station. If we don't see him along the way we'll have to take a look at the map again and try something different."

Peeta nodded and Bruda and Bligh headed back toward the Mighty Jolly. This time when they passed the Mighty Jolly Eyeball came out to watch them.

"What are you doing back here?" Eyeball asked gruffly.

"Nothing. Just taking a stroll."

"Why don't you take your strolls somewhere else?"

"It's a free city the last time I heard," Bruda noted.

"I can tell you're up to no good, so watch yourself or you'll have to deal with me."

"You don't scare me, you mutant scum!" Bruda replied.

Eyeball took a step toward Bruda. Bligh stepped out in support of his friend. Eyeball shook his head, turned and went back inside the Mighty Jolly. As they turned to resume walking they heard a growl from the alleyway across the street. Bruda looked over at Misty and smiled.

"Alright. Take it easy everyone. It's time to set the trap."

Peeta, Chalke and Raseen immediately moved toward the warehouses. Bruda and Bligh pretending not to be bothered by the rhutz, continued to walk toward the designated rendezvous point. Misty came out of the alley and followed them. Looking back at the rhutz they picked up their pace. In response, Misty started to trot after them. As they rounded the first warehouse, Bruda saw Peeta, Chalke, and Raseen turning into the walkway and getting into position. Bruda and Bligh started to run and the Misty did likewise, growling and baring his teeth. Suddenly, Bruda and Bligh stopped and faced the rhutz as Peeta, Chalke and Raseen stepped out to encircle him.

Misty looked around realizing he'd been lured into an ambush. Bligh pulled out his laser and took aim. The rhutz spun around, concentrated on the laser and it flew out of Bligh's hand. At the same time Peeta, Chalke and Raseen pulled out their lasers. Before Raseen could fire, his laser flew into the air as well, but Peeta managed to get a shot off hitting Misty in the leg. He let out a painful whimper. Then Chalke shot hit him in the chest causing his fur to catch on fire. Misty fell to the ground hard, then stumbled forward trying to struggle to his feet. Bruda finally took out his laser and fired, hitting the rhutz in the head. Misty let out one last painful whimper and then fell lifeless to the ground.

"What have you done?" Eyeball exclaimed as he came running around the corner.

"Quick! Let's get out of here!" Peeta yelled.

Everyone except Bruda took off running. Bruda raised his laser at Eyeball. Eyeball ignored him and ran over to Misty.

"Why did you shoot him, you lousy scutz?" Eyeball screamed as he quickly checked to see if the rhutz was still alive. Feeling no pulse, he turned to Bruda. "He's dead. You've murdered him!"

"It was self-defense," Bruda protested. "He attacked us."

Eyeball stood up, his fists clenched and started toward Bruda. "I'll kill you!"

Bruda fired the laser but Eyeball was wearing a thick leather belt that seemed to blunt the effectiveness of the laser. Bruda turned to run but Eyeball managed to grab his arm, yank him back and hit him hard across the face with the back of his hand. Bruda winced in pain as he fell backward onto the ground. Eyeball circled around ready to go in for the kill but didn't see Peeta taking aim at his back. This time the laser hit him in the leg and he fell to the ground with a loud thud.

Bruda scrambled to his feet and stumbled away out of Eyeball's reach. Peeta aimed the laser at Eyeball's head and fired again. There was a sizzling sound and then the big eyeball exploded. Peeta's face was pelted with the debris. Wiping his face, he holstered his laser and looked approvingly at his kill. Rupra came up beside him.

"Nice shot. Let's dispose of the body before someone comes this way."

They both took an arm and dragged the body to a debris station and dumped Eyeball into it. The big mutant disappeared into the industrial waste that was waiting for pick up. Then they did the same with the rhutz. Once satisfied the bodies were out of sight, Rupra and Peeta took off in a run. A few loons later they caught up with their friends at the tram station and boarded the first one heading for Capitol Square. Everyone grimaced when they saw Bruda's face and Peeta's blood-smeared clothing.

"Where did that one-eyed mutant come from?" Peeta asked out of breath.

"I don't know," Bruda replied. "He must have been watching from the Mighty Jolly."

"Why did you kill him?" Bligh asked worriedly.

Peeta looked at him. "He was a witness. I'm not going to jail for the rest of my life on account of some one-eyed monster."

"I know, but nobody would have cared if we killed a rhutz, but killing a mutant is technically murder."

"Don't worry, Bligh. Nobody saw anything. The warehouse was shut down for holiday and there was nobody around. That's why we picked that location. Had Eyeball minded his own business he'd still be alive drinking tekari in the Mighty Jolly."

Peeta looked at Rupra's face which was rapidly swelling and turning black. "Damn. Look at your face. You'll have to put some Rapid Cure on it when you get home."

Rupra felt his face tentatively. "It hurts like hell."

"Well, that rhutz won't ever be snarling at you again," Raseen said.

Bruda smiled. "Yes. We taught him a lesson, didn't we?"

They all laughed. "That was great," Chalke said excitedly. "We should do that again. I wonder how many rhutz there are in the city. We should kill every last one of them."

"I don't know about the rhutz, but there are plenty of mutants we could take on."

They all laughed.

Bruda nodded. "Perhaps we should—go after more rhutz. It would be too dangerous to target mutants, but who would miss a rhutz? Why don't you check around and see if anyone knows about other rhutz in Shisk? Tell them there's a new extermination service in town."

They laughed again, louder this time.

Chalke nodded. "Maybe I will."

They all said goodbye at Capitol Station and split up. Bruda went back to his hotel, tended to his injured face and ordered room service. While he was eating he worried about what would happen when Eyeball didn't show up at the Mighty Jolly. If they found the body and tried to pin the murder on him, he could claim self-defense but he'd have to hire a citizen defender and it could still get messy. *Why did Eyeball have to get involved? Damn him!*

12

Devastation

Although the nanomite's Ural Desert city was tough and durable it couldn't withstand a quantum eight tremor. When the tremor struck it ripped the city apart exposing it to strong winds and sudden downpours. Thousands of nanomite swarms died in the two loons the ground shook and split apart. Those who were not close to the point of fracture survived the initial quake but now faced the daunting task of survival in a suddenly hostile environment.

"We must prepare our swarms to reseal the exposed cells near or at the point of severance," the Speaker said. "There's no time to rejoin both sides of the severed city. Concentrate on getting a tight seal for now."

"Speaker," the Sentinel said. "There is a two-foot fissure separating the city from its raw material supply."

"How long to build a bridge across it?" the Speaker asked.

"It will take several loons," the Engineer replied.

"Get busy then. Time is critical. Rain or a strong wind will kill many swarms. We can't let that happen."

"Yes, Speaker. But ash is also beginning to fall from the sky from Mt. Alabash and it will hamper our efforts."

"Mt. Alabash?"

"Yes. It has erupted and is spewing out molten lava and incredible amounts of steam and ash. The sky is already gray and it's getting difficult to breath for those outside the city. There is also a possibility the lava might reach us here."

"If it comes, when do you think it will arrive?"

"In less than a kyloon," the Scholar replied.

"Can we evacuate?" the Speaker asked.

"No, Speaker," the Scholar replied. *"There is nowhere to go. Our best strategy is to seal the exposed inner walls and move as deep into the city as we can. If the lava covers us we will likely die, if not from the heat then from a lack of oxygen as the fire burns it off and sucks the life out of all of us."*

"Pray to God that doesn't happen," the Speaker said.

"What about a barricade, a wall to stop the molten lava or divert it around out city?" the Engineer asked.

"A barricade?" the Speaker asked. *"Would that work?"*

"If we could build a strong one between us and the lava, the lava would be diverted around us."

"Then we should split all available workers into two work parties—one to reseal the city and the other to building a wall to divert the lava around it."

The swarmmasters considered the suggestion and then the Speaker gave the order and the nanomites split into the two work parties as they had talked. Within a few loons a foot-wide line began to form to the north and east of the city. Since the wall wasn't intended to be inhabited by the nanomites it wasn't built with the usual nanomite care and skill. Speed and strength were the most critical attributes of this new wall. After a kyloon had gone by the interior repairs were almost halfway done and the wall was nearly three feet tall!

"How tall does the wall have to be?" the Speaker asked.

"At least six feet," the Scholar replied.

"That will take time. When will the lava be coming?"

"In less than two kyloons, so the workers must work harder than they have ever worked before."

"Yes, but the ash falling from the sky is causing problems. The swarms are having trouble breathing with so much toxins in the air."

"I wish there was a way to ease their discomfort, but I know of nothing that can be done," the Speaker replied.

Millions of nanomite swarms went to work on the wall and the exterior repairs despite the harsh conditions that confronted them. Thousands were dying every minute as they were smothered by the thick ash that now sat a half a foot deep above the city, but they had no choice but to drag their dead brothers aside and continue to construct the wall that they hoped and prayed would divert the lava and avoid certain doom.

As the wall grew to three feet the ash began falling harder and harder until a crack of thunder could be heard in the distance. The nanomites trembled at the sound. They knew a sudden downpour would be a disaster with their city split down the middle. They quickened their pace but it was to no avail as a sudden downpour drenched the nanomite city. Water began flooding inside the intricate structure drowning millions of nanomites. The only benefit of the rain was to clear the air and wash the ash away allowing the surviving nanomites to breath clearly again.

A kyloon later when the lava hit the wall it stood at nearly five feet. The nanomites inside the wall fled for their lives and took refuge back in their city. The searing heat from the molten lava sent the temperature within the city soaring to unbearable levels, but the wall held and the lava flowed around the city preventing the total annihilation of the nanomite population.

"God has saved our city," the Speaker announced to those who survived the ordeal. *"The cost in the lives of our brothers was dear but their sacrifice has ensured the survival of our life-form on Tarizon. We honor those who have died and shall remember this day forever."*

Threebeard paced back and forth nervously wondering if he'd ever see his sister and her companions again. Finally, he sat down at the computer terminal and started searching for information about the Mt. Alabash eruption. He gasped when he saw the report that the bridge over the Liehn River had collapsed during the tremor. *How will they get across the river?* He studied his map of Rigimol and finally decided they'd have to stay in Guhl until the bridge was repaired. *I wonder how much time that will take?* He closed his eyes and summoned his sister.

"Artis. Are you alright?"

"More or less," she thought. *"We can't travel very fast with all this ash coming down. We finally came to the highway so we're making a little better time. At least we don't have to worry about hitting rocks and cactus."*

"Listen. The bridge over the Liehn River is out. You're going to have to stay in Guhl until they get it repaired."

"Scutz! I wanted to get this replica back home where it will be safe. I'm so afraid something will happen to it."

"I know. I wish there were a way to get you home more quickly.

Unfortunately, all air traffic has been grounded with all the ash in the air."

"Oh, well. I guess we'll have to find an inn. Too bad there isn't a Mighty Jolly in Guhl."

"Yes, I'll have to do something about that," Threebeard said.

"Okay, I'll see you whenever."

As Threebeard was cutting his connection to Artis, his GC began beeping. He picked it up and saw it was from Armillo, his manager in Shisk.

"Threebeard," he said as he put the GC to his ear.

"Boss. I've got some bad news."

Threebeard grimaced. *All I need is more bad news.* "What is it?"

"Eyeball is missing."

"Missing? How could that be?"

"I don't know. He left the tavern in a hurry yesterday in the afternoon and hasn't been seen since."

"He's telepathic. Have you tried to link with him?"

"Yes, I have and others as well," Armillo advised. "He's not responding. No one can even find his mind."

"Did he say anything when he left?" Threebeard asked.

"He had been complaining about Rupra Bruda hanging around the neighborhood. He'd banned him from the Mighty Jolly a few days earlier and wasn't pleased to see him lurking about."

"Rupra Bruda? He's in Shisk?"

"Yes."

"I wondered where he'd gone. Why did he ban him?"

"I'm not sure. Something about killing a rhutz. Misty recognized Bruda when their paths crossed the other day. He told Eyeball what he had done in Tributon and Eyeball told Bruda never to come to the Mighty Jolly again."

"He must have found out Bruda murdered a rhutz in Tributon and was responsible for the Flat Meadow Massacre. It was a big scandal and his grandfather had to resign as speaker of the General Assembly to keep Rupra from going to jail. He disappeared shortly thereafter, and now we know where he went."

"What should I do?"

"File a missing person report with the public enforcer and tell them about your suspicions. I'll try to get to Shisk as soon as I can get away. Artis got caught in the Mt. Alabash eruption, so I can't leave until she gets back home safely. Have you seen Misty lately?"

"No. He's missing too."

Threebeard took a deep breath trying to control his growing rage. "So, now he's murdering mutants as well as rhutz. We can't let him get away with that. I'll be there as soon as I can to help prod the authorities into doing their duty."

Threebeard clicked off the GC and began reading everything he could find on Rupra Bruda and his family. Although Threebeard wasn't a violent man, he had no tolerance of those who killed for sport—whether it was rhutz or human beings. He wondered how the public prosecutor in Shisk would feel about it. It was no secret that many in Central Authority had opposed letting mutants live under the dome. They believed since the mutants were already physically impaired from the environment there was no reason to waste pure air and clean water on them now. They had learned to adapt outside the domes and they should stay there. The measure allowing them into the dome did pass, but only by a slim margin. Even after the vote Central Authority didn't make it easy for mutants to live in the cities. They segregated them into designated areas and made it clear they weren't to venture out of them. Fortunately, Threebeard had become wealthy enough that public officials couldn't ignore him. Whether they'd do what was right once an injustice was pointed out to them was another story.

When Artis arrived in Guhl she was shocked at the devastation left from the tremors. Most of the buildings had collapsed, fires were raging throughout the city, and many streets had cracked and buckled making it nearly impossible to travel. To make matters worse the ash was so thick it was nearly impossible to see or breathe and clean water was difficult to find. When they finally made it to the downtown area where most of the inns and taverns were located they discovered many had been destroyed and the ones that had survived were full of those who had lost their homes.

"Where are we going to stay tonight?" Artis asked worriedly.

"Not here, I'm afraid," Faruk replied. "It wouldn't be safe. You know what happens in a disaster. Looters and thugs take to the streets."

"Right. But where can we go?"

"Let's head on toward the river and set up camp away from all this turmoil. It will be a lot safer."

Artis nodded and they continued on through the city heading south toward the washed-out bridge over the Liehn River. As they maneuvered through the rubble Artis wondered if she'd ever see her home again. Liehn seemed so far away at that moment. Eventually they made it out of the city where they were expecting to find a secluded place to set up their camp and wait for the bridge to be repaired, but much to their shock and dismay thousands of people lined the road fleeing from the city. In every direction there were makeshift camps where people were huddled around campfires just trying to survive the night.

Ash was still falling heavily and Artis could hear hundreds of people coughing, wheezing and struggling to breathe. She wondered how many had already died.

"Where do you think all these people are going?" Artis asked.

"I don't know. Maybe to the river where they know they will at least be able to find water."

"Where is Central Authority? They should have a relief effort underway by now, don't you think?"

"Ordinarily, but with the bridge out and all aircraft grounded they're going to have to come in from Rizi and that's a long way off. It may be tomorrow before they get here."

"Damn! What are we going to do?"

"I don't know. If we unload our gear and try to set up camp I'm afraid we will attract a lot of unfriendly visitors looking for food and water. I think we should keep going and try to get away from the crowds. We can take the road to Rizi. It runs parallel with the river for quite a while until the river bends to the south. We can travel down it a while and maybe lose these crowds."

Artis swallowed hard. "Okay, sounds like a good plan."

Faruk called Giant on his communicator and advised him of the plan then started the ATV moving again. The crowds along the road seemed to be getting thicker and thicker and it was getting harder and harder to drive through them without hitting someone. Faruk honked his horn trying to get people to move out of the way but he got no response. Finally, six burly men turned and stood directly in front of them refusing to move.

"Give us your water and medical supplies," one of them screamed, "and we'll let you pass."

"What should we do?" Artis asked worriedly.

"Don't open your door. If you do they'll pull us all out and take everything we have."

"What if they try to break in?"

"They won't have any luck. These ATVs are built to military specifications. These mobs won't have anything that can hurt us as long as we stay inside."

The mob began kicking and shaking the ATV. Faruk looked around nervously, then gently accelerated forcing the men standing in front to move aside or suffer serious injury. They cursed and kicked the ATV as it passed. Someone swung a tire iron at the window causing Artis to nearly jump out of her skin.

Giant followed behind glaring at the men as he passed by. Soon they were picking up speed and clearing the hostile mob. A few kylods down the road they got to an intersection with a sign showing that Rizi was to their left. To their relief most of the crowds were headed for the river. They turned toward Rizi and after a few kylods had escaped the crowds of refugees fleeing from Guhl. Faruk relaxed and increased their speed but after only a few more kylods he slammed on his brakes.

"What the hell!" Artis screamed.

"Look ahead," Faruk said pointing.

She looked out and saw that the highway in front of them had disappeared. Faruk put a scarf around his mouth and nose and ventured outside. Giant got out and joined him in the gray darkness. The road had dropped nearly ten feet leaving them on the edge of a cliff. When he got back in the car his expression was glum.

"We'll have to set up camp here and see if there is a way around this sink hole in the morning. It's impossible to tell right now."

"What about the refugees?"

"We've traveled far enough we should be okay until morning."

Artis nodded. "Okay, I guess we don't have any choice in the matter."

Faruk shook his head and started backing up the car. They turned around and drove back to where they had seen a grove of trees that would provide them some protection from the falling ash. They considered setting up camp but after experiencing a few coughing attacks as the result of simply opening the door, they decided to sleep inside their vehicles as best they could.

They realized they were better off than most having enough food and water for at least ten days. They normally wouldn't have carried so much water but since they had planned to camp in the desert they had brought plenty. Still, they ate and drank sparingly, not knowing how long their supplies would have to last.

Faruk, being exhausted from the days' ordeal, quickly fell asleep, but Artis was wide awake, so she decided to link with Threebeard and advise him of their situation.

"Brother. Are you there?"

"Yes, Artis. Did you find a place to spend the night?"

She explained to him what they had found in Guhl and what had happened to them.

"I didn't realize Guhl had been hit so hard. There haven't been any reports of it on the news. Most of the coverage now is Mt. Nepat and Mt. Zillion. It seems they are about to erupt as well."

"Three volcanos erupting at the same time in Lemaine Shane! That's unprecedented."

"Yes. It hasn't happened in over a thousand cycles and it's not just in Lemaine Shane—it's all over the globe."

"What? There's other volcanoes erupting?"

"Not yet, but there have been many tremors and volcanic activity is likely in many other locations."

"Oh, God and Sandee! What's happening to Tarizon?"

"Super-volcanic eruptions. It's a rare event but does happen every five-hundred cycles or so."

"What are we going to do?"

"Just try to survive, I'm afraid. There's nothing we can do to stop it."

"Where is Central Authority? We've seen no relief efforts."

"I know. They will be concentrating on the domed cities. I'm afraid the people outside the domes are on their own as usual."

"That's a disgrace! We all pay our taxes and are equal under the Supreme Mandate."

"Yes, something needs to be done about that, but for now the only thing we can worry about is survival. I'm thinking about getting together with some other people to organize a relief effort—an army of mutants to go out and assist the citizens of Tarizon through this crisis."

"And when the crisis is over maybe you should train your Mutant Army as a military force," Artis suggested.

"Perhaps, but I fear we'd be no match for the TGA. Turning ordinary citizens into a fighting force is no simple task."

"True, but it's a thought."

"Yes, sister. It is an interesting idea."

13

Investigation

Armillo hung up the GC and stood up. He looked over at his assistant manager, Mira, and said, "I'm going over to the precinct office to file a missing person's report on Eyeball."

"A lot of good that will do," Mira replied. "The enforcers don't much like the lot of us."

"True, but they have a duty to treat us all alike. We are human after all."

"Not in their eyes."

"Well, it's what Threebeard wants, so I guess I better do it."

Mira nodded and went back to her work as Armillo strolled out of the office. Twenty loons later he was stepping out of the tram station and looking at a precinct office of the Public Enforcers.

Since the adoption of the Supreme Mandate justice on Tarizon was supposed to be truly blind. Every accused was provided a citizen defender at no cost. The rich weren't supposed to have any advantage over the poor nor were healthy humans supposed to be favored over the mutant. This was possible because on Tarizon a citizen did not have the right to obtain and pay for their own counsel. They had to accept the representation assigned to them. This ensured that everyone would be on an equal footing in the prosecution of a criminal matter. Under this system the prosecution and defense each had the same budget, time constraints, and access to the investigative arm of the judiciary, the inquisitors.

The inquisitors performed all criminal investigations and they do so in the interest of justice and not for the benefit of the prosecution or defense. This eliminated the common problem on Earth of tainted evidence being ruled inadmissible. It was rare for any evidence uncovered by the inquisitors to be thrown out. The use of inquisitors also eliminated the necessity of imposing a heavy burden of proof on the prosecution. There was still a presumption of innocence but the standard for conviction was simply the greater weight of the evidence rather than beyond all reasonable doubt. The careful use by the inquisitors of truth serums and sophisticated lie detection devices further ensured that the truth would be elicited from every witness.

Assignment of prosecutors and defenders was supposed to be made after a comprehensive computer analysis of each prosecutor or defender's background, experience, education, track record, the nature of the offense; the circumstances surrounding the crime; and the harm inflicted on the victim. This was supposed to ensure that each accused got a fair trial and a fair punishment if convicted.

Professional juries decided each case. These jurists were selected by computer from a professional jury panel to ensure each jury was fair and unbiased. Jurors were well paid for their services so they would have a positive attitude about their work and would not be susceptible to bribery. On Tarizon jury security was considered fundamental to the integrity of the judicial system and therefore jury tampering was a capital offense.

Armillo looked almost normal to the casual eye. His mutations were subtler than most—a few extra fingers and an eye in the back of his head. When he went out amongst the Purists he kept a hat on his head and his hands in his pockets to avoid uncomfortable frowns and stares. As he walked into the PE's office he did the same. An intake clerk looked up at him expectantly.

"What can I help you with?" she asked.

"I need to file a couple of missing person reports," Armillo said meekly.

"A couple," she said laughing. "Did they run off together?"

"I don't know. Nobody saw them leave and it's not likely they went off together—one of them is a rhutz."

"A rhutz? You want to file a missing person's report on a rhutz?"

"Yes, they've been recognized in Tributon as a sentient life-form and protected by the Supreme Mandate."

She laughed. "Yes, well this isn't Tributon. I'm not taking a missing person report for a beast. As far as I'm concerned they never should have been allowed under the dome."

"I'll need to talk to your supervising officer then," Armillo replied.

"Sure, but a lot of good it will do you."

"Nevertheless."

"Alright. Wait here and I'll go get him."

Armillo waited anxiously at the intake desk noticing that many officers and personnel were staring at him with amused looks on their faces. A few loons later a somber looking officer strolled up.

"Hello. I'm Inquisitor Griggs Wentz. What's this about wanting to file a missing person report on a rhutz?"

"A rhutz and a man named Eyeball."

"Eyeball? What kind of a name is that?"

"Actually, that's his nickname. His real name is Connell Riki. We call him Eyeball as, on account of him having just one big eye."

"So, you want to file missing person's reports for a mutant and a rhutz?"

"Exactly," Armillo said hopefully.

The inquisitor studied Armillo for a moment then shook his head. "Alright, we'll take the report on the mutant but not the rhutz. The rhutz isn't within our jurisdiction despite what the authorities in Tributon might think about it. When is the last time you saw this Eyeball fellow?"

"He walked out of the tavern in the middle of his shift two days ago for no apparent reason and hasn't been seen since."

"What tavern?"

"The Mighty Jolly."

The officer looked up. "You work for Threebeard?"

"Yes. He's the owner."

The inquisitor took a deep breath and let it out slowly. "So, what about the rhutz?"

"You're going to look into his disappearance too?"

"No, but there may be a relationship between the two since they disappeared at about the same time."

"Right," Armillo agreed. "Misty told Eyeball something that upset him. That might have been why he left in a hurry."

"Misty," Wentz repeated. "Does he have a last name?"

Armillo shook his head. "No. Rhutz only have one name. Their names are chosen based on what element of nature is most prominent at their birth."

"Really? Then there must be a slew of them named Toxic."

There was laughter in the squad room.

"No. Haven't heard one, but I know one named Thunder and another called Stormy."

"So, how are Misty and Eyeball connected in this case?"

"Well, a man named Rupra Bruda came to the Tavern. Misty lives in the alley behind the tavern and Eyeball feeds him the scraps from the kitchen. In exchange for the food Misty keep rats and other rodents away from the tavern and provides backup security if Eyeball needs it. Over the cycles they've become good friends. So, a week or so ago Bruda came to the tavern and Misty was patrolling the neighborhood and recognized him as the man who killed a rhutz in Tributon and was responsible for the Flat Meadow Massacre."

Wentz grimaced. "Was he sure? I mean, how could a rhutz know what this Bruda fellow looked like?"

"The rhutz can communicate over long distances. Apparently, the image of the man made it over here through the rhutz network."

"Hmm," Wentz muttered skeptically. "Well, I guess it doesn't matter. They're both still missing. I've got your report now, so I'll get an investigation going as soon as possible."

Armillo smiled. He wasn't sure if he believed Inquisitor Wentz, but he'd done what Threebeard had asked. "Thank you," he said respectfully, nodded and turned to leave.

"That's quite an establishment—the Mighty Jolly," Wentz added. "The men in the precinct have had some good times there and, of course, they appreciate the half price discount given to us, so we don't want anyone messing around with the place."

Armillo looked back grinning.

Wentz smiled wryly. "So, don't worry, we'll give this matter serious attention."

Armillo nodded and left.

Wentz went back to his office and pulled up everything he could on the Flat Creek Massacre and Rupra Bruda. He didn't care all that much for the rhutz or the mutants who lived in the city, but he detested anyone who believed they were above the law and, from what he had read, Rupra Bruda fit that category perfectly. His gut told him Bruda was involved in Eyeball's and Misty's disappearance and had probably killed them, but before he could go after him he'd have to find the bodies and some incriminating evidence to take to the prosecutors. It wouldn't be an easy task, but Wentz already disliked Bruda and was anxious to get started.

The next morning, he got another inquisitor on the task of finding Rupra Bruda. If he found the evidence he was looking for he didn't want there to be any delay in picking Bruda up. While they were looking for him, Wentz and an inquisitor named Luzzy Mollis paid a visit to the Mighty Jolly and interviewed everyone who had been there on the day of the disappearance. Only one employee had seen Eyeball take off, a kitchen boy named Garot.

"Bruda and some of his buddies came by the tavern like they were looking for something or somebody," Garot recalled. "They passed by and kept moving up the street. Eyeball saw them and became suspicious. He had told Bruda not to come back to the Mighty Jolly so he was concerned that Bruda was up to no good."

"I see. So, what did he do?" Wentz asked.

"It turned out they were looking for Misty because they had been wandering around aimlessly but as soon as he appeared they split up like it had all been prearranged."

"You don't know that for sure?" Wentz questioned. "You didn't overhear them."

"No."

"So, what happened then?"

"Bruda and one of his friends went back the way they'd come, going by the Mighty Jolly again and Misty followed them at a distance. Like I said, Eyeball knew they were up to no good so he followed Misty to make sure he'd be okay. They went toward the warehouse district and I haven't seen either one of them since."

"Alright. I think I'll go over to the warehouse district and have a look. Why don't you come along with me in case we find anything?"

Garot swallowed hard and then nodded. Wentz, along with Garot and several other officers drove over in their transport cruisers to the warehouse district and began searching the area and canvassing the occupants of the warehouses. He asked one of the maintenance workers where they disposed of their waste.

"There are two disposal units, one at each end of the warehouses," the man advised.

Wentz nodded and sent his men to search both disposal sites.

"Was there anyone working around here two days ago?" he asked.

"No. It was an off day. Nobody was working."

"That figures. They probably knew that would be the case."

They continued to talk until Wentz got a call on his communicator. "We found a couple bodies, sir. One is a rhutz and the other one is a human matching the description of Eyeball—except he no longer has one."

"Oh, God. Where are you?"

"At the south disposal unit of the second warehouse block."

"Alright. I'll be right there."

Wentz sighed. "Well, let's go see if it's your bouncer."

They drove the short distance to the disposal unit where the officers had found the bodies. Wentz and Garot got out and peered into the unit. Garot gagged and backed off quickly.

"Is that Eyeball?" Wentz asked.

Garot nodded.

"And Misty?"

"Right."

"It looks like they were carried here and dumped inside," Inspector Mollis said. "Luckily the disposal unit hasn't been processed yet. It was scheduled for 1400 today."

"Looks like they killed them with lasers," Wentz noted.

"It appears that way, although there is some bruising on Eyeball indicating some physical contact as well."

"Did you locate the crime scene?" Wentz asked.

"Yes. There are some burned spots in the grass up near the front of the landscaped area between the two buildings. We found blood splatter as well."

"Well, if there was physical contact we should find some trace evidence to link the murderers to the crime scene."

"So, what do you think happened?" Inspector Mollis asked.

"It looks like it was an ambush. Apparently Rupra Bruda is obsessed with killing rhutz," Wentz replied.

"Why?"

"His father and one of his friends were killed by rhutz and his grandfather had to resign from the Tributon General Assembly in disgrace over the Flat Meadow Massacre. I'm sure Mr. Bruda blames all his family misfortunes on the rhutz."

"Sounds like a motive to me," Inspector Mollis observed.

"Yes. When the lab results come back we'll have to pay a visit to Mr. Bruda and see what he has to say about all of this."

"That should be interesting."

"Indeed, it should."

14

Mt. Soni

Bruda and Essyria hired a Grinden for three days to take their mating party to Jedeva. It was expensive but Rupra considered it a good investment. He wanted to not only impress Essyria but also his friends. They reported to the rental lot just outside the dome, were assigned a driver, and began their journey to Jedeva. They could have taken the Jedeva Tube, but Rupra and Essyria were not in a rush and wanted to enjoy the spectacular scenery provided by the southern tip of the Weeping Mountains.

There were six in the mating party. Bruda brought Peeta and Chalke and Essyria brought Silla and her sister, Marga. The Grinden was fully stocked with food and drink so the party got off to a fast start.

"You're going to be in so much trouble when your mother finds out you've been mated," Silla teased.

"Too bad. It's my decision, not my mother's," Essyria replied.

"I know, but aren't you afraid your parents will cut you off?"

"No. Why would they do that? It's not like they had any control over who I ended up with anyway."

"True, but still."

"Once they get to know Rupra they'll approve of my choice."

"Then why didn't you introduce him to them before now?" Silla asked.

Essyria shrugged. "You know how parents overreact. I just wanted to avoid all that drama."

"If her parents had done a background check on me, they probably would have opposed the mating," Bruda interjected.

Silla looked over at Bruda expectantly.

"Ah. I was testing an experimental rifle for my father and there were some rhutz stalking a herd of range deer. About the time I pulled the trigger there was a tremor and I accidentally shot a rhutz."

"Accidentally?" Chalke laughed.

Bruda smiled smugly. "Well, at least that's my official position."

"So, what's wrong with killing a rhutz?" Silla asked.

Everyone laughed.

"Nothing?" Bruda admitted. "But there are some rhutz lovers who believe the ugly beasts are like humans, so there was a big stink and my grandfather had to resign from the Tributon Assembly."

"That's ridiculous," Silla said taking a drink of her tekari. "What a bunch of slubdubs."

"Anyway," Bruda continued. "We didn't want that little incident to get in the way of our mating."

Silla nodded.

Bruda thought of his friend Romas Lantra who he'd strangled for betraying him. It wasn't that he felt guilty for murdering his friend, but more sadness over his death. Bruda had liked Romas and missed him.

"What's wrong?" Essyria asked, seeing Bruda's contemplative stare.

Bruda looked at Essyria and smiled. "I was thinking of a friend back in Tributon, Romas Lantra. He was found dead for no apparent reason."

"Oh, I'm so sorry. They don't know the cause of death?"

Bruda sighed. "No, but I suspect he committed suicide. The inquisitors were looking for him. I'm sure he was trying to protect me. He knew if the inquisitors got a hold of him, he could be forced to say anything."

"Yeah. The inquisitors are a bunch of scutz," Peeta said.

Bruda looked at Peeta. Reading his mind Bruda knew he was worried about the public enforcers investigating Eyeball's death.

"Luckily, they're incompetent too," Bruda replied. "Even if they gave a crap about a mutant, they wouldn't waste much time worrying about his death."

"Mutant?" Essyria questioned.

"Ah. I mean, rhutz."

"Then why did Romas commit suicide? If the PE's were incompetent?" Essyria asked with a look of confusion on her face.

"Ah. Well. Because they're incompetent they have to resort to intimidation and out right fabrication of evidence to do the bidding of whoever is pulling their strings."

Essyria frowned.

"Anyway. That's ancient history," Bruda said. "Let's talk about something more interesting—like our future."

Silla sat forward excitedly. "Yes. What are you going to do after you're mated?"

Essyria's frown vanished as she contemplated the question. "Well, after we're mated, Rupra will have to find a job. I'm sure once my father gets used to the idea of he and I being together, he'll offer him a position."

"I don't know if that's a good idea," Bruda replied. "What I'd like to do is go into politics."

Essyria nodded. "Sure, but that takes time. You'll have to establish yourself first. My father can help you."

Bruda smiled. "Of course," he said out loud but he had no intention of working for Essyria's father. He liked his independence and couldn't stand the thought of someone looking over his shoulder all the time. That didn't mean he couldn't use Essyria's father's help. He planned to tap into that resource as often as he could.

It was early in the afternoon when they finally arrived at their hotel in Jedeva. After they had settled into their three adjacent suites on the seventh floor, Bruda and Essyria went to pay off the doctor for the pregnancy test. When they got back they all went to dinner at a Tunisu restaurant. Tunisu was a large island at the tip of Turvin that was well known for its unique way of cooking seafood. As they were finishing up their meal the topic of the next day's activities came up.

"Why don't we climb to the observation point at Mt. Soni? I heard there's been a lot of smoke coming out of it lately," Essyria suggested.

"I don't know. Do you think the observation point is still open? Aren't they worried about it erupting?" Chalke replied.

"No. It's not going to erupt. It just has to relieve the pressure once in a while so a lot of steam comes out."

"What about the tremor the last time I was here?" Bruda reminded her.

Essyria sighed. "You guys are a bunch of twits."

A twit was a nervous bird that jumped and squawked excitedly at the slightest provocation. Bruda was annoyed by the observation and glared at Essyria.

"All right," Bruda finally said. "If you want to live dangerously. We'll drive up to the observation point."

Chalke and Peeta glared at Bruda. He smiled back at them, amused by their discomfort.

"Sure, that should be fun," Marga agreed. "Will it be cold up there? I didn't bring warm clothes."

"I've got an extra jacket," Silla advised. "It will be cool, since the observation area is over eight thousand feet high."

"It will be warm in the Grinden, anyway," Essyria noted, "and we'll have plenty of tekari to keep us warm."

They all nodded in agreement.

The next morning, after breakfast, they piled into the Grinden and started their journey to Mt. Soni. It was a spectacular ride through the dense forests of the Weeping Mountains. Even though the road was narrow and winding the Grinden took it with ease and there was little discomfort for the riders inside. As they got closer to the big volcano they could see the large plumes of steam streaming out of it. Had they'd been outside they would have smelled the pungent odor of volcanic ash as well, but the Grinden's air filtration system eliminated the odor inside. They all looked up when the driver suddenly stopped.

Bruda hit his com button. "What's wrong? Why are you stopping?"

"Ah. Sorry, sir. But the road to the summit appears to be closed."

"What? I didn't hear anything about that," Essyria complained.

Bruda sighed. "Wait here. I'll get out and have a look."

Bruda got out of the Grinden and saw that a gate had been swung around blocking the road. There was a sign that said the observation area was closed due to recent volcanic activity. Essyria got out of the Grinden and came up beside him.

"You mean we came all the way up here for nothing," Essyria complained. "I really wanted to see the volcano up close."

Bruda shrugged. "I'm sorry."

Essyria glared at Bruda. "Come on. You're not going to let a little gate stop us, are you?"

Bruda sighed and went over to the gate. He looked at the padlock and willed it to open. Suddenly the metal rod popped out allowing him to remove the lock. Then he swung the gate open to let the Grinden pass through. After locking the gate behind them, they continued up the mountain.

"Do you think this is smart?" Chalke asked. "I mean, what if there's an eruption?"

"Don't be silly," Essyria said. "Mt. Soni's been dormant for over a hundred cycles."

"Yes. But on the VC, they've been saying volcanoes all over Tarizon have become active. Some experts predict there will be a lot of eruptions all over the globe."

"Maybe. But Mt. Soni isn't going to erupt today. We'll just go up to the observation area, take a quick look around, and then go back to Jedeva. You wouldn't want to spoil my mating by being a twit, would you?"

"No," Chalke said nervously. "Let's just not linger once we get there."

"We won't," Bruda promised, smiling at Essyria. "We'll just look around, take a few stills, and then come back down the mountain."

"Look," Silla said pointing ahead. "The sign says it's only three more kylods to the observation point."

"Good," Chalke replied. "I'll feel better when we're traveling away from this place."

As they traveled on the dense forest suddenly disappeared and they crossed a rocky area devoid of any vegetation. A few kyloons later they reached the south observation area reserved for tourists. Across the volcano at the government monitoring station there were many people, some civilian and others military. When the driver stopped they all got out, walked to the fence along the edge of the cone, and peered down into the volcano. Steam was spewing out into the atmosphere like someone had poured cold water into a hot fry pan. The air reeked of sulphur and the noise was deafening. Suddenly the ground shook violently knocking Chalke and Peeta off their feet. The rest of them managed to latch onto the fence and hold on for dear life.

"I told you this was a bad idea," Chalke said as he got back on his feet. "Let's get out of here."

"Come on!" Essyria replied. "There are always tremors around a volcano. It's no big deal."

"Oh, my God!" Chalke yelled as a finger of hot lava shot up fifty feet into the air. "It's going to blow."

The ground began shaking again and a giant boulder not thirty strides from them broke off the cone and fell into the abyss. Bruda looked down following the big rock and for the first time saw molten lava slowly pushing up toward the rim of the volcano.

"You're right, Chalke," Bruda said nervously. "We should get out of here."

They all turned and ran back to the Grinden just as the ground below them began to break apart. They jumped in and told the driver to get them out of there. Fortunately, he'd turned around in preparation for their return trip and bolted away just as soon as he was told to do so. The parking lot collapsed beneath them as they reached the road leading back down the mountain. The Grinden rocked and tossed them about as it struggled to keep traction. When they finally reached solid ground, the car lurched from side to side as another tremor struck. As they held on in terror there was a tremendous explosion behind them as the south side of the mountain blew apart.

Debris and rubble began raining down upon them hitting the Grinden's roof and putting a huge dent in the bulletproof window. The driver swerved around trying to avoid rocks and debris that suddenly appeared before them. The girls screamed and Bruda looked back in horror at the exploding mountain.

As they raced down the mountain a combination of falling ash and steam cut visibility to just a few feet. The driver was forced to slow down to be sure he stayed on the road. When they stopped to open the gate Bruda jumped out. Looking to his left he saw a line of molten lava crashing through the trees like they were toothpicks. He quickly opened the gate and rushed back to the car.

"Step on it! If we let the lava beat us to the road, we'll be trapped!"

The driver nodded and stomped on the throttle. The big Grinden took off and they plunged down the mountain at nightmarish speed. Chalke looked to his left in horror as the lava flowed through the trees like water through grass. As they reached the curve where the lava would cut them off if it beat them, the driver slowed, then accelerated through the turn. A ten-foot wall of lava spewed over the highway just a few feet behind them. A big glob hit the top of the Grinden with a loud thud making the girls scream.

Bruda looked back and sighed. "Alright. We made it," Bruda said.

"We should be able to outrun it now."

Chalke glared at Essyria. "Yeah. Mt. Soni won't erupt."

She shrugged. "Ah, don't be a slubdub. That was fun."

Silla looked over at Essyria and raised here eyebrows.

"Well, it will be a great story to tell our children," Peeta noted. "I'm not sure I'd do it again, though."

When they got down off the mountain traffic became heavy as local residents rushed to evacuate the area. Ash was already falling like snow and visibility was only a few strides. It was nearly nightfall when they made it back to Jedeva.

The tranquil hotel they'd left had turned into a bustling refugee center by the time they'd returned. The desk clerk summoned them over to the front desk when he saw them enter.

"Mr. Bruda. May I have a word?"

Bruda looked at the clerk warily, then walked over.

"Sir. I wonder if you would surrender two of your rooms. There are a lot of people who need shelter."

Bruda frowned. "You want all six of us to stay in one suite?"

"Yes. In light of the emergency."

"But we've come here to be mated. We want to be alone."

"Please, sir. People can't stay outside. It's not safe with all the ash in the air."

Bruda sighed. "You can have one of the rooms, but you can't expect my new mate and I to sleep in a dorm tonight."

The clerk bit his tongue. "Alright, sir. Thank you for that."

Bruda went back and gave them the bad news.

"Well, at least we can still be alone. I'm surprised they didn't want all of us to sleep together."

"They did," Bruda replied, "but I told them to forget it. This is a special time for us and I'm not going to let anything ruin it."

Essyria smiled. "Good. I'm glad I'm mating with a man with backbone."

Silla and Marga looked at each other and raised their eyebrows. Chalke turned away but Peeta smiled. "You don't have to worry about that, Essyria. Bruda's backbone is made of steel."

Bruda smiled. "Right. Well, let's not let a little volcano spoil our evening. Let's see if room service is still opened. If so, we can order up dinner and some drinks. We need to celebrate our narrow escape off the mountain."

They all nodded and headed for the elevator to go back to their rooms. The door opened and they got in. Chalke pushed the button for the sixth floor and the elevator began to rise, but before they reached the sixth floor the elevator began to rock back and forth. Silla screamed and Essyria grabbed Bruda's arm. Then the lights went out and the elevator came to a sudden halt.

15

Rescue Duty

Captain Grenz Lozich looked out over the light cruiser *Revenge's* bow as the ship glided through the calm waters of the Dark Sea. They were hugging Rigimol's shoreline hoping to spot any slavers who had gone ashore hunting for Seafolken to kidnap and fill up their holds for the slave markets of Ock Mezan and Lower Azollo.

It was a clear moonlit night and Grenz could see ahead for many kylods. Suddenly a strange sight to his port caught his attention. It looked like a wall of foaming water. He squinted trying to make the image focus. Finally, he rushed to the bridge and grabbed some binoculars.

"Holy Sandee! Look at that wave. It must be thirty feet," he screamed to his engineer. "Turn to port. We must hit it face on!"

Captain Lozich reached out with his mind to his crew. *"All hands! Secure your persons—tidal wave in twenty tiks. Repeat! Secure your persons immediately—tidal wave in fifteen tiks."*

The ship turned slowly to meet the huge wave but before it could get in an optimal position the wave lifted *Revenge* straight up into the air until it fell back on itself. A tik before the ship began to fall Grenz ran to the bow of the ship and dove into the water hoping to avoid a crushing blow from the ship's hulk. Water suddenly engulfed the craft and filled its interior. The moment Grenz hit the water he dove downward and away from the *Revenge* praying he wouldn't be struck. Finally, he stopped, realizing he was in the clear. Looking back he saw the ship's hull gradually sinking. He swam sideways until he was clear of the craft and far enough away not to be sucked down with it.

As he watched the ship sinking he saw many of his crew escaping. Fortunately, being a seafolken he didn't have to worry about breathing. His gills, positioned just below his rib cage, immediately began working when he was submerged in water. His hands and feet also swelled to provide natural fins to give him greater propulsion underwater.

Grenz reached out to his crew trying to establish a link. He felt a presence in his mind. *"Lt. Yels. Are you alright?"*

"Yes, I think so. Just a few bruises here and there. I was strapped in at the helm so I didn't get thrown around too much."

"What about the rest of the crew?" Captain Lozich asked.

"All but one is accounted for, Sir. Grinnel was asleep in his bunk and may not have gotten your warning. I was hoping he'd make his way out of the ship but he might have been struck by debris on the way down."

Grinnel was the ships cook and liked by everyone.

"Send down a rescue squad to find him. Perhaps he's still alive."

"Yes, sir," Lt. Yels replied.

Captain Lozich swam to the surface and scanned the horizon. He looked toward shore and saw where the tidal wave had struck. In his mind's eye he imagined the devastation in Dona Uza, a city of some two hundred and fifty thousand people directly in the tidal wave's path. As he was thinking crew members began popping up around him. He reached out to them.

"Swim to shore. We should help the people of Dona Uza. I'm sure there will be many who will need rescuing. Wait for me on the beach for further orders."

"Where did that wave come from?" a crewman asked.

"A tremor under the sea would be my guess. There have been reports of many tremors and volcanic activity all over Tarizon. We are not too far from Mt. Alabash that began erupting a few days ago. Perhaps there is a fault line that goes out to sea."

As the crewmen began swimming toward shore, Lt. Yels popped up. *"They're bringing Grinnel's body up. He was dead—must have hit his head when he was thrown from his bunk."*

Captain Lozich grimaced. *"Okay. Bring him to shore and we will give him a proper burial."*

About a kylod later Captain Lozich and his crewmen arrived on the beach just south of where the tidal wave had hit. Ash from Mt. Alabash was already a foot thick and still falling from the sky at an alarming rate. After burying the cook's body they left to see what help they could render to the victims of the massive wave. The devastation in the city was sobering. Homes and businesses that had once stood proudly were gone, lifted off their foundations and carried half a kylod inland.

The crew of the *Revenge* immediately began searching demolished structures and vehicles for victims. For many kyloons they pulled people trapped in their PTVs, businesses, and homes to safety. They even helped a rhutz, stranded on the top of a floating house, get to safety. Unfortunately, they also stacked many dead bodies on dry land for the authorities to find. At day's end they returned to the beach where they had buried their fallen comrade and conducted a memorial ceremony. As they concluded the ceremony Captain Lozich discussed their current situation.

"Without a ship there's not much we can do to interrupt the slave trade. I'm going to contact officials of the Dark Sea Alliance and see if they can find us a new ship. In the meantime, we can continue helping the victims of the tidal wave."

As everyone was nodding their agreement a human stepped out from behind a rock and pressed a gun against Captain Lozich's ear. One of the crew members took a step toward the gunman only to see three more appear behind them.

"One more step and your beloved captain will die," the man warned.

"Who are you and what do you want?" Lt. Yels asked.

"I'm Captain Shameus. We lost our cargo of seafolken in the tidal wave, so we were delighted to see all of you being so helpful today. But, now you will be coming with us."

"If you lost your cargo," Lt. Yels asked, "you must have lost your ship as well."

"True enough, but ships are easy to steal, particularly when the owners have fled and left them to the tidal wave. In fact, we've already found a nice replacement for the one we lost."

Fear and hatred welled in Captain Lozich. He couldn't believe he and his men had been captured by slavers. As they tied his hands he racked his brain trying to come up with a way out, but without weapons, the situation seemed hopeless. Still, he kept alert for an opportunity to escape.

"This way," Captain Shameus ordered.

Captain Lozich and his crewmen were led down the beach to a small fishing boat anchored off shore. Several flat boats had been pulled up on the beach for transport out to the ship. Once the Seafolken were in the flat boats they were blindfolded so they couldn't use their telekinetic abilities to untie their hands and escape into the sea. But before Captain Lozich had been blindfolded he saw the rhutz they'd saved earlier watching them from a distance. He had heard recently that the rhutz communicated telepathically and had learned to speak Tari, so he tried to establish a link.

"I am Captain Lozich, General of the Deep Sea Alliance. We are being kidnapped. Please contact the local authorities or any Seafolken you may run across of our plight. Ask them to find this fishing boat and rescue us."

"I am Dusk. I will forward your message, but perhaps I can help you escape."

"No, my friend. It would be too dangerous and too many lives have been lost today already. If you pass on my message, that will be enough."

"It is done," Dusk replied as he opened his mind and spread the message to all the rhutz in the area and told them to pass it on.

Once on board the fishing boat Captain Lozich and his crew were stashed in the hold for the long journey to the slave markets.

A rhutz named Windy living on the streets of Fasoon perked up when she got the message from Dusk. She knew a Seafolken dancer named Seductress who worked at the Mighty Jolly, so she went to her immediately and gave her the message. Seductress immediately got on the GC and called Threebeard.

"You said Captain Lozich?" Threebeard asked.

"Yes. He and his crew have been taken aboard a fishing boat called the *Seabreeze* off the coast of Rigimol. The rhutz who saw them kidnaped reported the boat was headed south."

"It must be slavers looking to take them to Ock Mezan."

"What can you do?"

"I don't know. Ordinarily I could link to the TGA satellite network and find them quite easily, but with the skies full of ash that won't be possible. They must be intercepted while they are close to land and before they get to Pogo Island. Once they get into the Coral Sea it will be nearly impossible to find them."

"Can I do anything?" Seductress asked.

"Do you know if there was anyone with the Dark Sea Defense Alliance that wasn't with Captain Lozich?"

"Yes," Seductress said. "There are several other ships patrolling the eastern coast of Azollo, but they are too far away to be of much help."

"Is there a base somewhere?"

"No, but there are Seafolken settlements along the coast of Allso and on Pogo Island that might be able to help."

"Can you communicate with them?"

"I don't know. I'll try."

"Do that. Notify them of the kidnaping and, if nothing else, have them keep a lookout for the *Seabreeze* so if we find the ship in the area we'll have a position for them."

"Will do," Seductress said and hung up.

Threebeard drew in a long breath. Between the daily tremors, volcanic ash polluting the air and water, Artis being trapped in Rigimol, and Eyeball's murder Threebeard didn't need another crisis. But Captain Lozich was his friend and he knew he had to find a way to rescue him. He got on his GC and called the TGA naval base at Gallion. After being given the run around he finally was connected to a Colonel Zitor.

"Hello."

"Colonel Zitor. My name is Tribius Nocteris, but most people know me as Threebeard."

"Okay. I understand you have a kidnaping to report?"

"Yes, Captain Lozich and the crew of the light cruiser, *Revenge*. They lost their ship in the tidal wave at Dona Uza and were forced to swim ashore."

"They must have been good swimmers to make it to shore after their ship was sunk by a tidal wave," Colonel Zitor observed.

"Well, actually they are Seafolken so it wasn't difficult for them. Although, they did lose their cook."

"I see."

"After they'd buried their cook they spent the rest of day helping victims of the tidal wave."

"Oh. I heard about them. They saved hundreds of people's lives. Everyone was wondering where they came from."

"Yes. They are good people and we can't let them be taken to the slave markets."

"No. We can't," Colonel Zitor agreed. "Where are these slave markets?"

"Ock Mezan is the closest. They're probably half way to Pogo Island by now."

"That's a lot of ocean to cover," Colonel Zitor observed, "and with visibility so low trying to find them would be nearly impossible."

"True, but they will probably stay close to shore, so we've got Seafolken all along the coast of Quori watching for them."

"Good. Well, if you can give me a location I can see if we have any ships in the area. If not, I may be able to send out a team by air."

"Thank you, Colonel. I'll get working on that right away and call you when I have a location."

"Do that and after we've rescued your friends I'd like to meet with you and Captain Lozich. I have actually heard about both of you and wanted to meet you."

"That would be an honor, Colonel. Let's hope that meeting will be soon."

"Yes, indeed."

Threebeard hung up elated that he'd gotten such a positive response from Colonel Zitor. He actually hadn't expected to get much help from the TGA given the environmental crisis that was quickly spreading throughout Tarizon. The fact that Colonel Zitor wanted to talk to him and Captain Lozich was even more surprising. Threebeard couldn't imagine what the topic of that conversation would be.

16

A Prominent Family

A dull emergency light came on when the elevator stopped. Essyria picked up the emergency phone but it was dead.

"Rupra, what are we going to do?" Essyria asked.

Rupra sighed. "Just relax. They'll get the power back on in a tik, I'm sure."

"I don't know," Chalke said. "The lines may have been taken down by the lava flow."

"I'm sure they must have a backup generator," Peeta replied.

"I'm claustrophobic," Silla advised. "If we don't get out of here quickly I'm going to be sick."

"Just relax," Essyria said. "Rupra will think of something."

Rupra looked up at the escape hatch above them. "Peeta, why don't you climb up and see how close we are to one of the floors?"

Peeta frowned. "Why me?"

"You're lighter than me. I'll give you a boost."

Peeta sighed and then nodded. Rupra gave him a boost and he was able to push the door open. Then he stepped on Rupra's shoulders and pulled himself up.

"It's only a few feet. If I can get the door opened we can climb out."

"See what you can do?" Rupra urged.

"Okay. I'll give it a try. I got it."

Rupra boosted the girls up and they managed to climb out onto the fourth floor. Getting Rupra out was the biggest challenge as there was no one to give him a boost. Finally, Silla ripped a curtain down from an adjacent room and they were able to use it as a rope. A few loons later they were up in their rooms totally exhausted from the ordeal and very hungry. Unfortunately, the power outage had shut down room service so they had to make do with the small stock of food in their rooms.

The following day didn't turn out much better with the hotel full of refugees and the air so foul that they couldn't leave their hotel. They did manage to have the mating ceremony but only after paying twice the bribes they had expected. It seemed most everyone in Jedeva had decided to cash in on Mr. Soni's eruption and the shortage of supplies and necessary services.

When they returned to Shisk they were shocked to see thousands of people lined up seeking entry into the city. Inside the dome the air and water was filtered and there was no ash. At first Central Authority was letting everyone in but it soon became apparent that the city couldn't support all those who wanted to enter. In fact, only with the intervention of Essyria and Peeta's parents did the mating party make it back into the city.

Needless to say, Essyria's parents were shocked to learn their daughter had been mated. After making it back into the city they went to Essyria's parents' home to explain themselves. Essyria's father, Sigor Tomaso, was a short man with a mustache and curly black hair. His mate Tulia was a slim blond with intense green eyes.

"Rupra was one of my patients," Essyria explained. "He was so sick I had to give him special attention, so, that gave us an opportunity to get to know each other. As we spent more time together we realized we had a lot in common."

"What could you possibly have in common?" Tulia spat.

"For one thing we are both telepathic. It is so refreshing not to be able to know what someone is thinking."

"I don't understand," Sigor said. "I thought it would be better if you knew someone's thoughts."

She shook her head. "No. People have horrible thoughts and fears that should never be shared with anyone. Because we are both telepathic we know how to guard our thoughts and keep them private. It's hard to explain, but there has to be some mystery in a relationship to make it interesting enough to sustain."

"Well, that's one thing you have in common, but not enough by itself," Tulia argued.

"I know, but that's just one thing. We are both very intelligent and share similar beliefs—plus we're good in bed."

"Yes, but that will become less important as you get older," Sigor noted.

"Maybe," Essyria conceded, "but it's still an important aspect of mating."

"You should have let the computers pick your mate. You have only considered a few of the factors that should be considered in mating. The computers would have considered hundreds."

Bruda, who had remained silent during the exchange, finally spoke up. "There is one thing the computers wouldn't have considered."

Everyone looked at Rupra. He cleared his throat. "They wouldn't have considered the fact that we are in love and couldn't possibly be mated with anyone else."

Essyria smiled at Rupra.

"When I was near death," Rupra continued, "an angel from God appeared at my side and her name was Essyria."

Tulia just stared at Bruda in shock. Finally, she smiled and relaxed a bit. "Well, you didn't tell me Rupra was a romantic."

Essyria laughed. "There's a lot you don't know about him, Mother. You should withhold your judgment until you get to know him." She turned to her father. "He's a hell of a salesman too, Father. With a little help I know he'll be successful."

"Okay," Sigor said. "It doesn't look like we have any choice in the matter, so I guess we should make the best of it. Rupra, tell us what you plan to do with your life."

"Well, my father was a manufacturer's rep for an armaments company. He liked it because it allowed him to be independent yet connected to a lot of good people. So, I was thinking along the same lines except I'm not necessarily tied to armaments or just one product."

"Health care is a growing industry," Tulia suggested.

"That's true. There are several industries that could be lucrative."

"Rupra's real ambition is politics," Essyria advised.

Rupra nodded. "Yes, my grandfather was a politician and I admired him very much."

"Well, success in business or a profession is usually required before politics comes into play," Sigor noted.

"True," Rupra conceded, "but opportunity doesn't always come when you expect it. If it does come I'm not going to let it slip through my hands."

Sigor nodded. "I suppose you're right. Anyway, I know a few politicians I could introduce you to, if you like."

"Yes. That would be much appreciated," Bruda said appreciatively.

As the conversation continued Essyria relaxed, satisfied her parents would accept Rupra into the family. Bruda was happy too as he was beginning to appreciate how much Essyria's family could help him advance his career and political ambitions. Previously a nobody in Shisk, now he was a member of an elite family and wherever he went he'd be taken seriously. It was amazing to him how everything was falling into place so quickly. *It surely is a sign from God that what I am doing is right. He wants me to rid Tarizon of the impure human population and any of the other life-forms who threaten or in any way diminish the human race. Everything I have done was God's will and everything I do henceforth will be to fulfill God's design for the world.*

17

Aftermath

Faruk and Giant, with their mouth and nose covered with a wet rag to filter the foul air, got out of their vehicles and began to inspect the sinkhole that had stopped their journey abruptly the previous night. The entire highway had fallen into it so Faruk and Giant hiked north and south looking for a way around the big hole. Unfortunately, the ash was so thick it was difficult to even walk safely let alone determine if a vehicle could travel through the gray soot.

Eventually Faruk found himself a long staff and used it to prod the ground in front of him. After about a kyloon he had managed to make it around the sinkhole, marking the trail with stakes along the way. When he'd retraced his steps back to the two ATVs Artis looked at him expectantly.

"Okay. I think we can make it. It will be a little bumpy but the ATVs should be able to handle it."

Artis nodded. "Let's get going then."

They all piled back in their vehicles and slowly followed the staked-out trail around the sinkhole until they were back on the highway again. Fortunately, the wind had picked up blowing a lot of the ash off the highway and making it possible to travel much faster. After about fifty kylods they passed a large convoy of rescue trucks heading for Guhl. One of them slowed and its window rolled down.

"Did you come from Guhl?" he asked.

"Yes, we were up in the desert doing research and left when the tremors started," Artis replied.

"What's it look like in Guhl?"

Artis shook her head. "It's pretty bad. Most of the city was destroyed. I hope you brought lots of food, water and medical supplies."

"We did. Where are you headed?"

"To Rizi, I guess, since the bridge is out, and then to our home in Liehn."

"It's pretty clear to Rizi so you should be alright. You got plenty of food and water?"

"Yes. We have enough."

"What about breathers? This ash will clog up your lungs pretty quick without protection."

"Ah. Right. We could use a few breathers if you have any?"

"Sure," he said reaching behind his seat and pulling out two of them. "Here are a couple for you."

"Thanks," Artis said taking the breathers. "What do we owe you?"

"Nothing. These are for the general public. Thanks for the information. See you later."

"No problem," Artis said as the truck drove off.

Three kyloons later they arrived in Rizi and stopped at the Mighty Jolly. Artis knew the tavern's manager well and they embraced as soon as she walked in the door. After Artis had linked with Threebeard to tell him they'd safely arrived, she went to her room and took a long hot shower. That night after they'd eaten a hearty meal the staff and some of the regular customers gathered around to hear their tale of the encounter with the nanomites, the tremors and the gray ash from Mt. Alabash. As the evening came to a close Artis wondered how the nanomites had fared after they'd left. She hoped somehow their desert city had survived and vowed to return as soon as possible.

Once the lava cooled the nanomite scouts began surveying the casualties to their swarms and damage to their city. The dead were removed and placed in burial chambers where they would decompose and provide precious chemicals needed by the swarms. By their count nearly thirty percent of the swarms had been killed and another twenty percent were suffering from the effects of the heat or toxic air and weren't expected to live but for a few days. The life span of a nanomite was short and any serious injury meant imminent death. Consequently, nanomites didn't view death like humans did. Death was a daily reality and the only concern for nanomites was survival of the swarms.

"Sentinel reporting."

"Proceed," the Speaker replied.

"Temperatures have returned to normal. Reconstruction of the center split in the city has begun."

"How long do you think it will take to repair?"

"At least eight days, Speaker," the Engineer said.

"Why so long?" the Speaker asked.

"We have only a few swarms and they are hampered by the toxic air. Although the lava has cooled the ground is still covered in ash. Until the rains come and wash the ash away it will be difficult for our brothers to work."

"Any sign of the humans?"

"No." The Sentinel replied. "They left with the first tremors."

"I wonder if they will return once the mountain is quiet."

"I don't know. They may have suffered damage to their cities as we have."

"It's unfortunate that the tremors came just when we were beginning to communicate."

"Yes, indeed," the Scholar replied. "That was bad luck but I am optimistic that they will return. We could learn much from them."

As they were talking the ground began to shake again, but this time there was a strange rumbling sound below them. An ominous feeling came over the swarmmasters. Then the ground beneath them gave way and the nanomite city split apart—then collapsed into the abyss. When the ground settled a few loons later the nanomite city was gone!

18

Rescue

Captain Lozich struggled to breathe in the hot hold of the fishing boat. Blindfolded and his hands and feet bound he was in excruciating pain. His men were crammed in the hold with him and he could feel their pain as well as his own. He wondered how long it would be before his captors would open the door to the hold and give them water. If it didn't happen soon he feared someone might die. Their treatment of he and his men didn't make sense. If they wanted to kill them why hadn't they just shot them and be done with it. Unless they wanted them to suffer. That was possible, he supposed, but it didn't make any sense. He finally decided the problem was the limited space of the fishing boat. Their captors obviously feared the Seafolken and wanted them in a place they couldn't escape. On a fishing boat the hold was the only secure location.

Finally, as the day began to wane the crew began allowing one Seafolken at a time to leave the hold to eat, drink and relieve themselves. When Captain Lozich was brought on deck he demanded to speak to Captain Shameus. Before he was put back in the hold the ship's captain came over to talk to him.

"I hear you've got a complaint, Cap?" Captain Shameus said haughtily.

"Yes, I do. It's too hot and crowded down there in the hold for me and my men. If you leave us down there much longer we won't be in any condition to sell when you get to the slave markets."

"If you think I'm going to fall for your tricks, forget it. I know about your kind. You've got powers and you can talk with your minds, so we won't be letting our guard down, I promise you."

"If you tie us up on deck, I give you my word we'll give you no trouble. I'm just afraid my men may get dehydrated or suffocate down there."

"I thought you didn't need air. Can't you breathe underwater?"

"Underwater, sure. Water has oxygen in it, but there's not much of it in the hold, particularly with the atmosphere so polluted."

"There may not be much, but it's enough to keep you alive and if you're not feeling so good, then you'll be less likely to be causing us trouble."

Captain Lozich clenched his fists angrily and started to protest some more but the captain cut him off.

"That's all," he said. "Take him back to the hold and be sure his ropes are tight and his eyes covered."

"Yes, Captain," a crewman said.

The crewman bound Captain Lozich's feet again, covered his eyes with a blindfold and then pushed him into the hold. Since his men were also blindfolded and couldn't see to get out of the way, he fell on one of them hard and then dropped to the floor landing on his shoulder. He cursed under his breath.

"You alright, Captain," Lt. Yels asked helping the captain up.

"Not really," Captain Lozich replied. "I think it's about time we got the hell out of here and cut a few throats."

His crew members growled their agreement as the door to the hold was fastened shut and it became pitch black.

"How can we get out of here tied up the way we are?" Lt. Yels asked.

"No more talking," Captain Lozich ordered. "They are listening to us."

Captain Lozich then reached out to his crew telepathically. *"All right. The longer we're down here the weaker we will become. If we are going to escape we must do it now,"* he thought.

"Yes, Captain. What's your plan?" Lt. Yels asked.

"We are in the middle of the Dark Sea. If the ship sinks we are at home and in no danger, but the slavers will die. I say we sink the ship."

"That's a good idea, but how will we do it?"

"I need this blindfold off so I can use my invisible hand to bore a hole in the hull. Whoever is closest to me needs to rip off my blindfold with his teeth."

"I think I can do it," Lt. Yels said maneuvering himself in front of the captain. Pushing his head against the Captain's shoulder he inched his mouth up to his face and found the edge of the blindfold. Once he felt the edge he gripped it with his teeth and worked it up until the captain's eyes were exposed.

"Excellent," Captain Lozich said silently. "Now let me see your hands, Lieutenant."

Lt. Yels turned so the Captain could see the ropes binding his hands. Captain Lozich concentrated on the rope and the knots began to unravel. In a couple of loons Lt. Yels' hands were free and he ripped off his blindfold and untied his legs. Then he freed the Captain and the rest of the crew.

"Now, all of you with a third hand on my mark concentrate on cutting a hole in the bottom of the ship large enough for us to escape." Captain Lozich and several members positioned themselves over the targeted area and began clearing their minds. "Ready, mark!" the Captain thought.

Immediately the bottom of the wooden craft began to creak and groan like it was under intense pressure. Suddenly a board split and water began spraying into the hold. The hole widened and water began flooding in. As soon as the hole was wide enough crew members began diving through it into the sea.

The noise could be heard on deck so it wasn't long before the Captain ordered his crew to open the hold to see what was going on. Much to his shock and dismay their Seafolken cargo had disappeared. Suddenly the boat listed heavily to port.

"To the lifeboat! The ship is sinking," Captain Shameus screamed but to everyone's dismay the lifeboat had been reduced to splinters. As the ship began to slowly sink into the Dark Sea, Captain Shameus looked out over the rail and saw the Seafolken in the distance treading water and watching them.

"There they are! Shoot them!" he ordered.

The crew members who were armed began firing at the Seafolken so they dove underwater to avoid being easy targets. Soon, the crew had spent their ammunition and stood helpless on the deck of their sinking ship.

Threebeard was awakened by persistent beeps from his GC. He rolled his feet off the side of his bed, sat up and pushed the accept button. "Hello."

"Threebeard!" an excited voice exclaimed.

"Yes."

"We've spotted the fishing boat 20 kylods northwest of Hisa Usa. I'm sending you the coordinates right now."

"Excellent," Threebeard said sleepily. "I'll pass on the information to the TGA. Hopefully they'll have a ship in the area that can intercept it."

"Tell them to hurry!" the frantic voice added. "The ship seems to be sinking!"

Threebeard straightened up. "What?"

"It's listing badly and the crew seems to be firing their weapons at something."

"Alright. I'll report it as being urgent. Thanks," Threebeard said clicking off.

He immediately punched in the number for Colonel Zitor.

"Hello."

"Colonel. Sorry to bother you so early, but the ships been sighted."

"Great. Do you have coordinates?"

"Yes, but I've been told the ship is in distress and may be sinking."

"Sinking?"

"Yes, apparently there is some conflict on the vessel. It could be the Seafolken are trying to escape. The crew has been seen firing their weapons."

"Alright. I'll send out a search and rescue team and some assault copters for support. Send me the coordinates."

"Will do," Threebeard said forwarding the numbers he'd just received.

"I'll let you know as soon as I hear something," Colonel Zitor said and then hung up.

Threebeard got up, put on some clothes and went into the tavern's kitchen to see if he could get some breakfast. He was delighted to see Poldra back in the kitchen.

"You made it back," Threebeard said exuberantly.

"Yes, we got in a few kyloons ago."

"Excellent! How is Artis?"

"She's fine. She was exhausted so she went straight to bed."

"I can imagine. Why aren't you doing the same thing?"

"I didn't have to drive, so I got some sleep while we were traveling. Would you like some breakfast?"

"Yes, six eggs and seven or eight bacon strips would be perfect."

The standard egg on Tarizon came from a small bird called the squit and bacon came from the river hogs that foraged in the swamps created when the Liehn River overflowed during the heavy rains each spring and fall. After Threebeard had poured himself a large cup of sankee, he sat down to await his breakfast. While he was waiting Faruk and Giant came in carrying the replica of the nanomite city. Threebeard got up and helped them set it on a table.

"God almighty! Look at that!" Threebeard said in awe.

"Yes, isn't it magnificent?" Faruk said. "We were lucky to get it back here in one piece."

Threebeard sighed. "Yes. This is a truly a miracle. Finally, we have proof the nanomites are sentient beings."

"I hope they weren't all killed when the lava struck," Faruk said worriedly.

Threebeard shook his head. "My concern as well. The lava flow must have gone right over their city. It may well have killed them all."

"Was that the only nanomite city on Tarizon?" Giant asked.

"No. Most desert regions on Tarizon have a few cities. They live in the desert because too much water disrupts their ability to move freely and they can easily be swept away if there is too much of it. Also, they need a chemical called bacuum that is plentiful in the desert."

"I wonder how long it will be before we can go back and check on them," Faruk asked.

"It may be quite a while," Threebeard replied. "Mt. Alabash is still active and now two other volcanoes on Lamaine Shane are erupting."

"Really?" Faruk said. "Which ones?"

"Mt. Cebat in the northeast and Mt. Kudath in the south."

"It's almost impossible to breathe now," Giant noted. "We had to use breathers whenever we went outside in Rizi."

Threebeard nodded dejectedly. "Yes, breathers may become a way of life outside the domes, I'm afraid. With so much toxic ash in the atmosphere and on the ground, it could be many cycles before we see the sun again."

"Many cycles?" Faruk asked alarmed by the thought.

"I'm afraid so. Our atmosphere was just starting to recover from the great wars, but now we may face an even greater threat."

"What's that?" Giant asked.

"This ever-thickening shroud of ash encircling the globe is blocking the sun's rays. If it continues for any period of time it will kill our agricultural production and still our solar energy plants."

"You mean we won't have electricity?"

"That's right. Since nuclear and fossil fuel energy production was banned cycles ago, eighty percent of our electrical production comes from solar energy and the rest from wind and thermal generation. But with the sun's rays blocked the world's energy production will be cut by eighty percent. In fact, solar energy production is already down by thirty percent with only four volcanoes active. What will happen if nine or ten more erupt which is quite likely?"

Faruk sighed. "I'm really scared. What will we do?"

Threebeard stroked his middle beard. "That's a good question, my friend. A very good question indeed."

Poldra brought Threebeard's breakfast over to the table and set it down. Seeing it, Threebeard perked up and returned to his table.

"Well, I'm going to get some sleep," Giant advised. "I'm exhausted."

"Me too," Faruk said.

Threebeard looked up from his plate and waved his approval for them to leave. After they were gone he noticed a disturbed look on Poldra's face. "What's wrong, Poldra?" he asked.

Poldra looked over at Threebeard. "My mother lives in Behn Lat. That's not too far from Mt. Kudath."

"Hmm," Threebeard moaned. "Yes, she could be in trouble. The winds in that area come in from the south this time of cycle."

"Maybe she could go to Mapi and find a place to live under the dome," Poldra said.

Threebeard shook his head. "That's a good idea, but Central Authority isn't letting mutants into the domes."

"What!" Poldra said, incredulous.

"I know. It's ridiculous and violates the Supreme Mandate but the Purists control the General Assembly in Quori and they are putting a lot of pressure on Central Authority to protect the domed cities from *overcrowding* as they call it."

"That's outrageous!" Poldra exclaimed.

"My sentiments exactly, but for now that's the way it is."

Poldra nodded and went back to his work. Anger began welling in Threebeard as it often did when he contemplated the injustices that existed on Tarizon. It wasn't supposed to be this way after the world was unified and the Supreme Mandate became the law of the land, but the harsh reality was the promise of freedom and equality for all was but a sham. Although this depressed him, he knew he couldn't let it debilitate him, as he believed its promise could yet be fulfilled. He was interrupted by beeping from his GC.

"Yes?"

"Colonel Zitor here. We've picked up Captain Lozich and his crew. There was only one crew member lost."

"Oh, thank God and Sandee! What about the crew of the fishing boat?"

"They were all lost when the ship sank."

Colonel Zitor explained what had happened.

"So, where are you taking them?"

"To Gallion."

"Good. Tell Captain Lozich he and his crew are welcome to stay at the Mighty Jolly in Gallion until he gets a new ship."

"I'll tell him, but I'd like you to come here tomorrow if you can. It's time we had that meeting we discussed."

"Well, I would but all air traffic has been grounded."

"I know. I'll send a low altitude jet copter to pick you up. We've rigged a special filtration system to allow it to fly through the ash."

"Sounds good. I'm anxious to meet you."

"Alright, I'll have the copter pick you up tomorrow morning."

Threebeard hung up feeling good that his friend had been rescued. His delight however faded as he contemplated what would be discussed in the meeting with Colonel Zitor and his unidentified friends. What exactly was the colonel cooking up? Did it have to do with the super-volcanic eruptions all over Tarizon? He didn't think that was likely. Perhaps the colonel wanted his help communicating with the rhutz or wanted help in recruiting mutants for the TGA? Those were all plausible topics of discussion, but somehow, he figured it would be something more complicated.

That evening Threebeard built a display case for the nanomite city and set it up in a special event room in the Mighty Jolly. He wanted it somewhere where people could see it, but also a place it would be secure. The security at every Mighty Jolly was tight as they had to deal daily with customers who'd drank too much, taken drugs, or were feeling the effects of their encounters with the Seafolken women. Even so, the presence of a one-of-a-kind artifact of incalculable value, brought new concerns. Many humans opposed the recognition of any competing life-forms and would see the existence of the nanomite city replica as a threat. This would mean around the clock security would be necessary and careful scrutiny of anyone viewing the exhibit.

The next morning word had already gotten out about the nanomite city and hundreds of people were lined up to view the exhibit. Threebeard, who was trying to get off to the heliport, instructed Giant on the extra security needed. He was glad everyone was interested in the exhibit but feared something might happen to it before he even had a chance to study it carefully. Twenty loons later he was climbing aboard the jet copter that Colonel Zitor had sent for him. As the copter took off into the thick gray sky he became sad and depressed at what had become of his beloved Tarizon. He loved to fly and observe the beautiful landscape from above, but today he saw no rivers, lakes or grassy plains. All there was today was dismal gray and a burnt odor in the air that forewarned of disaster and devastation. He rubbed his eyes as they had started to burn. A crewman seeing his discomfort offered him a breather which he took appreciatively and put it over his mouth and nose. Even with the breather he was relieved when they landed at Gallion and he was transferred to an air-conditioned ATV for transport to base headquarters. He was feeling better when they pulled up in front of the building and went inside. Colonel Zitor greeted him as he came in and escorted him to a conference room.

The large conference room seated twenty-six, had a display of charts and maps on one wall and a myriad of video monitors on the other. Threebeard saw Captain Lozich and his executive officer, Ullum Yels, and nodded toward them. Colonel Zitor then introduced the other three persons present, Tobin Sandinista, Rammel Garciah, and Basset Als.

"Basset is the new chairman of the Tributon General Assembly," Colonel Zitor explained. "He was elected after Cornelius Bruda resigned over the Flat Meadow Massacre. Being the chairman of the General Assembly also makes him a member of the Tarizon World Assembly."

"Right. Excellent," Threebeard said nodding.

"Rammel Garciah is the new appointee to the Council of Interpreters in Shisk. You may have heard of him as the headmaster of Vaceen."

"Yes, I've heard good things about Councilor Garciah and Chairman Als," Threebeard acknowledged.

"Yes, and finally you may have heard of Tobin Sandinista, a counselor in Urunes, who was approached by the rhutz about the Flat Meadow Massacre."

"Yes, we've met and my son Nic, with the Councilor's help, has been working with Starlight and Shadow to set up a communication network with the rhutz throughout Lemaine Shane."

"Yes, that's correct," Sandinista acknowledged.

"Alright. I know you are all busy men so, I'll get right to the point. I gathered all of you together because you have one important thing in common—belief in and allegiance to the Supreme Mandate, not only as a governing document, but in what it stands for. Many people adhere to the Supreme Mandate because it is the law, but if it were not the law they would do what was in their own self-interest. None of you are like that. You believe in freedom, justice and equality for all sentient life-forms as an ideal that should always be the norm. Am I right?"

Everyone nodded.

"Well, sadly, I have observed a growing movement that, if not checked, will soon seek and have the capacity to destroy the Supreme Mandate and all the principals for which it stands. I'm sure you've seen it too in the acts of those who would keep the mutants out of the domed cities, kill the rhutz as if they were rodents, and, due to the current emergency, suspend the freedoms we all have become accustomed to and cherish so much."

Everyone looked around the table and nodded. Colonel Zitor

continued. "So far those strongly behind the Supreme Mandate have managed to prevail and keep Tarizon on a straight and narrow course, but I fear with us facing a worldwide disaster of unprecedented magnitude the forces of evil may be too much for our young democracy."

"Why do you think that?" Threebeard asked.

"Before I go into detail I must advise you that what I plan to tell you today will be considered by my superiors as a breach of my oath as an officer of the TGA and even treasonous. So, if you stay and listen you might be considered a conspirator."

"If it will be a breach of your oath as an officer why are you doing it?" Rammel asked.

"Because not to do it would be a breach of my oath to honor and defend the Supreme Mandate."

Rammel nodded. "Then I'll stay."

Colonel Zitor looked around the room and, seeing the others nodding as well, continued. "I've overheard some of my superiors talk about orders coming in suggesting that the civil rights of our citizens should be suspended during the current crisis. Specifically, the mutants and Seafolken are to be excluded from the domed cities."

"What!" Threebeard exclaimed. "That's going to be an official policy?"

"Apparently, that's what the Generals are saying."

"How do they feel about it?" Rammel asked.

"Many of them agree it's necessary given the limited resources available. The rationale is that it will be impossible to save everyone, so what resources are available should be targeted to normal, healthy humans."

"That's outrageous," Threebeard spat.

"Yes, it is, my friend," Captain Lozich agreed, "but it doesn't surprise me."

"I apologize to both of you," Chairman Als said sadly. "Although, I have no abnormalities I do not consider myself superior to any other human or life-form here on Tarizon. We were all created equal by the Master and should live together in peace and love. It shames me that any human would think himself superior to other humans or other life-forms."

"No apology is necessary," Rammel replied. "You have no control over the evil in men's minds."

"I know, but it's still an embarrassment. The Seafolken don't seem to be inflicted with such evil."

Captain Lozich shook his head. "Seafolken are susceptible to evil too," he said, "but living in and around the sea we have been preoccupied with survival. There is no politics in the Seafolken world nor the temptations of the city."

"Alright," Chairman Als said. "So, what makes you think these Purists can prevail? So far, we've been able to keep them under control."

"Yes, but this current crisis plays right into their hands. They have wanted to exclude the seafolken and the mutants out of the mainstream for some time, but the scarcity of resources now gives them a good reason for it."

"True. It will make it more difficult to convince the people to do what is right, but I'm confident we can do it," Chairman Als argued.

"Can we?" Colonel Zitor said. "These people do not share our values. They don't care about the Supreme Mandate or civil laws. They will do whatever it takes to gain power."

"What's worse," Threebeard interjected. "They believe what they are doing is the will of God. I've been monitoring some of their communication channels and it's quite alarming."

"How do you monitor their communications channels?" Colonel Zitor asked.

Threebeard smiled. "I've become very proficient on the computer and have been able to access just about anything on the global network."

Colonel Zitor nodded. "That's good to know. Your talents will come in handy for what we need to do."

"What is that exactly?" Threebeard asked.

Colonel Zitor sighed. "Well, it should be fairly obvious. We need to prepare for the day the Purists take control of the General Assembly and abolish the Supreme Mandate."

Everyone just stared at Colonel Zitor. Threebeard tried to tell himself that couldn't happen but the more he thought about it the more he realized Colonel Zitor was right. Finally, he sighed. "So, assuming that happens, how do we prepare for something like that?"

"Well, as the leader of the mutants, you need to start organizing a mutant army."

Threebeard laughed. "Leader of the mutants? I don't remember being elected to that position, if there were such a thing."

"True, but you are by far the most intelligent, talented and successful mutant on Tarizon. You own a very lucrative business, you've made contact with the rhutz and the nanomites, and today I've just learned you're a premier computer hacker. I think all of that qualifies you as the best candidate to lead the mutants in the coming civil war."

"What about me?" Captain Lozich asked. "Do you want me to organize a seafolken army?"

"Yes, exactly, but both of you will have to be discreet about it. What I'd suggest is you tell everyone that you are organizing a relief effort. You can use that as your cover until the time comes that your armies are needed."

"But I have no military training nor do any other mutants."

"Yes, that's why I have convinced TGA command to start allowing mutants to volunteer for military service. Of course, seafolken already serve in the military, so you can draw from those with experience to build your seafolken army. As I understand it you've already begun with the Deep Sea Defense League."

"That's true, but it's been limited to putting slavers out of business. We've never faced a real military force."

"I understand. But you will have an easier time of it than Threebeard. He'll be starting from scratch."

"Right," Captain Lozich said.

"So, Threebeard. You and ninety-nine thousand other mutants will be allowed to go through TGA boot camp on the Isle of Muhl."

"The TGA has never taken mutants before," Threebeard replied. "How did you convince them to allow it?"

"I pointed out that with the current crisis they were going to need a lot more troops and the mutants were already acclimated to a polluted environment. Plus, they'd need troops to keep the mutant population outside the domes under control and who better to do it than mutant soldiers."

"I've never had any ambition to be a soldier," Threebeard confessed. "I really have no desire to go to boot camp."

"You need to do it, though. The 99,000 troops that come out of training will be the backbone of the mutant army and they will need a leader."

"Backbone. How many mutants do you expect to finally be in this army?"

"A million is my hope. We'll need every last one of them."

"What about the TGA? Who will it back if there is a civil war?"

"The soldiers are very loyal to their generals, so they will likely follow their lead. That will be my job along with Councilor Garciah. We will be courting the TGA generals and trying to convince them to side with the Loyalists."

"What about me?" Chairman Als asked. "What is my role?"

"Your role, Mr. Chairman, is to become Chancellor and keep the Purists from gaining control of the World Assembly. Hopefully you will succeed and there never will be a civil war, but if you fail we want to be ready to fight and win back freedom and democracy for the people of Tarizon."

"What makes you think I can become Chancellor?"

"Because you have natural charisma and you're a very intelligent and cunning politician. With our help, I'm sure we can get you elected. Keeping you in office will be the challenge."

Chairman Als swallowed hard. "You really think the Purists will do anything to gain power?"

Colonel Zitor nodded. "Yes, they are ruthless and they will do anything including bribery, intimidating and murder."

"Murder?" Sandista asked. "Do you think they would really resort to murder?"

"Yes, and to quell any doubts about their intentions, let me share one more thing."

"What's that?" Threebeard asked.

Colonel Zitor pulled out a sheet of paper from a file and began reading. "This document is called the Mutant Manifesto. It is currently circulating amongst delegates of the World Assembly."

"If the crisis brings about a catastrophic shortage of medical supplies, food, and other necessities, the most practical solution would be the elimination of the mutant population as well as any other burdensome elements of the population living outside the domes. Although this may

seem extreme to some, in the long run it will be the best solution for people of Tarizon."

Everyone shook their heads in disbelief. "The World Assembly is discussing genocide as a solution to the current problem?"

"Not everyone. Only the Purists. The Loyalist obviously won't even discuss it. But the fact that it is being considered should be enough to make it clear what we are up against."

"Indeed," Rammel agreed. "We must all take on our tasks with great diligence for the sake of Tarizon."

Everyone nodded somberly as the meeting broke up. Threebeard wasn't thrilled about becoming a military leader. It was the last thing he wanted to do, but he knew Colonel Zitor was right. If there was a civil war they'd need armies to fight, but the task of building a mutant army was daunting. He didn't know how he could possibly pull it off and he wasn't looking forward to TGA boot camp. It was bad enough for regular soldiers but for the mutants he knew the drill sergeants would have but one objective, to wash every last one of them out and prove that mutants couldn't be good soldiers.

<h1 style="text-align:center">19</h1>

<h1 style="text-align:center">The Network</h1>

Before Threebeard left the meeting with Colonel Zitor and the other Loyalist leaders he was stopped by Rammel Garciah. Threebeard was in awe of the newly appointed Justice to Tarizon's Council of Interpreters and felt a bit nervous.

"Listen. I know we've dumped a lot of responsibility on you, but remember you're not alone. If you need any help with anything just ask. We'll get you whatever you need to be successful."

"Thank you, Councilor. I'm sure I'll need a lot of guidance, particularly on military matters. This is all new territory for me."

"Colonel Zitor will soon be a General. He's up for promotion and we're doing everything in our power to make that happen. He'll make sure you get all the help you need."

"Right. But I don't even know where to begin."

"Yes. I understand, but you are very intelligent and quite resourceful, so I'm sure you will figure it out."

"I hope so."

"I'm very impressed with your work with the nanomites, by the way. I understand you have a replica of one of their cities they built for you."

"You heard about that?"

"Oh yes, I've got Loyalist cells all over Lemaine Shane so if there is any news I hear about it quickly. I understand you are building a communications network with the rhutz."

"Yes, my son Nic is working on that," Threebeard replied.

"Well, we should link our two networks. The rhutz would be a great ally if the civil war actually does materialize."

"I don't know if they'd join in any war. They are a peaceful life-form."

"I understand, but if there is a civil war they will be at risk as much as mutants. You saw what happened at Flat Meadow. Mutants won't be the only life-form facing genocide if the Purists gain control of the government."

Threebeard nodded somberly. "I'll discuss it with them and, I'm sure, when they realize the threat the Purists pose to them, they will cooperate."

"Good. I'll have someone contact Nic to start working on linking the two networks."

"Okay. I'll let him know to expect to hear from you."

Rammel slapped Threebeard on the shoulder. "Excellent! Looking forward to working with you."

Threebeard laughed and shook the Councilor's hand warmly. "Likewise."

On the way back to Liehn Threebeard's mind raced trying to grasp what he had gotten himself into. He wondered why such notable persons had selected him for such an important role in the Loyalist movement. Politics had never been something he expected to get involved in. He hadn't told anyone he had any political ambition, yet they had come to him asking for help in preserving the Supreme Mandate. He was honored but also shocked and overwhelmed. When he got back to the Mighty Jolly he found Nic and took him aside.

"How's your work with the rhutz coming?" he asked.

Nic smiled. "Pretty good. I've got five or six contacts set up in Tributon, two or three in Rigimol and one in Quori."

"Well, you're going to have to accelerate your work. I just came from a meeting with some government officials and they want you to expand the network throughout the globe."

Nic's eyes widened. "Wow. That sounds like a lot of work."

"Yes, it is and they want you to merge it with a Loyalist network that is being created."

"A Loyalist network?"

Threebeard nodded and briefed Nic on the Purists threat and the Loyalists intended response. Like Threebeard, Nic was a little overwhelmed by it all and the role that he was to play.

"Don't worry. You'll have plenty of help. In fact, someone from

Councilor Garciah's staff will be contacting you soon to coordinate things."

Nic took a deep breath. "All right. This should be interesting."

"Don't discuss any of this with anyone other than the people involved. If the Purists get wind of it they could cause us a lot of grief. For now, everything we are doing is for the relief effort. Understand?"

Nic nodded and went back to what he was doing. Threebeard went to find Giant to see how things had gone with the nanomite exhibit. He was shocked when he saw the throng of people waiting to see the replica of the nanomite city. Giant was standing by the door to the exhibit room.

"So, everything okay?" Threebeard asked.

"No problems. There has been a steady stream of people to see the exhibit. The good news is a lot of them are hanging around the tavern to socialize after they see the replica of the city. Sales are up dramatically."

"Excellent. I hadn't realized it would be such a great draw. Too bad we don't have a few more replicas to display."

Giant laughed. "Isn't that the truth. The media has been here too filming the crowds and the exhibit. I hope that's okay."

"Sure. I want all the people of Tarizon to learn about the nanomites so they will appreciate and respect them as a sentient life-form."

"That's what I thought."

Threebeard put his hand on Giant's shoulder and smiled. When he got back to his office he took a deep breath and sat down in front of his computer monitor. After punching in a few commands, the TGN came up and he searched for the TGA training base on the Isle of Muhl. If he were going to go to boot camp he knew he needed to find out what it was going to be like, so he could prepare himself and the recruits that came with him. After quickly examining the contents of the site a feeling of complete dread came over him. Boot camp was not going to be a pleasant experience.

20

Protests

Rupra Bruda was relieved when the meeting with Essyria's parents was over. He had worried a lot about it, fearing his past would come back to haunt him. Apparently Essyria's parents hadn't bothered to check him out, or if they did, they didn't have a problem with what he'd done.

He was at Essyria's compartment waiting for her to return from work. Bored, he turned on the VC to catch the evening news. The camera was focused on the mobs of people outside the wall trying to get into the domed city. Presidius Tash, a member of the General Assembly was being interviewed about the refusal of Central Authority to let more people into the city.

"The government has no right to deny citizens of Tarizon from the protection of the dome while Mt. Soni is erupting. Many of these citizens will die if they are not allowed into the city."

"But, Assemblyman," the reporter said. "The city can only support so many people."

He shrugged. "It's true the citizens of Shisk may be inconvenienced for a while, but they must share the burden of this natural disaster too. If Central Authority won't open the doors of the city to the refugees, they have a responsibility to find them suitable protection elsewhere."

"Well, that sounds good, Assemblyman, but you and I both know Central Authority doesn't have the resources to protect people outside the dome. It's just not feasible."

"That's why they should be let in."

Rupra listened intently to the debate for a while until he realized he'd just been given one of those political opportunities he'd been talking about. He knew the citizens of Shisk did not want to let the refugees into the city because they feared food rationing and overloading the cities' environmental system. It wasn't that they wanted to see their fellow citizens die, only that their own self-preservation was more important. He knew if he offered them a reasonable alternative they'd take it. He called Peeta and his other friends and suggested they meet the following day for lunch. To pique their interest, he told them he wanted to organize another rhutz hunt.

They all gathered the next day at a small café. After a round of Tekari's had been brought to them, Bruda began.

"Since we came back to Shisk and ran into the crowds seeking refuge in the city, I've been thinking about the situation. Many of our citizens will die on the outside as the air gets more contaminated. Already there are two more volcanoes erupting in Turvin, Mt. Rumbia and Mt. Drala. The situation won't be getting better anytime soon."

"So, what can we do about it?" Peeta asked.

"There are thousands of mutants and rhutz in the city. Why should they be allowed to stay? The mutants are already impaired. Why let healthy humans die and allow those already spoiled to survive. And the rhutz have no rights under the Supreme Mandate, so why should they be breathing our precious oxygen?"

Everyone just stared at Rupra in silence, so he continued. "I know it sounds a little callous, but think about it. The mutants' lives have already been ruined. It's unfortunate that it happened, but you can't change the past. We must look to the future. Our health systems are already taxed to the hilt by the crisis. Mutants require forty percent more of our health resources and they only represent less than five percent of the population under the domed cities. If we expel them from the city and replace them with healthy humans our health costs will decline dramatically and more people can be accommodated."

"Sounds good to me," Chalke said.

Peeta shrugged. "Okay. So, what? What does that have to do with us?"

"We should organize protests and put pressure on Central Authority to expel the mutants and let in healthy humans to take their places."

"What makes you think that would work?"

"Have you been watching the news?" Bruda asked. "People are conflicted over leaving healthy humans outside the domes but they are afraid to let them in because it might jeopardize their health and welfare. If we offer them a viable alternative we'll be heroes."

Peeta nodded. "Good plan. You sold me. How do we get started?"

"We should go to the east entrance to the city where the crowds trying to get in are the biggest and start picketing. We can picket, give speeches and have people sign a petition to deliver to the General Assembly. I know just the assemblyman to present it to. I was just watching him on the VC."

"There aren't enough of us and I'm not good at giving speeches," Chalke complained.

"Don't worry. I'll give the speeches. The rest of you can picket or sign up new recruits."

"What about the rhutz. I thought we were going on another rhutz hunt," Raseen complained.

"We will. Don't worry," Bruda said. "Right now rallying support for our cause is more important."

"So are we going to the east gate now?" Bligh asked.

"No," Bruda replied. "Tomorrow morning." Bruda pulled out two big stacks of handbills and dropped them on the table. "We need to post these on every public bulletin board and hand out as many as possible. Everyone grabbed a handbill and read it."

MOVE OUT THE MUTANTS
CPC RALLY

SHISK'S EAST GATE
TOMORROW 800 KYLOONS

IT'S TIME TO PUT THE MUTANTS IN THEIR PLACE, MOVE THEM OUT OF SHISK AND LET NORMAL HUMANS TAKE THEIR PLACE. COME SHOW YOUR SUPPORT AND SIGN A PETITION TO FORCE THE WORLD ASSEMBLY TO DO THE RIGHT THING. MUTANTS ARE A MISTAKE AND NOT PART OF GOD'S DIVINE PLAN.

Rupra Bruda, Chairman
Citizens for a Pure City
CPC

Everyone but Bruda took some of the handbills and began distributing them throughout the city. Bruda spent the rest of the day contacting the media and advising them of the rally. He also met with Assemblyman Tash and asked him to sponsor a bill in the World Assembly calling for the eviction of the mutants. Tash thought it was a great idea and agreed to introduce it immediately.

Late in the day Bruda went to the East Gate and picked out a good location for the rally. He decided on a public park built as a place for people entering the city to rest and relax. It had lots of big trees, beautiful flower gardens, and a large grassy area with picnic tables. Bruda figured the grassy area could accommodate a large crowd and they could put a few picnic tables together to create a small stage from which he could give his speeches. When he got to Essyria's compartment in the early evening she was waiting for him.

"Where have you been?" she asked irritably. "I thought you'd be home when I got off work."

"I told you I was getting together with the guys and planning a protest rally."

"Yeah, but I didn't think it would take all day. I'm starving."

"I'm sorry," Bruda said taking Essyria in his arms. "Let's go get something to eat and I'll tell you about the rally tomorrow."

"Tomorrow? That soon?"

"Yes. We have to strike while Mt. Soni is still erupting and people are pounding on the gates of the city demanding to be let in."

They went down the street to a restaurant they both liked and put in their order. While they were waiting for their dinner they drank tekari and Bruda showed her one of the handbills and explained his plans.

"That's a pretty bold approach. Aren't you afraid the mutants will try to string you up?"

"If they try to make trouble they'll regret it. The boys will be bringing their lasers."

"I don't know. You could get hurt."

"Don't worry. There will be security at the gate so, I doubt anyone will start any trouble."

As they were talking Essyria noticed a picture of Bruda on the VC over the bar. "Look! You're on the VC."

Bruda looked over at the bar and saw that there was a story about his rally on the news. He got up and asked the bartender to turn up the sound. Essyria followed him over and watched over his shoulder.

"The Citizens for a Pure City will be rallying at the East Gate tomorrow according to its founder, Rupra Bruda. Bruda tells Central Soni News that the rally is designed to drum up support for the Mutant Relocation Act, a bill he claims will be introduced in the World Assembly tomorrow. The bill will provide that all mutants in the city are to be expelled, so that normal, healthy humans stuck on the outside can be admitted. Bruda claims the mutants should have never been allowed in the city as they are unhealthy, unruly, and a drain on the city's economy. He claims the areas of the city they occupy have a high crime rate, are run-down, and a danger to the good citizens of Shisk. The rally will be at 800 kyloons at East Gate Park.

"Assemblyman Shelona Pulma who represents the mutant district said he's never heard of the CPC and doubts any respectable citizen of Shisk will support the group's proposal. When we asked several prominent mutants in the area about the proposal the general consensus was that it was an abomination and Rupra Bruda must be a lunatic."

Bruda turned around angrily and retreated back to his table. "A lunatic, huh," he spat. "We'll see about that."

"Well, what did you expect the reaction from the mutants to be?" Essyria laughed. "You're proposing to root them out of their homes and throw them out of the city to their likely death. You didn't think they'd be happy about that, did you?"

Bruda took a deep breath. "Yeah, I suppose you're right. Anyway, the best way to put them in their place is to make the rally tomorrow a big success."

"Well, that VC story should bring out a lot of curious citizens if nothing else."

Bruda nodded as their food was being served. After they'd eaten they took a leisurely walk and then returned to their compartment. Before they'd even had a chance to take their coats off, the doorbell rang. Bruda looked at the door irritably and then reluctantly went over to answer it. A tall man flashed a badge in Rupra's face indicating he was an inquisitor from the PE's office named Griggs Wentz.

"May I come in?" Wentz asked politely.

Bruda hesitated, not knowing what to do. The timing of the visit made him think the inquisitor was there because of the rally—perhaps to warn him not to cause any trouble? He hoped that was all it was. Finally, he stepped back and let the officer in. Essyria gave him a wary look.

"Please, have a seat," Essyria said.

Wentz took a seat, pulled out a small notebook, and turned to one of its pages. "Forgive the intrusion, but I'm here to ask you about an incident that recently occurred in the mutant section of town near the Mighty Jolly tavern."

Bruda's stomach twisted and Essyria gave him a worried look.

"Are you familiar with the tavern, Mr. Bruda?" Wentz asked.

"Yes," Bruda admitted, fearful he'd bring up his encounter with the Seafolken woman.

"I understand you had a run in with a rhutz while you were there."

"One growled at us is all. It wasn't anything unusual. Rhutz aren't known for being too friendly."

"Yes, you should know that better than anyone, I suppose," Wentz said. "I've read about your encounters with the rhutz back in Tributon."

Rupra shrugged. "So, it was all a big mistake. I killed the rhutz by accident. I was aiming at a range deer when—"

"I know. There was a tremor. I've seen all the news reports."

"Okay. So what do you want?"

"Well, it seems you paid a second visit to the Mighty Jolly ten days ago. Several witnesses saw you and some of your friends tracking that same rhutz, ah, Misty I think was his name."

"No. It was the other way around. We were just minding our own business when the rhutz started following us."

"Is that why you killed it?"

"We didn't kill it. We just went back to the tram station and left the area."

"What I don't understand is why you went to a mutant neighborhood in the first place. You weren't going to the Mighty Jolly."

"Ah. Yes, we were, until the rhutz started following us. It scared us, so we decided just to return to the tram station rather than risk getting torn apart by a rhutz."

"Really? I thought you had been barred from the Mighty Jolly."

Bruda shook his head. "Who told you that?"

"The manager informed us that his bouncer had banned you because of your involvement in the Flat Meadow Massacre."

Bruda didn't say anything.

"Don't think you can lie to me. If I find out anything you tell me is not true, I can make you take the truth serum."

A cold chill came over Bruda. The truth serum was something he feared. He didn't know what effect it would have on him. He thought with his abilities he might be able to put up a barrier in his mind and withstand it, but he didn't know for sure, so he said nothing.

Wentz continued, "The funny thing is, the rhutz is now dead."

"Dead? Really?"

Wentz nodded. "Yes, I'm afraid so. It seems you and your friends were the last ones to see it alive."

Bruda shrugged. "Hmm. That's strange."

"Yes, it is particularly strange since his body was found in the same disposal unit as Connell Riki."

"Who?" Bruda asked.

"Eyeball, the bouncer at the Mighty Jolly. Connell Riki is his real name."

"Oh. The bouncer. He's dead?" Bruda asked feigning surprise.

"Right. The very same mutant you had a run in with the last time you frequented the Mighty Jolly."

Bruda shook his head. "I wouldn't kill someone just because he didn't want me in his tavern. That's ridiculous."

"I understand you don't like rhutz, but what do you have against mutants? I see you're leading a rally trying to have them expelled from the city."

"That's true. It's not that I have anything against them. It's just a question of resources. We can't protect everyone from the contamination, so we have to make some hard choices. Obviously, we should protect those people who are normal and healthy. It's just common sense."

Wentz shook his head in disgust. "Well, unfortunately I can't prove you and your friends killed Eyeball and the rhutz right now, but I know you did it and I promise you I won't rest until I have established good cause for you to be compelled to take the truth serum. Then we'll find out what really happened."

"Don't waste your time. You'll never find the proof because we didn't do it."

"Sure, you didn't and Mt. Soni isn't erupting right now," Wentz spat as he got up to leave. He went to the door, then turned back. "Don't leave the city."

Bruda didn't reply but just glared at Wentz. Finally, Wentz turned and left. Bruda got up quickly and closed the door behind him and then turned to look at Essyria. "What a skutz! If he thinks he can mess with me, he's sorely mistaken."

"What are you going to do?" Essyria asked.

Bruda smiled thinly. "Make sure his investigation comes to an abrupt halt. He's out of his league but he doesn't know it."

"Did you read his mind?" Essyria asked.

"Yes. He has no evidence."

"So, why don't you leave it alone?"

"Because if he keeps digging he might find something. It's better to derail him right now while there aren't many involved in the investigation."

Bruda's concern about Wentz's investigation wasn't that he'd find any evidence to go forward with a case, but that he'd make an accusation, a prosecutor would be appointed and Bruda would be forced to accept the representation of a defender. That would create a lot of bad publicity and be a disaster at this early stage in his political career. He knew what he had to do—get rid of Inquisitor Wentz that very night.

"I'm going out for a while," he said.

"Where are you going?" Essyria asked worriedly.

"To take care of business. I'll be back in a few kyloons. If anyone asks you where I was tonight, well, tomorrow is a big day so I went to bed early. You can vouch for me."

"What about your tracking chip? Central Authority will know you went out."

"My tracking chip is in the bedroom. I removed it shortly after I got to Shisk. If anybody is tracking me they'll think I'm in bed."

Essyria nodded. "Okay. But what if they examine your body and find the chip missing?"

"I replaced the real chip with a deactivated one, so if they x-ray me it will appear to be there."

"Okay, so do you know where to find Wentz?"

"Yes, he's stopping at the Lonely Tavern for a drink before he goes home. He likes to flirt with the barmaid there."

Essyria smiled. "Reading minds comes in handy?"

"Yes, it does," Bruda said. "I'll need some zilium capsules."

Essyria nodded and went into the bathroom where she kept a good supply of the strong painkiller. She counted out eight pills and put them in a plastic bag. When she returned to the living room she handed them to Bruda.

"This should do it," Essyria said, then gave Bruda a kiss goodbye. "Be careful. Inquisitor Wentz may be more dangerous than you think."

Bruda nodded, then left and walked six blocks to the Lonely Tavern. There was an alley across the street, so he hid in the shadows where he had a good view of the tavern's front door. Closing his eyes, he concentrated, searching for Wentz' thoughts. Having just read his mind it was easy to find his brain waves amongst the customers in the tavern. He established a link and then relaxed. He knew now it was just a matter of time until his problem would be solved.

Wentz had a few drinks and flirted with the barmaid for about twenty loons, then he came staggering out of the tavern and headed toward his compartment. As he passed the alley Bruda took hold of Wentz's lungs with his invisible hand and crushed them with all his might. Wentz gasped in pain, grabbed his chest struggling to breathe. Panic stricken, eyes bulging, his entire body began to burn from a lack of oxygen. He began to convulse until he finally passed out and collapsed in a heap.

Bruda came out quickly from the shadows and dragged him back into the alley. After propping his body against the side of the building, he took the pills out of his pocket and stuffed them into Wentz's mouth. Then with his invisible hand, he forced the pills down his throat. Satisfied with his work, he scanned the area in all directions. Seeing no one about he walked out of the alley and went back to Essyria's compartment. She was relieved to see him.

"How did it go?" Essyria asked.

"No problem. He was half drunk when he came out of the bar so there was no way he could fight me off."

"Good. Did anyone see you?"

"No. The street was deserted. They probably won't find him until morning."

"He'll be long dead by then," Essyria noted.

"I hope so."

The next day Bruda and Essyria got up early and went to East Gate Park. Peeta and Bligh were already there setting up tables and putting pickets together. Several public enforcers were stationed at the edge of the park watching them warily. As the morning wore on more and more supporters showed up to help get things organized. When the hour came for the rally several thousand people were mingling around the grassy area between the park and Shisk's East Gate and several news reporters and their camera crews were on the scene. Noting it was time for the rally to begin, Bruda climbed up on the makeshift stage and addressed the crowd.

"Citizens of Shisk. My name is Rupra Bruda and I stand before you to protest an intolerable state of affairs. If you look out through the East Gate to our beloved city, you will see thousands and thousands of citizens of Soni waiting to be allowed into the safety of our dome. Yet, according to our leaders, none of them will be allowed in. Instead they will be left outside to die from the toxic air and polluted water.

"These officials say that Shisk does not have the resources to accommodate everyone who wants into the city. This may be true but who decides who has the right to the protection of the city? Should it be Central Authority or the people of Shisk? . . . My friends, we are a democratic city, and who is allowed to live here should be determined by the people not a bunch of bureaucrats. The World Assembly should put the matter to a vote and decide who can stay and who must leave.

"If you will remember when the dome was first constructed Central Authority, without the people's consent, let over 50,000 mutants into the city. What right did they have to do this? Did you vote to allow them? No, you didn't. Some bureaucrat took it upon himself to let them in."

There were cheers and nods of agreement from many in the crowd, but many others shook their heads in disbelief. A contingent of mutants on the fringe of the crowd scowled at Bruda looking like they wanted to come over and expel *him* from the city immediately.

Bruda continued. "I know it's tempting to feel sorry for the plight of the mutants, but for some reason God has chosen them for a different destiny than the rest of us. Perhaps they are paying for their sins or the sins of their fathers. None of us mere mortals can possibly understand God's will, but when it is clear, as it is with the mutants, we shouldn't interfere with it.

"The mutants are a sick people and if you let them mingle amongst us their diseases will spread to the rest of us. Let us right a horrible wrong by expelling the mutants and letting as many normal and healthy humans in the city as it can hold without jeopardizing the citizens that already live here. Let not mere mortals interfere with the will of the Lord!

"So, come up and sign our petition demanding the General Assembly take this matter up and vote to evict all mutants from the city immediately to make room for those who truly deserve to be protected. I have been assured a bill will be introduced today proposing that very thing. So, let's let everyone know that the majority of the citizens of Shisk support it and want it passed without delay. Let the will of the people prevail!"

Again, there were many who cheered but an equal number who just stared at Bruda as if he were the diseased one. Bruda stepped down and picked up a picket. A hundred other demonstrators joined him as he marched to the East Gate. As the people outside the city saw the picketers marching toward them, they began to cheer and move in closer to get a better view, but when the marchers got too close the contingent of public enforcers stepped in front of them blocking their march. Bruda stopped and stared at the officers for a long minute and then turned and began marching along the street that led into the city. Crowds along the way cheered and jeered the picketers in equal numbers. It was apparent that Bruda had opened up a painful wound that would cause much grief to the inhabitants of Shisk in the days to come.

21

Recruitment

Word of Rupra Bruda's blatant attempts to get mutants expelled from Shisk outraged mutants all over Tarizon. Never had they been so callously attacked and told they were second class citizens; not worthy to live inside the domed cities. This outrage made it easy for Threebeard to begin the recruitment of soldiers for the Mutant Army. He began spreading the word that soldiers were needed to aid and protect mutants who were being excluded from the domed cities. The fact that the TGA was promising to train the first 99,000 recruits amazed and excited most mutants as in the past they'd always been excluded from military service. The twenty-two Mighty Jolly Taverns located throughout Lemaine Shane became recruitment centers and young mutants were soon lining up to enlist.

Raising an army was a daunting task but Threebeard knew all the technical knowledge for the task was at his fingertips on the TGN. He dove into the task and discovered a wealth of information from the TGA archives and even found several detailed mobilization plans used by the military in the past. Fortunately, he wouldn't need to feed and house his army in the beginning. He'd simply have to enroll them in the TGA training program being set up by Colonel Zitor and then wait for them to serve their two-cycle tour of duty. But at the end of their initial tour of duty he'd have to be ready to house, feed, and equip 99,000 soldiers immediately and eventually ten times that many. Since he would be in training himself, he'd have to have others in charge of locating or building, a military base, acquiring uniforms, equipment, armaments, and support personnel.

While Threebeard was busy with recruiting, Nic accelerated his work on setting up contacts with the rhutz packs throughout Tarizon. He worked closely with Councilor Garciah's staff member, Thomilius Tomel, who'd been assigned to coordinate with him in integrating the two networks.

Thom, as Nic called him, a tall, slim man with a light complexion, was young like Nic and very outgoing. The work involved much traveling so the two spent a lot of time together and became good friends. They started in Lemaine Shane but fortunately they'd both already done a lot of work there, so it only took them a few phases to finish up and move on. They next traveled to the continent of Turvin, started in Drasha in the far north and traveled by ATV along the north coast to Elish. This was slow, tedious work as they had to locate human contacts and then find local rhutz packs telepathically so meetings could be arranged at which they would explain what they were trying to do.

The political situation in Turvin was different too. The people of Tuht, Synclare, Pohl and Merria were more interested in trade and commerce than social justice. Whereas they generally accepted and approved of the Supreme Mandate they only did so because it ensured greater freedom and independence from the government. Now with the world's commerce coming to a standstill due to tremors, volcanic eruptions and the thickening cloud of ash encircling the globe, it was hard for them to think ahead to the political threat that they were facing.

Neither had the people of this region encountered problems with the rhutz. They'd heard about Flat Meadow but found it hard to comprehend. There were plenty of rhutz around but they'd scarcely given them a thought. Now to find out they were a sentient life-form was a little hard to swallow. Fortunately, a rhutz named Falling Star traveled around with them to help convince the cell leaders that the rhutz were an intelligent life-form. One such gathering took place just outside of Roshaunda in Synclare. Nic, Thom and Falling Star were standing on an outdoor stage used for theatrical performances. Their audience of some twenty-five local citizens watched them attentively.

"My name is Nicirius Nocteris, but you can call me Nic. You may have heard of my brother, Tribius Nocteris, also known as Threebeard."

Many heads nodded as the name *Threebeard* had become well known due to the spread of the Mighty Jolly Taverns all over Turvin. Many smiles could be seen over the faces of the men in the crowd, no doubt caused by memories of their encounters with the Seafolken women featured at the popular taverns.

"With me I have Thom Tomel, a member of Councilor Garciah's

staff, and the rhutz, Falling Star."

Some of the people in the front rows leaned back fearfully as Falling Star took a few steps forward and dipped her head slightly.

Nic continued. "The purpose of our visit is to establish a cell here in Roshaunda where information about the global crisis as well as the political situation can be disseminated quickly and confidentially. All of you were chosen because of your fundamental belief in the Supreme Mandate, the peace it has provided Tarizon, and a strong desire to see it survive the global crisis that now faces Tarizon.

"My expertise will be in helping you establish a relationship with the local rhutz population and Thom will concentrate his efforts on setting up a communications link with other cells throughout Turvin. Falling Star is traveling with us to show you a side of the rhutz that you may not have ever seen before. As I understand it, there are a few of you with telepathic abilities. Raise your hands if you have that ability."

A few hands went up.

"Okay. If each of you would come up we'll see if we can establish a connection with Falling Star," Nic said. The five with their hands raised made their way up to the stage and faced the audience. "A few phases ago very few rhutz could think in Tari, but because of the hard work of Starlight and Shadow back in Tributon thousands of rhutz now can do it. Falling Star is one of them, so just look into her eyes as you would to read anyone's mind."

The group concentrated and focused on Falling Star. A woman in the group stiffened as a link was established. Her eyes widened as Falling Stars memories exploded in her mind. Another flinched as the connection was established. Soon all of them were smiling as they entered the world of the rhutz.

"It's a pleasure to make your acquaintance," Falling Star thought. *"As you marvel at my world I am awed by yours. For hundreds of cycles we have walked in this world on separate paths, but now we must unite to meet the challenges of nature and of evil men. I can't say I understand the human race. I don't know how it is that some are good and others evil as the rhutz are of but one will—what is best for all rhutz. But at least there are many humans, like all of you, who are honorable and trustworthy who we would be proud to join in the struggle to save our beloved planet, Tarizon."*

The five locals on stage smiled and nodded their approval to Falling Star and then blended back into the audience. Thom then addressed the group. "Our plan is to set up a cell in each urban area. The purpose of a cell is to identify those in the area who are sympathetic to our cause and bring them into the fold. When each cell grows to sixteen members it should split geographically into four new cells. Each cell will have someone devoted to keeping a line of communication open to the other cells so that information and orders can be sent out and received quickly. One person in each cell will be devoted to identification and recruitment of members, another to security and another to fund raising. While the Loyalist network is growing we will keep it secret, but should the time come when action is called for we will be ready."

Thom, Nic and Falling Star continued their work in Turvin zig zagging back and forth through Soni, Rour and Merria until they reached the southern tip of the continent. At Crystal Uza they took a ferry to the Tunisu Islands where they met Threebeard and Rammel at a tropical resort called Emerald Cove to debrief.

"You did well," Threebeard said slapping Nic on the back. "I knew I could trust you to do a fine job."

"Well, Falling Star was the hit of the show. She's quite an inspiration."

"I bet she was," Rammel said. "Unfortunately, we're going to be desperately needing your network very soon. I don't know if you heard, but the General Assembly is considering a vote calling for the relocation of all the mutants in Shisk to facilities outside the dome."

"Yes, we heard that when we were in the city," Nic said. "Do you really think it will pass?"

"I don't know," Rammel replied. "It might. Rupra Bruda has done a good job of stirring up the citizens. He's got people everywhere protesting about the healthy, productive humans left outside the city while worthless mutants are taking up valuable real estate within the dome."

"What an evil bastard he is!" Thom said.

"You don't know the half of it? I'm sure he was responsible for killing Eyeball and Misty the rhutz who lived near the Mighty Jolly in Shisk."

"Yes," Threebeard agreed. "I had our manager go to the public enforcer's office and insist on an investigation. They found both of their bodies in the warehouse district adjacent to the Mighty Jolly. Now, the enforcer assigned to the case has died under suspicious circumstances."

"What suspicious circumstances?" Thom asked.

"Shortly after questioning Rupra Bruda, he was found dead in an alley across from a tavern where they say he'd been drinking heavily—no evidence of trauma other than bruised lungs and a toxic level of pain medication. The medical inquisitor doesn't know what to make of it, so he concludes it was the result of his being drunk and mistakenly taking too many pills."

"So, you think Bruda did it?" Nic asked.

"Absolutely," Rammel said. "Back in Tributon Bruda's friend died the same way—no apparent trauma to the body other than bruised lungs. Everybody knows Bruda has a strong invisible hand as well as being telepathic. I'm sure he read the enforcer's mind to find out where he was going, then killed him and made it look like an accident."

"Skutz. That's scary. How do you defend yourself against someone like that?" Thom asked.

"You don't, unless you have similar powers and can guard against his probing mind," Threebeard replied. "Nic and I were lucky we inherited the gifts. We can stand up to Bruda, but many others will be defenseless. That's why he's so dangerous and we must be sure he never gains any political power."

"But what can we do?" Nic asked.

"Alert your cells in Shisk to the threat and have them launch protests against the resolution in the General Assembly to remove the mutants from the city."

"Sure. But will that be enough?"

"Not by itself," Rammel admitted. "Basset Als, Thom and I will be working behind the scenes with members of the World Assembly trying to get the resolution defeated, but we need some public outcry as well."

Threebeard nodded. "And I'll go to the public enforcer and the media and expose Rupra Bruda. The people need to know the kind of man who is soliciting their support."

Nic wasn't so sure his cells, who had only been recently established, would be capable of launching much of a protest against the resolution in the World Assembly, but it would certainly provide an opportunity for them to get some needed experience. The media attention from the protests would also help them identify people sympathetic to their cause which was one of their biggest problems. It was delicate work talking to citizens to determine their politics without exposing the existence of the cells to the enemy. Presumably if someone showed up for a rally called in support of the mutants the people attending would be safe to approach for cell membership. They'd still have to be careful, though, as spies often showed up to these rallies to obtain information about their enemy. Nevertheless, Nic believed the controversy would ultimately be a boon to the growth and expansion of the cell network in Shisk. They all left together for Shisk but once inside the dome they separated. Threebeard, Falling Star, and Nic went to the Mighty Jolly and Thom and Councilor Garciah went to Garciah's new residence near the Capitol Building.

The Council of Interpreters was beginning its new session in a few days so Councilor Garciah would be tied up, so this left Thom to work with Basset Als with the responsibility for applying pressure on delegates of the World Assembly. While Nic worked with the cell leaders, Threebeard went to the public enforcer's office to see how the investigation of the death of Inquisitor Wentz was coming. He met with Public Enforcer, Chief Ert Stegis in his office.

"Sorry to hear about the death of Inquisitor Wentz," Threebeard said.

Chief Stegis sighed. "Yes, it was quite shocking and unexpected."

"So, the medical inquisitor ruled it an accident?"

"Yes, an unfortunate mixture of alcohol and drugs, I'm afraid."

"What about the bruising on his lungs?" Threebeard asked.

"How did you know about that?" Chief Stegis asked.

"Reports from the medical inquisitor are public records. I accessed it as soon as it came out."

Stegis nodded. "Right. Well, that was odd, indeed. The medical inquisitor stated he thought it might have been some sort of lung disease or trauma caused when Inquisitor Wentz fell on a trash can in the alley."

"But if that were the case there would be external bruising, right?"

"True, the ME explanation wasn't all that convincing, but with no witnesses, what other explanation is there?"

"What about Rupra Bruda? Hadn't Inquisitor Wentz just interrogated him at his compartment?"

"True. But his tracking records have him at his mate's compartment the entire evening."

"His mate's compartment? I didn't know he had a mate?"

"Yes, it happened quite recently. He mated into a rather prominent family in Shisk, the Tomaso family, Sigor and Tulia."

"Of Tomaso Industries? The medical equipment and supply manufacturer?"

"Yes, that's the one."

"Hmm," Threebeard muttered bitterly. He knew that was bad news. With money and power behind Bruda he'd be ever harder to stop. But that wasn't an issue he needed to discuss with PE Stegis.

"Well, there are ways to disable a tracking device."

"Yes, I suppose, but without any evidence of that, we have to assume it was working properly."

"The reason I'd like you to take a second look at Rupra Bruda is that he has telekinetic abilities—rather strong ones. If you will check the records of a suspicious death in Ce Lat a cycle or so ago, you'll find one with the same type of internal injury to the lungs. The victim was Romas Lantra, a close friend of Bruda, who was scheduled to be interrogated by the inquisitors in connection with the Flat Meadow Massacre."

"Really? That *is* interesting. I'll check it out, but unless you can shed some light on how he managed to manipulate his tracking chip, I don't think it will make much difference."

"Right. I understand," Threebeard said thoughtfully. "I'll work on that while you're looking into Lantra's death."

Threebeard left feeling less than enthusiastic about the results of his visit with Chief Stegis. The tracking chip issue intrigued him so he went back to the Mighty Jolly to get on the TGN and find out if there were any other reports of citizens manipulating their tracking chips. He quickly discovered it had been a chronic problem for Central Authority as many individuals had simply removed their chips. Central Authority's response to this was to make the removal or disabling of a tracking chip a major crime. This gave Threebeard an idea. Even if they couldn't prove Rupra Bruda had killed Eyeball or Inquisitor Wentz, they might be able to prove he altered his tracking chip which would give the inquisitors the right to compel him to take the truth serum. If he was their killer, he'd likely confess it once he'd taken the serum.

For the rest of the day Threebeard researched tracking chip technology and discovered they were manufactured at Pullit Engineering right there in Shisk. To expedite his research, he decided to pay a visit to the company. Since they wouldn't have any reason to talk to him, he called Chief Stegis and asked him to call over to them and ask them to cooperate. Chief Stegis wasn't thrilled about the idea but finally, after Threebeard dropped Councilor Garciah's name, decided it couldn't hurt and made the call. Upon his arrival Threebeard was taken to a small conference room and told to have a seat. After a few loons two men came in and sat down.

"Hello," a lean, gray-haired man said. "I'm Tollis Linden, assistant plant manager, and this is Tod Gucilli, from research and development. What is it we can help you with?"

Threebeard nodded. "Nice to meet you. I just wanted to say your tracking chip technology is fascinating. I have been studying up on it lately. To think you can know the location of every citizen, monitor their vital signs, and even listen to the sounds around them is truly amazing."

"Yes, we are rather proud of what we have accomplished here. Of course, it is illegal to monitor conversations of citizens under the Supreme Mandate without a council order, so that part of the device is rarely used."

"Still, to have that capability is mind boggling," Threebeard marveled.

"Yes, thank you. So, how can we help you?"

"Well, there is a certain suspect in a murder case who I suspect may have disabled or manipulated his tracking chip in order to provide an alibi for the murder."

The two men looked at each other nervously, then Tod said, "No, that's not possible."

Threebeard looked intently at Tod searching his mind. It didn't take but a tik to determine he was lying. Anger welled up in Threebeard but he managed to hide it. "Are you sure about that?"

"Yes, the moment a tracking chip is tampered with a signal is emitted and Central Authority is notified."

"Who monitors these signals?"

"It goes out into the network as a priority alert."

"I understand, but who monitors the alerts?"

"Ah. Every city has a monitoring station and there are regional stations outside the cities. For Shisk the station is right here in this building."

"Could the person on duty when an alert is sounded disregard the alert?"

Tod shrugged. "Sure, but why would they do that?"

"Ah. They could have fallen asleep. Someone could have paid them money to ignore the alarm, perhaps?"

Linden shook his head. "No. Not possible. All our employees are carefully screened before hiring and closely monitored once employed. It couldn't happen."

"Then why did you fire someone for that very offense just last month. Let me think. His name was Ethenius Holdins, I believe."

Linden paled. "How did you know about Holdins?"

Threebeard shrugged. "Your terminations are a public record and it isn't hard to put two and two together. I'm very well informed, so I'd refrain from lying to me. If it turns out you knew about someone tampering with a tracking chip and didn't report it, you could be in serious trouble."

Linden swallowed hard. "No. We didn't know exactly what happened, but there was an alert that somehow got misdirected and lost. We questioned the employee involved, but when he was less than cooperative, we fired him."

"I see. I'll need the employee's name. I'm sure Chief Stegis will want to talk to him, and if he lies, petition the council of interpreters to have him put under the truth serum."

"Of course. I'll write it down for you."

When Threebeard got back to the Mighty Jolly he called Chief Stegis and gave him the information on the terminated employee. Stegis agreed to follow up on it.

Threebeard then began researching the Tomaso family and soon realized Rupra Bruda's threat was much greater than he first imagined. He was convinced more than ever that he had to make sure Bruda was arrested for killing Misty, Eyeball, and Inquisitor Wentz. That was the only way to keep him permanently out of politics where he posed the most danger. His wrist array beeped.

"Yes," Threebeard said.

"Ah. This is Chief Stegis. I'm afraid I have bad news."

Threebeard's heart sank. "What is it?"

"Ethenius Holdins is dead."

Threebeard sighed. "Crushed lungs?"

"No. A bullet to the head. It looks like a suicide."

"Yes, of course," Threebeard replied bitterly.

22

Mutant Relocation Act

Basset Als grew up in Shini the capitol of Rigimol. He was tall, standing well over six feet, black hair and blue eyes. A good-looking man but, more importantly, a dynamic individual with a keen intellect and a fiery tongue. It was not surprising that he had risen quickly up the political ladder to become the youngest member of Tarizon's World Assembly. He commanded such great respect and allegiance that many believed someday he would be chancellor.

It was fitting that the first bill that he took the forefront in opposing was the proposed Mutant Relocation Act. He felt strongly about this issue not only because it subverted the intentions of the Supreme Mandate, but also due to the fact that he had two mutant children himself that he dearly loved. They would be exempt according to the fine print in the Mutant Relocation Act exempting families of assemblymen, but nevertheless he abhorred the concept of treating human beings differently on account of their health or one life-form as being better than another.

Thom Tomel was an intellect and a great speech writer. He had written the first draft of Basset's speech to be delivered to the World Assembly the next day and the two were going over it.

"The people are so scared with all the tremors, tidal waves, and volcanos erupting that they are not thinking rationally," Thom said. "Don't expect them to be too worried about civil rights."

"So, I just need to reassure them that they will be safe," Basset replied.

"Not just them but those outside the dome as well. Many of the people outside the dome trying to get in are friends and family of the people inside the dome. We have to convince them that those people somehow will be protected from the atmosphere."

"Right," Basset said. "But how can we make such a promise."

"Perhaps we could set up camocubes outside the door and filter the air and water," Thom suggested.

"An interesting idea, but I doubt there are enough camocubes available in all of Tarizon for such a structure."

"True, and we don't have time to manufacture them," Thom mused.

"Wait a minute," Als said. "What about the shuttles?"

Thom frowned. "The shuttles?"

"Yes, there are thousands of shuttles in suspension yards that were used to ferry people back and forth to Earth during the 8th World War. There are also an equal number of survival pods used to keep citizens alive in orbit around Tarizon. If we could get some of them operational we would have a place to put the refugees seeking entry into the city so that mutants would not have to be evicted."

"What about all the mutants outside the dome," Thom asked.

Basset sighed. "Well, there are too many of them, I'm afraid. That's a different problem that the World Assembly will have to take up later. I'm just worried about defeating this bill that is before the World Assembly right now."

"It might work. We'll need to contact the TGA and see if our plan is even feasible."

"Let's see what your brother has to say about it," Basset said as he picked up his GC and punched in the Colonel's number. After a few moments Colonel Rei Tomel came on the line.

"Chairman Als, how are you?" Colonel Tomel asked.

"Not too well. We are trying to figure out how to defeat the Mutant Relocation Act."

The Colonel groaned. "Ah, a daunting task, I'm afraid."

"Yes, but we have an idea and we need you to tell us if it is feasible."

"Okay. What is it?"

"There are a lot of Earth shuttles in dry storage as I recall."

"That's right."

"If I remember correctly they each can house about 10,000 passengers and could provide a regulated environment for them."

Colonel Tomel thought a moment. "Yes, I think that is correct."

"What I'm wondering is if we could park ten or fifteen of them just outside of Shisk. That would be a safe place the refugees could be taken."

"Yes, that makes sense. I'm just not sure how quickly the shuttles could be activated."

"Could you check into it. I'd like to propose this as an alternative to the eviction of the mutants from Shisk."

"Yes. Absolutely. This is something we could do all over Tarizon and perhaps save thousands of lives."

"Good. Check into it and get back with me would you, Colonel?"

"I will, Mr. Chairman. Nice talking to you."

Thom looked at Basset and smiled. "Great idea. I'll revise your speech and incorporate the idea."

"Yes. Just pray to God and Sandee that it will work."

While Nic was meeting with cell leaders in Shisk planning to disrupt Rupra Bruda's rallies in favor of the Mutant Relocation Act, Falling Star reached out to the rhutz in and about Shisk. She quickly learned that there were seven packs inside Shisk and eleven in the country within a few kylods of the city.

"Brothers and sisters. I am Falling Star from Tributon sent here by Shadow and Starlight to link the rhutz and the humans in the Loyalist Party. This is a time of great peril for the rhutz on Tarizon. Not only has nature unleashed its fury against us, but many of the humans conspire against us as well.

"You have heard of the Flat Meadow Massacre perpetrated by Rupra Bruda and his followers. With great regret I am here to inform you that Bruda has killed yet another of our brothers and is plotting to kill many more. This time it was Misty who lived under the dome in Shisk. Misty recognized Bruda, confronted him and was killed for it.

"Bruda now is trying to get the mutants and rhutz of Shisk evicted to make room for more healthy, unimpaired humans who he claims are superior to the mutants on Tarizon. This is a dangerous time for us and you must all be alert to this terrible danger. Stay out of public places and lay low for a while until this danger is over.

"We are in the process of forging an alliance between the Loyalists, the mutants, and the Seafolken to fight Bruda and his evil Purists. But our alliance is young so we are all vulnerable and must be vigilant.

"During the next few days we will be working hard to defeat this legislation in Tarizon's World Assembly. It may be that we will need you for security or to show our support to those who oppose the new law. Be ready and respond quickly should you get the call.

"God and Misty be with you," Falling Star concluded.

Later that day Colonel Tomel called Basset Als with a report on the Earth shuttle situation. "I've checked with Intergalactic Command and they report that most of the Earth shuttles have been out of service for so long that it would take considerable time and effort to repair and refit them for intergalactic travel."

Basset sighed fearing his idea wasn't feasible.

"But, since you don't need them to travel off Tarizon they don't think it will be too difficult to move some of them to sites near the cities and get their environmental systems online."

"Excellent," Basset replied. "Would you start organizing a team to implement the plan. I'm going to propose it to the World Assembly later today and I'm pretty sure it will adopted."

"I'll get right on it," Colonel Tomel assured him.

Basset hung up and called Threebeard and gave him the good news. When he had finished, Threebeard told him about his progress on the investigation of Rupra Bruda. Basset was disappointed but not surprised by the setback. "It's going to be next to impossible to take down Bruda legally."

"Perhaps someone ought to just put a bullet bomb in his head," Threebeard replied.

"That is tempting, but we are pledged to uphold the Supreme Mandate," Basset reminded him. "We can't let Rupra Bruda drag us down to his level."

"I know. Just a thought," Threebeard chuckled. "I just got off the GC a few tiks ago with Nic and he says there should be a good crowd of our supporters at the East Gate tomorrow. Apparently, a lot of people are appalled at what Rupra is trying to do and want to help us stop him."

"That's good news."

"It should be an interesting confrontation. I just hope it doesn't turn violent."

"The public enforcers should be out in force, so hopefully everyone will remain calm," Basset reasoned.

"Bruda may want it to turn violent particularly if it gives his supporters good cause to kill a few mutants and rhutz."

"You're probably right. I'll remind Nic to tell our supporters that it should be a peaceful demonstration, to expect the CPC to try to provoke them, but not to let it happen."

The following morning Bruda was shocked at the size of the crowds at East Gate Park. He'd expected the ranks of his supporters to have grown because of the news reports and the publicity he'd gotten out but he was not prepared to see so many Loyalist supporters picketing against the mutant evictions. He wondered how that had come about. He couldn't imagine anyone caring that much about the mutants.

A group of mutants jeered at him as he and Essyria walked by. He shook his head in revulsion and walked on to the group of tables he'd staked out the day before to be the CPC headquarters for addressing his followers and signing up new members. Chalke and Peeta were already there enrolling new recruits.

"So, it looks like we've got the attention of the city," Bruda said.

Peeta glanced around the crowd nodding. "You could say that. What did you do to get all these people out?"

"I talked Assemblyman Tash into introducing a bill this morning to evict the mutants and allow as many healthy humans into the city as possible. I guess now people are taking us more seriously."

"They have no choice," Essyria noted. "They have to be responsive to the people."

"I'm a little surprised to see the opposition so well organized," Bruda said.

"Yes, I was surprised too when I got here early this morning," Peeta agreed. "There was a large contingent of Loyalist organizers at work."

"Did you recognize anyone?" Bruda asked.

"No, but a three-chinned mutant seemed to be in charge."

"Threebeard," Bruda said. "I'd heard he was in town."

"There were a lot of rhutz and Seafolken as well."

Bruda sighed. "Well, I guess that's to be expected. They suspect we killed Eyeball and Misty. I guess that's got them riled up."

"Too bad we can't have that rhutz hunt today," Chalke said. "There are plenty of them around."

Bruda smiled wryly. "Maybe we can do better than that."

Everyone turned to Bruda expectantly. He told them his idea. Essyria's eyes widened.

The World Assembly was called to order by the Chairman, Ruskin Wallt. The Great Hall was filled to capacity with assemblymen, staff members, the media and hundreds of spectators. The Chairman announced that this was a special session called by Chancellor Chlovus Hock to address the current global crisis brought about by the super-volcanic eruptions occurring all over Tarizon and the devastation they were causing. An environmental expert from Central Authority was called first to report on the current situation throughout Tarizon. He told of thirteen volcanoes currently erupting all over the globe. He explained that these were not just ordinary eruptions but unprecedented eruptions coupled with devastating tremors, lava flows, tidal waves, and huge toxic emissions of volcanic ash. He then explained Central Authorities' response to the disasters but warned that its resources were already stretched and overtaxed.

"These cataclysmic events that we are experiencing today will impact Tarizon not just for the immediate future, but for cycles and cycles to come. Thousands, maybe millions will die, even if we mobilize all of our resources to deal with the effects of these tragic events."

The expert left the podium. "We are all greatly concerned about all these disasters happening all over Tarizon and we will take whatever time is necessary to deal with them in the days to come, but right now we face a crisis right here in the capital. As you know there are thousands of refugees lined up at our gates seeking entry into the dome. Unfortunately, we cannot facilitate everyone who seeks to come in. To address that problem, Assemblyman Tash has asked for the floor to introduce a bill. Assembly

Tash. You have the podium. Assemblyman Tash, a skinny, gray-haired man with a scowl on his face, walked up the stairs to the podium and looked out over the crowd.

"Mr. Chairman, members, and citizens of Tarizon. I hate to have to interrupt the Assembly's deliberations over these terrible disasters all over our planet, but as you know the World Assembly is responsible for the affairs of its capital city, Shisk. As the chairman explained, we are facing an immediate crisis that must be dealt with swiftly and effectively. Thousands of our citizens are pounding on our door seeking refuge from the toxic ash that is spewing out of Mt. Soni. The air quality outside the dome is so bad people are having to use breathers to avoid the deadly toxins in the air. But even with breathers they still must find clean water and food, all of which are in short supply with all traditional distribution outlets out of service.

"The tragic fact is we cannot protect and provide for everyone outside the dome. This is a disaster beyond any of our imaginations and could not have been anticipated. Accordingly, we must make difficult choices and tough decisions to protect as many citizens as possible. It is with this backdrop that I propose the Mutant Relocation Act for your consideration.

"Many cycles ago when Shisk was first built Central Authority sought to allow a cross section of the population of Tarizon into its capital city dome. Perhaps when this was done it made sense. The effects of the 8th World War were waning and Tarizon was gradually recovering from centuries of abuse, so many people were able to stay outside the dome and live in good health. But the situation today has changed. Now, since we cannot protect all of our population, we must decide who we should protect.

"I think it is obvious who those should be. The normal, healthy human population that will provide the greatest future for Tarizon.

There were screams of disapproval from the delegates and spectators in the crowd. The Chairman called for order.

"We cannot be selfish in this decision. We must consider what is best for Tarizon. Accordingly, this bill orders the immediate eviction from the city of all non-human life-forms and humans with abnormal defects or afflictions that might cause them to be a burden on the resources of the city. Once the mutants and others are gone we then will be able to allow in thousands of citizens who would otherwise die."

There were screams of protest. One delegate yelled, "You're advocating genocide, what's wrong with you?"

The Chairman stood up and glared at the delegate. "We will have order. You'll have your turn to speak."

Tash continued. "As you know many citizens have taken to the streets demanding this action. If you don't address this issue immediately and take swift action, I fear that the city will erupt into anarchy. As you know the people outside the dome can only survive for a few days, so this is not a matter that can be delayed. Thank you."

Tash left the podium and the Chairman stood up. The chair recognizes Assemblyman Als who has asked to speak on this issue. Basset Als climbed the stairs and went to the podium.

"Mr. Chairman, members, citizens of Tarizon. I can understand Assemblyman's Tash's concern for the refugees pounding at the gates of Shisk demanding they be let in. Of course, this is a tragic situation and something must be done, but his solution is not the answer. We must not panic and do something rash, something that will haunt us for the rest of our lives. We cannot let this disaster turn us away from the dictates of the Supreme Mandate. Whatever this body does to respond to the challenges that face Tarizon must be for the benefit of every sentient life-form equally.

"But talk doesn't solve problems in and of itself, so I have an alternative proposal that I think will be just as effective as what Assemblyman Tash has proposed, yet will not divide our people and undermine the very fabric of our society. As you all know during the 8th World War we faced a similar environmental disaster and faced the same situation we face today; too few resources to take care of all of those in need."

Basset reminded them of the Earth Shuttle and Orbital Hibernation programs. Many delegates nodded their memory of those difficult days.

"I have talked to Colonel Tomel of the TGA and he assures me that we can have twenty-five Earth shuttles parked outside Shisk within two days to take in at least 50,000 refugees. This should ease the situation immeasurably and avert the crisis we now face here in Shisk. He also assures me that many more Earth shuttles can be refitted and made available to other cities around Tarizon to provide housing with clean air, pure water, and nutritious food. Of course, this won't solve all our problems, but it is a much better solution than the Mutant Relocation Act, which I urge you to kill quickly as its introduction as a serious bill to consider is an outrage and a blemish on the history of this great body."

There was applause and shouts of approval. Assemblyman Tash looked dumbstruck. The Chairman called for order and asked if there was any more debate. Many hands were raised and the debate continued, but the general mood of the Assembly was clearly in favor of Basset Als proposal rather than the drastic provisions of the Mutant Relocation Act.

After Rupra Bruda informed the crowd of the introduction of the Mutant Relocation Act in the World Assembly and predicted its approval, he climbed down off his makeshift stage and began leading the march of the CPC members toward the East Gate. As they marched they chanted "Kick them out! Kick them out! ... Kick the filthy mutants out!"

At the same time the Loyalist crowd began marching from another location toward the East Gate putting the two groups on a collision course. Threebeard, Nic and Falling Star were leading the Loyalist group and Bruda, Chalke and Peeta were leading the CPC supporters. When the two groups got within a few strides of each other Tibor Raseen, his face covered by a mask, stepped out from the crowd and took a shot at Threebeard with his laser. The laser struck Threebeard in the shoulder and he fell to the ground. Falling Star immediately took after the assailant. Raseen ran to a jet bike parked nearby but before he could get on it and make his escape Falling Star pounced on him and began ripping him to shreds. At first the crowd looked on in shock but it wasn't but a few tiks before more guns and knives were drawn and the two groups were fighting in close combat.

Nic helped his brother to a picnic bench away from the melee and laid him upon it. He tore away Threebeard's shirt and examined the blackened wound. It smelled like smoldering flesh and was swelling rapidly. Two TGA medics arrived moments later and began cleaning the wound. His partner gave Threebeard an injection, plugged something into his wrist array and then helped his partner apply a dressing.

"We need to get him out of here. I've ordered a medicab. It should be here momentarily," a medic said.

"Is he going to be okay?" Nic asked worriedly.

"I don't know. His vitals are weak and that laser did some serious damages. You can ride with him to the casualty station."

"Thank you," Nic said giving Threebeard a concerned look.

Moments later the medicab landed nearby and the two medics loaded Threebeard on board, then left to tend to the next casualty of the East Gate riots. Nic climbed in solemnly beside Threebeard and the robot medicab took off. About ten loons later the medicab landed on the roof of the Northeast Casualty Station and took Threebeard inside. Nic watched as he was taken away and then went to the waiting room. Just as he sat down his wrist array beeped.

"Yes," he said.

"How is Threebeard?" a concerned Thom asked. "I just saw him shot on the VC."

"He's alive and fortunately received quick medical attention. The laser hit him in the shoulder, so I don't think any major organs were injured."

"Where are you now?"

"At the Northeast Casualty Center. I didn't see what happened to Falling Star. Is she okay?"

Thom hesitated. "No. After she killed the shooter someone picked up the shooter's laser and shot Falling Star. I'm afraid she is dead."

"Oh, my God! Have they identified the shooter?"

"Yes, a Tibor Raseen. He was a member of the CPC but Rupra Bruda is claiming he acted alone."

"Yeah. I bet. Was anyone else hurt?" Nic asked.

"Yes, seven others were killed by the rhutz who went on a rampage after Falling Star was killed. Many more were injured. It took the PEs twenty loons to restore order."

"What a nightmare," Nic said.

"Yes, and it was all for nothing. The World Assembly voted down the Mutant Relocation Act decisively."

"Oh. Thank God and Sandee."

"Let me know when you hear anything about Threebeard's condition. Basset and I are quite worried."

"Yes. You'll be my first call as soon as I hear anything."

Nic clicked off his wrist array and took a deep breath. He thought back to everything he and his brother had been through. He couldn't imagine life without Threebeard. He wasn't just a brother but a father and best friend. He had to survive. Not only did he and Artis need him but Tarizon needed him as well. God had given him such wonderful gifts to help him make Tarizon a better world. He couldn't let him die this way. Then a horrible thought came over him. What if there wasn't a God?

23

Unpopular Orders

Captain Vin Lugart, the commanding officer of Earth Shuttle Command, received the urgent call from Colonel Tomel asking about the availability of Earth shuttles for temporary duty as housing for refugees. He was aghast with the news that his shuttles would be used for such a purpose. He had hoped when he got the command that he would get an opportunity to travel to Earth but that hadn't happened. Of the 1,937 Earth shuttles in his inventory only about twenty-five were fully operational and ready for service. He had been ordered to place the others in long term storage as it wasn't anticipated that there would be a need for Earth travel in the immediate future.

Since he had been rather bored with this command he was glad, at least, that he finally would be doing something. He immediately gave orders to begin the process of bringing the fleet out of storage and getting the shuttles ready for use. Then he prepared to personally supervise the deployment of the twenty-five Earth shuttles that were flight worthy to Shisk. Although he could have assigned the task to underlings, he decided since this was just the first of many deployments of Earth shuttles around Tarizon, that he should make sure it was done quickly and efficiently.

Sixty-three kyloons after Captain Lugart got his orders the first shuttles began landing in a large field just outside Shisk. Fortunately, the shuttle's thrusters were self-contained and didn't require the burning of oxygen or elements in the atmosphere, so the ash-laden air had no impact in their proper functioning. An advance team had surveyed the location selected for the shuttles to land and sent back landing instructions for each of the shuttles. It was an incredible sight to see twenty-five huge Earth shuttles descend upon Shisk at one time and settle down just outside the city.

The crowds that had gathered at each of Shisk's eight gates now flocked to the area that the media had dubbed "Shuttle City." The TGA had cordoned off the area to prevent refugees from getting injured when the shuttles landed, but the sight of the shuttles landing caused near bedlam and the soldiers on duty had a difficult time containing the anxious crowds.

The shuttles had the capability of burrowing underground for the purpose of stealth when they landed on Earth, but it was determined not to be necessary for the purpose of handling refugees. When all the ships had landed Captain Lugart stepped out and surveyed the new city that had suddenly appeared out of nowhere. Looking to his left he saw a jet copter approaching from Shisk. It set down a hundred strides from his shuttle, officially known as *Tormenter*, and Assemblyman Basset Als stepped out and waved to the captain. Moments later Basset Als and his aides were whisked aboard *Tormenter* and followed the captain to the officer's conference room.

"I appreciate you responding so quickly," Basset said.

"Well, I'm glad I got the call. I've been rather bored babysitting a fleet of old ships."

"I can imagine. I was so relieved when I was told you had twenty-five ships flight-ready. I can't imagine what would have happened had that not been the case."

"Well, Central Command felt a few ships needed to be ready in case of an emergency, although I doubt this is the type of emergency they had in mind."

"No, probably not," Basset agreed. "So, I have brought you the Assembly's resolution. It instructs you to house as many of the refugees as you can. Unfortunately, there are many more than you will be able to accommodate, but do the best that you can."

"As I understand it, since the mutants were allowed to stay in the city that I am only to house unimpaired humans aboard the shuttles."

Bassett grimaced. "Well, I am afraid the Assembly did not address that issue. I fear had they tried the resolution would not have been passed."

"So, what am I to do?" Captain Lugart asked.

"Use your discretion. I know it's a terrible burden to thrust upon you, but it would take the Assembly several phases to agree on the criteria for selecting which refugees to be allowed on the shuttles."

"So, you are asking me to play God—selecting who shall live and who shall die?"

Basset shrugged. "Hopefully, it won't be that bad. We are looking into other ways to help the people outside the domes. One idea is to shut down all the transport tubes and turn them into housing."

Captain Lugart grimaced trying to picture how that would work. The tubes were protected from the environment but they didn't have a water filtration system since the traffic that flowed through them was self-contained. There were periodic fuel stations, restaurants and rest stops but not nearly enough to take care of any sizeable population. Plus, once the tubes were shut down to traffic there would be no way to supply the facilities that were in place.

"Well, I'll do the best I can," Lugart said.

As Bassett was leaving he introduced Captain Lugart to Lt. Lelfendix Fulty and told him he would be his liaison with the ground troops assigned to protect the city. When Basset left Lt. Fulty stayed behind and was given quarters on the ship to be close to Captain Lugart. Early the next morning Captain Lugart, Lt. Fulty, the ships executive officer, Lt. Sitch Elmst and the ship's medical officer met with the officers of the other twenty-four shuttles by video conference to discuss the criteria for the selection of refugees. Captain Lugart stood to address the group.

"Much to my chagrin, I have been given the task of deciding which refugees should be housed on our twenty-five shuttles. Since it is a matter that we could debate for kyloons on end, I have decided just to make the determination myself based on the information that is available to me. From what I can determine the idea of using Earth shuttles to house refugees came about to avoid having to deal with a proposal to evict the mutants from Shisk. That being the case it only makes sense that only non-mutated humans should be allowed on the shuttles.

"I know that this may be offensive to many of you, but I believe that was the spirit of the compromise that was made. Accordingly, only non-mutated humans will be allowed aboard the shuttles. The next criteria for selection shall be the state of each refugee's health. The shuttles are not hospitals. We have limited medical facilities, so we should avoid persons with serious medical issues. Our goal isn't saving lives, but preserving life on Tarizon for the long run. I know this may seem callous to some of you, but it is the reality that we face and we do not have time to debate it.

"Should anyone disagree with my orders you are free to contact your assemblyman and complain, but don't bother me with your concerns. They made the decision to lay this responsibility on me and I will gladly give the task back to them should you convince them they have made a mistake.

"Are there any questions?" Captain Lugart asked.

One of the shuttle captains beeped in indicating he wanted to ask a question. Captain Lugart opened a link for him to speak.

"Yes, Captain. Am I to understand that no mutants, rhutz, or Seafolken will be allowed aboard the shuttles?"

"That is correct," Captain Lugart said.

"Sir. Whereas I understand the order quite clearly there are many Seafolken who serve on this ship and who will be highly offended by the criteria that you have established."

Captain Lugart shrugged. "I am sure you are right, Captain. But like I said, no matter what decision I made on the issue, someone is sure to be unhappy. But the reality is, I have made my decision and I don't have the time or patience to deal with any dissent. So, tell your crews that if anyone fails to carry out my orders they will be subject to immediate court martial. Is that understood?"

"Yes, Captain."

When the meeting broke up Lt. Fulty forwarded Captain Lugart's orders to the TGA troops and they began processing them and delivering those that met Captain Lugart's criteria to the shuttles. It was a long tedious process and there was much bitterness among those who were sent away to fend for themselves in the toxic haze that hung over the desolate countryside. By morning the crowds around Shisk had disappeared for it was clear Shisk was closed to those from the outside and there were no vacancies in Shuttle City.

Once Threebeard had been placed in the capable hands of the doctors at the Northeast Casualty Center he was stabilized and sent into surgery. Two kyloons later he emerged with a rebuilt shoulder better than the natural one that had been destroyed by the laser. Nic was delighted when they rolled him into the recovery room where he had been allowed to wait. He rushed over to where they parked his bed.

"Hey, brother. How do you feel?"

Threebeard opened an eye and looked up at him. "Is that you, Nic?"

"Yes, how do you feel? You just came out of a long surgery."

"I feel like I've been run over by a zodillo."

"I bet. You've got a new shoulder. They say it will be twice as strong as the old one."

"Really. Good. That might come in handy someday. Say, what happened after I was shot?"

"Falling Star ripped apart the skutz who shot you."

"She did? Good. You'll have to thank her for me."

Nic's face dropped. "Well, I would if I could, but I'm afraid I won't be able to. She was killed."

"Oh. No. Don't tell me that."

"I'm sorry. There was a riot and many died."

"What about the bill? The Mutant Relocation Act?"

"It was defeated."

Threebeard let out a long sigh of relief. "Thank God and Sandee."

"But now we have another problem"

"What's that?"

"Captain Lugart who has been placed in charge of Shuttle City won't let mutants, humans in need of medical attention, or Seafolken onto the shuttles. It also seems Central Authority has abandoned any effort to save them."

"Well, I better get well so I can start building my mutant army. It sounds like we're going to need it."

Nic laughed. "You've got that right. Oh, Inquisitor Waldreen, is in the waiting room. He needs to talk to you."

Threebeard nodded. "Okay. Go ahead and send him in."

Nic left and returned a few moments later with Inquisitor Waldreen. Waldreen was a tall, slender man with a somber face.

"I am so glad to see that you are recovering," Waldreen said. "I've talked to the doctors and they say had the laser hit you a little lower you would have died instantly."

Threebeard smiled. "Yes, Sandee was with me. So, do you know who the shooter was?"

"Yes, a man named Tibor Raseen. He was a member of the CPC and apparently close to Rupra Bruda."

Threebeard shook his head. "Is there nothing Bruda won't do to get what he wants? The man has no conscience whatsoever."

"Obviously not. Anyway, Bruda was seen fleeing with a woman on a jet cycle right after the attack. There is a citywide alert out for his arrest but he may have left the city."

"How do you know?"

"His tracking chip went dark minutes before you were attacked and no one has seen him since."

"What about his companion?" Threebeard asked.

"We believe it is his mate and her tracking chip is not functioning either."

"What do her parents have to say about it?"

"They are very upset that she has disappeared and claim not to know anything."

"They may not. Bruda is a sly one and I doubt he'd tell anyone where he was going."

"That may be and with travel outside the dome nearly impossible, I can't promise there will be much of an effort to find him."

"In that case, am I free to leave the city? I need to get back to Tributon."

"Yes, but if we get lucky and find him we will need you to return to aid the public prosecutors."

Threebeard nodded. "Don't worry. I would be most pleased to respond to such a call, but I seriously doubt it will ever come."

Inquisitor Waldreen bowed slightly, then took his leave. Threebeard thought about Rupra Bruda and wondered where he might have gone. Unfortunately, with Tarizon in chaos he knew he could have gone just about anywhere outside the dome and easily disappeared. He thought about getting on the computer and searching the TGN for any sign of him, but he knew that would not likely be fruitful. Finally, he decided to forget about Rupra Bruda. As long as he was on the run he'd not likely be a threat. At least he hoped that were the case.

In the next few days Threebeard had recovered enough so he could travel back to Tributon. Since all but emergency air traffic had been grounded he was forced to take a freighter from Shisk to Behn Lat. With most of the volcanoes around the globe still erupting a thick shroud of volcanic ash hung over Tarizon. The ash was so thick Tarizon was plunged into a state of perpetual darkness. It took Threebeard nearly a week to get to Behn Lat, so he took advantage of the time to get a lot of sleep and accelerate his recovery. When he finally made it back to the Mighty Jolly he was anxious to start gathering together his troops as he knew for sure now that civil war was inevitable.

As soon as Threebeard was shot, Rupra Bruda and Essyria got on their jet cycles and made their escape. They knew if they delayed they'd be drawn into the riot. Bruda saw Falling Star attack his friend Raseen but knew he could do nothing about it. He cursed himself for underestimating again how quickly the rhutz would counterattack. A wave of guilt washed over him for Raseen's death but it quickly vanished as his and Essyria's safety became a more pressing issue. He had expected Raseen to escape after the assassination attempt making it impossible for the PE to determine who was responsible, but once Raseen was identified as one of his friends, an arrest warrant would be issued for all of them. After they were far away from the East Gate they stopped to talk and consider their options.

"I told you killing Threebeard was too dangerous," Essyria spat. "But you wouldn't listen to me."

Bruda looked back toward the East Gate with a worried look on his face. "That idiot just stood there for ten tiks after he made his shot. If he hadn't delayed he'd have gotten to his jet cycle and made a clean escape."

"I think he wanted to see if Threebeard was dead," Essyria replied.

"Yeah, well he could have read about it in the newspaper rather than compromising all of us. The incompetent skutz!"

"So, what do we do now?"

"We don't have any choice but to leave the city," Bruda replied. "There were too many witnesses and the PE is going to have to nail somebody for the riots."

Essyria sighed. "Where can we go? The air is toxic outside the city and the ash so thick on the ground that it is difficult to travel."

"That's actually good. Once we leave the city no one will follow us. We just need a good ATV with an air filtration system."

"My father has several," Essyria advised. "They are solar powered but they have a CNG backup propulsion system."

"CNG?"

"Compressed natural gas. It's a rather archaic system but it works. We can bring along extra tanks."

"How will your father feel about that?" Bruda asked.

"He won't mind if we borrow one to avoid capture and the humiliation to the family if I went on trial."

"I suppose not. Where are they?"

Essyria started her jet cycle. "Just follow me."

Essyria took off and led them to the northwest part of the city where her father had his business. It wasn't a workday so the office and warehouse was closed. They drove around the back, parked their jet cycles out of view and then went in the side door of the warehouse. Essyria looked into the retinal scanner, the keypad on the door flashed green, and the door unlocked. Inside, there was an assortment of construction vehicles, tractors, and three ATVs. Essyria pointed to them and they rushed over.

"Okay, I'll go get the keys out of the office. There's food and bottled water in the closet," she said pointing to a door not too far away.

Rupra nodded and went to the closet and opened it. He was pleasantly surprised at the good stock of provisions available to them and began picking out what he thought they would need. Essyria found the keys in the office and wrote her father a note.

Father,

We borrowed an ATV. You'll understand why when you listen to the news. Don't worry about us, we will be okay and will return your vehicle in good condition. Just need to lay low for a while.

Love,

Essyria.

Essyria went back into the warehouse and helped Rupra finish loading the ATV. Soon they were on the road heading toward the Northwest gate. As they approached they wondered if anyone would try to stop them. It had been less than two kyloons since the riot had started so they reasoned it was unlikely anybody would be looking for them yet, but they couldn't be absolutely sure so they approached the gate cautiously. A guard waved for them to stop as they drove through. Rupra swallowed hard as the window rolled down.

"You're not going to leave the city, are you?" the guard asked. "The air is toxic and travel is extremely dangerous."

Rupra looked at Essyria. "Ah, my brother is stranded in Lilial," Essyria said. "He was visiting a friend and we're going to get him and bring him back."

The guard nodded. "Well, I hope you have plenty of food and fresh water. I'm not sure you'll be able to find fuel either."

"My brother knows where we can get fuel to make the trip back," Essyria assured him. "We'll be okay."

The guard shrugged. "Okay, then. Good luck."

Rupra accelerated the ATV out of the gate and gradually built up speed. The ash was falling so hard visibility was but a few feet, so he couldn't go very fast for fear of hitting something.

"Is that where we are going?" Rupra asked. "Lilial?"

"No. That's just the next big city. Actually, we should go to Dangali. My parents have a cabin up there. It's always kept fully stocked with food and has a deep water well. It's one of the most beautiful places on the planet, right on the edge of the Weeping Mountains. It will be an excellent hiding place as long as nobody is traveling. Ordinarily it's crowded with tourists but I don't think that will be the case now."

"No. That sounds fine," Bruda said smiling. "I'm sure we'll find ways to occupy our time."

Essyria smiled back wryly. "Yes, I imagine that won't be a problem."

Fortunately, there was very little traffic on the roads but even so as night fell traveling became quite treacherous. The light from the ATV's big front lamps reflected off the falling ash making it impossible to see more than a few feet ahead. The fact that the ash now was several feet deep also made it hard to follow the road and several times Bruda felt the big ATV straying off the pavement. Finally, just before dawn, Essyria pointed to a sign informing them that they were but ten kylods from Dangali.

"Okay, just ahead there will be another road called the Weeping Mountains Highway. We will need to take it. Our cabin is about five kylods up that road."

Bruda nodded and took the turnoff. Half a kyloon later they pulled onto a small feeder road and drove up to the cabin. Although Essyria had called it a cabin it was quite large and luxurious. Bruda smiled when he saw it and looked over at Essyria.

"Very nice," Bruda said. "Are you sure nobody will be here?"

"Yes. The caretaker came back to the city when the volcano began to erupt."

They drove down the long driveway and Essyria pointed to a large garage. "We should park the ATV inside out of sight."

She got out, walked to a control panel next to the garage, and peered into a retinal scanner. The door began to rise and as soon as it was opened Bruda pulled the ATV inside. He got out and was immediately embraced by Essyria.

"We made it! Thank God."

Bruda lifted her off her feet and swung her around. "Yes, we did. Now, let's go inside, take a shower and see if your father has any tekari."

"Oh, don't worry about that," Essyria replied. "This is a vacation home. It's well stocked for partying."

They went inside the lavish cabin and headed straight for the shower. Soon they were washing each other's body under a steady stream of hot steamy water. As soon as they felt clean again the fear and anxieties that had consumed them since their narrow escape from the angry mobs melted away into passionate lovemaking. When they were spent they went to the kitchen to find something to eat. While Essyria was fixing them a sandwich Bruda turned on the VC. A news report was in progress. A view of Mt. Soni's continuing eruption was on the screen.

"There is no sign of the massive eruption ending anytime soon. Scientists fear the eruption could last for a phase or more given the fact that Mt. Soni's eruption is connected to numerous other volcanic eruptions all over Tarizon. Reports are coming in that Mt. Drala in Rour is now erupting as well as Mt. Makuta and Mt. Rumbia in Merria. Central Authority is urging all citizens to stay off the highways, stay indoors, and keep windows and doors closed to prevent the invasion of the toxic gases being emitted by the volcanoes."

The view shifted to Shisk's massive dome. It glowed in the darkness with bolts of dry lightning striking the ground about it. Essyria came up next to Bruda and handed him a bottle of Tekari.

"What do you think is going to happen? Is the world coming to an end?"

Bruda turned and looked at Essyria thoughtfully. "No. Not the end, but a new beginning."

Essyria grimaced not sure she wanted an explanation of that remark. She was tired and in no mood for politics. All she wanted to do was go to bed and sleep for a phase.

The reporter continued. "In Shisk rioting has ended at the East Gate as shuttles began landing to house the crowds trying to enter the city. The TGA is coordinating population of what is being called *Shuttle City* and the process is expected to take several days. Although only about 50,000 citizens will be able to board the shuttles more than 1900 more shuttles are being readied for service in the near future.

"A citywide alert has been issued by the public enforcer's office for five persons thought to be responsible for the attempted murder of the mutant known as Threebeard. Threebeard is the proprietor of the popular Mighty Jolly tavern chain with taverns in Lemaine Shane as well as Turvin. Although the shooter, Tibor Raseen was slain by a rhutz shortly after the attack, his suspected co-conspirators got away."

Five pictures displayed on the screen. "They are Rupra Bruda, Essyria Tomaso, Peeta Rufalus, Allie Chalke and Blinh Bligh. A spokesman for the Tomaso family indicates that Essyria Tomaso was secretly mated recently to Rupra Bruda and may be an unwitting accomplice. A global alert has been issued for detention of these fugitives and anyone who has knowledge of their whereabouts are urged to contact your local PE."

"Skutz!" Bruda said angrily. "Tibor was such an idiot. I should have killed Threebeard myself."

"Don't worry about it tonight. There is nothing you can do about it now. Let's just go to bed. Tomorrow is another day."

Bruda nodded. He'd go to bed but he doubted he could sleep. All his plans had been upset due to one idiot's blunder. He shook his head in disgust and vowed he'd never let that happen again.

24

Isle of Muhl

The big transport plane took off from Gallion headed for Pegaport, the TGA training center on the Isle of Muhl. It was the first of twenty planes bringing five thousand mutants for their basic training. Threebeard unfurled the map Colonel Zitor had given him. He wondered if Muhl was manmade. Except for its jagged and jittery form, it was almost a perfect square, 257 kylods in length and 258.1 kylods in width. The western third of the island was separated north to south by the Drogal Mountains climbing to a modest 3,254 feet at its highest peak. The Pegaport Training Center at Muhl was located on the southwest corner of the island, west of the Drogal Mountains. To the south lay the Southern Sea and to the northwest the Yulev River. The Yulev River looked to be quite wide and there appeared to be but one bridge across it isolating the base from the rest of the island.

On the bottom left corner of the map was the layout of the training facility itself. It lay in the shape of a triangle with a large airstrip and athletic field to the north. Along the river were hangars, fuel tanks, and the enlisted men's barracks. At the foot of the Drogal Mountains were an armory, officers' quarters, and endurance course. A road wound through the center of the base making a large circle, within which lay the base headquarters, the nutrition center, classrooms, a detention center, and parade ground. A wide beach separated the base from the Southern Sea. Eight guard towers were situated along the river and the beach, but there were no towers along the foothills of the Drogal Mountains.

Threebeard remembered reading about the Drogals, the big, feathery birds that were native to the Drogal Mountains. Its natural prey were mountain rats, dirkbirds, and range deer but if it was hungry or felt threatened it might eat humans as well. The mountains contained rich mineral deposits and before WW VIII mining had been attempted. But working the mines was dangerous business with the Drogals on the prowl. Eventually the Drogals won the battle and the mines were shut down. As the plane began to make its descent a second lieutenant came by and sat next to Threebeard.

"You must be Threebeard," the lieutenant said.

Threebeard looked up from his map and nodded. "Yes."

"I am Lt. Marsen. Colonel Zitor asked me to make contact with you and keep him apprised of your progress."

"Oh. Excellent. I was hoping I would be able to stay in contact with the colonel."

"You won't be able to talk to him directly but you can send messages through me."

"Good," Threebeard said.

"Anyway, I just wanted to give you a little orientation before we land. There are some things you should know about."

"Okay. Like what?"

"Pegaport is a high motivation facility. The people brought here are usually conscripts who have little desire to be soldiers."

"But we all volunteered," Threebeard protested.

"I know. Colonel Zitor tried to get them to send you to Dalo but Central Command thought mutants would need special attention."

"Great," Threebeard spat. "So, what do we have to look forward to?"

"Well, the drill sergeants at Pegaport are tough and mean. They think they have to be to keep the conscripts motivated. Most of recruits who graduate will be foot soldiers. They have to be in top physical condition, so a special emphasis is put on PT. Long morning runs, rigorous weight training, and strict discipline is the norm. Those who can't maintain the pace or follow the rigid rules end up in Hell Squad."

"Hell squad?" Threebeard repeated warily.

"Yes. In Hell Squad recruits are treated differently. Central Command believes that they have to be given special motivation to break their independent spirit. It's their philosophy that there is no room for independent thinkers—second guessers—in the TGA. Orders must be carried out quickly and precisely as given—command thinks, soldiers obey."

Threebeard felt his stomach tightening. He wished he had been given this orientation back at Gallion where he could have changed his mind about becoming a soldier.

Lt. Marsen continued, "Motivation is dished out in a number of interesting ways in Hell Squad—stick therapy, food or sleep deprivation, buzz gun motivation, or, if all else fails, electric implants. Stick therapy is pretty simple. The drill sergeant carries around a long white stick made of a hard rubber. It has a nasty sting and has been known to cause permanent scaring. It's used across a candidate's arm or back if he's not cooperating."

Threebeard squirmed nervously, not particularly liking what he was hearing.

"Food or sleep deprivation is employed in cases where candidates have a high pain tolerance, or actually enjoy pain. It's pretty self-explanatory. Meals and kyloons of sleep are taken away for bad behavior. Recruits who need food and sleep tend to become much more cooperative. But even that is not enough for some. The buzz gun is harmless but very painful—ten times the pain of the stick. Electric implants allow the drill sergeant to impose pain from a distance for substandard performance or disobedience."

Threebeard swallowed hard. He was becoming angry at what lay ahead. "So, why are you telling me this. Are you trying to scare me?"

"No. I just want you to know what you are up against so you'll be careful. Do exactly what your drill sergeant says and don't give him any reason to discipline you. Try to be inconspicuous."

"Inconspicuous is a little difficult when you have three chins," Threebeard noted bitterly.

Lt. Marsen laughed tentatively. "Right. Well, luckily with an entire class of mutants you won't stick out as much. Anyway, your training here will be less than a phase, then you will be on to Pogo Island for officer training. You'll be treated much better there."

Threebeard sighed deeply. "Right. If I live that long."

After Threebeard left for TGA training, Artis went back to the Ural Desert to see how the nanomite city had fared in the wake of the quakes and Mt. Alabash's eruption. It had been six phases since the volcanoes on Tarizon finally became silent and the roads had been repaired enough for travel. The skies were still a dark gray and very little sunlight penetrated the shroud of ash surrounding Tarizon. Artis felt sad looking out over the ugly gray landscape remembering how magnificent it had been on her last trip. She was also fearful as to what she would find when she reached the site of the nanomite city. *Could it have survived the quakes and the lava?* She feared the worst.

Once they got off the main highway locating the nanomite city was extremely difficult as all GPS navigation was down due to the general power outage over the entire planet. When Central Authority decided to suspend nuclear power, and rely primarily on solar energy it had seemed like a prudent idea. Solar energy was cheap, clean, and there was an inexhaustible supply, or so they thought. Fortunately, Giant had a good sense of direction and eventually got them to their destination.

"I believe our camp was right over there on that bluff. We'll be able to tell for sure if our monitoring station is still intact."

Before they had left, Giant had set up a camera to monitor the nanomite city until they got back. He had done it hastily so he wasn't sure if it had survived. The camera was usually solar powered but it had a battery backup attached that was good for about ten kyloons. He thought that would have been long enough to capture the fate of the city, but he wasn't sure.

"Over there," Giant said, "pointing to a four-foot square box sitting precariously on the edge of the bluff."

Artis looked over at where the nanomite city had been and her heart sank. There was nothing there. The nanomite city had vanished!

"Where did it go?" Artis moaned. "How could it just disappear?"

Giant shook his head. "I don't know. Hopefully, the camera will tell us."

Giant rushed over to the monitoring station and examined the camera inside. "It looks okay. After we set up camp we can take a look at the footage and see what happened."

Artis closed her eyes and tried to focus on the nanomites. If there were any alive she thought perhaps she could make contact with them. Feeling nothing, she walked over to where she remembered the nanomite city to be and tried again. After a kyloon without success she went back to where Giant and Faruk had just finished setting up camp.

"Give me a minute and we can look at the footage," Giant said when he saw Artis walking grimly into camp.

Artis nodded. She wasn't sure she wanted to see the demise of nanomites that it had taken her so long to befriend. She felt sick inside, but she knew Threebeard would want to know for sure what had happened. "Okay. I'm going to get me a tekari. You want one?"

Giant nodded. "Sure. We'll probably need it."

Giant typed in the commands to view the tape in fast forward mode as they couldn't possibly watch it in real time. The view showed the city motionless in its splendor. Then suddenly the ash began falling making it difficult to see anything. A little while later the ground shook violently and when it stopped a crack down the middle of the city could be seen. Ash continued to fall but Artis and her friends could see the nanomites fighting back.

"What's that?" Faruk asked.

"It looks like they are building a wall?" Artis replied.

"A wall for what?" Giant asked.

But before anyone could comment the sky turned red and they got their answer as the lava hit the nanomite wall. Artis gasped in shock and wonder at how the wall diverted the lava around the nanomite city. They all laughed and cried tears of joy as the rains came and the nanomite city had somehow survived. But they knew the story wasn't over and waited for the final chapter. It came quickly. Just as the city seemed miraculously to have been repaired, the ground shook violently.

"Oh, my God! Another tremor!" Faruk gasped.

Artis leaned forward willing the tremor to end but instead the nanomite city collapsed and disappeared.

Giant stood up abruptly. "What happened?" Giant asked. "Where did it go?"

"The earth swallowed it," Artis replied dejectedly.

They watched in silence as the quake stilled and the camera continued to shoot at the spot where the nanomite city had been. Then suddenly clouds began to build and it got very dark. An ominous feeling came over Artis as torrential rains came followed by a flash flood that poured into the sinkhole that had swallowed the nanomite city. Artis had been hopeful that some of the nanomites had survived the quake, but she knew there'd be no survivors of the flash flood.

Giant shut off the video. "Skutz! I can't believe after all they went through, God would let them die that way."

Artis looked at Giant. She loved God but shared Giant's dismay at how He would let tragedies like this happen. She wondered what purpose God had for all the volcanic eruptions and the destruction of Tarizon's atmosphere. Hadn't man done enough with its nuclear wars? Was this God's punishment for all the evil in the world? If so, why punish the good along with the evil? Why destroy innocent nanomites who only sought to live in peace? She got up and gazed out over the landscape and saw the nanomite city in her mind's eye. *Thank God, I still have the replica.* Finally, she decided she better let Threebeard know what happened. She closed her eyes and established a link.

"Brother."

"Yes, Artis. I hope you have good news."

"I'm afraid I don't."

She explained what had happened to the nanomites.

"I feared that would be their fate. They were too close to the volcano."

"Do you think there are any nanomites that have survived?" Artis asked.

"Hopefully. I believe there are other desert locations where they live. You will have to search for them. We can't let all our hard work go to waste. The nanomites are a wondrous life-form and we must make contact with them again and help them recover from this terrible disaster.

"I will search the corners of the world until I find more of them," Artis promised him.

"Good. I wish I could help you but I will be tied up here in Muhl for some time. Then I have to go to Pogo Island."

"Why Pogo Island?"

"Colonel Zitor has arranged for twenty of us to go to officer training school. It's critical that we get this training so we can train officers for the mutant army."

"How is your training so far?" Artis thought.

"Incredibly demanding. Our drill sergeant, Sgt. Greer, obviously wasn't happy being assigned to a mutant squad and he's taking it out of us. I think he wants us to fail."

"Oh, I'm so sorry. I've been worried about you."

"I'll survive, but there are some in the squad who may not. I have tried to help them but I can't be seen doing it or I'll get in trouble."

"I'll pray for you, brother," Artis said.

"I'll do the same for your quest to find nanomites who have survived the tremors and volcanos."

Artis broke the link and went back to camp. She found Faruk and Giant sitting where she'd left them and looking rather forlorn.

"All right. Our next task is to find any nanomites who have survived. We'll stay here a few days in case there are any here. If we don't find any we will have to search other deserts for them."

"Other deserts?"

"Yes, nanomites have been seen in the Duesi Desert in Synclare and Rezoon Desert in Darkland. Hopefully, some will have survived."

That night before Artis went to bed she tried to connect with the nanomites but got no response. After finally giving up she went to bed but had trouble falling asleep. Finally, when she dropped into a shallow slumber she began to dream about the nanomites and the memories they had shared with her. In the middle of the night she woke up, tears flowing down her cheeks. She wondered if she'd ever share their thoughts again. She feared she wouldn't.

Threebeard's mental clock woke him up just a few loons before the lights would come on in the barracks. He dropped to the floor and then began shaking beds to wake everyone up. Satisfied everyone was awake and preparing for the drill sergeant's arrival, Threebeard quickly dressed, made this bed, and took a quick trip to the relief station. As he was walking back to his bunk the lights came on and to his horror he noticed Gin Slitter was still sound asleep. He remembered shaking him and telling him to get up, but apparently it hadn't worked. Threebeard rushed over and began shaking him again.

"Gin! Get up. Come on. You only have a few tiks!" Threebeard said.

Gin blinked a few times. Noticed the lights on and jumped out of his bunk.

"Get dressed. I'll take care of your bunk."

It was strictly forbidden for one recruit to do another recruit's job, but Threebeard didn't care. He wanted all his men to survive boot camp, and he would do whatever it took to ensure they would. The door to the drill sergeant's quarters opened and Sgt. Greer stepped out with a malicious smile on his face. He quickly scanned the room until his eyes fell on Threebeard helping Gin make his bunk. He walked over briskly and stood before them.

"So, is Gin incapable of making his own bunk?" Sgt. Greer spat.

Threebeard turned around and stood at attention. Gin, who had very large, barrel-shaped arms, pulled on his last boot and straightened up. Sgt. Greer looked at him in disgust.

"No, sir. He is quite capable," Threebeard replied.

"Then why are you making it for him?"

"Ah. Just helping him out, Sergeant."

Sgt. Greer looked at his watch. "Well, could it be that he had trouble getting up this morning?"

"Ah. I don't know, Sergeant. I just noticed he was running late and decided to pitch in and help."

The Sergeant got up close and looked in Gin's eyes. "You have trouble getting up, you little slubdub? Are we working you too hard? You going to complain to your mommy?"

Gin leaned back in terror. Stuttering, he replied. "N...n...no, sergeant. Just ov...ah...ov...overslept. Sorry."

"Sorry? You're sorry?" the sergeant taunted. "When you are a soldier, sorry is not good enough!"

"Yes, Sergeant. It won't happen again."

The sergeant turned back to Threebeard. "As for you. I've had my eye on you from the very first day you arrived. Who the skutz do you think you are? Getting up early and rousting everyone out of their bed before the lights come on? Reminding everyone of what they're supposed to be doing? Keeping everyone out of trouble. What are you trying to do? Take my job?"

Threebeard shook his head. "No, sergeant. Just trying to keep everything running smoothly."

"Well. That's not your job! That's my job. So, since there isn't room for two drill sergeants in this squad, I'm going to ship you out somewhere where your talents might actually be appreciated."

Threebeard frowned. He didn't like where this was going but he didn't know what he could do about it.,

"Where would that be, sergeant?" he asked warily.

The sergeant laughed. "That would be Hell Squad, son. I'm shipping you out to Hell Squad and I've already talked to Hell Squad's drill sergeant, Sgt. Zolt Hovic, and he can't wait to see your sorry ass. He said he's been wanting to go on holiday."

Threebeard swallowed hard. Somehow, he didn't think Sgt. Hovic would be going on holiday.

After studying her brother's research on the nanomites, Artis decided that the Duesi Desert in south central Synclare was her best bet for finding living nanomites. Numerous formations had been spotted there and they were far enough away from the two closest volcanoes, Mt. Pohl and Mt. Rumbia, that they wouldn't have been destroyed by lava flow. Fearing that the nanomite life-form might be in danger, Artis, Giant and Faruk took a freighter from Bama Uza in southern Tributon to Keba in southern Tuht. From Keba they acquired an ATV from the local cell there and drove to Roshaunda, the capital of Synclare which sat just fifty kylods southwest of the Duesi Desert. There they picked up a local guide named Phen Cantis.

Roshaunda was situated in a dense forest just north of the Weeping Mountains. Usually the landscape in this area was breathtaking, but Artis and her companions found it bleak and depressing. Six phases without the sun and a hard coating of ash had turned the dense green forest into a dismally gray wasteland. Artis couldn't tell for sure, but it appeared fires must have rampaged through the area leaving nothing but devastation in their path. Whereas, normally a forest fire would only cause temporary damage and trees and vegetation would immediately begin to emerge from the fire's ashes, this hadn't been the case this time. Without the sun's rays nothing could grow and the destruction appeared to be permanent.

Artis hoped this wasn't the case. Threebeard had told her that he believed Tarizon's atmosphere would gradually heal itself over time, but it may take twenty cycles for that to happen. As they drove through the dismal landscape she hoped it wouldn't take that long.

The Duesi Desert was no more picturesque than the Weeping

Mountains. Whereas the sky was lighter and visibility much better, the endless gray landscape made Artis long for color. She remembered the Ural Desert the first time she had visited it, and tried to imagine what the landscape around her would have looked like had it not been for the volcanoes wreaking havoc on the world. She wished for a yellow flower of a green cactus, but saw nothing but depressing black and gray. When they finally reached their destination, a stark valley where nanomite formations had been reported just two cycles earlier, Artis was depressed and not optimistic they would find anything living in the desolate valley where they found themselves. Nevertheless, they set up camp and started searching for anything that remotely resembled a nanomite formation.

Hell wasn't a strong enough term for what Threebeard found in his new squad. They were a diverse group of recruits who now had one thing in common, they were all terrified of Sgt. Hovic. Most of them had already felt the sting of his white rubber stick and many had already spent time in solitary confinement. Threebeard was appalled at the tactics being employed and one day made the mistake of complaining about it.

Sgt. Hovic had been picking on a mutant named Tuckh who was a slow runner due to his feet being slightly out of alignment. Threebeard knew he was running as best he could but Sgt. Hovic insisted his problem was laziness. One afternoon Sgt. Hovic decided to place a motivation collar on Tuckh. It was the first time such a training tool had been employed and Threebeard was sick watching the sergeant placing it around his neck. Once it was in place he ordered Tuckh to run five laps. Tuckh tried to comply but every time the sergeant thought he wasn't running fast enough he'd give Tuckh a little jolt. Finally, Threebeard couldn't take it anymore.

"Sergeant. Stop doing that. It won't help. He's slow because he has a congenital defect in his feet. Haven't you seen it?"

Sgt. Hovic glared at Threebeard. "Did I ask for your opinion, soldier?" Sgt. Hovic spat.

"No, but—"

"Shut your mouth then, you dirty slubdub! If I want your opinion I'll ask for it. If he's been assigned to this platoon then Central Command must think he's physically fit and who am I to second guess them?"

"Just look at his feet," Threebeard pressed. "They are not fit for running with any speed."

"I said shut up!" Sgt. Hovic snarled. "You don't get to provide input unless I ask for it."

"It's just that this man has volunteered for service to Tarizon and this is the way he is treated?"

Sgt. Hovic tapped his wrist array and spoke into the microphone. "Corporal Leether, get out here at once. I need you to escort someone to the tank."

A jolt of fear stabbed Threebeard. He'd read about the sensory deprivation chamber and how mentally debilitating it could be. The tank was the last place he wanted to be taken, but he knew resistance would be futile as the sergeant could summon the MPs with his wrist array. His stomach was in knots when Corporal Leether came to get him. He took deep breaths trying to calm himself. He thought perhaps it wouldn't be so bad in the tank since he knew what to expect and could take counter measures to keep from going mad. Still, he was tempted to squeeze Corporal Leether's lungs with his third hand until he passed out and then escape into the Drogal Mountains. Unfortunately, that would end all hope of raising a mutant army and, therefore, wasn't an option. He'd simply have to survive the tank somehow. He wondered how long Sgt. Hovic would keep him there.

The tank was in a bunker below ground. Several platoons were marched to the bunker so they could watch the insubordinate recruit being led inside to the tank. Just watching a fellow recruit being subjected to the sensory deprivation chamber was a tremendous deterrent to future disobedience, so all of the drill sergeants brought their platoons to watch as often as possible. Threebeard noticed a group of officers loitering around with bemused expressions on their faces. He couldn't imagine how anyone could get a thrill out of torturing another human being. He cursed the sadistic group of skutz and vowed someday to wipe the smiles off their faces.

Once inside Threebeard was stripped naked, dropped into the tank of green slimy water, and secured so his head was barely above the water line. He had no idea how long he was to be subjected to this torture as Sgt. Hovic hadn't bothered to tell him. He tried to relax and suppress the terror that was stabbing at him. He knew from his study of the sensory deprivation tanks that he was in no physical danger. This was mental torture so all he had to do was go to another place in his mind and ignore what was happening to him. Just as he was starting to feel a little better the chamber door was rudely closed and Threebeard was plunged into total darkness.

He let out a gasp and struggled to get free but this movement just caused the water to slap over his face and get into his nose and mouth. He swallowed a mouthful of the green gunk and nearly choked to death. When he finally quit coughing he held his breath until the water calmed. He didn't dare move after that and resolved not to ingest anymore of the wretched liquid. *Get hold of yourself. Calm down. Relax.* He told himself.

After finally calming down he thought about Artis and tried to connect with her but felt nothing. *How could that be? I've always been able to connect with Artis no matter how far away she was.* He finally realized the tank must be made of lead or some other dense substance that could not be penetrated. A sick feeling came over him knowing that he was isolated from the rest of the world. Then he wondered if somehow the Purists had found out about the Loyalist plan to build a mutant army and decided to kill the one responsible for its creation. Depression consumed him and he wondered if he'd ever again see the light of day.

Artis and her companions searched every square foot of the valley where the nanomites had been seen but found nothing. Between the tremors and the ash all signs of the nanomites had vanished. After traveling to the other sites in the Duesi Desert with similar results, she decided to contact Threebeard and see if he had any ideas. But, when she tried to make contact with him she felt nothing. Alarmed she thought about Nic and immediately made contact.

"Nic. Have you talked to your brother lately?"

"No. Why? What's wrong?"

"I've tried to make contact with him but I can't do it. I wonder if anything has happened to him."

"I don't think he's in any danger. Colonel Zitor assured him he would be safe. He said the training would be tough, but nothing he couldn't handle."

"Well, something is wrong. I've always been able to connect with him. I'm scared."

"Okay, sis. I'll try to connect with him. If I can't I'll call Colonel Zitor and have him check on him."

"Good. Thank you. I'll feel better once I know he is okay."

"So, how is your search coming?" Nic asked.

"Not good," Artis thought. *"There is no sign of them here in Synclare."*

"What are you going to do?"

"Go on to the Rezoon desert, I guess."

"That's a long way," Nic noted.

"I know, but we can't let an entire life-form be destroyed. We have to help them survive somehow."

"Right. Is there anything I can do?"

"No. We're going to travel to Rallis on the coast of Merria and take a freighter to Pulugas in Darkland. It will probably take us fifteen days to get there."

"Well, be safe. I hope you find the nanomites."

"I hope so too. I can't believe they are all dead. How could that be."

"Well, there is no guarantee that any of us will survive. On the news they say twenty million humans have already died."

"Oh, dear God. How could that be?"

"Be careful of marauders. There are a lot of desperate people out there trying to survive."

"Yes, so I have heard. So far, we've managed to avoid them."

"Keep in touch. I'll pray your quest is fruitful."

"Thank you, brother. I love you."

"Me too. Be safe."

Artis opened her eyes and looked around. She felt better having talked to Nic but still was worried about Threebeard. She couldn't imagine what could have happened to him. The next day they left Synclare and traveled to the coast for their voyage to Pulugas in Darkland. She'd heard that Azollo had been hit particularly hard by tremors, volcanic eruptions, tsunamis and wildfires. This was to be expected since there were eight volcanoes currently erupting on the continent. So, she wasn't optimistic about finding any nanomites alive there, but she still had to try.

25

Accidental Death

Threebeard lost track of time in the tank. He didn't know if he'd been there one day or three. There was no change in his environment—just complete and absolute darkness and silence. He felt cold and wet. His muscles ached from lack of use and being held in one position for countless kyloons. He had an urge to flex them and move around but knew he couldn't do that because the churning of the water could easily drown him. It was pure mental torture and had been much harder to endure than he could have ever imagined.

Finally, he was startled by a blinding light. He closed his eyes tightly trying to fend off the painful rays of the sun. He felt arms rudely pulling him out of the tank but he didn't dare open his eyes for fear of permanent injury to them. He was pulled onto a metal platform where he fell onto his side being too weak to stand up. They gave him a towel to dry himself and his clothes. After he'd struggled back into his uniform, they helped him climb the stairs out of the hold. The warm air felt wonderful until he took a breath of it and nearly gagged.

"Give him a breather," a voice commanded.

A breather was put over his face and he took several deep breaths.

"Threebeard, are you okay?" a voice said.

Threebeard tried to speak but nothing came out. He tried again. "I don't know. I'm still alive, I think."

"Yes, you are," the voice agreed.

Threebeard gradually opened one eye and was delighted to see a hazy Lt. Marsen. "How long was I in there?" he asked.

"Eight days, I'm afraid. That's quite a bit longer than usual."

Threebeard opened his other eye half way, looked around and noticed he and Lt. Marsen were alone. "So, why so long?"

Lt. Marsen swallowed hard. "I'm sorry to say your identity has been compromised. The commandant knows who you are. He ordered the extra five days."

"Who's the commandant?" Threebeard asked. "And how did he find out who I was?"

"Captain Videl Lai is his name. He's not sympathetic to mutants or any non-human life-form. He was vehemently against allowing the mutants into the TGA. When he found out the leader of the mutants had made it into Hell Squad he was, needless to say, delighted."

"Yeah. I bet. So, what now?"

Lt. Marsen sighed. "I'm afraid you'll have to go back to the squad now. I'm to deliver you there at 1700 kyloons. The squad is in firearms training: lasers and rifles."

"Good. That's the kind of training I need. Lead the way."

"You sure you're up to it? I could take you to the casualty department for a checkup before we report."

"No. I'm sure I'm already way behind the other recruits. I don't want to miss any more training."

Lt. Marsen led him to classroom B22 where his platoon was listening to a lecture on the armaments the recruits would be learning to use. Sgt. Hovic frowned when they walked in. He pointed to a chair and Threebeard took a seat. Lt. Marsen stood in the back to make sure Threebeard's integration back into the platoon went smoothly. The instructor was speaking.

"This is the C31 pistol. It is a semiautomatic, magazine fed, recoil operated, double action pistol. Its magazine holds fifteen rounds and it's light and versatile. There is a heat-seeking version in development but it will be a few cycles before it is perfected. Imagine if you didn't have a straight shot. With the heat-seeking technology you could simply shoot as close to your target as possible and if the ball detected a heat pattern it would veer towards it."

Next he picked up a rifle and said, "This is the R6, the standard issue rifle for the TGA. Lightweight, durable, and always dependable. The R6 can fire either semi-automatic (single-shot) or 6-round bursts. It also can fire heat-seeking balls. Become proficient with the R6. It is your most versatile weapon, able to engage targets at long range and in close quarters. As a general rule, select single-shot mode when attacking at long range. However, when you are going to be up close, such as in urban operations, go to burst mode."

The instructor set the R6 down and picked up another rifle and held it up. "This is the T6. It's a modular light rifle weapon system that delivers a coherent, directed lethal laser beam over a range in excess of 200 strides against visible targets. The T7 provides a total integrated weapons system, including high energy density power source, laser medium resonator and focusing system. It weighs approximately the same as the R6 and is capable of delivering a maximum rate of fire of approximately three lethal laser bursts per tik. Differing from other individual small arms, the T6 does not employ ammunition in the conventional sense, relying upon the thermal energy provided by a D33 power source. The T6 may be fielded for continuous tactical use for a period of over 45 days which gives it a significant advantage over the R6."

The instructor put down the T6 and continued, "Now this afternoon each of you will be issued a C34 pistol and either an R6 rifle or T6 laser rifle. You will be instructed in the proper use, handling, and care of these weapons. Over the course of your training you will become proficient in their use. These three weapons are the ones you will be using most often in your combat operations, but there are many more weapons that you will be trained to use in the course of your time here at Pegaport."

Threebeard left the classroom with the platoon and went back to the barracks. While they were getting ready to go to the nutrition center for dinner several of the recruits inquired as how Threebeard was feeling. Later he struck up a conversation with a mutant who had recently be sent to Hell Squad named Stixx Leode.

"What was it like in the tank?" Leode asked.

"Cold, desolate, and very lonely. It's like you don't exist except in your mind."

"How did you survive it without going crazy?" he asked.

Threebeard took a deep breath. "Fortunately, I was familiar with the concept of the chamber and knew there was no use trying to fight it. It was difficult at first, but finally I just let my mind wander wherever it wanted to go. It was like a long night full of sweet dreams and horrible nightmares from which you could not wake up. But I knew eventually it would be over, so I kept telling myself not to panic and get overwhelmed."

Leode shook his head. "It sounds horrible to me."

Threebeard nodded. "No, I wouldn't recommend it. It did give me a lot of time to think."

"Sgt. Hovic is a scutz. It's too bad somebody can't give him some of his own medicine."

"Well, I've given that idea some serious thought, believe me."

"You have?"

"Sure, I had plenty of time to think about it—not much else to do in the tank. I came up with quite a few fun ways to kill him."

"I bet," Leode laughed.

"So, how is everyone holding up in the platoon?" Threebeard asked.

"Well, things are settling down a little bit. Everyone is being very careful to follow orders meticulously and not to do anything to piss off the sergeant. He's still picking on Tuckh, though. Yesterday he beat him pretty badly when he couldn't make it over the obstacle course wall quickly enough."

"The dirty scutz," Threebeard spat shaking his head. "With those feet it's a wonder he can even get over it at all."

"I know. I wanted to help him, but there wasn't much I could do."

"No. You would have ended up in the tank just like me. So, what's the schedule tomorrow?" Threebeard asked.

"Right after lunch we're running to the rifle range to learn how to shoot the T7 and our lasers."

"Good. I'm anxious to learn how to shoot. I hope I can do it with six eyes."

"You'll have to close five of them and aim with just one," Leode suggested.

"Yeah. I figured that. I just don't know if I'll be able to hold a rifle properly. They weren't exactly made for three-headed mutants."

Leode laughed. "Probably not."

The next morning the recruits were awakened early and paraded double time to the shooting range. On the way Tuckh stumbled and fell and Sgt. Hovic took the opportunity to beat him severely again while the recruits looked on in dismay. It was all Threebeard could do to restrain himself from choking the sergeant with his third hand.

The range personnel distributed a laser to each of the recruits. Threebeard inspected his laser carefully and Tuckh looked at his warily. While everyone watched, the instructor took apart a laser and put it back together again. Then he showed them how to fire it properly. When he was done he directed everyone to practice on the targets. Threebeard aimed the laser as he'd been told and fired it straight ahead. The laser blast missed the target and hit the wall behind it. Others began firing with most of the shots missing the targets.

"Keep your lasers steady and squeeze the trigger gently," Sgt. Hovic screamed. "Don't jerk it."

Threebeard tried again and this time burned a hole through the upper left quadrant of the target. He laughed in delight for the first time since he'd returned from the tank. Then he noticed Tuckh having trouble holding his laser steady and Sgt. Hovic rushing over to give him hell. Anger welled in Threebeard as he recalled his eight days in the tank. Memories of all the abuse the sergeant had shown the recruits rushed through his head. Then he thought of Videl Lai and how he'd added five days to his punishment for doing nothing but caring for another human being. He thought of Eyeball and Misty and how they'd been brutally murdered by those who despised the Supreme Mandate and wanted to destroy it.

Without conscious thought he reached out with his third hand and tripped him. Sgt. Hovic fell forward crashing into Tuckh. Tuckh twisted in shock losing his grip on the laser. Suddenly, there was a flash from the laser and a scream of utter agony from Sgt. Hovic. Tuckh dropped the laser and backed away. Several members of the range staff rushed over and huddled over the sergeant. There were calls for a medic, but Threebeard knew there'd be no need for one. A laser blast through the chest at point-blank range would, he knew, be fatal.

Artis was growing weary from her journey. The freighter they took from Rallis was diverted to Dalo to deliver supplies there. Millions on the small island had been killed when the islands sole volcano, Mt. Tiberius, erupted and spewed lava over seventy percent of the island. By the time the ship sailed into Pulguras Harbor in Darkland twenty days had passed. The only thing that had made the trip tolerable was a sudden connection to Threebeard eight days into the journey.

"*Where have you been brother?*" Artis asked joyfully.

"*Submerged in an iron tank. That's why we couldn't communicate.*"

"*An iron tank? God and Sandee save us. What are you talking about.*"

Threebeard explained what had happened and told her about the accident and Sgt. Hovic's death.

"*So, are you in trouble again?*"

"*No. They have no reason to suspect me. It was just a tragic accident.*"

"*You don't think anyone will be suspicious?*"

"*The commandant, Videl Lai, may question what happened but he will have no way of proving it was anything but an accident.*"

"*I'm so worried about you, brother. You must be careful. I don't want to lose you.*"

"*Don't worry. My training at Pegaport is almost over. I'm told officer training on Pogo Island will be much easier. They treat the candidates very well there. But, what about you? I'm sorry you had no luck in the Duesi Desert.*"

"*Yes,*" Artis said. "*It was very depressing there. I hope it is different in the Rezoon Desert.*"

"*Me too. Perhaps the tremors haven't been so devastating. Keep me updated.*"

"*I will. May God and Sandee be with you.*"

Artis disconnected feeling much better that her brother was safe. Two days later when they finally docked in Pulguras Harbor she felt slightly optimistic that they'd eventually find a nanomite city. She reasoned that God wouldn't allow her six thousand kylod journey to be in vain. Unfortunately, the situation in Pulguras was desperate and Giant had great difficulty procuring transportation for their journey inland. There were no ATVs with internal filtration systems available so the group had to settle for an old hover taxi that had gone out of service when the volcanoes began to erupt.

One advantage of the hover taxi was that it didn't have to travel on ordinary roadways. It could travel over any flat surface. This came in handy when they came to large cracks in the road. Usually a small detour off road would get them moving again. The downside to the hover taxi, however, was its small size and lack of adequate storage for water and provisions. It also lacked the strength and stability of an ATV and even a modest wind made it difficult to drive.

Once they got out of the city the roads were nearly deserted which made travel easier but also made them apprehensive. If no one was traveling there had to be a reason. Half way to their destination they found out why there were no travelers. As they came over a hill and began to descend into a valley they were confronted by a dozen men on jet cycles. Having been warned about marauders Giant didn't stop but rather turned the hover taxi off road in an effort to get around the cyclists. The maneuver was partially successful but two cyclists managed to circle around and head them off before they got back to the road. Giant nearly collided with one of the cyclists and in his effort to avoid one of the bikes he sideswiped the other one.

The collision damaged the propulsion unit and the hover taxi fell to the ground and slid 150 feet before it came to a stop. Giant immediately sprang from the car and turned to face their assailants. A few tiks later the cyclists were encircling the hover taxi waiting for the command to attack. When the command came, the lead cyclist began bearing down on Giant, but before he reached him Giant reached out with his third hand and dislodged the cyclist from his bike. The startled biker rolled head over heels several times before crashing into a tree.

Artis emerged from the other side of the hover taxi and began knocking the attackers off their bikes with her third hand almost as adroitly as Giant. Several cyclists charged at Giant on foot but were no match for him. He dispatched one with a crushing blow to the skull and lifted the other one high in the air and threw him thirty feet into a pile of boulders. He didn't get up.

Artis had more difficulty subduing her attackers but with Faruk's help she managed to stand her ground until Giant was free to help out. Soon the bikers were rethinking the propriety of their attack, picking up their wounded, and making their escape.

"We better get out of here," Giant warned. "They'll be back soon with a more effective attack strategy, I'm sure."

"What about the propulsion unit?" Artis asked.

Giant looked at the disabled hover taxi and then at one of the abandoned jet cycles laying in the sand. "I guess we'll have to appropriate these jet cycles. We don't want to be around here when the marauders return."

Faruk looked at the jet cycle and frowned. "You want me to ride one of those?"

Giant smiled. "Either that or wait for us here and we'll pick you up in a few days on the way home."

Faruk looked around warily and shook his head. "No. That's alright. You'll have to show me how to ride this thing."

"It's really quite simple," Giant said picking up one of the cycles and rolling it over to Faruk.

After he'd given him a short lesson on the operation of the cycle they packed as much gear as they could load on the bikes, put on their breathers and helmets and took off. Three kyloons later they reached the Rezoon Desert and drove to the first location where the nanomite formations had last been seen. It was dark when they arrived, so they set up camp, built a campfire and cooked dinner. After they'd eaten they sat around the campfire and chatted.

"So, Faruk. How did you like riding a jet cycle?" Artis asked.

"It was fun for a while, but I think I prefer an ATV. I'm exhausted and my butt is sore."

Artis laughed. "Yes, I agree. Particularly having to wear a helmet and breather. It got very tiresome."

"It beats walking," Giant noted.

"True," Artis agreed. "So, tomorrow hopefully we'll be able to find one of the nanomite formations and make contact with them."

"So, once we make contact, then what?" Faruk asked.

"It will depend on the nanomites. If they are in distress we'll see if there is anything we can do to help them survive. If they don't need or want our help, we'll go home."

"Are you going to have to teach them Tari again?"

"Probably. I doubt the nanomites back in Tributon had time to pass on the new language to the other colonies."

"Well, I hope we find them," Faruk said. "I'd hate to think that every last nanomite has been killed."

Artis smiled confidently. "I'm sure we'll find some. Don't worry."

Giant doused the fire and they all retreated to the tent to try to get a good night's sleep. Giant and Faruk fell asleep immediately, but Artis twisted and turned but couldn't get comfortable. Her mind was racing trying to think of the best approach to make contact with the nanomites. Then she remembered Threebeard had said not to fight it, just let her subconscious mind seek them out. So, she took a deep breath and tried to relax. Soon she drifted off and began a silent search for her new-found friends.

The next day she tried to remember her dreams but came up blank. After breakfast they started searching for the nanomite formations. The dark sky and endless gray landscape made it difficult to see any kind of rock formations. Everything looked alike, so Artis began searching with her mind for any sign of a nanomite presence. They searched all day hitting each of the suspected nanomite locations but they found nothing. Discouraged they made camp again that night with the intention of leaving at first light the next morning.

During the night, however, a nanomite speaker came to Artis in a dream and revealed that nearly all of the nanomites had been killed in the aftermath of the volcanic eruptions, except a very few who had taken sanctuary in a safe place. Unfortunately, the speaker did not reveal where the few remaining nanomites were located. Artis wasn't sure if the dream had been real, but nevertheless it gave her hope that somehow a few nanomites had survived and could be rescued.

The next day they climbed on their jet cycles and began their journey back to Tributon feeling sad and dejected that they had been unable to save the nanomite life-form on Tarizon. On the way, however, Artis made contact with Threebeard and gave him the bad news. He was disappointed as well, but told Artis not to give up hope for he too had been contacted in a dream by a living nanomite speaker claiming that somewhere on Tarizon a colony of nanomites had survived and could yet be saved.

26

Summons

After several phases in hiding, Rupra Bruda and Essyria were getting cabin fever. Although living in luxury they were both bored and starting to get on each other's nerves. The unchanging dull gray landscape didn't help their demeanor much either, so when the communicator buzzed unexpectedly one day they both perked up wondering who was calling them.

They didn't answer the call at first. No one was supposed to know where they were. So, they waited until the caller had hung up and then checked for messages. The mysterious caller turned out to be Essyria's mother who said it was imperative that Essyria call her back.

"How does your mother know we are here?" Bruda asked irritably.

Essyria shrugged. "I guess it was obvious. We borrowed their ATV and took off. Where else would we go?"

"Do you think she told anyone we were here? Maybe that's why she is calling. She wants to warn us that the PE is coming to arrest us."

"I doubt that is it, but I suppose we better call her and find out."

Bruda nodded so Essyria picked up the communicator and punched in her mother's number.

"So, you *are* at the cabin," Tulia said. "I told your father that's where you must be."

"You didn't tell anyone else, did you?" Essyria asked nervously.

"No. Of course not, but the PE has been by several times looking for you. They say you were involved in the attempted murder of that mutant, Threebeard."

"Well, we were there when it happened but we had nothing to do with it," she lied.

"So, why don't you come back and tell that to the PE? You can't hide forever."

"We can't take that risk. We have enemies in Shisk who will do anything to destroy us."

"Well, there are other people in Shisk looking for Rupra. They say they are friends who want to help him."

"Who are they?"

"They are military men from the TGA. They say they sympathize with his efforts to rid Shisk of the mutants and the rhutz and would like to discuss working together in the future."

"Okay. Let me discuss it with Rupra and I'll get back with you. If he is interested where do they want to meet?"

"I don't know. They just said if I heard from him to have him contact Lt. Elmst at Shuttle City. I have his number."

Essyria wrote down the number and then hung up. She relayed the conversation to Bruda.

"Do you think it's a trap to get me to show myself?" Bruda asked. "I can't imagine a lieutenant in the TGA would be sympathetic with our cause."

"I don't know. On the news they say no mutants, Seafolken or rhutz have been allowed in Shuttle City. Perhaps we do have some supporters there."

"I suppose," Bruda mused. "I guess it won't hurt to call the Lieutenant and see what he has to say. We can use a secure communicator to make the call, so it won't be traceable."

Essyria nodded. "Do you have one?"

"Yes. I always keep one handy. You never know when you'll need it."

Bruda went into their bedroom and returned with a small communicator. He punched in the number and put the device to his ear.

"Shuttle City Command," a voice said.

"Ah. Lt. Elmst, please," Bruda said.

"Just a minute."

A few tiks later Lt. Elmst came on the line. "Lt. Elmst."

"Yes. Lt. Elmst. Rupra Bruda here. I was told you wanted to talk to me."

"Oh, yes. Captain Lugart asked me to try to locate you. He's organizing a conference of political leaders and thought you should attend."

"What kind of political leaders?" Bruda asked warily.

"Politicians, councilors, businessmen and military officers who share your views when it comes to the rhutz and the mutant problem on Tarizon. Do you think you could make it?"

"Ah. I don't know. When will it be held?"

"Soon. Perhaps tomorrow or the next day. We will come pick you up and take you to the conference."

"Where is it going to be held?" Bruda asked.

"The Isle of Muhl. We'll fly you down there by shuttle and bring you back when it is over."

Bruda was shocked by the transportation arrangements but the idea of traveling in an Earth shuttle intrigued him. He'd never ridden in a shuttle before and he'd always wanted to.

"Who else will be at the conference?" Bruda asked.

"The base commandant, Videl Lai. Lt. General Bratford, Colonel Lugwin, myself and a few others."

Rupra was shocked and amazed to be included with such a distinguished group. He was equally intrigued as to the purpose of the meeting.

"Okay. I'd be honored to attend. Can I bring my mate? She's a cofounder of the CPC."

"Yes. I'm sure that would be fine. If you give us your coordinates the shuttle will pick you up tomorrow at 0900 kyloons."

Bruda hesitated a moment. He gave Essyria a questioning look. She nodded, so he gave the lieutenant their coordinates. After he'd hung up he swallowed hard.

"Well, I hope that wasn't a mistake," Bruda said.

"It seemed like a legitimate invitation. I can't imagine any PE being that creative in luring in a fugitive. Plus, how would they get their hands on an Earth shuttle?"

Bruda shrugged. "Well, we'll find out soon enough if it's a trap."

The next day at 0845 Bruda and Essyria were outside in the pasture next to their cabin looking up into the gray sky. They had bags packed and were excited about the adventure upon which they were about to embark. Suddenly they heard a rumbling sound like distant thunder. They looked up and saw the huge shuttle slowly descending. The ground shook when the shuttle made contact. A few tiks later a hatch opened, a ramp was lowered and Lt. Elmst stepped out.

"Good morning. Come on aboard," Lt. Elmst said waving his arm enthusiastically.

Rupra picked up their bags and followed Essyria up the ramp and into the ship. Once inside someone took their bags and Lt. Elmst showed them to their quarters.

"The flight won't take but five or six kyloons but we may not be returning for a day or two, so these will be your quarters until we get back."

"Excellent," Bruda said admiring the fine accommodations. "Any chance we can see the rest of the ship?"

"Of course. Why don't you settle in I'll come and get you in a little while and take you to the bridge? I think you'll find it quite interesting."

Bruda smiled broadly. "Yes, that would be most satisfactory."

Lt. Elmst nodded and left. After the door closed Essyria took Bruda's hand and squeezed it tightly. "This is so exciting. I can't believe this is happening."

Bruda nodded. "I know. Who would have thought one day we're fugitives from the law and the next day on our way to meet with a TGA general?"

Essyria put her arms around Rupra's neck and kissed him passionately. Rupra pulled her up close and was about to unzip her dress when there was a knock at the door. They broke apart quickly and straightened their clothing.

"Yes," Bruda said.

"The captain has requested you and your mate's presence on the bridge," a voice said.

Bruda opened the door and smiled at the crewman. "Okay, we're ready."

"Follow me, then," the crewman said.

They followed him through a maze of corridors until they came to a double hatch. The crewman opened the right hatch and nodded for them to enter. Inside they found themselves in a large circular room. A huge blank screen was the focus of the room, facing it was a central console where the captain sat and workstations were set all along the perimeter for the crew. The instrumentation around the central console and around the workstations was breathtaking. The captain stood up as they entered and smiled.

"Welcome to *Tormenter*," Captain Lugart said enthusiastically.

Bruda smiled appreciatively. "Thank you, Captain. Essyria and I were delighted when we learned we'd be transported to the Isle of Muhl on your shuttle. It is quite an honor."

"Well, it's imperative that we have this meeting soon and the participants are scattered all over the globe, so this seemed the best way to get everybody together."

Bruda nodded.

"This is a spectacular ship," Essyria noted. "I've always wanted to travel on one."

"Well, it's a bit of a relic but it still does its job."

"So, I've heard about the remarkable job you've done in Shuttle City," Bruda said. "Who would have thought the Earth shuttle fleet would be used as housing."

Captain Lugart shook his head. "Indeed, but at least when the crisis is over we'll have an up to date fleet of Earth shuttles."

"Right. Too bad you won't need them," Essyria said.

Captain Lugart looked at Essyria. "Don't be so sure about that."

Essyria raised her eyebrows. She wondered what the captain meant. *Are there plans to go to Earth?* She looked at Rupra but he just shrugged. After the ship got underway again Rupra and Essyria were escorted back to their quarters where they found food and refreshments. They ate and drank and discussed their first impressions of the ship, Captain Lugart, and the mysterious conference they were to attend. The ship landed several times apparently to pick up more guests but Bruda and Essyria were not summoned from their quarters until they finally landed on the Isle of Muhl.

It was late afternoon and what little light made it through the thick cloud of ash that hovered overhead was rapidly waning. As they walked down the ramp to the ground Bruda noticed they were on a military base. He assumed it was Pegaport, the only TGA facility on Muhl. Several crew members directed the passengers along a path leading to a large building Bruda assumed was the base's headquarters. Once inside they were escorted into a large conference room.

The room had a long table that seated twenty-four, large video monitors on one wall, maps of Tarizon's five continents and eight large islands on another and various communications equipment hanging from the ceiling. Bruda and Essyria were directed to a seat at one end of the table. Captain Lugart took a seat at the other end next to the officer who appeared to be in charge. When the last seat at the table was filled the man at the end of the table rose.

"Good evening and welcome to Pegaport," the officer said. "My name is Videl Lai. I am the Commandant here and I have been asked to preside over this meeting.

"Some of you know why you are here, but others I'm sure have no idea why you have been summoned. Hopefully as I begin to explain the purpose of this gathering it will become clear to you why you were chosen to participate. If, however, you at any time feel uncomfortable or are less than enthusiastic about our purpose, please feel free to get up and leave. Your participation is strictly voluntary.

"Now. we have a lot to cover so let's get down to business. As you are all painfully aware Tarizon is in danger of becoming uninhabitable. Even if the worst of the volcanic eruptions are over, it will be fifty cycles before the planet's ecosystem repairs itself to the level before the eruptions. The reason we are here today is to discuss a long-term strategy for survival. A strategy that is realistic and one that is best for the people of Tarizon.

"In developing such a strategy one harsh reality must be accepted. We cannot save every citizen on the planet. That is simply impossible and a waste of our precious resources to even try. It will be a great challenge just to save the people under the domes. As you know food is already in short supply. Most of our farms outside the domes have ceased production due to a lack of sunlight. This means we will have to grow our crops indoors with artificial light. We all know this will be exceedingly difficult and it will be many cycles before production levels reach the minimum requirements of our citizens under the domes.

"So, what do we do with all the millions outside the dome? What are our options? Do we divert precious resources to try to save them or do we just let them fend for themselves? These are the tough questions. Realistically, however, there is just one course of action that makes any sense and that is to let them die. After all, the tremors and volcanic eruptions were not caused by man, so if millions outside the dome die it is not the fault of the human race but the will of God.

Bruda was enjoying Videl's presentation. He liked his realistic thinking and understood now why he'd been invited to the conference. Videl Lai obviously didn't like mutants or non-human life-forms. He could see where Videl Lai was going and it made a lot of sense to him.

"Unfortunately, the World Assembly is controlled by the worshipers of the Supreme Mandate. They believe that everyone including mutants, Seafolken, rhutz and nanomites all have equal rights. We all know this is not true. None of these life-forms are mentioned in the Supreme Mandate and even if they were it's just not possible to save them all. Realistically all those who live outside the dome are doomed and the sooner that we accept that fact and deal with it, the better.

"So, each of you have been summoned here today because you all possess unique talents that we believe would be useful in our efforts to persuade the World Assembly to adopt our policies for dealing with the mutants and inferior life-forms during this global crisis. Later on, this evening we will break off into groups and each of you will be told exactly what we would like you to do. At that time, you can ask questions and decide if you want to make this commitment.

"Finally, even if we are successful in gaining control over the World Assembly, it may be that Tarizon can't be saved. We won't know if that is the case for many cycles but we must be ready to face that reality. That is why we are immediately beginning the creation of a plan to relocate as much of our population to Earth as we can. This would be a tremendous undertaking but it may be necessary to save the people of Tarizon from extinction. The reactivation of the Earth Shuttles to act as shelters during this ecological crisis was a brilliant stroke of good fortune. Fortunately, Captain Lugart was in control of the Earth Shuttle fleet so he is ensuring that only those who support our cause will be allowed on the shuttles. When the time is right we will start sending them to Earth and begin the process of taking control over our sister planet.

"Now, I know this argument doesn't apply to the nanomites and the rhutz. They have always been able to adapt to the environmental changes and somehow have survived. So, why do we consider these life-forms to be the enemy? As to the rhutz you have all heard of the Flat Meadow Massacre. That most shocking event illustrates the power and cunning of the rhutz and the threat they pose to the human race. It's true they have not generally been belligerent to man so far, but as the resources of the planet are strained that could change. You may have heard of an assassination attempt on the three-headed mutant named Threebeard. Unfortunately, Threebeard survived the attack. I say unfortunately, because Threebeard has enlisted the rhutz as allies in the Loyalists' efforts to resist our cause. Further, Threebeard has managed to communicate with the nanomites and, I fear, they too will support the Loyalist cause.

"Now, you all know of the great power of the rhutz, but few of you probably appreciate the even greater threat of the nanomites. Can you imagine an enemy so small you cannot see it? An enemy that can pass through solid objects like you and I walk through air. An enemy that can build strong and durable buildings in a fraction of the time it takes humans. An enemy that is everywhere and can spy on you without you even knowing it.

"This is why we must destroy both of these life-forms if we are to achieve our goal of bringing Tarizon back to its Golden Age. The age before the first world war when the air was clean, the skies were blue, and the human race was unblemished!

"So, now we are going to split up into groups and give out individual assignments. When that task is complete there will be a banquet in the nutrition center followed by a party to celebrate a new beginning for Tarizon. Thank you."

The attendees gave Videl Lai a round of applause and then began filing out to attend their individual meetings. When Bruda and Essyria got up to leave Videl Lai came over to them.

"Rupra Bruda! Thank you for coming," Videl said.

"Oh. It's our pleasure."

They shook hands and then Videl turned to Essyria. "And you were most kind to bring such a beautiful young lady."

"Thank you. This is my mate, Essyria."

"I know. What a lucky man you are," Videl said giving Essyria a big smile.

"So, where are we to go now?" Bruda asked.

"Oh, you're staying here. Captain Lugart and I will be meeting with you and your lovely mate."

Bruda nodded, shocked that he'd become an overnight hero for his campaign against the mutants and the rhutz. He was flattered and felt vindicated that so many supported his actions. In his mind he was just getting started in his political career and was a nobody, yet here he was amongst some of the most powerful men on Tarizon. He was glad when he finally saw Captain Lugart coming to join them. They took seats around one end of the conference table.

"So, I guess you are curious as to your assignment," Videl said.

Bruda nodded. "Yes, I am."

"Well, I have been watching you very closely since the Flat Meadow Massacre. It took a lot of courage to take on a pack of rhutz."

"Well, my grandfather was a rancher and the rhutz caused him a lot of trouble breaking down his fences and killing his stock. I guess I inherited his hatred for them."

"Your grandfather is a good man. I was sorry to see him resign. I hope you didn't blame yourself for that happening."

"Well, it was kind of my fault."

"Nonsense. Your grandfather should have never resigned. He should have backed you and made sure the amendment to the Animal Control Act passed."

"How could he have done that?" Bruda asked.

"Oh, I think you know. Like I said I have been watching you closely. You know how to punish people who get in your way. I know at least one inquisitor who underestimated you in that regard."

Bruda turned a little red. He wondered how much Videl Lai knew about him. He looked at Essyria and she raised her eyebrows.

"Ah. Well, I don't take failure very well, so I'll do whatever it takes to get the job done."

"That is exactly why you are here," Videl said. "We need someone to take charge of the new Purist Party. Someone who will, as you say, do what it takes to get the job done."

Bruda was shocked but elated with the opportunity that had suddenly been thrust his way. He couldn't quite believe what he was hearing. "You mean in Shisk?" he asked.

"No, I mean for all of Tarizon. Shisk will be your headquarters but I want you to organize the party on every continent, in every state and in all the domed cities."

"But what about you? I thought you were in charge of the party," Bruda questioned.

"No. No. I'm not an organizer. I'm a politician. With your help I'll be elected chancellor one day."

Bruda nodded. "Oh, right. I understand."

"So, will you do it? We'll provide you with whatever resources you'll need. I want the job done as quickly as possible, hopefully within one cycle, so we will be in full operation when the campaigning begins for seats on the World Assembly."

Bruda swallowed hard. He desperately wanted the job but it was an incredible undertaking and he didn't have all that much experience in politics. He looked at Essyria. She smiled broadly.

"You can do it. I have faith in you," she assured him.

Bruda nodded. "Okay, I'll do it, but I'm going to need some help. I've never organized anything at this level."

"Don't worry," Captain Lugart said. "We've recruited many seasoned politicians to assist you."

"Really? Then why didn't you pick one of them as chairman and let me help them?"

Videl shook his head. "No. They are old men set in their ways. They wouldn't have the guts to do the things that need to be done to assure the party's success. You can draw on their experience to initially set up the party organization but once that is done it will be up to you to mold the party into an efficient and powerful force."

"Ah. What about the PE in Shisk? I believe he has a city-wide alert for my arrest."

"That's been taken care of," Captain Lugart replied. "The PE in charge of the case has been presented evidence to show that someone else was responsible for the attack on Threebeard. You and Essyria have been cleared of all charges."

A surge of relief came over Bruda. He'd been worried sick about the warrants for his arrest. "Really. That's excellent news," Bruda said looking over at Essyria. "It will be great to be able to go home."

"You will have to be more careful in the future," Videl said. "Don't ever hire an assassin who can be linked to you. You need to have people that are well insulated from the party for that type of operation. That way if they are caught, no one in the party can be blamed."

Bruda just looked at Videl Lai trying not to reveal his shock. He couldn't believe what he was hearing. Not that murder bothered him all that much. It would be nice to have the authority to do anything he wanted to ensure the party's success, including killing anyone who got in his way. But the implication of Videl Lai's words of caution was that assassination would be a common tool to achieve the goals of the Purist Party. That thought was a bit sobering, but the more he thought about it the more comfortable he became with it. *Yes, I'm going to like running this Purist Party!*

"Of course. That was rather amateurish of me. I'll never let that happen again."

"Good. Then let's go on over to the banquet. I've worked up a pretty good appetite."

They all stood up and made their way out of the conference room. Soon they were issued breathers so they could take the short walk to the nutrition center. The pungent odor of fire and ash hit Bruda the moment he stepped outside. He immediately pulled the breather over his head and turned to make sure Essyria had hers in place as well. Inside the nutrition center a banquet was in progress. Hundreds of people were seated awaiting the event to begin. Bruda and Essyria were escorted to a table in the front of the room and seated next to Lt. Commander Rugge Brunns and his companion, Ensign Aerial Muri. They each introduced themselves and shook hands. When Bruda took Ensign Muri's hand in his, a pleasant feeling came over him. The feeling startled him and he stared at the beautiful TGA officer. When he'd held on to her hand a little too long Essyria elbowed him gently. He let loose and looked at her irritably.

"So, I understand you're to be the head of the party," Lt. Commander Brunns said.

Bruda smiled. "Yes. So, it seems. I'm honored, of course, but a little at a loss. All this has happened so fast."

"Oh, yes. Well, my job will be challenging as well. I have the simple job of transporting millions of citizens across the universe to Earth."

Bruda laughed. "Well, I guess we both have our work cut out for us. At least traveling to Earth has been done before."

"Yes, but I have to convince the current occupants of the planet to accept us with open arms. Otherwise I'll have to bring a fleet of warships to force them to cooperate."

Essyria shook her head. "That may be difficult. I've heard the humans there, particularly the Americans, are quite protective of their territory."

"Yes, but they are also very competitive with other nations on the planet, so I think we can use that as leverage to get their cooperation."

Bruda nodded. "Yes, and like humans here on Tarizon they are rather greedy as well. So, if you bribe the right people you will be able to get them to look the other way when the shuttles start landing."

"Ensign Muri squirmed uncomfortably in her chair. "You all make it sound so easy. The Americans are greedy, sure, but they love their freedom even more. As soon as they understand our true intentions they will fight like a wounded rhutz."

Lt. Commander Brunns shrugged. "I hope you are wrong, my dear, but if they try to fight us they will regret it."

Bruda frowned. "Correct me if I am wrong, Commander, but I wasn't aware that Tarizon had any military capability in space."

Brunns nodded. "Yes, you're right, but that will be changing. One of my first projects is to begin construction of an intergalactic fleet. Of course, when I go to the World Assembly for the funding I'm not going to reveal its true purpose."

"Right. That wouldn't be prudent," Bruda agreed.

Bruda sat back trying to digest everything that had been thrown at him. It was all so overwhelming, but at the same time, wonderful. For the first time in his life he felt like he was a part of something important and meaningful. He looked at Essyria who could feel his happiness. She took his hand and squeezed it as the waiters began serving them one course after another until they couldn't eat anymore. Then everyone moved to an adjoining room that had been converted into a ballroom. Bruda and Essyria danced and mingled with the guests until the party finally ended, and they went back to their quarters to celebrate their good fortune in each other's arms.

27

The Will of God

Threebeard felt a great relief when the big transport plane landed on Pogo Island. Somehow, he had miraculously survived basic training and Hell Squad. After Sgt. Hovic's death there was a general inquiry and the sergeant's death was finally determined to have been an accident, but the new drill sergeant treated the squad with much greater respect nonetheless. He apparently still had his suspicions. After graduation the best mutants, including Threebeard, were sent on to Pogo Island for officer training. Although OTS was intense, Threebeard knew he had a lot to learn if he was going to raise a mutant army, so he relished the opportunity to learn all he could.

It was not surprising that he graduated number one in his class by a large margin and gained the respect of his fellow mutant officers. After the graduation ceremonies each of the new 2nd Lieutenants or Ensigns, depending on whether they were being deployed into the Army or Navy, were granted ten days leave before having to report for duty. Threebeard took that opportunity to go home to Liehn and check on his sister Artis who was in a deep depression over the apparent extinction of the nanomite life-form on Tarizon. Threebeard felt equally distraught by the loss of the nanomites. Just as they were about to establish a link between the two life-forms the volcanoes began erupting. He knew they had done all they could but that didn't make the loss any easier to swallow. But now they needed to press on if they were going to stop the mutants and the rhutz from suffering the same fate.

The situation in Liehn, like all the cities without a dome, was desperate. Food production had taken a nosedive since the planet had been encompassed by a shroud of ash and toxic gases. Water was another problem. Most of the rivers and lakes that had provided water in the past had been polluted by the endless ash that fell from the sky. Before any of it could be used it had to go through extensive filtration which took time and was expensive. This shortage of food and water was a major problem for the Mighty Jolly taverns which had turned into refugee centers since the volcanoes began to erupt.

To get Artis out of the doldrums Threebeard assigned her the task of setting up large camocube greenhouses near every Mighty Jolly so they could grow all of their own fruits and vegetables. Realizing the importance of the task and knowing Threebeard's time in Liehn was short, she immediately jumped on the task and, within a few days had a camocube farm, complete with a water filtration system and artificial light, up and running just outside the city limits. Unfortunately, it would take several phases for the new crops to grow and mature enough for harvesting, but at least it was a start and gave everyone hope for the future. Her actions attracted much attention too, and inspired the town council to get busy with their own projects to ease the food shortage in the city.

A more immediate problem was the health of the citizens outside the dome. Before the great eruptions the air quality was poor but now it is so toxic no one could live without breathers outside or air filtration systems in their homes and businesses. Unfortunately, there weren't enough breathers for every citizen nor did many of the homes have air filtration systems. As a result, the hospitals and clinics were flooded with far more patients than they could possibly treat. With the world's transportation system at a standstill, the inventory of medical supplies and drugs were rapidly being depleted.

With so many mutants not getting the medical attention they needed to survive the respiratory ailments that plagued almost everyone, the death rate began to soar. This created another problem—what to do with all the dead bodies. Central Authority had dictated that the dead be cremated but the crematoriums were working at full capacity yet bodies were stacking up so quickly in their inventory rooms that they were becoming a health hazard. Finally, temporary burning sites had to be cleared where thousands upon thousands of the dead were incinerated in mass fires much to the horror of their families and loved ones.

When Threebeard reported to his duty station at Gallion he was exhausted. His ten day leave had been anything but relaxing. Trying to deal with Artis' depression, all the problems his Mighty Jolly taverns were experiencing, and seeing so many of his friends and neighbors in such desperate straits had taken a toll on him. He was fighting off depression himself, wondering if there was any hope for those outside the domed cities.

Shortly after he had reported to his assigned barracks, Threebeard was summoned to base headquarters by Colonel Zitor. His barracks were located adjacent to the docks so as he was walking to headquarters he couldn't help but admire the hundreds of naval vessels in port and notice how many Seafolken were on the ships and working on the docks. It made sense as the Seafolken were at home in the sea, but he wondered what they would do if civil war broke out. Would they remain loyal to the TGA if they backed the Purists in the war, or would they break their oath and join the Loyalists? He hoped the latter would be the case.

When he got to headquarters, he pulled off his breather, left it in the anteroom and stepped inside to the reception area. A Seafolken woman manned the front desk. She immediately perked up when she saw Threebeard.

"You must be Lt. Nocteris," she said with a broad smile. "It's an honor to meet you, sir."

Threebeard nodded and looked around to see if they were alone. "You can call me Threebeard," he said, "if we are alone. I hate formality. What's your name?"

"Corporal Londoria," she replied. "Colonel Zitor is waiting for you. Go right in. Down the hall, third door on the right."

Threebeard nodded and started down the hallway. When he saw a door with Colonel Zitor's name on it, he knocked.

"Come in," a voice said.

Threebeard opened the door and stepped inside. There were three desks in a row flanked by various pieces of office equipment and communication devices. A secretary motioned to Threebeard to come over.

"Lt. Nocteris?" she asked as she stood up.

"Yes."

"Right this way."

The woman led Threebeard down the hall to a conference room where he found Colonel Zitor and Lt. Stixx Leode.

"Threebeard. Come in. You know Lt. Leode."

Threebeard nodded, happy to see his friend from Hell Squad.

"Yes. Stixx, how are you?"

"Excellent now that Hell Squad is behind us."

Threebeard laughed. "Yes, that was an experience you would never want to relive."

"Sit down," the colonel said. "We've got a lot of ground to cover."

Everyone sat down and the colonel began. "Stixx, you are here because Threebeard requested you be assigned to him to help build the mutant army. You'll be his executive officer. I'm assigning both of you officially to our base in Mapi, however, you will actually be quartered fifty kylods north of there, along the north fork of the Rini River. That's where you will begin assembling your mutant army. You'll initially be assigned ten thousand mutants and you'll have six phases to get them organized and trained for deployment around Lemaine Shane for humanitarian duty. Once they have moved out they will be replaced by twenty thousand new recruits. After that our funding runs out, so we'll just have to see how things are going. If your troops are doing a good job, we may be able to convince the World Assembly to increase the number of mutant troops.

"In case we lose our support in the World Assembly you should be working on alternative funding sources and also be prepared to restock the supplies and armaments you'll be needing for your troops. You'll have to find alternative sources of supply. Do you understand?"

Threebeard nodded solemnly. "Yes, sir."

Colonel Zitor swallowed hard. "I have recently received some disturbing news which you need to know about. Just after you left boot camp on Muhl there was a gathering of Purist leaders led by Commandant Videl Lai. Among the attendees was the man who orchestrated the attempt on your life, Threebeard."

"Rupra Bruda?"

"Yes. Word is he has been personally selected by Videl Lai to remake the Purist Party into a ruthless and soulless political force."

Threebeard shook his head. "Well, they picked the right person for that job. Bruda has no conscience and cares only for himself."

"They brought his mate Essyria along too, apparently."

"She's just as evil as he," Threebeard noted.

"Who else was there?" Lt. Leode asked.

"Captain Lugart, Lt. General Bratford, Colonel Lugwin and quite a few others. Oh. Lt. Commander Rugge Brunns was there."

"How did you hear about this?"

"Ensign Aerial Muri provides us with intelligence. You should get to know her. She's part Seafolken but Brunns doesn't know it. She sleeps around and keeps us informed as to what's going on. "

"How can I meet her?"

"I'll make sure she has an occasion to go to Mapi and I'll alert you to her arrival and assign you to show her around. Since you both have telepathic abilities you can establish a link while you are together. That will make it easy for her to report to you."

Threebeard laughed. "And she's Lt. Commander Brunns' lover?"

"Not only his. None of the officers can keep their hands off of her. They say Videl Lai has his eye on her. He's just waiting for the right opportunity to steal her away from him."

They all laughed hard.

Later that day Threebeard and Lt. Leode met with twelve other mutants who had been at Pogo Island with them and discussed the organization of the ten thousand troops they were soon to be assigned. They decided to split the troops into ten divisions—two medical, two engineering, four infantry, one airborne, and one logistics. This organization would be optimal for their current disaster relief assignment but could easily be modified for military action if need be. When the first class graduated ten percent would remain behind to train the next class coming in.

Before they returned to Mapi, Threebeard took a three day leave and returned to Liehn. When he arrived back at the Mighty Jolly he was amazed with how much progress Artis had made at getting agricultural production up and running at all the Mighty Jolly locations around the globe. Nic was also there and reported that he had established cells in every state in Lemaine Shane, Turvin and Azollo. In fact, he was packing to go to Lower Azollo when Threebeard arrived.

"So, there was a lot of support for our cause in Azollo?" Threebeard asked.

"Not as much as in Turvin. The people are very independent and would prefer just to be left alone. I explained to them that the Purists wouldn't let that happen. If they wanted to be remain free they needed to support our cause. So, most reluctantly agreed."

"Good. When you are in Lower Azollo I want you to contact the Seafolken commanders down there and get them linked into our network. They are very strong there and can be a big help."

"I'll do that. Who should I contact?"

"Quirken. General Quirken in Zangor. Just ask anyone down at the docks. They'll be able to lead you to him."

"Okay. I'll do it."

After talking to Nic Threebeard went to check on the replica of the nanomite city. He was still morning the harsh reality of their extinction. He looked down at the intricate design of the crystal facade and thought of how incredible it was that something so small could be intelligent and build structures millions of times larger than themselves. As he was mourning their loss Artis walked in.

"I can't bear to come in here anymore," she said quietly. "I wanted so much to learn about them and become their friend."

"I know. I had such high hopes of establishing a partnership with them. I dreamed of them building great cities for humans and in return helping their swarms multiply throughout Tarizon. It would have been a glorious partnership."

Artis began to weep. "I know. It is such a tragedy. If only there had been a way to protect them from the volcano."

"You did all you could. There was no way you could have prevented the sinkhole."

They both felt it at the same time. A weak presence in their mind. They looked at each other not daring to hope.

"Concentrate," Threebeard said closing his eyes. The presence became stronger and stronger until—

"We are not extinct!" a voice in their heads said.

Artis felt her heart skip a beat. *"Swarmmasters?"*

"Yes," the Speaker said. *"We have been waiting a long time for you to speak to us."*

Threebeard smiled joyfully. *"We didn't realize there were any of you in the replica of your city. If we had known we would have communicated earlier."*

"Why did you think we left you the replica? It was our contingency plan in case the volcano consumed our city."

"Thank God and Sandee!" Artis said weeping tears of joy. *"You are so wise."*

"We have strong instincts for self-preservation."

"I am so sorry about your brothers and sisters who perished in the Ural Desert and all over Tarizon."

"Yes, it is sad for every life-form, but the important thing is that we all have survived."

"Yes, indeed," Threebeard agreed. *"Somehow, no matter what happens, we'll all survive."*

"And if we help each another as God has commanded, all our life-forms shall flourish together in peace and harmony."

Threebeard closed his eyes thinking of the growing Purist threat. He swallowed hard. *"But, I'm afraid there are those who would subvert God's will and try to take all His gifts to the exclusion of all others."* Threebeard unleashed his memories of Rupra Bruda and the atrocities at Shisk. He wanted the nanomites to realize the full extent of the threat that confronted them.

The swarmmasters reeled at the revelation. *"Why are these Purists so full of evil and hatred?"* the Speaker asked. *"What have any of us done to them to warrant such wretched plots and schemes?"*

"They are greedy and selfish. They want all of God's gifts for themselves and care nothing for God's other creations."

"We are a peaceful life-form but we can and will kill those who attack us. Survival is paramount. Tell us how we can help thwart the plans of these soulless Purists. We will be your ally and will fight to victory or death, as is the will of God!"

28

Grave Measures

Although the volcanoes had been quiet for two cycles, the situation on Tarizon worsened each day as the thick layers of ash encircling the globe refused to dissipate. Although the scientific community had non-stop debates on how to deal with the situation, it became apparent the world's climate was too vast a beast to tame. If Tarizon's ecosystem could ever be restored it wouldn't be by act of man but by the grace of God. With this realization the ash encircling Tarizon became to many a shroud of doom, a hopeless condition that might never be fixed. Because of this many believed the only option left was to evacuate Tarizon and transport its population to Earth, the closest planet in the universe where human life was known to exist.

When the matter came up for debate, Assemblyman Basset Als took the podium to state his views on the subject. "Although the situation on Tarizon is desperate, evacuation is not an option for the vast majority of our population. It is not logistically possible to transport a billion people to Earth. The experts say the best-case scenario would be twenty percent would make it off the planet and it's anyone's guess how many would actually make it to Earth.

"But even if they did, how do you think the authorities on Earth would take to the sudden arrival of 20 million refugees? Well, that's not hard to imagine. They'd likely blow our shuttles out of the sky before we even landed. And if we sent an advance party to arrange for them to accept us, what is the likelihood of the authorities on Earth agreeing to such an invasion of refugees?"

Als paused for a moment to let his words sink in. It was a ridiculous proposal placed on the docket by the radical Purists but, unfortunately, it had some support so he had to take the proposal seriously. "Put yourself in the place of the Americans or the Chinese. They are not like us. They are an unenlightened people. They don't even know we exist. They will fear us because they don't know us. They will be suspicious and careful. It would take many cycles to gain the trust necessary to even begin talks about them accepting our refugees.

"So, let's not waste any more time on options that are not realistic. We have to accept our situation and deal with it. Thank you."

Als sat down and Assemblyman Presidius Tash stood. "Mr. Chairman, fellow assemblymen, and citizens of Tarizon. Assemblyman Als says we should be realistic. Well I couldn't agree more. But the reality is Tarizon is finished." The crowd stirred at the statement. The chairman asked for order. "I know we all love our planet and it's hard to accept the fact that it may soon be uninhabitable, but what centuries of war couldn't do God and mother nature have accomplished in but one cycle. Thirteen super volcanic eruptions, 22,003 tremors, 111 tidal waves, and 4,110 wildfires have plunged Tarizon into darkness and chaos. There is no way we can survive this and the only realistic thing to do is start planning the planet's evacuation.

"Now, nobody said evacuation would be easy, but we are talking about the survival of our people. We cannot allow our civilization to die. We have accomplished too much to sit back and accept our perceived destiny. We are better than that. So, I say to all of you, we must get all of the existing 1,900 or so shuttles ready to transport as many people off Tarizon as is possible. When the shuttles reach Earth, they can orbit the planet until arrangements are made for them to land. And if the authorities on Earth won't welcome us with open arms then we'll find a suitable place to land and stake a claim."

Many assemblymen stood up screaming their outrage while others clapped in enthusiastic support. Tash continued, "Assemblyman Als said only 20 million of our citizens could be successfully evacuated to Earth. I think his estimate is a little conservative, but let's just say he's right. Unfortunately, I'm afraid we'll be hard pressed to find even 20 million citizens physically able to make the trip to Earth and that number will be dropping dramatically each day we delay in getting off this God forsaken planet!"

The assembly broke out again in urgent conversation. Tash patiently waited for the room to quiet. "So, I urge each of you to vote in favor of the resolution pending before this assembly to immediately begin development of an evacuation plan to ensure that our civilization is not lost. Thank you."

The debate continued until the Chairman adjourned the session for lunch. Assemblyman Als went back to his office where Councilor Garciah, Thom Tomel and several others were waiting. They all went into a small conference room where food and drink were available to them while they talked.

"Assemblyman Tash is such an idiot," Thom said. "There is no way an evacuation to Earth will work."

"Yes, but a lot of assemblymen agree we have no other choice," Rammel noted.

"That's right, so we have to come up with a compromise. It would be a mistake to devote all our resources to an evacuation. The citizens left behind would pay dearly for such an eventuality," Basset said.

"Yes, it would be a disaster for the mutants, the rhutz and the nanomites. That's for sure," Rammel agreed.

"I'm afraid, however, if it went to a vote right now, we might lose," Basset said.

They all were quiet a moment as they filled their plates with food and found something to drink. Basset took a seat at the end of the table, grabbed a tablet and began writing something. After a moment he looked up. "What if we proposed to immediately send an envoy to Earth to see if they would accept our refugees? We could offer them gold, diamonds and other items they cherish as compensation."

"I don't think money would be enough," Rammel said. "I think you have to give them something so valuable that once they hear about it, they'd have to have it."

"Like what?" Thom asked.

"Like technology. The Americans, in particular, are very competitive and if we offered them technology that would make them superior to all other nations on Earth, how could they turn that down."

"Yes," Basset agreed. "We should offer them superiority and power. That is something much more valuable than money."

"So, how would it work?" Thom asked.

"Our emissary would make the journey to Earth, negotiate a treaty and then return to Tarizon. By the time he arrived back home the refugees would be ready to leave immediately."

"But the Purists won't want to wait," Thom said.

"Of course, they won't, but fortunately most of the assembly will understand our plan is much more feasible and realistic. They will go for it I think, rather than a plan proposed in fear and panic."

"Who would the emissary be?" Thom asked.

"Well, it has to be one who is articulate, persuasive and someone everyone trusts."

"I agree, but they will want to hear a name," Thom persisted. "If we don't offer a name the Purists will come up with someone we don't like."

Basset nodded. "I was going to suggest Councilor Garciah."

Rammel stiffened. "You want me to go to Earth?"

"Yes," Basset replied. "You're the obvious choice. You're a councilor, your impartiality and integrity is impeccable, you are articulate and, most importantly, you speak English."

Thom's mouth dropped open. "What? You speak English?"

Rammel sighed. "I've studied it, although I'm not sure how much of it I remember. It was a dream of my father to go to Earth back when that option was being considered."

"You can brush up on it."

"I suppose."

"So, will you do it? If anyone can pull it off, I trust it will be you."

"I will but my mate will be quite distraught when she learns of it."

"Take her with you."

He laughed. "I'm not sure she would like to be put to sleep for a cycle."

Basset shrugged. "From what I have been told it is like going to bed on Tarizon and waking up the next morning on Earth. Only the thought of it is troublesome. In reality it is nothing."

"Hmm. I don't know."

"Tell her she won't age for two cycles. When she gets back she'll be younger than all her friends."

"That's right. You don't age when you travel FTL."

Basset nodded. "So, you'll do it?"

Rammel shrugged. "Why not?"

Basset smiled and looked down at his notes. After a moment he looked up. "Okay, when the debate comes to an end I'll make a motion to amend the evacuation resolution on the table and we'll see what happens."

When the group broke up Basset got on his communicator to start lining up support for his amendment. In the meantime, Thom called Threebeard and Colonel Zitor to advise them of the latest developments and Rammel called his mate to give her the startling news. When the general assembly reconvened, the debate went on until late in the afternoon until the last assemblyman who had wanted to speak on the matter took his seat.

Assemblyman Als stood up. "Mr. Chairman. I wish to propose an amendment to the resolution before the assembly."

The chairman nodded," The chair recognizes Assemblyman Basset Als."

"Mr. Chairman. I move to amend the Emergency Evacuation Act by adding a stipulation that before any evacuation takes place that an envoy be sent to negotiate a suitable treaty with the government of the United States for the peaceful acceptance of refugees to there. Further, I propose that the United States be offered valuable technology as consideration for the treaty, such that they would be given superiority over other nations on Earth. Finally, I would propose that the envoy be Councilor Rammel Garciah since he is uniquely qualified for the appointment as he has already learned the English language which is spoken by the Americans."

Basset sat down and another delegate immediately rose. "I second the motion."

There was a moment of silence as the assemblymen digested the motion. Then excited conversation broke out for several moments until the chairman quieted the assembly and asked for debate. Assemblyman Tash rose. "Mr. Chairman. I'd like to be heard on this amendment."

"Very well, the chair recognizes Assemblyman Tash."

"Mr. Chairman. Assemblymen. We don't like Mr. Als' amendment but we know there are others who feel the same way, so we would not oppose it if while these negotiations were going on with the Americans that a fleet of combat warships were constructed to force the nations on Earth to accept our citizens should they decline to enter into a treaty voluntarily.

Therefore, I move to amend Mr. Als' amendment by stipulating that Deep Space Authority immediately begin construction of a fleet of at least seven battle cruisers, 2500 fighters and 50 support ships at the DSA Space Port on Clarion to be completed and ready for combat in two cycles so they will be ready to accompany the evacuation shuttles to Earth."

Another delegate stood up and seconded the motion. The chairman took a moment to discuss the situation with an aide and then replied. "Very well, there is an amendment to Mr. Als amendment to Mr. Tash's motion. Is there any debate?"

Many assemblymen spoke up wanting to discuss the amendments before the general assembly. While the debate went on Assemblyman Als went back to his office to confer with Thom, Rammel and his staff.

"So, it appears our move has been anticipated," Basset said sighing deeply.

"Yes, indeed," Thom replied.

"We played right into their hands. They knew their plan for an immediate evacuation wasn't feasible, so they used it as a diversion from their real plan to build an intergalactic fleet," Basset mused.

"So, what do we do?" Rammel asked. "It makes sense to bring along a military force to Earth in case we cannot negotiate a treaty. We can't leave 20 million citizens orbiting around Earth forever."

"Yes, I'm afraid you're right," Basset said. "We have to agree to the fleet or it will make us appear to be unreasonable and reckless. I fear; however, the Purists' intent is not to protect the citizens of Tarizon, but to gain the might to enslave them."

"So, what should we do to prevent that?" Thom asked.

"If it is built, we'll have to make sure the Purists don't get control of it."

A few loons later Basset was back on the floor of the assembly. When the last assemblyman sat down, Basset rose. "Mr. Chairman, I believe the amendment proposed by Mr. Tash is reasonable, although I don't know where we will find the resources to build this intergalactic fleet. But that issue can be dealt with later. I move to call the question."

Another assemblyman stood up. "I second the motion."

The chairman nodded. "Very well, please cast your vote on the amendment to the amendment to the original motion. Specifically, if an envoy is sent to Earth to negotiate a treaty to accept our citizens and the evacuation is postponed for 2 or 3 cycles, that, in the meantime we authorize the construction of an intergalactic fleet as specified earlier by Mr. Tash."

Lights began flashing on the vote tabulation board and after just a moment it was clear the amendment had passed. "Alright, the second motion has passed. Please cast your ballot on the first amendment, as amended, to the original motion to immediately begin the evacuation of the citizens of Tarizon to Earth utilizing our existing fleet of Earth shuttles."

The voting board lit up again and the amendment passed 423/377 with 23 abstaining. "Alright, the amendment carries. Now cast your vote on the original motion as amended. To summarize, the vote is on Mr. Tash's motion which now provides that Central Authority will immediately send Councilor Rammel Garciah to lead a delegation of diplomats and appropriate staff to Earth to negotiate a treaty for the settlement of citizens of Tarizon on Earth. Further, that in the two to three cycle period that it takes to travel to Earth, negotiate the treaty, and return to Tarizon that Central Authority shall commence preparation for the evacuation of 20 million citizens and construct an intergalactic fleet consisting of 7 battle cruisers, 2500 fighters and 50 support vessels for the purpose of accompanying the evacuation shuttles to Earth."

The voting board lit up again and Basset held his breath. The Loyalists would vote against the measure as it was generally felt that an evacuation to Earth was a futile enterprise and Tarizon could not afford to divert needed resources to the building of a fleet of warships that wasn't really needed. Nor did the Loyalist have any desire to force the people of Earth to accept 20 million refugees, if they did not consent. It ran contrary to their belief in the rule of law and the protection of the rights of all life-forms.

The tally reached 337/321 quickly and then the board was quiet. The chairman looked up patiently and waited another loon. Then he said, "Alright, you have one more loon to cast your vote before I close the voting."

The board lit up again and reset at 382/393. Basset felt a surge of hope but it was quickly dashed when the board reset again at 404/401. "You have one-half loon to place your vote," the chairman noted.

The total switched again to 407/405. There was a collective groan amongst the Loyalist assemblymen. Everyone knew 412 vote would be a majority. "Ten tiks," the chairman advised.

There were eleven votes yet to be cast. Basset looked around to see if he could tell who hadn't voted yet but saw nothing telling in the faces of his colleagues. Finally, the total reset one last time. "Alright, the voting is now closed. Mr. Secretary do we have a final count?" The tally changed one last time to 413/408 with 2 abstentions. "The motion carries."

There was cheering and general excitement amongst the delegates who favored the resolution. Basset shook his head in dismay, turned and went back to his office. Councilor Garciah was waiting for him in his office.

"Well, Councilor. I guess you better start packing. You're going to Earth."

Rammel groaned. "Skutz. That's all I need is to be asleep for two cycles."

"I know. What a waste of time and resources."

"Do you have any idea how to approach the Americans?"

"No. Not really. The hardest obstacle will be getting an audience with someone in the government. If we mention we're from another planet they'll throw us all in a mental institution."

"Do you think you will have any problem landing?"

"No. Since they have the mistaken belief that they are the only sentient life-form in the universe, they have no defenses against an enemy who would come from above."

"Well, you better go break the news to your mate."

"Yes. I can't wait to see her face when I tell her."

Threebeard was in his office at the TGA base in Mapi going over his budget projections for the next cycle when he was told he had a call from Colonel Zitor. He picked up his communicator and accepted the call.

"Colonel. How are you?"

"Annoyed," Colonel Zitor replied. "I've just been ordered by my superiors to produce you for another assignment."

"Another assignment? What are you talking about? I thought it was arranged that I could stay here and organize the Mutant Army."

"That was my plan but apparently your services have been

requested by a Berne Baldrige. Do you know him?"

Threebeard sighed. "Right. He asked me to see if I could make contact with the nanomites. I'd almost forgotten about him."

"You did establish contact, didn't you?"

"Yes, but most of the nanomites were killed by the volcanoes and the tremors."

"Well, Baldrige and Central Authority want you to try to get the nanomites to help on some construction projects."

"That's ridiculous. There are only a few nanomites still living."

"That may be, but I have my orders. You are to report to the TGA Science Laboratory at Fasoon tomorrow at 1100 kyloons."

"Did they say how long this assignment will take?"

"I asked them that and their answer was evasive. It all depends on how long it takes to make contact with the nanomites and then to enlist their help."

"Alright. I'll start packing, but I'm reluctant to put the nanomites in contact with Central Authority. I'm not sure it would be in their best interest."

"Well, we don't even know if the nanomites are capable of doing what Central Authority wants them to do. Anyway, they can't force them to cooperate if they don't want to."

Threebeard disconnected and went to his second in command, Lt. Stixx Leode. He told him he'd have to take over while Threebeard was on assignment in Fasoon. Lt. Leode assured him they could get along without him for a while and not to worry about it.

Reluctantly Threebeard reported the science lab the next morning. It was an imposing facility covering some 120,000 sq. ft. and a hub of activity. A long line of PTV's and trucks were lined up to enter through the TGA security gate at the main entrance. A copter port sat just north of the facility where they landed. An escort was waiting for Threebeard when he disembarked and he took him to Baldrige's office.

Baldrige stood up, came around his desk and extended his hand. "Lt. Nocteris, it's so good to finally meet you."

Threebeard shook his hand and nodded. "Yes, this was an unexpected pleasure."

"Have a seat," Baldrige said pointing to a wooden chair in front of his desk. "Sorry to drag you away from whatever you were doing, but when

I told my superiors that you had successfully communicated with the nanomites, they insisted I follow through with you to see if the nanomites could help us with the current building crisis."

"Building crisis?"

"Yes, as you can imagine there has been an extensive damage to buildings throughout Tarizon. It is estimated forty percent of all the structures on Tarizon were severely damaged or destroyed. If this isn't enough 80 percent of construction related laborers are unfit to work. Of course, that doesn't make much difference since construction materials are almost impossible to find right now."

Threebeard took a deep breath. "I'm aware of the problem, but I don't see how the nanomites can help."

"Well, you and I both know they are capable of constructing some pretty elaborate structures and they do it with materials that are apparently close at hand."

"That's true and the city we studied in the Ural Desert was remarkably strong and durable. It withstood the lava flow of Mt. Alabash, but was lost when a tremor opened up a huge sink hole that swallowed the city."

"That's what I heard, but I understand some of the nanomites survived."

"Yes. There are some swarms back at the Mighty Jolly in Liehn."

"Good. I'd like you to bring them here so we can make contact and determine if we can be of mutual assistance."

"Mutual?"

"Well, I'm sure they don't want their life-form to become extinct."

"No. Survival is their strongest instinct. They will do anything to survive."

"Well, perhaps if we help them they would be willing to help us. It's at least an idea that should be explored."

"But how could so few nanomites help when the building crisis on Tarizon is so widespread?"

"Well, I have studied the nanomites for a long time and one of the most astonishing facts about them is that given the right conditions they can reproduce remarkably fast. I have seen them increase their number tenfold in just a few phases."

"Really? That is impressive. Unfortunately, the eruptions began just as we made contact with them so I'm afraid I don't know that much about them. Artis, my sister, is the one who has spent time with them and knows them the best. If they do agree to come I'd like to bring her along. It may be that she will be of more help to you than I could be. If that is the case, I'd like to get back to Mapi as I'm needed there desperately."

"That's fine. If Artis can assist us with what we need, perhaps I can convince my superiors to let you go. We'll just have to see what happens. In the meantime, how long will it take you to bring the nanomite city here?"

Threebeard shrugged. "Probably three or four days. We have to be very careful how we transport them since these are the last ones on Tarizon that we know about."

"Alright. Go get them and take whatever precautions you deem appropriate to ensure their safe arrival. I'll be anxiously awaiting your return."

Threebeard nodded and stood up. "Alright, if I can get transport to Liehn I would appreciate it."

"Not a problem. The copter you came in is at your disposal as long as you need it."

Threebeard left the building and went straight to the copter port. As promised his jet copter was waiting. The flight took several kyloons but he still managed to make it home before sunset. Artis was shocked when he strolled through the front door of the Mighty Jolly.

"What are you doing here? I thought you went to Fasoon?"

"Yes. That's where I just came from. I thought I'd surprise you."

They embraced.

"It's so good to see you. What's going on?"

"It's seems Central Authority has suddenly become interested in the nanomites. They are looking for ways to start rebuilding all the structures that were damaged or destroyed by the tremors. Unfortunately, the construction industry has totally collapsed so they are desperate to find ways to get things moving again."

"How do they expect a few swarms of nanomites to help?"

"I'm afraid Baldrige has misled them. He's speculated that they can multiply geometrically and that they will be able to start constructing useful buildings in no time."

"Well, that's ridiculous. We've barely started communicating with them."

"They are desperate. What can I tell you?"

"So, why are you here? To get the nanomites?"

"Yes, and to talk you into joining the project."

"You want me to go to Fasoon?"

"Yes. I need to get back to Mapi to continue building the mutant army. This distraction is coming at a bad time. If you come and can do what they wanted me to do, then they will let me get back to what I was doing."

"But I don't think what they want is possible."

"It probably isn't, but I guess it won't hurt to try. If it turns out not to be feasible or if the nanomites don't want to do it, then you can come home."

"Right. But if they want to keep the nanomites? I don't want to lose the opportunity to forge a strong relationship with them."

"I know. I don't like this anymore than you do, but I've got my orders. I can't disobey them."

Artis sighed deeply. "Okay. I guess I have no choice."

"Thank you. Let's talk to the nanomites and see if they are even willing to give this a try. Perhaps we can leave some of them here in case the project fails. Then when you come back you can continue with your work."

"Okay. That's a good idea."

Late that night, after the nanomite exhibit was closed, Artis and Threebeard went to them and established a link. It was an easy thing for Artis to do now since she had been talking with them almost every day. Often, she'd dream about them and realize she had been communicating with them subconsciously during the night. It was a strange but wonderful feeling.

"*Swarmmaster. I have good news. Threebeard has returned from Mapi.*"

"*Indeed, that is good news,*" the Speaker said. "*We very much enjoyed our last communication. What brings you home?*"

"*As happened to your nanomite city many of the buildings throughout Tarizon have been severely damaged or collapsed. This is causing great turmoil and upheaval for the human population.*"

"*That is understandable. How is reconstruction coming?*"

"*It's not. That's the problem. Our construction workers are too sick to work, we have a shortage of materials and most of our roads and bridges*" cannot be traveled on. The situation is desperate."

"I'm sorry to hear that."

"Our government, which we call Central Authority has an idea they wanted me to discuss with you."

"Really? What idea?"

"They have seen what wondrous buildings you have built out in your desert homelands and they wonder if they might hire you to construct buildings for them."

"We build cities because they are necessary to protect our swarms," the Speaker said. "Our primary objective in life is survival. We must devote all our efforts to that. Why would we want to build structures for humans? We have no desire for your gold or credits."

"So, would it be fair to say a growing population would be one of your primary goals?" Threebeard asked.

"Yes. That is of paramount importance. The more nanomite swarms there are the more our survival is guaranteed."

"Well, I think what Central Authority would offer you if you could build for them would be a safe environment where your swarms could grow, not only in the desert but in every city in Tarizon. Your population could multiply to levels well beyond anything you have ever imagined."

"Your idea is worth considering," the Speaker admitted. "I would have to consult with the others, but if your government could provide us what we need to flourish then we might be willing to try to build the structures you desire. We don't know if what you ask is possible, but we would be willing to try if it benefitted both humans and nanomites."

"Good. Consider this idea and if you are willing to go forward I will need to transport some of your swarms to the human science lab at Fasoon where we can start working on the project."

"Very well. Gives us a day to consider this idea and come back to us."

"We will," Threebeard said. "We'll talk tomorrow."

After Threebeard and Artis had left the swarmmasters began their deliberations. We can't trust the humans...With unlimited bacuum our numbers will grow quickly...But we will become their slaves...They could withhold bacuum and then what would we do?...The humans are evil...Why should we help them, they are our enemy....We could live on all corners of *the planet...Central Authority can't be trusted....We will die and our life-form will become extinct if we don't cooperate...It would be better to be dead than to be someone's slave...We must live...If we are alive there is always hope...Artis and Threebeard will protect us.*

29

Picking a Delegation

Petrina Garciah, their son, Eroh, and daughter, Ellah, sat spellbound by what their father was saying.

"We're going to Earth. I have been appointed Ambassador to the United States of America and must leave at once for important negotiations."

"We're all going?" Petrina asked.

"Yes. I'll be gone for three cycles and with the state of affairs on Tarizon I wouldn't feel comfortable leaving you behind."

"But won't it be dangerous?" Petrina objected.

"No, mama. It will be fun," Eroh argued. "We should go."

"It will have its risks, but I think it will probably be less risky than staying here. The purpose of the trip is to negotiate the acceptance of 20 million Tarizonian citizens for permanent settlement in the United States. If we are successful you would be going to Earth eventually anyway. So, why wait?"

"What about the rest of the population?" Petrina asked.

"That's the most we could possibly hope to transport to Earth. Even that number is probably unrealistic."

"So, how will this work?" Petrina asked warily.

"There is an Earth shuttle being prepared for the trip as we speak. It is commanded by Captain Sarrin Shilling. She apparently has been to Earth before on several reconnaissance missions. We will take with us twelve diplomats, three representatives from each of our life-forms on Tarizon, and six scientists to explain the technology we are offering to exchange for allowing us to settle on Earth."

"Technology?"

"Yes. The nations of Earth are very competitive and we feel by offering them technology that will ensure their dominance over the other nations will be too alluring to resist."

Petrina nodded. "If they are like the politicians on Tarizon that should work like a charm."

"So, will you come?"

Petrina sighed.

"Yes, mama! Say, yes?" Eroh urged.

Petrina smiled at her enthusiastic son and then turned to Ellah. "What do you think, Ellah? Should we go to Earth?"

Ellah swallowed hard. "How long will it take to get there?"

Rammel frowned. "Well, my love. About a year but it will only seem like a single night. The way it works is once we get out of Tarizon's atmosphere the ship goes FTL, so you have to be put in a sleeping chamber for the duration of the trip. That means you'll go to sleep and when you wake up we'll be on Earth."

Ellah's eyes widened. "I'm going to sleep for a year?"

Rammel laughed. "Yes, but you won't age but a day. And you'll love Earth. The air is pure, the trees are bright green and there is plenty of food for everyone."

Ellah tilted her head. "I should like to see Earth and it would be nice to be able to go outside without a breather."

"You'll love it," Eroh said excitedly. "It's like Tarizon used to be three hundred cycles ago."

Ellah shrugged. "Okay, it should be fun," she said tentatively.

"Good. Then it is settled," Rammel said. "You'll need to start packing. We'll leave in just a few days."

The following morning Rammel and his family left by jet copter to the Spaceport at Gallion. When they arrived Rammel's family was taken to barracks set aside to house the crew and other passengers going on the trip. He was taken to headquarters to meet the captain and the other diplomats making the trip. Colonel Zitor greeted him when he arrived and took him into a conference room.

"So, who has been selected to accompany me on this trip?" Rammel asked.

"The Purists insisted they be represented, so they have sent Lt. Commander Brunns as your first deputy. Or, I should say, Commander Brunns, he's been promoted for this assignment. His aide is Ensign Aerial Muri."

"What's his authority? I don't want someone second guessing everything I do."

"He's just along for the ride. You have complete authority to negotiate the treaty. Just don't get sick or die. If that happens he'd be in charge."

"Well, if he or one of the other Purists don't poison me, we should be okay."

"That's actually a concern, so I'd be careful."

"Wonderful," Rammel moaned.

"Don't worry, all the cooks are Seafolken, so the Purists won't be able to buy them off."

"That's a comfort."

"You'll also have Lucillia Reppa, as your assistant. She's one quarter Seafolken, speaks English and has strong telepathic and telekinetic abilities."

"How is it that she speaks English?" Rammel asked.

"She apparently leaned it at one of Threebeard's classes at Mapi. When Central Authority found out Threebeard spoke English they had him set up a class to teach it to shuttle pilots and their crews. Ensign Reppa was one of his pupils as was Ensign Muri."

As they were talking Captain Shilling walked in.

"Oh, Captain Shilling," Colonel Zitor said. "I'd like you to meet Rammel Garciah."

"It's a pleasure, Ambassador."

"Ambassador? That sounds strange," Rammel said.

"Well, you better get used to it," Colonel Zitor replied. "That's your new title."

Rammel gave the pretty Captain a long look. "So, Captain. I understand you have been to Earth before."

"Yes, I have."

"Did it bother you going to sleep and trusting the computers to wake you up when you got to Earth?"

Captain Shilling smiled. "Yes, Ambassador. It was a bit unsettling, but as a pilot I'm placing myself at the mercy of the computers every day. Fortunately, they have triple redundancy, so it's unlikely anything will go wrong."

"Well, that's good to hear," Rammel said tentatively.

An aide stepped in the room followed by three other officers. They saluted Captain Shilling. "This is Ensign Muri, Ensign Reppa, and Lt. Rossi Sincini. I have told you about Ensign Muri and Reppa. Lt. Sincini is my engineering officer. He'll have a dual function for this trip as the ship's engineering officer and the delegation's science consultant. He'll have the responsibility of explaining to the Americans what technology we will be offering."

"Excellent, it's a pleasure to meet you Lieutenant.

"The pleasure is mine, Mr. Ambassador."

When everyone had arrived and taken their seats, Ambassador Rammel began the meeting.

"Ladies and gentlemen. It's a pleasure to meet such a distinguished group of officers and private citizens. This is an historic occasion. Although we have known about our sister planet Earth and studied it from a distance for many cycles, we have never attempted to make contact with our brothers and sisters who live there. It has always been our objective to one day make contact, but our leaders knew such contact would be fraught with peril, so they didn't want to do it until we understood the situation on Earth well enough to avoid causing panic and hysteria. But the current crisis on Tarizon makes contact now imperative. There is no guarantee that anyone on Tarizon will survive another ten cycles under current conditions. We have to evacuate as much of our population on Tarizon as we can before our citizens are so sick that they cannot travel.

"Therefore this mission is of the utmost importance. The very survival of our people is at stake. Now, with that said I'd like to discuss the best way to approach the American government. Obviously, if an Earth shuttle suddenly lands in Central Park in New York City there could be very serious consequences."

Captain Shilling smiled. "Mr. Ambassador. There are many lightly populated areas north of New York City where we could land without the likelihood of being seen."

"Why are we going to New York City?" Ensign Reppa asked.

"That's where the United Nations is situated," Rammel replied. "I have been told the proper person to make contact with would be the American Ambassador to the United Nations. Although he technically isn't authorized to represent the U.S. government in its relations with other planets, since they have no such Ambassador he's our best bet, I believe."

"How do we know this?" Lucillia asked.

"Apparently we have been studying the American government for many cycles. Their media broadcast thousands of video and audio programs every day. By monitoring those broadcasts, we have learned a lot."

Lucilla nodded. "Can we see some of those videos before we leave to give us an idea of what to expect?"

"No. There is no time now. You'll have plenty of time, though, when you get there. We expect it to take up to six phases, or months, as they call them on Earth to make contact once we arrive. During this time, you will have to learn English fluently, pick up their customs, dress, and gain insights into their political institutions. It is imperative that we not attract attention when we get there. It will not be easy to get an audience with the U.N. Ambassador. If we all end up in jail or dead the mission will be a failure."

When Threebeard and Artis went to the nanomite replica the next morning, the nanomites indicated their willingness to at least to discuss with Central Authority the proposal to enlist the help of the nanomites in rebuilding Tarizon. As Threebeard requested the nanomites agreed to leave some swarms at the Mighty Jolly in case something went wrong with the building experiments and the nanomites somehow perished.

"So, what is the best way to divide your swarms and transport you to Fasoon?" Artis thought.

"If you will find a sandy location nearby and set our city next to it we will build transport cubes which will make it easy for you to transport us."

Artis and Threebeard agreed and went out to find a suitable location. Once they had found it they carefully carried the nanomite replica to the location and set it down on the ground.

"Now, give us until tomorrow to build our blocks. Come early in the morning and we will be ready."

Threebeard left Giant and several others to guard the nanomites and then went back to the Mighty Jolly to arrange for the pickup. The next morning when Threebeard and Artis arrived at the site where they'd left the nanomites, there were four large cubes of hard white crystal in a neat row where the nanomites had been left. Giant took one of the cubes back to the Mighty Jolly and the other three were picked up by a TGA jet copter and flown to Fasoon along with Artis and Threebeard.

When they arrived, the cubes were transported to a laboratory where Baldrige along with three other scientists were waiting patiently. Baldrige introduced his assistants as Drs. Eristeff, Vogels, and Sturvin. When the cubes were in place Threebeard cleared his throat. "So, here they are. They have agreed to explore the possibility of helping Central Authority as we discussed."

Everyone stared at the three beautifully crafted cubes. Baldrige shook his head. "This is absolutely amazing. I am so excited to finally be communicating with the nanomites. Unfortunately, I don't have the gift of telepathy, so you'll have to talk to them for me for now. Later on we'll need to train others to communicate with them as I know you have other responsibilities to attend to."

Threebeard nodded. "Artis can communicate with them and she has agreed to stay with you as long as you need her."

Baldrige smiled at Artis. "That is very generous of you."

"Well, I'm very interested in the welfare of the nanomites, so I'm hopeful your plan will work. We almost thought we had lost the entire life-form after the volcanoes began erupting."

"Yes, Threebeard told me about your journeys to find any survivors. That was very brave of you to venture out under such bad conditions."

"Foolhardy is probably more accurate," Artis replied with a grin.

"Nevertheless, I am honored to be working with you."

"So," Threebeard interjected. "How do you propose we proceed."

"Well, I think the first thing is for you to introduce us and then my team has a lot of questions for starters. We need to understand how the nanomites work so we can figure out how best to communicate to them the specifications for the buildings we need."

"Alright, do you have the questions written down?"

"Yes, I have an initial set right here," Baldrige said handing them to Threebeard.

Threebeard took the list of questions and began reading them. When he was done he closed his eyes and made a connection with the nanomites.

"Swarmmasters. We are ready to get started if you are?"

"Yes, Threebeard," the Speaker said. *"Who are these men with Artis?"*

"The man in the white coat is called Baldrige. He has been studying your life-form for many cycles and will be in charge of the experiment. The others are Doctors Eristeff, Vogels, and Sturvin."

"Doctors?"

"Yes, a doctor is someone who has studied a particular subject and is recognized as having a lot of knowledge about it."

"I see. So, how shall we begin?"

"They have some questions for you to start with, which I will read to you and then relay to them your response."

"Very well?" the Speaker replied. *"We are ready."*

"Okay. What is the physical structure of the nanomite body?"

"Each nanomite has a head, neck, torso, four legs for movement forward or laterally, two arms for manipulation, and two wings for flight."

"Does each nanomite determine his own movement or does he respond to a central command."

"Each nanomite moves with the will of the swarmmaster in one single fluid movement."

"Who directs the movement of the swarms?"

"Each nanomite swarm is part of the local nanomite colony. All of the swarmmasters in the colony have equal voice in the Council of the Colony. If there is a dispute the majority rules."

"Where does this council meet?"

"It meets in our minds. We just begin talking among ourselves until we reach a consensus."

"Who is in charge of the debate?"

"No one. Everyone just starts thinking and our thoughts are exchanged and processed."

"Do you ever have a deadlock?"

"No. We almost always reach a consensus since our interests are

identical."

"So, how do you go about designing your beautiful homes?"

"The ideal building structure for a nanomite city has been known for as long as there have been nanomites. We simple follow the same process each time we have to build."

"Do you think you would be able to alter your design and process if we told you exactly how we wanted a building built."

"We don't know for sure, but we will try. Theoretically we can build a structure differently if there is a good reason. For instance, when the lava flow threatened our city in the Ural Desert we built a wall to divert the lava flow. So, it can be done."

The question and answer session went on for several kyloons until Baldrige suggested they stop for lunch. This prompted questions about how the nanomites received nourishment.

"We are very small so we don't require a lot of food from your standpoint. Usually the air is full of pollen, plant matter, seeds, and water. All the things that we need to survive. We also need a certain chemical which your scientist call bacuum. This chemical is necessary for our reproduction process and therefore critical to our survival."

"We have bacuum," Threebeard thought. *"How do you ingest it?"*

"We send a swarm through the rock or sand that contains it and carry it back to the other swarms."

"Okay, we can bring you bacuum that we have filtered and ground into a powder. Will that do?"

"Yes, just make a small pile of it next to one of our stones."

"Is there anything else we can bring you right now for lunch?"

"Yes, some dried grass or grain would be fine."

"Alright, I'll have someone supply you with that and we will come back to talk some more in a few kyloons."

"That will be acceptable," the Speaker thought.

Earth Shuttle 26 landed softly on the landing field at the Spaceport at Gallion. The crew and passengers that were assembled several hundred strides away watched in awe as their new home settled down casting off a cloud of ash in all directions. Fortunately, they all had breathers so they simply closed their eyes until the cloud had dissipated. A few seconds later the main hatches opened and eight gangways were lowered to the ground to allow passengers and crew to board.

Rammel smiled at his daughter who looked a little pale. "Don't worry, Ellah. Everything will be fine."

Ellah had been worried, not about the spaceflight, but by the thought of being asleep for a full cycle. She had asked many questions about how such a thing could be possible. In particular she was concerned about practical things like eating, going to the bathroom, and taking a shower. Petrina had explained how all of that was taken care of by tubes and monitors that would be regulated by the ship's computers, but that had not been much comfort to her.

"Why can't we just stay awake?" Ellah complained.

Eroh rolled his eyes. "You're such a dirkbird."

"Don't be cruel to your sister," Rammel scolded. "Like we talked about before, love, it's because the shuttles were built to transport a large number of people and that's much easier to do if everyone is in a sleeping chamber. Plus sleeping people don't eat and drink nearly as much as people who are awake."

A bell rang signaling that it was safe to board the ship. Eroh immediately rushed on board. Rammel took Ellah's hand and she reluctantly followed him up the ramp with Petrina close behind. Once on board they were taken to a large room where the ship's medical staff was preparing passengers to be put in their sleeping chambers.

"I'll go first," Eroh said bravely, "so Ellah will see that it's nothing to fear."

Rammel felt a sense of great pride for his son's gesture. Eroh had always been very mature and responsible. He'd filled in for Rammel as a father figure for Ellah when he'd been appointed to the Council of Interpreters and forced to spend long periods away from home.

A crew member helped Eroh take off his shirt and climb into the chamber, then she placed monitors at various points on his body and inserted several tubes.

"See you on Earth," Eroh said as he was given an injection and gradually drifted off to sleep.

The crew member closed the sleeping chamber and then looked up. Ellah squeezed Rammel's hand. "No, father. I'm scared."

"I know, but it will be fine. It's just like going to bed and waking up in the morning."

Ellah took a deep breath as Rammel picked her up and placed her in the sleeping chamber. She started to squirm but the medical tech quickly injected her and she immediately became limp. After she had been hooked up to her monitors and the various tubes inserted, the door was closed.

"Well, I guess it is good night, dear," Rammel said. "Pleasant dreams."

Rammel and Petrina kissed and then went to their sleeping chambers. Moments later they were both in a deep sleep. A sleep of a thousand dreams. Dreams of past triumphs and tragedies and hopes and fears for the future. A kyloon later Earth Shuttle 26 lifted off for its long journey to Earth with Captain Shilling at the helm along with six crew members who would be awake during the journey guiding the ship through space to its final destination, Earth.

30

First Contact

Rammel and his staff was awakened from their sleeping chambers ten days before their expected arrival on Earth. This was to allow them to hit the ground running the moment they arrived. Although they knew it would take time to actually make contact, they didn't want to waste any of their limited time on Earth. Earth Shuttle 26 sat down in a soft meadow about ten miles from the nearest inhabited area. Scans of the area before the landing detected no human life-forms in the area.

The Earth shuttles were circular in design and could immediately corkscrew underground so that their presence could not be easily detected. From above the landing area simply appeared to be a recently plowed field. A topside hatch allowed egress to the shuttle from above. To minimize possible detection Earth Shuttle 26 came in at 3 a.m. and descended quickly so as to appear as if it were a falling meteor. Rammel had decided not to immediately exit the shuttle once it was safely underground, just in case their entry into the atmosphere had been detected. If jets were scrambled to investigate he didn't want them to find anything.

Once the sun had risen the hatch was opened and Rammel climbed out of the shuttle and looked around. He marveled at the clear blue sky, the green grass and the yellow flowers that adorned the meadow. It had been many cycles since he'd seen such wonders and seeing Earth in such splendor gave him great determination to make his mission a success.

Once the full delegation had climbed out of the shuttle and got their gear readied for travel, they began to hike in the general direction of the closest city. After hiking all morning they came to the crest of a hill and saw the small town that had been their destination. There were eight in this initial party and they had no weapons. This was a peaceful mission and they wanted to be sure there was no doubt about that, so they left their laser rifles and other personal armaments in their shuttle. They could have brought a hover vehicle for transportation, but that would have prematurely made it apparent that visitors had arrived from another world.

Commander Brunns, Lt. Ziegfield Kulchz, and Aerial Muri stepped a few strides away from the group to talk privately. They were the representatives selected by the Purist Party to accompany the mission and they had their own agenda while they were on Earth.

"This is just how I imagined Earth to be. It's a paradise," Brunns said. "I shall bring my family with me the next time I come. This must be our new home."

Kulchz took a deep breath and let it out slowly. "Yes, it is nice to be able to actually breathe. The air is so cool and fresh. It's exhilarating."

"Well, if the Americans are as greedy as we think, we should have no problem coming to an agreement," Aerial remarked.

"I don't care if the Americans agree or not, the people of Tarizon are coming to Earth, like it or not," Brunns replied.

"Yes, when we return to Earth we will have an intergalactic fleet that will be invincible. If need be we'll simply take control by force."

"It won't be that easy," Aerial said. "The Americans are fighters. They won't just sit back and let us take over their world."

"They will have no choice," Commander Brunns disagreed. He laughed. "We are so ahead of them technologically a war with them would be a joke."

"So, what are we going to do to make sure the Americans go for out deal?" Kulchz asked.

"We're going to bypass the bureaucrats and get in tight with the military. They are the ones with the real power. I'm sure they will want the new weapons technology we brought with us and will do anything to get it."

"Excellent plan," Aerial said. "You are a genius, Commander."

The delegation began moving out forcing them to end their private discussion. They fell in behind the group as the delegates moved single file through the meadow.

They had brought many things with them—gifts for the U.S. President, their credentials, a letter from the Chancellor, and things that would prove they came from another solar system. They knew that it might be difficult for the government to accept the fact that human life existed on other planets. If they weren't convincing they knew they could easily end up in a prison cell for the rest of their lives.

Their immediate problem was to get into town unnoticed, obtain transportation, local currency, and get something to eat. They had eaten rations on the ship but they weren't very satisfying.

On the outskirts of town, they hid their backpacks and walked in like they'd been out on an afternoon stroll. Although many people looked at them in their unusual attire, nobody seemed alarmed or distressed that they were in town. So far, their arrival had been perfect. They hadn't stuck out. Now they needed local currency and their plan was to find a pawn shop or jewelry store.

They got directions and found a jewelry store where they were able to sell an assortment of precious stones. The proprietor must have thought he was dealing with a bunch of idiots when he showed them out the door having parted with less than 5,000 U.S. dollars for stones worth ten times that. But they'd gotten enough money to buy a used car, get new clothes, gasoline, food, and a hotel room when they got to New York City.

They arrived in New York on a Sunday, a few days before the next session of the United Nations General Assembly. Once they were settled in their rooms the question was how to approach the Ambassador.

"You will have to call his office and try to get an appointment," Lt. Reppa said. "Without an appointment he won't talk to you."

"Yes, but they will try to make us see an underling first, I'm sure. But, that won't work. We can't afford to show our hand to anyone but the Ambassador. If the word gets out that we claim to be from outer space there is no telling what will happen," Ensign Muri said.

"So, I guess we need to make up some kind of a story to pique the interest of the Ambassador so he'll be compelled to meet with us," Rammel concluded.

"Why don't you tell him you represent a nation that wants to be admitted to the United Nations? Tell him that your country is very rich and if the United States sponsors us you will make it very much worthwhile,"

Aerial suggested.

"That's a good idea and not a big stretch from the truth," Rammel replied. "I'll try that."

Rammel nervously picked up the telephone to make the call. He was not used to the clumsy American telephones as all communications on Tarizon were hands free. The operator finally connected him to the Ambassador's secretary.

"Hello," the voice said.

"Hello. Hi. This is Rammel Garciah."

"Who?"

"Rammel Garciah, an emissary from Turvin. I'd like to make an appointment with the Ambassador."

"What's the nature of your visit?" she asked.

"I've come all the way from Shisk. We'd like to obtain membership in the United Nations and wanted to see if the United States would support us."

"Well, I'll discuss the matter with the Ambassador but he's very busy. I can't promise you he'll be able to see you."

"Tell him our government has much to offer in return for his support."

"Well, okay. I'll do that. Give me your number and we'll get back with you."

Rammel gave the secretary their hotel telephone number and then hung up.

Aerial looked at Rammel expectantly. "So, how did it go?"

"About as expected. I'm not going to hold my breath waiting for a return call. We'll just have to wait a day or two and call back. In the meantime, we should all start learning about America. I think I'll go to the library and see what they have there that would be useful."

"I'll go with you," Commander Brunns said.

Rammel nodded. "The rest of you are on your own for a few days. Check out the city and learn as much as you can, but don't be conspicuous and stay out of trouble."

"I think I'll go visit the United Nations building and observe its security protocols. We'll need to know that when we get an appointment," Lt. Sincini said.

"I'll go with you," Lucilla added.

Lt. Sincini nodded and they turned and left. The others wandered off talking amongst themselves about what they should do for the rest of the day.

At the library Rammel was amazed at the vast amount of information available. He and Commander Brunns went off in different directions and soon got lost in the stacks. Rammel thought about the telephone call to the U.N. Ambassador's office. He knew there wouldn't be a return call that day. In fact, he didn't really expect a return phone call at all since, when the Ambassador tried to find *Turvin* and *Shisk*, he obviously wouldn't have any luck. His intention was simply to get the Ambassador curious.

When they grew weary of the library Rammel and Commander Brunns walked the streets of New York just taking in the wonders of the city. As they talked they both agreed as distant as Tarizon was from Earth the cities had a lot in common. Although the buildings and transportation systems were quite different, the people of New York seemed much like the humans on Tarizon in the way they lived and interacted with each other. Rammel wondered if the physiology of the humans on Tarizon and Earth differed. This would be an important thing to know. Would an American doctor examining a citizen of Tarizon know he was from another planet? The Seafolken would be easily spotted as their gills and membranes between their hands and feet would stand out, but a normal human, he thought, might be mistaken for being from Earth.

The following day Rammel called the Ambassador's office again and was told the Ambassador had gotten his message but hadn't been able to fit him into his schedule yet. After he hung up he noticed Lt. Sincini standing by the door.

"Lieutenant. What did you find out about security at the United Nations?"

"It's pretty tight. Each delegation has its private security. Then there is the U.N. security and finally the New York police. If they can't handle a situation then the government's FBI or the state's national guard can be called in."

"Well, that's to be expected."

"Their electronics are not very sophisticated. It wouldn't be hard to break in during the night when there is no business going on."

"Well, we won't need to do that, hopefully. We must gain the Americans' trust so we can avoid a confrontation. It's not in any of our interests to destroy the last habitable planet for humanity. "

"If anyone can convince the Americans to cooperate I'm sure you can do it."

"Well, a lot will depend on how well you sell our technology. You need to get their scientists drooling over the thought of obtaining it."

"Don't worry, Ambassador. From what I've seen these last few days it won't be hard to impress them."

"Well, I wish you had something that would make the Ambassador agree to talk to me."

Sincini thought a moment. "I might have something. Let me think about it a day or two and I'll get back with you."

Sincini left leaving Rammel hopeful he did indeed have a trick to make the Ambassador agree to a meeting.

Rammel called again the next day and again got the cold shoulder. This went on each day for a week until the secretary finally asked, "Where is Turvin anyway? The Ambassador says he's never heard of it. Is it in South America? I noticed your name was Spanish."

"My name is Spanish?" Rammel said amused.

"Yes, Garcia is a common Spanish name."

Rammel didn't say anything for a moment but eventually decided not to correct her. "It's a new nation very rich in oil and diamonds. If the Ambassador will see me, I'll show him where it is on the map and let him see some of the stones mined in our great nation. I have a gift for the President too, from our Chancellor."

"A gift?"

"Yes, something quite magnificent. We were hopeful the Ambassador would see that he got it."

"Well, he might do that. I'll tell him what you said and get back with you."

"Thank you. And tell him again that we can provide the United States much in return for its support."

"Alright. I'll remind him."

Artis was pleasantly surprised how quickly the nanomites had embraced the concept of building structures for Central Authority. She had envisioned it being a long drawn out affair to convince them to do it and then many cycles to actually come up with a viable way to actually build something. But when promised the opportunity for unlimited expansion throughout Tarizon the nanomites put out an extraordinary effort to make the project work.

The biggest difficulty that had to be overcome was communicating to the nanomites the specifications for the buildings that humans would inhabit. Since nanomites could not read plans or written specifications they had to come up with a different way to communicate the desired structure and look of the building. This was finally accomplished by detailed computer simulations of every foot of the construction project. Artis would then study the simulations and communicate those images to the nanomites.

Over the first phase there had been many small experimental building projects conducted in the lab, but the real test came about in the sixth phase when the nanomites were given the task of building a small warehouse on the science lab campus. It was to be a simple rectangular building with a flat roof and a string of offices along one side of the building. The remainder was open space for storage.

By this time living under optimal conditions the nanomites had grown tenfold to over 5,000 swarms. Nobody knew for sure how many nanomites would be needed for the project but everyone was anxious to find out. All of the materials the nanomites would need were dumped next to the building site and a nanomite cube was set at each of the corners of the buildings' perimeter. Additional cubes were placed at uniform intervals within the interior of the warehouse site. For several days it didn't appear that anything was happening but then gradually the ground began to swell almost imperceptibly.

In order to measure the progress of the building, Baldrige installed sensors to detect even the smallest of changes in the structure. In talking to the nanomites Artis learned that the slow progress was due to the fact that the project was much more complex than anything they had ever done and realistically required many more nanomites than those available. This wasn't a problem for the swarmmasters as they relished the growth of their numbers, but it did take time.

It was almost a phase before the foundation of the warehouse was completed, but progress began to accelerate thereafter and it was an impressive sight to see walls seem to grow out of the ground like a plant or a tree. Over the next phase public officials from all over Tarizon descended on the science lab at Fasoon to see this wondrous sight. On one such occasion the group of official guests included Rupra Bruda. Artis didn't recognize Bruda by his looks but when she saw the name on the guest roster she almost died. She immediately linked with Threebeard.

"Yes, Artis. How are you?" Threebeard thought, delighted to hear from his sister.

"I was fine until just a minute ago."

"What happened?"

"You won't believe who's on the guest roster today."

"Who?"

"Rupra Bruda."

Threebeard didn't respond right away, but eventually he thought. *"Yes, I've heard he's ingratiated himself with Videl Lai and his group. Apparently, he is no longer a suspect in my assassination attempt."*

"How do you know this?"

"The public enforcers in Shisk informed me someone else confessed to the conspiracy and denied Bruda was involved."

"That's a lie," Artis spat.

"I know, but there is nothing we can do about it other than keep a close eye on him."

"How can we do that?"

"Oh, I already have that taken care of."

"How?"

"It's best kept as my secret. It's not that I don't trust you, but Bruda is developing a Purist intelligence core. He's teaching any purist with telepathic abilities how to enhance their capabilities. They will be very good at reading unsuspecting minds, so it's best to keep our secrets to ourselves and not transport them through space where they might be intercepted."

"Is that possible? Could they be intercepting our conversation right now?"

"I don't know, but Bruda has a very strong gift and he will use it in any way possible to forward the Purists' agenda. We can't be too careful."

"I understand."

"Have you been able to train any of the other scientists to communicate with the nanomites?"

"No. I don't know what the problem is but there are three of them with the gift but the nanomites only talk to me."

"What do the nanomites have to say about that?"

"They say they don't hear the other's thoughts, only mine."

"Hmm. That's interesting. I guess you're going to be stuck there until we can find someone with strong enough abilities to make contact with them. I'll talk to some of my Seafolken friends. There are some of them with strong abilities that might be able to assist you."

"Thank you, brother. It's a lot of pressure on me to be the only one who can talk to them. It has been a long time since I have been home, but I can't leave under the circumstances."

"I know. I'll talk to the Seafolken immediately. Be careful with Bruda around. He's the evillest man I have ever known and if he realizes you are my sister, he may try to harm you."

"I'll be on my guard."

Two days passed before the Ambassador's secretary finally called back and said the Ambassador could see Rammel and the delegation the next day for ten minutes during the noon recess of the General Assembly. They were instructed to meet him at one of the conference rooms in the United Nations building and told where they could get credentials and directions to the room.

Rammel was ecstatic that he'd finally gotten his audience with the Ambassador. He knew the Ambassador would be very skeptical about this nation of Turvin that nobody on his staff could find on a map, but he was sure his curiosity would give him a few minutes to make an impression. He didn't think he'd need long.

The following day the delegation went to the United Nations building as instructed, picked up their badges, went through a security check, and were escorted to the conference room where they were to meet the Ambassador. He hadn't arrived yet so they were asked to wait. While they were waiting, a young staff member questioned them.

"Where is Turvin, anyway? We couldn't find it on any map. Is it in South America?"

"No. It's a very small nation. It's not on the map."

"So why do you think there is any chance it could get a seat in the United Nations General Assembly? The Ambassador doesn't have time to waste on hopeless causes."

"It's not a hopeless cause. Believe me, we will make it very worthwhile for the United States to support us."

The young staff member was about to ask another question, when the Ambassador walked in. Rammel stood, smiled and bowed to the Ambassador. The Ambassador nodded and motioned for them to come into the conference room. The young staff member shook his head and walked away. Rammel and the delegation followed him in the conference room where the Ambassador's staff was already seated. Security guards were posted at the door.

"Okay, tell me about this mysterious country called Turvin," the Ambassador said.

"Yes, actually Turvin is a continent like North America. Shisk is the capital city of Soni which was once an independent nation but now is a state on Tarizon."

"What? Tarizon? I'm afraid I don't understand."

"Tarizon is not of this world. It's a planet in another solar system. We have traveled for more than a year to get here."

The Ambassador started to laugh. "Is this some kind of joke?" He looked at his assistant. "Who put you up to this?"

"I assure you, Mr. Ambassador this is not a joke," Rammel said strongly. "We have been sent by the Chancellor and Tarizon's World Assembly to establish diplomatic relations with the United States. I have a letter from the Chancellor himself if you'd like to see it."

The Ambassador laughed again and glanced over to his assistant skeptically. The assistant shrugged. The Ambassador turned back to Rammel, took the letter from him, and opened it. It was in Tari so the Ambassador handed it back and said, "Would you read it for me? I speak eight languages but certainly not one from another world." He stifled another laugh and then forced himself to listen.

Rammel pulled out a small square metallic object from his pocket and placed it on the table. "Actually," he said. "The Chancellor will read the message himself." Rammel tapped the box and immediately a circular area on the top of the object lit up; a hologram of the Chancellor appeared above the box. He immediately began giving his message in English.

To the Most Honorable United States Ambassador to the United Nations:

Greetings from the people of Tarizon.

Forgive me for the manner in which we made first contact, but I think you can understand the need for the greatest discretion. Because our two worlds know nothing of each other and the greatest fear humans can face is fear of the unknown, we are making this first contact with you, America's greatest diplomat, and have sent our most esteemed emissary, Rammel Garciah to bring our message. We trust that the two of you can breach the great gulf that stands between our two worlds so that a great alliance can be forged.

My emissary will explain our predicament and what assistance we will require. We pray that you will hear him out and help us in this time of great crisis. Your nation's aid will be remembered and rewarded tenfold. I look forward to a long and profitable relationship between our worlds.

Malnor Artiss
Chancellor of Tarizon
Protector of the Supreme Mandate

The image disappeared and the room was so quiet you could have heard a feather drop. The Ambassador looked at Rammel and then at one of his staff members. Finally, he spoke. "Well, that is quite a little device, but that doesn't prove you are from another planet. Scientists have been working on holograms for years but, I'll admit I haven't seen one quite like that."

"We knew you would be skeptical so we brought a lot of proof to convince you," Rammel said. He took a stone out of his pocket and tossed it to the Ambassador. "Give this to your geologists. I think they will attest there is nothing like it on Earth." Before the Ambassador could respond Rammel snapped his fingers and Lucillia came forward, put her arm on the table and pulled out a small knife. The security guards drew their weapons. The Ambassador gasped and came to his feet. Before anyone could stop her, Lucillia slashed the knife across her forearm. Blood immediately began to bubble out of the wound. The Ambassador looked at Rammel in horror.

"Don't be alarmed Ambassador," Rammel said. "This is just a simple demonstration of some of our medical technology that we hope to be able to share with your government." Everyone in the room gathered around the woman to watch Rammel, who had pulled out a small jar and unscrewed the lid. The woman wiped the blood away with a rag and Rammel began applying the white liquid contained in the bottle on the wound. The bleeding immediately stopped and before their eyes the skin began repairing itself. In just a minute the horrible gash was gone.

The Ambassador looked up in astonishment. "Very impressive." He laughed. "You're going to make a believer out of me yet."

"Yes, but I can see you're not a hundred percent certain quite yet. I think what I'm about to show you will change that. I'll need a glass of water for this next demonstration."

The Ambassador motioned to one of his aides. The aide produced a glass of water and handed it to Rammel. Lucillia who was still standing amongst the eager onlookers began to disrobe. The Ambassador looked around nervously. Some of the male aides were unable to stifle their amusement until the Ambassador gave them a dirty look. When Lucillia was finished she was standing before them in a bikini. Beneath the bra there were gills that were slowly moving in and out as she breathed. Several of the onlookers gasped in amazement.

"Lucilia is one quarter Seafolken. The Seafolken are a race of humans on Tarizon that has adapted to life in the sea. A full blood Seafolken has a tough light green skin, feet and hands that become webbed while in water, and is amazingly strong. Quite interestingly the quarter-breeds can look almost like you and I, except for the gills." Rammel took the glass of water and began pouring it on Lucilia' s feet. Immediately they began to transform until they were much wider and webs began to form between her toes. Again, there were gasps from the onlookers. Lucillia extended her hands and Rammel poured water on them as well. They began the same sort of transformation. "A quarter-breed can swim underwater for up to twenty minutes without surfacing. A full blood Seafolken can stay under water for hours."

The Ambassador shook his head. "All right. I'm a believer. Can I see your ship?" he said smiling broadly.

"Of course," Rammel replied, "but only when we leave to go back to Tarizon. We can't disclose its location yet."

"I understand," the Ambassador said. "This is indeed a momentous occasion. I am honored that you chose to make first contact with me. I promise I will do everything in my power to persuade our government to assist you in any way it can."

Rammel bowed. "Thank you, Mr. Ambassador."

"Tony," the Ambassador said to one of his aides, "I want you to assign a full security detail to our guests and I want you to move them to the Hilton. No one is to talk to them. Put them on their own floor. Also, contact the director of the CIA and tell him I have to meet with him ASAP and I'll need to see the President!"

31

Deceit

Events moved quickly once the U.N. Ambassador had accepted the fact that Rammel's delegation was really from another world. A permanent liaison to the delegation was immediately assigned and from that moment forward there was always a link between Rammel and the United States government.

The first serious meeting took place a few days later when the Director of the Central Intelligence Agency came by Rammel's suite at the Hilton. He was accompanied by representatives from the State Department and the Pentagon. Everyone introduced themselves and took a seat around a small conference table.

"This is indeed an historic occasion," the Director noted. "Honestly, I never believed that I would be having such a meeting. The idea that we have a sister planet is quite a shock."

"Yes," Rammel said. "I can imagine it would be hard to believe. I'm not sure why, but we have always known about Earth. In fact, we have studied your planet from a distance for over a hundred Earth-years. We call them cycles on Tarizon. The time they represent is not exactly the same, as our planet is a little bigger than yours, but they are approximately equivalent."

"So, why did it take so long for you to make contact?"

"We knew our arrival might not be welcomed—at least at first. Humans fear the unknown and we didn't want to create panic. We had to figure a way to make contact discreetly so that we could let you know that we are here in peace."

"Along that vein," the Director said. "We don't think it would be wise to make your presence known yet to the American people. You are right about fear of the unknown. The people will have to be prepared for the news that life exists on another planet. It will be a delicate task and will take some

331

time."

"We totally understand and will leave that up to your discretion," Rammel agreed. "We did not come here to cause any kind of an upheaval."

"So, why *did* you come?" the Director asked.

Everyone looked at Rammel expectantly. He sighed deeply. "I am sad to say it, but Tarizon is in turmoil. Just when a world government was finally established and we'd enjoyed twenty cycles of peace, the world was struck by super volcanic eruptions, thousands of tremors, tidal waves, fires, and every other imaginable catastrophe that could beset a planet."

"Oh, my God!" the Director said. "I'm so sorry."

"Thank you. The net effect of these disasters has been loss of millions of lives, the destruction of much of our world's infrastructure, the loss of forty percent of all our homes and buildings, the pollution of our air and water, and, worst of all, the loss of light from the sun."

"Loss of light from the sun?" the Director questioned.

"Yes, Tarizon has been engulfed in a shroud of ash and other toxins that are blocking seventy-eight percent of the light that normally would fall on our planet. Besides the constant state of near darkness, the loss of this light has destroyed our primary energy source as well as most of our agricultural production."

"So, how can we help?" the Director asked.

"Well, what I was sent here to negotiate was the resettlement of 20 million Tarizonians to your planet."

The Director just stared at Rammel, thunderstruck by what he was hearing. General Stout, one of the representatives from the Pentagon cleared his throat. "So, you're proposing to bring 20 million refugees to Earth?"

"Yes," Rammel said. "That's exactly what we are asking but we don't expect you to do it out of the kindness of your heart. We will make it worth your while."

"Assuming we agreed to this, which is by no means a certainty, what could you possibly offer us to make it worthwhile to accept your people, find a place for them to live, feed them, and deal with the incredible backlash that something like this could cause?" the Director asked.

"Well, what we are offering is technology. Technology that will advance the United States by 50 years and insure that you are the dominate nation on Earth for a long time to come."

"What kind of technology?" General Stout asked.

Rammel gestured toward Lt. Sincini. "Well, I brought with me Lt. Sincini. He's our scientific director and he and your scientist can get together later to discuss this technology in more detail, but we can offer you the ability to travel through space faster than light, conceal your jets so they can fly anywhere undetected, set up a defense system that will ensure no missiles will ever hit a target on U.S. soil, and generate enough solar power that you will never have to burn coal or oil again."

General Stout raised his eyebrows. "Okay, you've got our attention. Perhaps we can set up a meeting with Lt. Sincini with some of our scientists tomorrow. We will want a detailed report on this technology you are offering to show the President when we meet with him."

"That will be fine," Rammel said.

"Yes," the Director said. "And my people will want more details on these 20 million refugees. We'll have to figure out the logistics of handling so many people. The President will want to know if it is even feasible. You know, where would we put them? How would we feed them? Do we build a new city or integrate them within our own population? There's just so much to consider."

"We are at your disposal. I know this is a monumental task and it will take some time to sort out, so just let us know how we can help."

Commander Brunns, Commander Kulchz and Ensign Muri left Rammel's suite and went down to the coffee shop in the lobby to talk. They had, so far, been silent observers, being content to watch how the negotiations were developing. But now some decisions had to be made.

"So, what do you think the Americans will do now?" Kulchz asked.

"I don't know, but I know what I'm going to do."

"What's that?" Aerial asked.

"I'm going to get assigned to Rossi Sincini's delegation to explain the technology incentive to the scientists and military. You should do the same Kulchz. We need to start making friends."

"Okay," Kulchz replied.

"What about me?" Aerial asked.

"You better stick with the Ambassador so you can keep me apprised as to the progress of the negotiations."

"Yes, sir. No problem," Aerial agreed.

"I brought a few things of my own to help mold a few friendships," Brunns advised.

"Like what?" Kulchz asked.

"Like gold and diamonds. I understand they are a very hot commodity here on earth."

Kulchz smiled wryly. "How much did you bring?"

"Enough to make them very wealthy if they agree to cooperate."

"Do you think they will betray their own government?" Aerial asked.

"They are human, so I suppose they will for the right price."

"But I understand patriotism is very strong in America," Aerial argued.

"Well, if money doesn't do the trick I'm sure you could seduce them and we could get some compromising photos. Who could resist the opportunity to be the first man on Earth to sleep with a woman from another world?"

"I'm not a prostitute," Aerial objected.

"No, but you are an officer and you will obey orders."

Aerial gave Commander Brunns a scathing look. "What about us?"

"There is no *us*. You will do as you're told."

"But, how—"

"Enough!" Brunns spat. "You'll do what is expected of you to make this mission a success. Do you understand?"

"Yes, sir," Aerial conceded bitterly.

"Now, you can start by going up to Ambassador Garciah's suite and becoming his constant companion. I want to know everything that is going on."

"He has a mate and two children back at the ship. I doubt he'll feel comfortable having me hang around."

"He's a man. He won't mind, I promise you."

"This isn't what I signed up for when I joined the party. I'm a military officer not a sex toy."

"Quit moaning and obey your orders. I know this is a diplomatic mission but I can still put a bullet in your head for insubordination."

Aerial signed deeply and stood up. "Alright, I'm going."

"Stay close by the Ambassador. Make sure you are in earshot at all times."

"Yes, sir," Aerial said as she stomped off angrily.

Commander Brunns shook his head and smiled at Kulchz. "What a frustrating woman."

"Why do you put up with her?" Kulchz inquired. "I would have shot her the first time she refused a direct order."

"She didn't refuse. She just wanted me to know she didn't like the assignment."

"Too bad. I don't like many of my assignments, but I do them without question."

"Well, the truth is I like having her around so I put up with more than I should. She's a very alluring woman. It gets lonely at night and being with her can be quite intoxicating."

Kulchz laughed. "Oh, I see. I'm surprised you gave her up to the Ambassador, then."

"Well, sometimes you have to make short term sacrifices to achieve your long-term goals, right?"

They both laughed heartily.

"Besides, have you seen some of the American wenches hanging around in the downstairs lobby?"

Kulchz nodded excitedly. "Oh, yes. Indeed."

"Well, I needed to make room in my bed for one of them."

They both laughed again.

"So, what are we waiting for?" Kulchz asked eagerly.

"Nothing," Brunns said. "Let's go downstairs, get drunk, and find us a couple of nice wenches to bring back with us."

They both got up laughing and set out eagerly on their quest for a memorable evening.

After the successful construction of a warehouse at the science laboratory in less than two phases, Central Authority decided to divide the nanomite swarms and start five new projects at Gallion, Mapi, Shini, and Vaceen. The projects were simple government buildings for bureaucrats who were working rather inefficiently in temporary structures. When Artis informed the nanomites of the move, they objected.

"Central Authority is very pleased with the construction of the warehouse and would like you to do five projects now at other sites in Lemaine Shane. They propose to divide your hives by five and move you to these new locations."

"Some of the swarms can be moved, but not all of them. We agreed to build structures for the humans but they are also our homes now and some nanomites will have to be allowed to live there."

Artis relayed this to Baldrige who was surprised by it. He consulted with Central Authority who didn't like the idea.

"Central Authority doesn't want nanomites to remain in the structures they build. They say they will provide you with farms where you can live between construction projects."

"No, we won't build something we cannot live in. Besides, our structures will require maintenance which the inhabitants will happily perform."

Artis relayed this to Baldrige and asked him why it made a difference. The humans inhabiting the buildings would never even know the nanomites were still there. It wasn't like the nanomites would play loud music or anything. Finally, after much debate Baldrige and Central Authority finally gave in and agreed that some of the nanomites could stay. Once this was ironed out twenty-five nanomite blocks were sent to each of the five sites selected for new government office buildings. This meant Artis had to do a lot of traveling to provide the necessary communication between Baldrige and his engineers and the nanomite speakers. The upside to this was a dramatic increase in the number of nanomite swarms. In less than a cycle the nanomite swarm population on Tarizon went from an estimated five million to 750 million, and this was just the beginning of the Nanomite's entry into the construction industry on Tarizon.

The President accepted the U.N. Ambassador, General Stout and the CIA Director into the Oval Office. After being served coffee and exchanging pleasantries, the President started the meeting.

"So, it is true. There are aliens here from another planet?"

"Yes," General Stout replied. "It appears that way, although we haven't seen their spaceship yet. They say it is hidden somewhere close by but won't tell us where."

"So, it still could be a clever ruse. I could see the Chinese or the Russians doing something like this to embarrass us."

"I don't think so," Stout said. "We've had a meeting with their science officer, Lt. Sincini. He's obviously a brilliant man and quite knowledgeable. He's given us some rock and materials samples that are quite extraordinary. One material called limbidium is as light as aluminum but much stronger and tougher than any steel alloy we have on Earth. They claim it is nearly indestructible, but, whether it is or not, either way it is something that would revolutionize the construction of military equipment from tanks to supersonic fighters."

"They say they have fighters on Tarizon that travel mach 8," the Director added.

"What about this alien life-form, the Seafolken? Did our medical people check her out?"

"Yes, they say she is very much a human but has adapted to live also in the sea," the Director replied.

"Could she just be some kind of mutation born here on Earth?"

"I don't know. They claim there were once Seafolken here on Earth—the mythical mermaid. They believe Tarizon is a sister planet and the original human settlers brought with them the same plants, trees, insects, birds, and animals to both planets. Although humans are the only sentient life-form on Earth there are several other sentient life-forms on Tarizon that have lived in harmony for thousands of years."

The President stood up and began pacing. "This is just so mind boggling, I'm having trouble getting my head around it."

"Yes, sir," General Stout agreed. "It is a lot to comprehend."

"I mean, the ramifications of this becoming public knowledge are staggering. There will be a media frenzy beyond belief."

"Yes, and since these aliens have superior technology what is to stop them from just taking control of the Earth once they get 20 million of their kind here?" the Director warned.

"But, you've got to admit, they seem sincere," the Ambassador said. "Particularly Ambassador Rammel. He's obviously an honorable man, a statesman, you can tell."

"Yes, but with their 20 million people there will have to be thousands of spaceships, spaceships that most likely will be equipped with weaponry," General Stout said. "What if this is just a ploy to get a foothold on Earth and then take over?"

"What I think, Mr. President," the Ambassador said, "is that the government of Tarizon is desperate. They have shown us video footage of the volcanic eruptions, tremors, tidal waves, and fires. The situation is cataclysmic. They are coming here whether we like it or not, so it is better that we accept them as brothers rather than as conquerors. We don't want Earth to end up like Tarizon."

The President shook his head and sat down. "Alright. What you say makes sense. I assume Earth is the only suitable place for them to settle."

"So they say," General Stout agreed.

"Well, it doesn't look like we have much choice. Why don't we propose a compromise? There is no way we can allow 20 million people to come all at once. It would create a general worldwide panic."

"Yes, you're right, Mr. President," General Stout said. "I would propose a covert operation. We allow maybe one million to come spread out over a few years. We can let them assimilate into population centers all over the United States so they won't be noticed."

"But with that many aliens there is no way their existence won't be noticed," the Ambassador argued. "I think it would be better to be forthright with the American people and the world. It would be impossible to keep something like this under wraps. Either accept them or tell them no. That's the right thing to do."

"No, we need their technology," General Stout argued. "Once we have it we can better defend ourselves should they turn out to be hostile."

"You're right. It may be impossible to keep a lid on this," the President acknowledged.

"Not necessarily," the CIA Director replied. "It may be possible to swear the Tarizonians to secrecy. It would have to be a CIA operation, of course."

"Well, look into it. If Ambassador Rammel can guarantee to keep the project secret and the CIA agrees it can be done, then maybe we can work something out. But not 20 million! Get them to be more realistic. Won't things get better on Tarizon eventually? Can't we just help them get through this calamity somehow without bringing them all here?"

"Yes, Mr. President. Perhaps if we just let them conceive their children here on Earth in a toxin free environment, then when they return to Tarizon their children will be strong and healthy," the Director suggested. "That should guarantee that the human race survives."

The Ambassador shook his head. "I think this is a mistake, Mr. President. You should be honest with the American people and the Tarizonians. Either accept them here openly or refuse them. Even letting them breed on Earth is a huge risk. There is no way it could be kept secret."

"Right. Refuse them and suffer the consequences," General Stout spat. "If they have the technology to travel millions of miles through space, do you think we'd have even the slightest chance of repelling their attack? Give me a break!"

"Okay," the President said. "See if we can't work out a compromise and keep a lid on this. Only those who need to know will be brought in on this secret. And, for the record, this meeting never happened."

Rammel smiled when Ensign Muri walked into his suite. He liked Ensign Muri. She was quite beautiful and had a most pleasant demeanor. Just having her around made him feel good for some reason. He couldn't put his finger on it, but the woman was like medicine. If he was tired or melancholy just seeing her picked him up.

"Ensign Muri. To what do I owe the pleasure?"

"Well, I thought maybe you might need a dinner companion. Commander Brunns and Kulchz are out enriching their cultural experience, so I was left all alone."

"Really. Well, that's their loss and my gain. I would love to have dinner with you."

"Good. I've heard there is a Chinese restaurant down the street."

"Chinese. I don't think I know what that is?"

"It's a land on the other side of the globe. Apparently, many of their people have immigrated to the United States and set up a Chinatown in every major city."

"How interesting. Let me get my coat and we will give it a try."

Rammel left the room for a moment and Aerial waited. She wondered if she should be honest with him or keep her assignment to herself. It would be dangerous for her to talk freely to him. She didn't want to compromise such a good man. She knew if she tried to seduce him, no matter how much he loved his mate, he would be unable to resist her. When he stepped back into the room with his coat on she took his arm.

When they left the suite the security team the CIA had assigned to them insisted on accompanying them, so they walked out of the hotel with two men following several strides behind them. It was a pleasant night and Rammel felt exhilarated with Aerial on his arm. He looked around taking in the bright lights and mass of people walking the streets, talking, laughing and enjoying the evening. When they got to their destination Aerial pointed up to the neon dragon that adorned the building.

"That looks like one of our drogals on Tarizon."

"Yes, it does. Maybe it is a drogal but on Earth it's called a dragon."

They opened the door and walked inside the restaurant ornately decorated like an emperor's palace with soft music playing in the background. A beautiful Chinese woman bowed and then took Garciah's coat. Another woman showed them to a booth and gave them menus.

"This is wonderful," Aerial said. "It's so different than anything on Tarizon."

"Yes. It is quite enchanting. America has a very rich culture."

The waitress returned with a pot of tea, poured them a cup and then asked for their orders. Neither of them knew what to order so they asked the waitress for a recommendation.

"You should order a buffet and then you can take a little of everything and see what you like."

"Excellent idea," the Ambassador agreed.

"Yes. That sounds good."

The waitress escorted them to the buffet table and gave them plates. A few minutes later they were back at their booth with food piled high on their plates.

"Oh, this is wonderful," Aerial said as she stuffed her mouth with cashew chicken.

The Ambassador nodded but was too busy eating to respond. They ate with little conversation until their plates were nearly empty.

"Hmm. What a good idea it was to come here," the Ambassador said. "I'm so glad you came by."

"Me too," Aerial said, her tone suddenly getting serious. "Ambassador, I need to tell you something in confidence. Can I do that?"

Rammel gave Aerial a hard look. "Confidential? What are we talking about? Something personal?"

"No. Something about me. I'd like to let you in on a little secret that you have to promise not to mention to anyone else."

Rammel frowned. "Well, this is highly irregular. I don't know if I can make that promise."

"If I tell you and you betray me, I will likely be killed."

Rammel sighed. "If I make you this promise, will I compromise our mission?"

"No. Not at all. In fact it will make it more likely to succeed."

"Well, then I promise to keep your secret, whatever it is."

Aerial smiled. "Wonderful. You know I am a member of the Purist Party."

"Yes. That was made clear to me when you were added to the delegation. In fact, I was hoping to show you the error of your ways."

Aerial laughed. "Well, that won't be necessary. I am part Seafolken and I detest everything the Purists stand for."

Rammel's eyes widened. "Really? That is quite a shock."

"Yes, nobody knows but Colonel Zitor, Threebeard and now you. So, you must never mention this to anyone, even your mate."

"No. I wouldn't. But, why are you with the Purists if you don't believe in what they stand for?"

"We cannot let the Purists ever get control of the government. That would be the end of the Supreme Mandate and the end of freedom for all life-forms on Tarizon. I couldn't let that happen, so I decided to be a spy and do everything I could to subvert the Purists' agenda."

"Well, this is a very dangerous path you have chosen, but I commend you for your courage."

"Thank you."

"So, does Commander Brunns know you are with me? Isn't it dangerous for you to go out to dinner with me?"

"No. In fact, my job is to seduce you and keep you close at all times, so I can report back to the commander everything you are doing."

"Oh. I see. Well, that's very interesting."

"Yes. So don't tell me anything you don't want the commander to hear."

"Right. I'll keep that in mind."

"But, I will tell you everything that Commander Brunns and Kulchz are up to, so they won't get the upper hand."

Rammel laughed. "Wow. Whose idea was this, Colonel Zitor or Threebeard's?"

"Mine. I only went to them because I needed someone to provide intelligence to. Threebeard was perfect since we could talk telepathically and nobody would ever know. But when I got assigned to the delegation going to Earth, I needed to find someone else to report to. Threebeard suggested you. He said I could trust your discretion."

"Indeed, you can."

"So, you won't mind me hanging around and pretending to be your lover. I don't want to cause problems with you and your mate."

"No. My staff will keep my secret. They will be surprised by my perceived indiscretion, but they won't say anything to Petrina."

"You can't tell her about our true relationship, even if she hears that we are spending a lot of time together."

Rammel swallowed hard. "I won't compromise you. I promise."

"Good then. This will be a very pleasant assignment."

Rammel smiled broadly.

<h1 style="text-align:center">32</h1>

<h1 style="text-align:center">Tarizon Repopulation Project</h1>

When negotiations resumed Mohammed Baba from the CIA was included in the U.S. Delegation as the person assigned to head up the project should an agreement be reached. Mo, as he preferred to be called, was thrilled with the unique assignment and determined to work out something mutually acceptable. Rammel, Mo, General Stout, and his aide, Lt. Wentworth sat across the table representing Tarizon. Mo took charge of the meeting.

"Alright, the President has considered your requests and is pleased to advise you that the United States will assist Tarizon in this time of need. However, it will not be possible to allow 20 million refugees to settle permanently on U.S. soil. The logistics of such a mass immigration is simply not possible for too many reasons to go into at this time. Suffice it to say, this is what we will be willing to do assuming we can get assurances that the project will at all times be kept top secret.

"With those assurances, the United States will allow the temporary acceptance of up to one million human guests from Tarizon to be spread out over twenty metropolitan areas at our discretion. No more than 100,000 guests will be admitted each month until the maximum number of permitted guests has been reached.

"This project will be jointly administered by the CIA and a local administrative arm of the Tarizon government who will be jointly responsible for keeping it top secret. All expenses incurred by these two agencies will be paid by Tarizon. To protect the secret nature of the project, the Tarizon government will provide medical clinics for its citizens so that no guests will ever be treated by U.S. doctors or at U.S. hospitals. Guest workers will at all times adhere to federal, state and local laws. The CIA will maintain a staff of attorneys, accountants, and other professionals to handle interactions between U.S. authorities and guest workers. All guest workers will file tax returns and pay taxes on earnings in accordance with the Internal Revenue Code.

"The purpose of the Tarizon Repopulation Project as it will be known, is to allow at least one generation of strong, healthy, normal citizens to be conceived and nourished on Earth so that they can be returned to help stabilize the dwindling population on Tarizon. All children of citizens of Tarizon will return to Tarizon upon reaching age five, however, no mothers who are U.S. citizens will be allowed to accompany her children to Tarizon.

"In exchange for allowing guest workers on U.S. soil Tarizon will provide the technology promised on a schedule to be mutually agreed upon by the parties, but to be delivered in full within five years.

"Now, with that on the table, are there any questions?" Mo asked.

Commander Brunns stood up. "Yes, I have not a question but a concern. Although we are appreciative of your offer of assistance, by allowing only one million citizens to come to Earth you are sentencing to death millions of Tarizonians. We must be allowed to bring as many of our citizens as we can safely transport."

Mo sighed. "Yes, we understand the grave situation you face at home, but even bringing a million of your people to Earth is an unprecedented undertaking that will require a monumental effort on the part of the United States to accomplish, particularly since it must be kept secret.

"Let me assure you that if this matter were made public there would be little likelihood that *any* of your citizens would be allowed to come to Earth. We are taking a big risk in allowing any of you to come to Earth as legally a treaty must be ratified by the Senate and if funding is needed then a bill must be passed by Congress. If knowledge of the Tarizon Repopulation Project ever comes out, all of us involved could lose our jobs and be criminally prosecuted."

Rammel stood up. "Yes, I know you are taking a great risk and even though we would like to bring more people here, we will be content with what you offer, however, the technology we offered was based on the allowance of 20 million guests. Therefore, the technology offered will have to be reduced."

Mo shook his head. "No, our offer is conditioned on receiving the full technology package. Like I said everyone involved in this project is taking a great risk. If this blows up in our faces it could cost the President his reelection. This is only going to get done if we get the entire technology package that Lt. Sincini presented to us."

Commander Brunns stood up angrily but Rammel put his hand on his shoulder. "I'll take care of this Commander. Take a seat."

Brunns started to protest but after a stern look from the Ambassador he relaxed and sat down.

"I can understand your disappointment now that you have seen the wonders of our technology, but you cannot expect to get it all if we only get 1/20th of what we asked for. But, in the spirit of compromise I can offer you everything in the package except our FTL technology which wouldn't have any practical value to you for many years anyway."

Mo considered this for a moment and then shrugged. "Okay, I'll discuss it with the President. Perhaps this will be acceptable."

"Good," Rammel said. "Now the biggest obstacle that I see remaining is the idea that this project can be kept secret. I don't know how you plan to do that."

Mo took a deep breath. "Yes. This won't be easy but it is an absolute necessity. An idea that we think might work is to claim that these guest workers are from other countries on Earth. There are always countries in turmoil who have refugees needing political asylum or nations at war who have citizens who have been displaced. We believe we can use these situations as cover for the Tarizon Repopulation Project."

"I see. Yes, that sounds like a good plan. We can possibly help you on that score with our memory guns."

"Memory guns?" Mo asked.

"Yes, we have developed a way to erase short term memory—a day, a few hours, or a few minutes depending on the situation. You simply point the gun at a person's eyes and a layer of his memory is destroyed taking the memories stored there with them. The duration of the beam determines the amount of the memory lost. So, if for some reason the project were to be discovered, if you got to the person quickly enough you could erase his memory back to the point where he learned of its existence."

"Yes, that could be useful," Mo agreed.

"In fact, that is how we could land our shuttles without fear of detection. We simply mount a memory beam on the ship and flash it periodically so that anyone who sees our ship will have their memory of it erased."

Mo nodded. "Yes, that's perfect. That will go a long way to solving our secrecy issues."

The meeting went on for hours but it was clear the parties had reached a tentative agreement. When the negotiations broke up Commander Kulchz took Lt. Wentworth aside.

"Lieutenant, I just wanted to say I'm looking forward to working with the U.S. military on this project."

"Yes, as am I," Lt. Wentworth said.

"I don't know how it is on Earth, but on Tarizon the politicians know very little about the practical needs of the military."

Wentworth laughed. "Yes, the situation is the same on Earth. Politicians are short sighted and focusing more on their reelection than what's good for the people."

"Exactly," Kulchz continued. "They don't understand that they would have nothing if the military wasn't there to guarantee that the people obeyed their policies."

"Yes, we are definitely underappreciated."

"Particularly when it comes to getting paid, right?"

Wentworth laughed. "Boy, ain't that the truth."

"So, Lieutenant. Just to show you our appreciation for what you are doing for the people of Tarizon, I have a gift for you."

"A gift?" Wentworth repeated.

"Yes," Kulchz said reaching into his pocket and pulling out a small cloth bag. He studied it a moment and then handed it to Lt. Wentworth.

Wentworth took the bag, opened it gingerly and then gasped, "Are these diamonds?"

"Yes. Fine diamonds as perfect as you will find anywhere."

Wentworth couldn't keep his eyes off the diamonds. "How many are there?"

"Twenty-five assorted diamonds ranging from two to five carats."

"And these are a gift to the delegation?"

"No. No. Not the delegation. This is just between you and me."

Wentworth grimaced. "What will you be expecting in return?"

"Nothing. This is just a gesture of friendship. We are both military men and I want you to be as enthusiastic about this project as I am."

Wentworth laughed. "Wow! Okay, then. Thank you."

"Of course, I am hopeful that Commander Brunns and I will be able to stay on Earth and help you administer the project. Neither of us has any desire to return to Tarizon."

Wentworth raised his eyebrows. "Well, I don't know if I can help you out on that score, but if I see a way I will certainly try."

"Good, because we both enjoy giving gifts to our friends. And we have a lot to give."

When the four new nanomite projects were completed several phases later the swarms were divided again and sixteen new, more ambitious, projects were started including the Hall of the Interpreters in Shisk. The Hall of the Interpreters was to be the beginning of Tarizon's rebirth. Situated on a hill it would be visible from almost anywhere in the dome and become a beacon of hope for Tarizon's future. Much to Central Authorities' delight, before long, nanomite buildings were springing up all over Tarizon and Baldrige had become a hero for harnessing this wonderful new force for the good of Tarizon.

Despite these early successes there still was one nagging problem. Artis and Threebeard were still the only two humans who could talk to them. Threebeard had tried to get the Seafolken to help Artis in this endeavor but every Seafolken he contacted refused to work for Central Authority since it had made no effort to end slavery on Tarizon and there were still thousands of Seafolken enslaved all over the world.

When Threebeard failed to find someone to assist Artis, Baldrige started spreading the word about his need for someone with very strong telepathic abilities to assist him. When Videl Lai heard about the problem he called Baldrige and suggested Rupra Bruda.

"Yes. Young Bruda has a remarkably strong gift as does his mate."

"Isn't he rather busy as your party chairman? I doubt he'd want to drop everything to come work with me."

"That's true but this is very important for the future of Tarizon. If the nanomites can actually build these structures as well as you say, then we ought to take advantage of their cheap labor."

"Yes, indeed," Baldrige agreed. "Will you inquire into weather Chairman Bruda can help us out?"

"Yes, right away. I'll call him now."

"Thank you," Baldrige said and the line went dead.

Videl punched in Bruda's number and waited.

"Bruda here."

"Rupra. This is Videl. How are you?"

"Fine."

"Listen, my friend. I know you are aware of the construction work being done by the nanomites."

"Yes. I visited the science lab and saw them at work."

"Well, apparently Central Authority is in need of nanomite handlers. You know, people with strong telepathic abilities who can communicate with them at each construction site. So far only Artis and Threebeard have been able to communicate with them."

"Is that right? I didn't know that."

"Yes, so I thought of you. Your abilities are about as strong as anyone I know and this would be a good opportunity to get the upper hand in this project."

"Yes. You're absolutely right. It would be good if we controlled all of that free labor," Bruda agreed.

"Exactly."

"Apparently the nanomites need only a few chemicals to keep them happy."

"Right, they can't be very smart. So, can you and your mate go up there and see if you can communicate with them? If so, I'll suggest to Baldrige that you two establish a training school for handlers. That way we can make sure we get our people in control of the swarms."

"Not a problem. We can wrap up what we're doing in a day or two and then go straight there."

"Excellent. I'll let Baldrige know you are coming."

Five days later Rupra Bruda and Essyria arrived at the science lab ready to get started. Unfortunately, Baldrige had failed to let Artis know they were coming and she was aghast when he told her they were there to learn how to communicate with the nanomites. She kept her distress to herself but excused herself to consult with Threebeard.

"Brother. I need your counsel immediately."

"What is it?" Threebeard replied, concerned with Artis' tone.

She opened her mind to his so he could understand the dilemma. He groaned in despair.

"Oh, God and Sandee. Now what are we going to do? I fear the nanomites will be in deep trouble if Bruda and his thugs get control over them."

"What should I do?"

"Warn the nanomites and resign immediately. Perhaps Mr. Bruda won't be able to make contact without your help."

"I hope that is the case."

"You cannot assist Bruda in any way. Try to make the nanomites understand the perilous position they will be in if Rupra Bruda gets control of them."

"I will, brother. Thank you for your counsel."

When Artis returned she called Baldrige aside and explained to him that she could not work with Rupra Bruda and his mate, as she believed he was involved in the plot to kill her brother.

"But he has been cleared of those charges," Baldrige argued.

"Yes, but he hates mutants and we know he has killed at least two rhutz for no reason."

"He claims the first one was an accident and he denies being involved in Misty's death."

"I don't care what he told you. Neither were by accident, believe me. They were both premeditated murder."

"So, you are refusing to assist them?"

"Yes, I am. And if they join our team then I must resign."

Baldrige frowned and shook his head slowly. "Alright, give me a few kyloons to consult with Central Authority."

Artis nodded and left Baldrige's office. She went straight to the warehouse to confer with the nanomites who had stayed behind. When she was inside she closed her eyes and concentrated.

"Swarmmasters"

"Yes, Artis," the Speaker said. *"How can we help you?"*

"Something has happened that we did not anticipate."

"What? Tell us."

"Central Authority has brought in a man, Rupra Bruda, who they want to assist me in communicating with you. Since you have been divided we need more than one human to be able to communicate with you."

"Yes. That makes sense."

"It does, but this man is no friend to the nanomites. He is evil and will not respect your wishes nor your rights. I have refused to work with him."

"That is good, then. What is the problem?"

"The problem is that Central Authority may still allow him to be a speaker for Central Authority. If this happens I fear for your safety and well-being."

"This is unfortunate news. We were very happy with the growth of our hives and the success of the project."

"I know. It is very distressful to me and Threebeard too. We don't know what to do."

"Stand firm. We will support you. If the humans want us to continue building on Tarizon, they will send this Rupra Bruda away. If not, we will stop building."

"Good. Thank you. I'll let you know how it turns out."

Artis left feeling a little better, but when she got back she could tell by the solemn look on Baldrige's face that she was in trouble.

"Central Authority insists you work with Rupra Bruda and his mate."

Artis shook her head in despair. "No. I won't. I guess I have no choice but to resign. And, for your information, the nanomites have advised me they will not work with Bruda and his mate and will stop building if I resign."

"Well, we'll see about that," Baldrige said signaling to two security guards stationed near the door. They came over immediately and stood behind Artis.

"These men will be showing you out."

Artis glared at Baldrige. "You're just going to throw away all we have accomplished?"

"No, we will have to proceed without you. I'm sorry. That's Central Authority's decision."

Artis shook her head. "Well, good luck with that," she said and stormed off.

When Artis was gone Rupra Bruda and Essyria walked over to where Baldrige was standing. "Don't worry. We'll handle the nanomites."

"How? Apparently Artis has already conferred with them and they are refusing to work with you."

"Maybe that's the case with the swarms here, but the other swarms don't know what is happening. The nanomites can't communicate over long distances like the rhutz. As long as we don't let these swarms anywhere near the other ones we will be okay."

"But with personnel going back and forth between construction sites it's likely the news will eventually get to the other swarms," Baldrige warned.

Bruda sighed. "Well, if that's true we have but one choice."

"What's that?" Baldrige asked.

"We must terminate them."

Baldrige grimaced, not grasping Bruda's words.

"Terminate them?"

"Yes, all the nanomites here at the science lab must die. Every last one of them so they can't alert the others to our intentions."

Aerial Muri and Rammel got out of the elevator and stumbled toward their suite. Their two bodyguards watched them with some amusement as they tried to unlock their door. When they finally managed to get the door open Rammel nodded to the men as he closed it.

Inside Aerial pulled her dress over her head and kicked off her high heels. Rammel took off his coat, stumbled to the sofa and collapsed. Aerial came over, took off his shoes, and began to loosen his belt. He looked up at her longingly.

"You want to sneak upstairs and take a swim?" Aerial asked. "The pool is closed, so we'll have it all to ourselves."

"A swim?" Rammel questioned.

"Yes, I long for the water. I'm a mermaid for the sake of Sandee. At least that's what they call girls like me on Earth. Mermaids."

"Well, that is tempting," Rammel replied. "But what if we are seen?"

"Your security team will keep away any intruders, won't they?"

"Yes, I suppose so."

"Then, come on. Let's go. I'll brief you on what Kulchz is up to while we swim, so if anybody asks what you were doing you can say you were working."

They both laughed.

After they stripped and put on bathrobes, they took the elevator up to the rooftop swimming pool. As expected the pool was deserted. Aerial dropped her robe and walked slowly into the pool giving Rammel an eyeful. His mouth fell slightly open as she began to transform before him.

"Don't gawk from out there. Come on in and take a closer look. You may never get an opportunity like this again."

Rammel reluctantly took off his bathrobe and dove into the pool. When he came up next to Aerial she was smiling broadly.

"So, are you glad you came?"

He nodded taking in her stunning breasts and the small set of gills beneath them. "Yeah, this will definitely be a memorable night. Although, I can imagine what my staff will think of me when they get wind of this."

"Don't worry. You'll go up a notch in the eyes of the men and the women will just think you're a typical male."

"Perhaps, but I should set a higher standard."

"Well, some day you can explain yourself and then they will understand."

"Right. So, what is Kulchz up to?"

"He and Commander Brunns are buying off every American officer they meet with diamonds and gold. They say they are just gifts of gratitude with no strings attached but that's obviously not the case."

"Really? I wonder what they hope to gain by it?"

"They don't want to go back to Tarizon and they are hoping their new military buddies will help convince you to let them stay."

"What do you think I should do about it?"

"Don't ask me. I'm just a spy. You're the politician."

"Right."

"Perhaps you should tell Mo so he will know what he's up against."

"Yes, but what will he think of us if we cannot even control our own delegation?"

"I wouldn't worry about that. He will appreciate your trust in him and it will help build a strong bond between you."

"You may be right. I will discuss it with the others and see what they think I should do."

"Good. And now I am going to swim a hundred laps if you don't mind."

"Go right ahead," Rammel said as he edged over to the side of the pool to give her room.

She glided away and began swimming laps. Her strokes were strong and graceful and she moved in the water with remarkable speed. Rammel was mesmerized watching such a beautiful creature swimming so effortlessly back and forth like the pendulum of a clock. When she was done she came over to him smiling.

"What are you so happy about?" he asked.

"I feel so good in the water. It's been a long time. Before we go, do you want me to make your day?"

He laughed tentatively. "What do you mean, make my day?"

"Have you ever felt the sting of the tortiac?"

Rammel blushed. "No, of course not."

"Well, mine isn't as strong as a full blood's, but have no doubt it will still be the most pleasant feeling you have ever experienced. It would be my honor to give you that pleasure."

Rammel swallowed hard. "Thank you, but as pleasurable as that would be, I couldn't justify allowing it."

Aerial frowned. "You sure? Nobody would know."

"You and I would know and once I'd experienced such pleasure I'd want more. Then our facade would crumble into reality. I must stay focused on the mission."

Aerial nodded. "You're right, of course."

She turned and strolled out of the pool giving the Ambassador one last magnificent look and then put on her robe. Her webbed hands and feet quickly resumed a normal human form. When they got back to the suite the door was ajar.

"Hmm. It looks like Kulchz and Commander Brunns have been here," Aerial said.

"Yes. It's a good thing you told me they were coming. I put everything important in the hotel safe."

"But you left them something to find, didn't you? I don't want them to think I warned you they were coming."

"Yes, I left a few classified documents that they should find interesting."

"A little misinformation, perhaps?"

"Why of course."

"Good. Now you better go report the burglary to the authorities to keep up the charade."

"Right. Sergeant! Someone has been in my suite!"

The two guards rushed over and shook their heads when they saw the room in shambles.

33

Hope for the Future

On the way back to Liehn, Artis connected with Threebeard and told him what had happened. He was upset and promised to call Baldrige and try to talk some sense into him. When she arrived at Liehn she went straight to the nanomite cube and explained what had happened.

"Why do the humans allow Bruda to live?" the Speaker asked. *"If he acts detrimental to the human race, he should be killed. We don't allow individual swarmmasters to do what they want. Everyone must act in concert with the collective will."*

"But how do you determine the collective will?" Artis asked.

"The swarmmasters confer and discuss the situation until a consensus is reached."

"But doesn't that take time?"

"No. Since we all have the same goal, the welfare of the swarms, most decisions are obvious and there is nothing to argue about."

"Yes, but it is much more complicated for humans. Humans often have different personalities, values and objectives, so it's easy for conflicts to arise."

"Is there anything you think we should do?" the Speaker asked.

"Yes, you need to warn the other swarmmasters about Bruda and his intentions. They need to know what he is capable of doing. Can you do that?"

"Not without getting close to them. Our communication ability is instantaneous, but we have to be within a kylod or so of the other nanomite swarmmasters."

"Do you think the other nanomite swarmmasters will talk to Rupra Bruda if he tries to connect with them?"

"They might if he has as strong a gift as you and Threebeard. Some human's thoughts are so weak we cannot hear them very well."

Artis sighed. "I've been told he has a strong gift. So, they might hear him."

"Can you go to the other sites and warn our brothers?" the Speaker asked.

"I guess that's what I'll have to do."

"Do you think Bruda would try to harm any of us?"

"I don't think so. Central Authority wants the building projects to go forward. It wouldn't make sense for him to harm you. He just wants to control you."

"Then there is probably nothing to worry about. We'll be alright, Artis. You've done all you can to help us. Now it is up to God what happens."

"I hope God can protect you. I'm so worried."

During the night following Artis's sudden departure from the science lab, Bruda had a fumigation tent placed over the new warehouse. Fumigation tents were used to eradicate rodents and insects that had been so infested a building that ordinary spraying techniques weren't effective. Bruda figured this would work well enough to rid the building of its nanomite population. The job was done at night so nobody at the lab would know that a mass murder had taken place right under their noses. Since nobody was left at the lab who could speak to the nanomites there, Bruda was sure his secret would be safe. The nanomite swarms were asleep when the toxic gas began invading the structure of the building.

"Swarmmasters. A strange fabric is being constructed on all sides and over the top of our warehouse," a sentry advised. *"We just noticed it while we were securing the perimeter for the night."*

"Who has placed it there? And for what purpose?" the Speaker asked.

"Six men are just finishing putting it in place and are now sealing the corners. I don't know what the purpose is but I have a bad feeling."

"Artis warned us about this human named Bruda. He is a murderer," the Speaker recalled. *"Perhaps we can flee through the foundation."*

"Yes, Speaker, but I don't think we will have much time."

"We will commence evacuation now. It is our only option."

As the evacuation commenced the swarmmasters complained bitterly amongst themselves. *"The humans are evil, we should never have trusted them...What can we do?...Evacuation will take too long...There isn't time to get everyone out of the building...They must plan to kill us...A toxic gas, no doubt...But why would they do this?...Because they want to enslave us like they did the Seafolken...But Artis wouldn't allow it?...Artis is probably dead...Yes, if they kill us our nanomite brothers won't know of the danger they are in...I smell something...Yes, it has begun...It is very bitter...It's making me sick...Oh, God! Save us...We must escape!...I can't feel my feet...What's happening to me?...You're dying brother, just like the rest of us...Oh! My arms and legs feel so heavy...I can't see...Why is this happening? We were trying to help the humans, why would they betray us?...The humans are evil...They kill for sport...We were foolish to trust them...They will pay for their treachery."*

Artis tried to make good on her promise to warn the other nanomite swarms about Rupra Bruda and the Purists, but much to her despair Central Authority would not allow her access to them. They told her she had done much damage to the program and they couldn't let her disrupt their efforts any further. When she complained to Threebeard he attempted to persuade Baldrige and Central Authority to allow her access, but his requests were flatly rejected.

Once the details of the Tarizon Repopulation Project had been agreed upon the difficult task of implementing it began. Because of the enormity of the task it was decided that most of the delegation would stay on Earth to help the CIA with the necessary preparations for the arrival of the first hundred thousand guests. Since Rammel knew that Commander Brunns had his own agenda on Earth he decided to stay and send Brunns back to Earth to present the accord to the Chancellor and the World

Assembly. Brunns wasn't happy about this turn of events but there was nothing he could do about it since Rammel outranked him.

This left Commander Kulchz, as the highest-ranking Purist on Earth, with the task of planning Phase One of Operation Conquest Earth—the forcible overthrow of the U.S. government in order to pave the way for the arrival of twenty million settlers from Tarizon. It would be Kulchz's job to make this happen and he had roughly two cycles to get it done.

Of course, Rammel knew of the Purists' agenda due to Aerial Muri's spying, but there wasn't much he could do about it other than keeping a close eye on Kulchz and his extracurricular activities. In order to make sure Threebeard and the Loyalist leaders on Tarizon got the complete picture of what was happening on Earth, he sent Aerial back there with Commander Brunns. He knew she could connect with Threebeard telepathically and he thought it was more important for her to be on Tarizon providing intelligence on Videl Lai and his cohorts rather than on Earth where her unique skills would be wasted.

As a further precaution against Kulchz's activities Rammel decided to advise Mo of the threat. He did it at Mo's office at Langley on the day before Earth Shuttle 26 was about to take off on its return trip to Earth.

"Thank you for agreeing to meet," Rammel said.

"It's always a pleasure, Mr. Ambassador, but I was a little surprised you didn't bring this up at our last joint meeting."

"Yes. Well, what I'm going to tell you is off the record, as you say here on Earth."

"Off the record?"

"Yes, I'm going to tell you something about our political situation on Tarizon since it impacts the TRP."

"Okay."

"As you may have observed there is some tension between members of our delegation."

"Yes, you and Commander Brunns don't always see eye to eye."

"Yes, that is because he is a Purist and I am a Loyalist. It's like being a Republican and a Democrat here on Earth except the stakes are higher due to the crisis we are in."

Mo nodded.

"We have told you about our Supreme Mandate which is similar to your Constitution. The difference between the situation here and on Tarizon, is that everyone on Earth supports the Constitution. I don't think I have heard anyone say they wanted to abolish it."

"No. It's the framework of our political system and everyone is sworn to defend it."

"Well, on Tarizon even though the Purists have sworn to uphold the Supreme Mandate, their real goal is to abolish it. They think that due to the crisis Tarizon faces, all civil liberties should be abolished and martial law be imposed on the population."

"Really? I didn't know that."

"It's true and you need to understand that in dealing with Kulchz and the other Purists who will be staying on Earth. I will try to keep him in line, but he is like a snake and I can't guarantee I will be successful."

Mo took a deep breath. "What do you think he will be doing?"

"The Loyalists want to bring all 20 million citizens to Earth, so he will be soliciting support among your people to allow that. He's already been spreading around gold and diamonds to your military officers in hopes of gaining their loyalty and support."

"What? He's bribing U.S. military personnel?"

"Yes, absolutely."

"How do you know this?"

"I have my spies. I will give you a full report."

"Yes. Do that. We can't have that kind of thing going on. It could subvert the entire program."

"But now that you know about it, perhaps you can enlist a few of your own spies so you will know what Kulchz and the Purists are up to."

Mo nodded his head slowly. "Yes, that's a good idea. I'll look into it."

"Please don't tell the Ambassador or the President about this. I don't want them to kill the accord. We must move forward as planned. I'm sure between you and I we can control the Purists."

"Okay. You're probably right and neither I or General Stout want anything to jeopardize getting the technology we have agreed upon."

"No, I wouldn't think so."

"Thank you for bringing this to my attention, Mr. Ambassador."

Rammel nodded and then got up to leave. "So, I will see you tomorrow for the take off."

Mo stood and smiled. "Yes, I'm anxious to see your ship."

"I'll give you a personal tour. It's quite extraordinary."

"I can imagine. I can't wait."

Mo escorted the Ambassador out of the building where a limo was waiting to take him back to his suite. He was ambivalent about leaving. He was anxious to see his wife and children and bring them to New York since, for security reasons, he hadn't seen them in six months. They hadn't dared go back to the ship for fear someone would follow them. But he was also a bit sad to have to say goodbye to Ensign Muri. Although he'd remained faithful to his mate, he had fallen in love with her and it had taken all his strength and will power to resist her. Fortunately, she had respected his situation and, except for a little flirting for show, hadn't pressured him to do anything compromising. He knew it was a good thing she was leaving as Petrina would sense his feelings if all three of them were in the same room.

The next day Rammel and the delegation led Mo, General Stout, the Ambassador, and several of their aides out to where Earth Shuttle 26 was buried. Captain Shilling and her crew came out of the main hatch to greet them. It had been agreed that there would be no personal cameras at the site as what pictures were to be made would be kept by the CIA at Langley.

Rammel and Lt. Sincini took Mo, the Ambassador and General Stout on a tour of the shuttle. They toured the bridge, the engine room, galley, and sleeping chambers. They were particularly interested in the FTL drive and Lt. Sincini's brief explanation as to how it worked.

While the touring was going on, Captain Shilling and the crew assisted those who were staying on Earth with their personal belongings and said their goodbyes. Commander Brunns and Ensign Muri reported back to the ship and got settled in their quarters. Since there were so few returning to Tarizon, Commander Brunns and Ensign Muri elected not to travel in the sleeping chambers but to remain awake on the long journey home.

When it was time for the shuttle to leave Rammel led everyone to the perimeter of the meadow to watch the ship take off. At the appointed hour the ground began to rumble as the ship began to rotate and screw itself out of the ground. A cloud of dust rose as the ship began to gradually rise out of its subterranean home. Rocks and dirt were spit outward forcing the observers to turn away to protect themselves from flying debris. When the ship had cleared the ground, it rose quickly in the air and shot upward through the clouds. Rammel watched it disappear and wondered if there was any way they'd be ready when fifty spacecrafts just like Earth Shuttle 26 came back in just two short years with a 100,000 passengers.

34

Retaliation

After Artis was denied access to the nanomite swarmmasters at the sixteen new construction sites in Lemaine Shane, she began to worry about the nanomites she'd left back at the science lab. Since they would no longer cooperate with Baldrige, she feared what he would do with them. The more she thought about it the more worried she became. She finally decided she had no choice but to try to rescue them. Unfortunately, she wouldn't be allowed anywhere near the science lab, so she'd have to find someone else to do it. When she expressed her concerns to Giant he agreed to visit the science lab and check on them. When she pointed out that he couldn't communicate with the nanomites, he said he'd bring along one of the seafolken dancers with him.

A few days later Giant and Ariela set out for the TGA science lab. Since it was well known that they both worked with Threebeard and Artis at the Mighty Jolly they realized they wouldn't be allowed into the lab, so they had to figure out how to get in surreptitiously. When they arrived, they watched the employees coming and going through the main gate for a while. The gate was quiet except at each shift change, so they decided they'd have to ambush two of the employees on their way home and steal their identification cards. They waited behind the subtram station outside the gate and when the first worker walked by Giant stepped out and grabbed him from behind and got him into a choke hold. Then he pulled him around the back of the station, out of sight, and applied just enough pressure to cut off his air supply until he fainted. He repeated this process with a woman leaving the lab. While the two workers lay unconscious on the ground Giant stole their employee identity cards and Ariela bit them both with her tortiac so they would have no memory of what happened to them when they awoke. Then they got in line to enter the facility.

Once in the lab grounds they went straight to the warehouse to make contact with the nanomites, but much to their chagrin Ariela could not feel their presence anywhere. Desperate, Ariela revealed herself to several employees and asked them if the nanomites still occupied the building. Unfortunately, none of them knew whether they did or didn't. After a few more loons, they decided they'd better leave before their illegal entry was discovered. On the way out they passed by an outbuilding used for storing small maintenance equipment and Ariela heard a voice in her mind.

"Ariela," the Speaker said.

Ariela stopped, startled by the voice in her head. Giant looked at her curiously.

"Yes, Speaker. I'm a friend of Artis," she thought. *"Why are you here and not in the warehouse?"*

"Baldrige and Bruda had most of us exterminated. They put a tent over the warehouse and pumped in toxic gas. Only a few of us escaped."

"Oh, my God! How many were killed?"

"Over 12 million swarms. We had very little warning. We've been hiding out here trying not to be discovered."

Ariela told Giant what the Speaker had said. He shook his head in disbelief.

"I can't believe they just killed them for no reason."

"Oh, they had a reason. They didn't want anyone interfering with their plans to enslave us."

Ariela let out a long breath. *"Yes, that is the Purist's mission; to enslave or exterminate all mutants and other life-forms, which includes all of us. Unfortunately, they are gaining strength in the government every day."*

"So, what should we do?"

"Let me see if I can establish a link with Artis. She'll know what to do."

Ariela thought of Artis and within a few tiks she responded.

"So what word do you have of the nanomites?" Artis asked.

"We found what's left of them."

"What's left of them?"

"Yes. Bruda exterminated twelve million swarms!"

"Oh, my God! How did the others escape?"

"They fled through the foundation and made it to an outbuilding."

"Okay. You must get the survivors out of there. In the meantime, I will contact Threebeard and see what can be done to punish Bruda for this atrocity."

"That may be easier said than done. They have tight security. Do you have any ideas how to get them out?"

"No. Nothing comes to mind," Artis said.

"That's okay. We'll figure something out. Pray for us."

"I will."

Suddenly an alarm sounded that could be heard all over the facility. Giant looked up realizing the workers they'd put out of commission must have awakened or their bodies discovered. Security would be looking for them now.

"You can hide here in the shed," the Speaker advised. *"We have built a hidden vault to store food and bacuum. There is plenty of room for both of you. We'll seal it off so if they try to open it they won't be able to do it."*

"Don't seal it completely. We don't want to suffocate."

"Don't worry, we'll leave air slits and make a back door so you can come and go as you please."

"Okay. Good," Ariela said. She told Giant the plan.

Ariela walked toward the spot where the vault was supposed to be located. She felt around until a portion of the surface moved. Pushing it inward she was able to climb inside. Giant followed her in. It was much roomier than she'd imagined. A few moments later she heard the voices of soldiers searching the shed. She held her breath until the voices went away. Then she felt a presence in her mind.

"Threebeard?"

"Yes, I've spoken with Artis. She told me what happened. Tell the Speaker that the humans responsible will be punished for what they have done. The governor of Quori has already called the Public Enforcer in Fasoon and ordered an investigation be started immediately. Quori has a large mutant population, so I'll make sure there is a lot of pressure on him to do a good job."

"I will open my mind so you can talk directly to them."

"We understand," the Speaker said sensing Threebeard's thoughts.

"But what about our brothers at the other construction sites? They are in grave danger. What if Bruda kills them too?"

"He won't as long as they continue building."

"If they hear about this genocide they will stop."

"True. But they don't read newspapers or listen to the VC, so how would they find out?"

"We could get word to them."

"I know, but that would only make things worse. Let the Public Enforcer send out their inquisitors. I'm sure they will work quickly and find good cause to arrest Bruda and refer the case for prosecution."

"I hope you are right, for if those responsible for the murder of our brothers and sisters are not brought to justice, we will have no choice but to punish those responsible ourselves."

"That won't be necessary. Just give them a little time to do their job."

"We will wait a while, but not forever."

While Ariel, Threebeard and the swarmmasters conversed, Giant went out and looked around and discovered a truck loaded with bricks at the construction site of a new building under construction. While the workers were on break he drove the truck to the shed and told the Speaker to have the nanomites move into the two pallets of bricks. They obliged and he drove the nanomites safely out of the main gate since the guards were screening trucks going in but ignoring those leaving. Not wanting the TGA to come after them when they discovered the truck missing, Giant and Ariela stopped in the next town and let the nanomites move out of the bricks and into the shell of a church that had been destroyed by tremors. Then they drove back to the science lab, left the truck by the side of the road and returned in their PTV. Since the speaker had assured them the nanomites would be fine in their temporary home, Giant and Ariela went directly to the Public Enforcers' office in Fasoon and filed a complaint against Baldrige and Bruda for genocide.

Inquisitors Petra Depp and Allie Pingh were assigned by the Fasoon PE to investigate the reported genocide of the nanomite workers at the science lab. They went out that afternoon and confronted Baldrige with the accusations.

"Extermination? I know nothing of this," Baldrige protested.

"Then where are the nanomites?" Inquisitor Depp asked.

"I don't know. We haven't heard from them for days."

"So, what happened to them?"

"I don't know. I can't communicate with them. Rupra Bruda and Essyria did all the communicating."

"So, Rupra Bruda told you they were no longer in the warehouse they built?"

"Yes. He said they left after Artis quit."

"Isn't it true a tent was placed over the warehouse?"

"Yes. I don't know who did that. I didn't authorize it. I had it removed as soon as I saw it."

"Then who constructed it?"

"No one will admit to it. I'm really at a loss."

"None of your employees know what happened?"

"No. They all admit seeing it put up but no one knows who ordered it and for what purpose."

"Come on," Inquisitor Pingh said. "You want us to believe you don't know the nanomites were exterminated. You're a scientist, surely you did tests on the warehouse and discovered residue of the toxic gases."

Baldrige paled. "Well, yes. We investigated the warehouse after the tent was removed and did find residue of the toxins."

"What did Rupra Bruda say about it?"

"He said nothing. He and Essyria left the day before it happened."

"Of course, they did. They wanted an alibi."

Baldrige shrugged. "I wouldn't know about that."

"So, where is Bruda now?"

"I don't know. He hasn't been seen since he left."

"What I want to know," Inquisitor Depp said, "is why you didn't report this to the Public Enforcer the moment you discovered the toxins?"

Baldrige squirmed in his chair. "Ah. I wasn't sure anything had happened. Bruda said the nanomites had fled."

"Well, it looks to me like you were a co-conspirator in this genocide. What do you think Pingh?"

Inquisitor Pingh nodded. "Yes. That's obvious."

"No," Baldrige protested. "I didn't know anything about it."

"Well, then give us a name of somebody who does know something about it."

Baldrige took a deep breath. "Okay. After we removed the tent, we tried to figure out who had erected it. We searched our entry logs and discovered a pest control crew had come in from Fasoon to take care of some rodent problems in one of the storage buildings. Apparently, this crew was responsible for erecting the tent and pumping in the toxic chemicals."

"Who was in charge of this crew?"

"According to our logs his name was Fellis Broggin. I don't know anything about him other than I'm told he is tall, has black hair, dark eyes, and a mustache."

"Alright. We will go talk to Mr. Broggin. In the meantime, don't try to disappear. We'll be monitoring your tracking chip."

From Baldrige's office Inquisitors Depp and Pingh went to the warehouse and inspected the site. A forensic team was already there, had cordoned off the site and was gathering evidence. Depp and Pingh looked around and then began interviewing employees who worked in the area. Many confirmed that a tent had been erected over the warehouse and that they had smelled some kind of chemical when they got close to it. Several employees confirmed that a tall, dark-haired man seemed to be in charge of the erection of the tent. When the two inquisitors came back to the warehouse the forensic team leader advised them microscopic analysis had confirmed remnants of dead nanomites in the walls of the warehouse.

The next morning the two inquisitors tracked down Fellis Broggin and brought him in for questioning.

"So, you admit you erected a tent and fumigated the warehouse?" Inquisitor Pingh asked.

"Yes. I was hired to do it."

"Who hired you?"

"We got the order from the science lab."

"Who at the science lab?"

"I don't know. The paperwork didn't say. It was just an ordinary order like we've gotten many times before."

"How were you paid?"

"Credits were applied to our account when we finished the job."

"Did you talk to anybody at the science lab?"

"No. We just went in and did the job per the specifications."

"Nobody signed off on your work?"

"No. We just finished up and left."

"What about the tent? You didn't come back and take it down."

"No. The tents are disposable. The order didn't require us to remove it. In fact, it specifically provided that science lab personnel would dispose of it."

"Isn't that dangerous to be pulling down a fumigation tent?"

"Not for humans."

"What about the fumigant? Was something specific requested?"

"No. They left that to us."

"What did they say they were fumigating?"

"Nanomites."

Inquisitor Pingh frowned. "They told you they wanted you to exterminate nanomites?"

"Yes. That's what the order stipulated."

"And you didn't have a problem with that?"

"No. I figured the science lab would know what they were doing."

"Do you understand that the nanomites are a sentient life-form?"

"No. They're not. They are a pest just like a common rat."

Inquisitor Pingh sighed. "Okay. So you intentionally killed millions of nanomites."

"Well, I don't know how many were there. You can't see them."

"But it was your intention to kill all of them, whether it was ten thousand or ten million."

"Whatever."

Later that day an inquisitor in Shisk tracked down Rupra Bruda and Essyria and questioned them at length about the genocide of the nanomites at the science lab. They both denied knowing anything about it and said they didn't know Broggin. Attempts to track down who ordered the fumigation and paid for it were unsuccessful.

The next day the Public Prosecutor opened a case against Fellis Broggin charging him with genocide. After a public defender was appointed for him the case was set for trial in thirty days. At the trial Broggin's defense was that the nanomites were not mentioned in the Supreme Mandate as a life-form and, therefore, had no civil rights. Quori's Supreme Council of Interpreters, who had exclusive jurisdiction over charges of genocide, rejected that defense and found Broggin guilty of genocide and sentenced him to public flogging followed by a lethal injection to be televised throughout Tarizon. The public defender immediately appealed the conviction to the Supreme Council of Interpreters in Shisk.

At about this same time another charge of genocide of the nanomites had been brought in Merria, a state on the east coast of Turvin. Here a nanomite handler, Hirah Zahn was convicted of the supreme capital offense of genocide when he had millions of swarms of nanomites exterminated because he couldn't find room at any of the nanomite farms to house them. Since he was anxious to go on holiday he opted for their extermination. Since these two cases had similar facts and turned on the same issue as to the status of the nanomites as a protected life-form, the Supreme Council of Interpreters decided to hear both cases at the same time.

35

The Genocide Decision

Being unable to leave his post Threebeard and his staff assembled in the communications room and turned on the VC to watch the proceedings of the Supreme Council of Interpreters. It was a solemn group as they feared there would be no justice for the nanomites who, despite their incredible contribution to the rebuilding of Tarizon, had yet to get a majority of the World Assembly to recognize them as a life-form protected by the Supreme Mandate.

The room became quiet as the coverage began. Lorina Lance stood in front of the media camera and adjusted her hair. A white light came on and a digital readout began the countdown 3, 2, 1. She smiled brightly.

"Good morning, this is Lorina Lance reporting on a cold, dark day from Shisk, the world's capital, where the fate of the nanomite life-form hangs in the balance. Ironically nanomites built this very structure dedicated to the pursuit of justice, where it will be determined today whether or not they too may enjoy the rights guaranteed by the Supreme Mandate, the foundation upon which our world is governed. The eight councilors of the Council of Interpreters must make this determination by upholding or overturning the convictions of Hirah Zahn and Fellis Broggin for the supreme capital offense of genocide.

"Earlier this year Zahn was in charge of the relocation of a nanomite construction colony after it had completed the construction of a subtram transfer station in northwest Dramapour. It was the beginning of the Unification holiday and witnesses testified that Zahn was anxious to return home because he had plans to go on holiday with his mate. Unfortunately, when he contacted the closest nanomite farm he was told it was full. When he tried other farms in the region he was told that they too were full, so he apparently determined that there was a surplus of nanomites and that those in his custody wouldn't be missed if they should happen to disappear. As the hour got later he became more and more distressed at the thought of missing out on his holiday and having to face the anger of his mate, so he ordered his men to fumigate the new structure with a chemical that he knew would kill the nanomites waiting within for transport. He may have gotten away with his crime had not several hundred swarms buried deep in the foundation of the building survived. Their speaker reported the crime and demanded Zahn be punished for his actions. After the slaughter was confirmed by the Public Enforcer, Zahn was arrested and charged with capital genocide. He was convicted and is now pursuing this appeal.

"Fellis Broggin's situation is a little different. He is in the fumigation business and was hired to fumigate a warehouse of nanomites at the TGA science lab in Fasoon, Quori. He didn't know who had hired him but he had done jobs at the science lab before so he didn't question the order. He admitted he knew he was killing millions of nanomites but didn't care since he considered them just another pest. He was convicted by the Fasoon Council of Interpreters and immediately appealed to this court.

"For those of you who haven't been to the Hall of the Interpreters, it sits proudly on the tallest hill of Shisk. Raised by nanomites in less than a cycle, it has now become the home of the Council of Interpreters. As are all nanomite structures, it is made of Bazillian Crystal which is a hard, durable material that shines quite radiantly even under the toxic clouds that hang as a shroud over Tarizon. This particular blend gives the structure a marble-look that is quite magnificent. Inside there isn't an empty seat as a court scribe rises to announce that the session is in order. We now take you to the Great Hall where the Chief Councilor is about to begin."

"Good Morning," Councilor Sidon said. "Today we have asked for oral arguments on the matters of the appeals of the final convictions of capital genocide determined by the Merria Council of Interpreters in matter number SM 2247, State of Merria vs. Hirah Zahn and matter number SQ 1121, State of Quori v. Fellis Broggin. The prosecution and defense will each have 20 loons to make their arguments and all other parties given leave to speak will each have 10 loons. Please be seated promptly when your time has expired. We will not extend oral arguments beyond today's session." The Councilor turned to a stout man dressed in a purple robe. "Mr. Sorhn, I believe you will be speaking for the prosecution?"

"That is correct."

"Then you may proceed."

"Thank you, Chief Councilor," Sorhn said as he took the lectern and faced the eight supreme councilors. "There is no dispute that Hirah Zahn exterminated the swarms in the building they were constructing in Dramapour for his own convenience and that Fellis Broggin fumigated the warehouse at the science lab in Fasoon for his standard fee for extermination of common rodents, each knowing their actions would kill millions of nanomites. Let's get that out of the way at the outset. Neither have disputed these facts, nor have they shown any remorse for their actions. The question that this supreme council must consider is whether the nanomite population of Tarizon enjoys the protections provided to other life-forms on Tarizon under the Supreme Mandate. We don't believe this would be an issue had contact with the nanomite life-form taken place before the ratification of the Supreme Mandate. For anyone who has studied the life of the author of the Supreme Mandate, our beloved Sandee Branh, knows that he not only championed equal rights for all the races of humans on Tarizon but also for other life-forms such as the Rhutz and the Seafolken. And why would he not also cherish a life-form that has the capacity to enter into covenants with Central Authority and to build not only this magnificent hall, but thousands of other similar structures throughout the five continents of Tarizon?

"These two men must pay for their crimes against the nanomites and the people of Tarizon. Their punishment must be most severe in order to deter others who would circumvent the Supreme Mandate and the laws of God and Sandee. If we allow these men to get away with this horrific act all nanomites will be at risk and construction on Tarizon will come to a standstill.

"We've already heard the Purists call for their extermination and the extermination of the rhutz. What right do we have to eliminate these God-given life-forms? If we allow the genocide of the nanomites, the rhutz will be next and then what? There is talk from the Purists that we'd be better off without the mutants and the Seafolken. Unless, of course, they would agree to become our slaves."

Councilor Thoripides stood and glared at Sorhn. "Wild speculation and slander will get you nowhere with this Court," Thoripides warned. "How do you dispute the clear language of the Supreme Mandate that '...all citizens of Tarizon shall enjoy the fundamental rights herein enumerated... and ...all citizens of the 29 states shall be citizens of Tarizon?' Since you admit that the very existence of the nanomites was unknown when the Supreme Mandate was ratified, they obviously could not have been citizens of any of the 29 states and therefore cannot be citizens of Tarizon today."

"Councilor Thoripides," Sorhn replied, "the nanomites should be considered citizens because the author of the Supreme Mandate intended all life-forms to be afforded liberty and civil rights under the new order. His writings and teachings are clear on this point."

"His other writings are irrelevant," Thoripides scowled. "We are bound only to consider the actual content of the Supreme Mandate, for that is what was ratified by the citizens of Tarizon."

The Court Scribe stood and motioned that time was up. The gallery erupted in a subdued chatter as Sorhn returned to his seat. The bailiff stood and admonished the crowd to be quiet or be arrested and escorted to a detention center for negative stimulation therapy.

Sidon looked at Sorhn. "Thank you, Mr. Sorhn. Now I believe it is time for the accused's' defender, Mr. Sorrbeth, to speak. Mr. Sorrbeth, you have 20 loons."

Sorrbeth rose slowly. He was a tall, imposing man who exuded great confidence. He strolled swiftly to the podium. "Chief Councilor, members of the Supreme Council of Interpreters. It is with great humility that I speak before such a distinguished body. Councilor Thoripides has already spoken directly to the heart of my client's case. The Supreme Mandate does not protect nanomites. That is clean and simple. Neither of the Supreme Courts of Merria or Quori had the right to try these defendants for genocide. Genocide by definition is the mass murder of a large number of people. People historically have referred to human. The mutants and Seafolken qualify because of their human origin, but no other life-form was actually mentioned in the Supreme Mandate. Now since the Supreme Mandate was adopted several states have recognized the nanomites and the Rhutz as sentient life-forms, but the acts of those states do not bind the citizens of other states."

Councilor Sidon sat up in his seat and peered out at Sorrbeth. "Mr. Sorrbeth. Do you deny that the nanomites are sentient beings—that they are self-aware and capable of rational thought and communication with human beings?"

"I concede nothing, Your Honor. I have never seen or talked to a nanomite. Only a few claim to have done so and then only telepathically. I don't deny that they are good at building their crystal structures, but how do we know whether they do it voluntarily or if Rupra Bruda and the other handlers have simply learned how to train them and modify their behavior?"

"If you could talk to a nanomite swarmmaster today, would that change your mind?" Sidon asked.

Sorrbeth chuckled. "Certainly, but we know that is not possible. They can't even be seen by the naked eye. Even if one shouted, we couldn't hear him."

The gallery erupted in laughter. Councilor Sidon grinned. "Well, Mr. Sorrbeth. Don't leave after you've finished making your argument today. I believe there is a nanomite who has asked to be heard."

Sorrbeth's eyes widened. "If it is true, I wouldn't miss it, but I fear this appearance will be but another trick of the mutant Threebeard."

The scribe stood up indicating Sorrbeth's time had elapsed. He returned to his seat and Councilor Sidon looked down at his docket sheet. "The court will now hear from Artis, known to most of us as Threebeard's sister."

Artis walked slowly to the podium. She was unknown to the delegates but they knew her brother Threebeard well. Not only was he psychic but telepathic and telekinetic as well. It was assumed Artis had inherited these same gifts. It was no secret that Central Authority feared Threebeard as the unofficial leader of the mutant population. As Artis walked by Sorrbeth's seat, a glass of water tumbled over and spilled its contents in his lap. The gallery erupted in laughter. Sorrbeth stood up and raised his fist at Artis.

Councilor Thoripides became rigid in his chair and glared at Artis. "Let me remind you this is the highest court of the land, mistress. We will not tolerate childish antics."

"Yet you will tolerate scoundrels who openly condone genocide and even suggest it would be a remedy for the millions of mutants who are suffering outside the domes and taxing the resources of Central Authority."

"Let's not get off the subject," Councilor Sidon interjected. "That is not an issue before this court today."

"My apologies, Chief Councilor. Since I am one of the few people who communicate with the nanomites I wanted to tell the Court what I have learned about them. My contact is with a nanomite speaker, a single nanomite swarmmaster who communicates for all the swarmmasters who collectively comprise the colony. This came about actually at the request of Central Authority. After the cataclysmic volcanic eruptions that devastated Tarizon less than three cycles ago, the construction industry was in ruins and Central Authority was looking for a way to rejuvenate it. The nanomites were well known for the crystal palaces that they inhabited in their desert homelands, yet no one knew how they did it. The one thing that was clear was these nanomites were geniuses when it came to engineering. It was thought if communication could be established, that perhaps the nanomites could build other structures, structures that could be used by humans.

"Since it was apparent the nanomites swarmmasters could communicate instantaneously with their individual nanomite workers and fellow swarmmasters, it was thought that perhaps communication could be established telepathically. So, my brother was asked to attempt to make contact. Since he did not have the time to do it, the project was delegated to me. It was a long and arduous task, the details of which I couldn't begin to explain in the short time I have to speak today, but the important thing is I did make contact. It was an exciting moment when I first felt a swarmmaster's presence in my mind. He and the other swarmmasters had resisted me because they had observed many evil deeds committed by the human race on Tarizon.

"Let me tell you about the nanomites. They are gentle, caring, beings. They experience joy and pain just like you and me. They have no politics because all act for the benefit of each other. Any one of them would sacrifice their life for the good of the swarm. There is no conflict, discord or jealousy in a nanomite swarm. They simply don't understand these concepts. Everyone looks out for each other in their constant battle for survival."

"Excuse me," Councilor Thoripides interrupted. "From your explanation these nanomites seem to me to be just another insect who live by instinct and don't have the ability for rational thought."

"Oh, but that is not the case at all, Councilor. Each swarmmaster has emotions. They worry about their swarms and the other swarms in the colonies. They communicate with other swarmmasters and they discuss options and make plans for how best to make their colonies thrive. They are as much a sentient life-form as human beings."

Councilor Thoripides shook his head and rolled his eyes. "Artis, if I can call you that—"

"Yes, please do, everyone does."

"Artis, how do we know you're not making all of this up? I know you've been able to get the nanomites to build magnificent structures all over Tarizon and I commend you for that, but many believe you have simply learned how to control and manipulate them. How do you respond to that?"

The scribe stood up and Councilor Sidon smiled. "I think, Councilor, that our next speaker may be able to answer that question better than anyone. Artis, would you ask the speaker for the nanomites to make his appearance?"

Artis nodded and closed her eyes. Councilor Thoripides snarled, "What is this?"

"Patience," the Chief Councilor said. "Give her a moment."

"Yes, I have him," Artis said without opening her eyes.

The Chief Councilor nodded. "Please translate his thoughts."

"I object!" Councilor Thoripides scowled. "This is outrageous."

Councilor Sidon sighed. "I suspected you would object, so I polled the other councilors and four of us want to hear from the speaker of the nanomites. Do I need to take a formal vote?"

Thoripides sat back in his chair and shook his head. "All right, then. Let's hear from the Speaker. Does he have a name?"

"No. But I sometimes call him Allo. It's just a name I made up to make it easier to communicate with him. You will actually be speaking to all the swarmmasters when you talk to Allo."

"Very well, proceed."

"*To answer your question, we act voluntarily after extensive discussion between all our swarmmasters. Artis and Threebeard are not forcing us to do anything we don't want to do.*"

"*Very well, Allo,*" Councilor Sidon said. "*Then why have your swarms built so many magnificent palaces, halls and buildings all over Tarizon?*"

"*Because we have agreed to a covenant for such construction work with Central Authority. We must honor our word."*

"But what do you get for all this hard work? From what I have heard it so little in comparison to what us humans get."

"What seems like nothing to you is monumental to our colonies. Before we knew of your human existence, life was very perilous for us. To thrive as a people, we must have certain chemical elements and specific environmental conditions. Only a few places on Tarizon are habitable for us. The Covenant makes it possible for us to migrate and multiply. Our colonies have increased a hundred-fold since we signed the Covenant. Like humans and all life-forms our most important instinct is for survival and increasing our swarms. It is our ultimate objective to make sure nanomites never become extinct."

"So, tell us how you feel about Broggin and Zahn and what they did."

"We feel a great sadness and depression over the loss of so many of our brothers and sisters. At times we regret that we ever came to know the human race. But mostly we feel outrage that someone could murder millions of swarms of nanomites and feel no remorse. We wonder if other human beings could do the same thing."

"I assure you that these are unique cases, Allo. We feel your outrage and that is why both the Quori and the Merria Councils of Interpreters convicted both of these men for these heinous crimes. Unfortunately, under the Supreme Mandate they are entitled to an appeal. I promise you I will urge my colleagues to uphold these convictions."

"Thank you, Chief Councilor. You are an honorable man and we hope the others who are deciding this appeal are as just and honorable, but we have our reservations judging by the arguments we have heard today."

"I understand, but the right to speak freely is protected under the Supreme Mandate and no one should be chastised for exercising that right."

"Then we will speak freely. If these two murderers are not executed for their crimes, we will see that justice is done in our own way. Also, we will consider the Covenant with Central Authority breached and no longer honor it. And if there are any further acts of genocide against the nanomites, we will take appropriate measures to protect ourselves and punish those who have done us harm."

The gallery erupted in hushed conversation. Councilor Thoripides' eyes narrowed. *"Are you threatening us?"* he asked.

"No," Allo replied evenly. *"I'm simply stating a fact which is my right as a citizen of Tarizon."*

The scribe stood up and Artis opened her eyes. Councilor Sidon coughed nervously. "Well, thank you Artis. Our final speaker will be Lt. Videl Lai."

Videl Lai, a tall, thin man walked deliberately up to the lectern. He didn't bow but rather glared at the Chief Councilor. "You may proceed," the Councilor advised.

"Since my time is short I will not belabor issues that have already been addressed. What I wanted to warn the Supreme Councilors about today is the growing threat that the nanomites pose to Central Authority and the human population of Tarizon. Are you aware that many nanomites swarms are left in each structure after they build it? They will deny it since current regulations require them to leave, but how do we know they haven't left spies for the militant mutants who are raising armies to overthrow Central Authority and seize control of the urban domes?"

The Chief Councilor shook his head. "Senator, do you have an argument relevant to the issues before this tribunal? We are not interested in your paranoia."

Videl Lai's eyes narrowed. "If you insist on ignoring the truth and won't heed my warning, then I just want to say that, as far as I am concerned, Broggin and Zahn are heroes and patriots and I applaud what they have done."

Many in the gallery cheered Videl as he returned to his seat, but most just sat in shock pondering his words. The Chief Councilor spoke up. "The council will take this matter under consideration and have a decision by the end of the day. Thank you," he said and stood up.

Councilor Thoripides leaned back in his chair and laughed. "Artis, you're a good actor. Allo of the nanomites? What a joke!" A few tiks later the Councilor's chair collapsed and he fell hard to the floor. He screamed and then scrambled to his feet staring at the pile of sawdust which was all that was left of his seat. Councilor Sidon stifled a laugh, but few in the gallery restrained their amusement over the nanomite speaker's clear message.

The media camera came back on and Lorina Lance was back in

front of it. "All right, the council has left the Great Hall and will now deliberate in private before taking a final vote. You saw that the Chief Councilor had mustered enough votes to let Allo be heard. There is no guarantee, however, that he will be able to muster the four votes necessary to uphold Zahn and Broggin's convictions. In addition to Councilor Thoripides, two other councilors are staunch allies of Videl Lai and the Purist Party. The other four councilors are known to be independent with allegiances to no one. Accordingly, the vote could go either way and since there is so much at stake deliberations may extend late into the night.

"If Broggin and Zahn's convictions are upheld they will be flogged, hung by their wrists in the public square, and then given a lethal injection. Experts tell me the public flogging is to ensure the condemned men suffer great pain and feel the public's outrage. Just after nightfall they will be given lethal injections, their bodies incinerated and their ashes put in a public disposal unit.

"While we are waiting for the decision of the Supreme Council of Interpreters we will return to our regular programming with a promise that coverage will resume just as soon as the Supreme Council reconvenes."

Threebeard and his staff took advantage of the recess to get some lunch. They met in the officer's club a few loon's later.

"Did you hear that?" Lt. Leode asked. "They know we are building a mutant army."

"Yes. Some people think that's what I'm doing, but they can't prove it and each of you should deny it if you're asked."

"I wonder what the other generals will think. They can't just stand by and let a mutant army be raised against them."

"Don't worry," Threebeard replied. "Commander General Zitor will protect us. They wouldn't dare make a play against us."

"Yes. It's a good thing he got a promotion. If he was still a colonel we'd be in trouble."

"I can't believe Videl Lai came out blatantly for the genocide of the mutants and congratulated the murderers, Broggin and Zahn," Lt. Leode said. "He must be a lunatic."

"Many believe he is, but what shocked me was Allo's threat to take appropriate measures if there is an acquittal. What do you think he meant by it? "

"I don't know," Threebeard replied, "but if they can sabotage Councilor Thoripides' chair in just a few tiks after he laughs at them, can you imagine what they could do to make life miserable for all of us if they decided to seek vengeance for the genocide committed against them?"

Lt. Leode nodded. Central Authority and the Purists have surely miscalculated the threat the nanomites pose for them. Six and a half hours after the lunch break, the session of the Supreme Council of Interpreters reconvened. Lorina Lance was back in front of the media camera when it went live.

"This is Lorina Lance back live in the Great Hall of the Interpreters. We've just been advised that the Supreme Council of Interpreters has made a decision and will be announcing it shortly. Councilor Sidon is taking the bench and looking rather somber which could be good news for Broggin and Zahn. We have been told that Councilor Thoripides will read the decision."

Councilor Thoripides began speaking from his seat. "Citizens of Tarizon, after careful consideration of the appeals of Fellis Broggin and Hirah Zahn of their convictions of capital genocide, it is our opinion that the convictions should be and are hereby reversed. After careful study and deliberation, it is clear that nanomites are not 'persons' within the meaning of the Supreme Mandate, nor were they citizens of any of the 29 consolidated states at the time the Supreme Mandate was adopted. Therefore, Broggin and Zahn's convictions for the crime of capital genocide are reversed and they shall be released immediately."

The camera switched back to Lorina Lance. "Well there you have it. Broggin and Zahn's convictions have been overturned and as we speak they are being congratulated by Senator Videl Lai and others who have shown their support for them since their arrests. This is a difficult day for Artis and the nanomites. It is unclear if they will indeed reject their covenant with Central Authority, but their speaker, Allo, seemed pretty adamant that there would be no further construction by nanomite swarms if the convictions were set aside. He even suggested the nanomites would find a way to exact revenge for the genocide of millions of their life-form. What that means is anyone's guess, but I'm sure Broggin and Zahn will be pondering that question carefully tonight when they rejoin their families."

"This is Lorina Lance reporting from the courtroom of the Supreme Council of Interpreters. Good night."

After the disappointing decision, Artis retreated from the Hall of Interpreters clutching the small cube which housed several nanomite swarms, including their speaker, Allo. Giant, Ariela and Nic met her outside the hall to escort her to the Mighty Jolly where she was staying.

An assemblyman saw her and pointed. "There she is with her cube full of bugs," the assemblyman said grinning broadly. The group turned and laughed heartily at Artis and her nanomite cube."

"Don't listen to them," Nic said as they left the Great Hall and walked over to a waiting Grinden. "They're a bunch of ignorant slubdubs."

They all got in and the Grinden took off.

"I know, but a majority feel the same way. I fear the nanomites will become slaves now and it's all my fault for forcing them to communicate with us."

"It's not your fault and if you hadn't taught them to communicate they would probably be extinct right now rather than as numerous as they have ever been in the history of Tarizon. How many nanomite swarms are there now?"

"I don't know."

"Billions by my count, so don't beat yourself up."

"I know. But they are a very fragile life-form and I'm worried about what is in store for them."

"Don't worry about what is in store for us," Allo interjected. *"Worry about the fate of Broggin and Zahn and those who protect them. We will have justice."*

Artis looked at Nic and Ariela. She didn't know how to respond to Allo. *"I'm sorry, Allo. Unfortunately, our system is not perfect. The nanomites were wronged today and I am ashamed of the Council of Interpreters. Please forgive my inability to make the World Assembly see the righteous and just path to follow."*

"We have no complaint with you," Allo thought. *"You and Threebeard have done your best. I have but one last thing I would like from you."*

"What's that?" Artis asked. *"Take us to the place where Broggin and Zahn will be staying tonight. I understand the Purists are hosting a party for them, and in the morning, they will be going home."*

"No. I will not be a part of your revenge," Artis said. *"I have sworn to uphold the Supreme Mandate and Broggin and Zahn were entitled to their appeal. There's nothing I can do but take you back to the Mighty Jolly and return you to Tributon."*

Ariela told Giant of Allo's request and they discussed the request briefly.

"Giant and I will take you there," Ariela thought. *"We believe in the Supreme Mandate but we don't believe in Central Authority or the Purists who have been pulling its strings lately. We would relish seeing you get your revenge and will help you in any way we can. We can probably find others to help as well."*

"That is most generous of you and Giant. We could use help in getting word to all our swarms and moving them to strategic locations."

"Is that all right with you, Artis?" Ariela asked. *"Can you spare us for a while?"*

"Yes, we can spare you but keep Threebeard and me out of whatever you do. We are trying to raise a mutant army and we cannot give Central Authority any excuse to shut that down."

"Understood. We will keep our assistance secret since we work for the Mighty Jolly. If we need a human spokesperson we'll get someone not associated with Threebeard or the Mighty Jolly to lend his name to the movement."

Artis handed Giant the nanomite cube. *"Okay, good luck."*

"What will you say if Central Authority asks you what you did with this cube?" Allo inquired.

"We will tell him we took it back to the Ural Desert. We'll make a point to go there for show. If they have agents following us, that will distract them for a while and give you time to do whatever you are planning."

"Thank you, Artis. And thank Giant for us. You two are true friends," Allo said.

Giant, who had stood as guardian over the model nanomite city for over a cycle, was very angry that the Supreme Council of Interpreters had denied them standing under the Supreme Mandate. He regretted the fact that Councilor Rammel Garciah hadn't been there to urge the other councilors to do the right thing. He was sure the outcome would have been different had Garciah not been on Earth.

Giant, Ariela and a rhutz named Daylight waited outside the Emerald City Hotel near the center of Shisk where the party was taking place. When it was over they followed them to a military base just inside the southwest entrance to the dome. Zahn and Broggin were dropped off in front of some barracks and went inside. A few tiks later Daylight walked around the perimeter of the building, checking on doors and windows available for ingress and egress. Daylight, having been with the local Loyalist cell for several phases already knew Tari and had no trouble linking with Allo. This gave the nanomite swarmmasters a pair of eyes that could be used to plan their revenge on Broggin and Zahn. Daylight was anxious to help as he knew Rupra Bruda had killed his friend Misty and was responsible for the Flat Meadow Massacre.

Allo noted that they were close to a nanomite farm that serviced Shisk. Since they were so close he was able to communicate with their speaker there and advise them of the current situation. He immediately initiated a conference between all the swarmmasters.

"The World Assembly has denied us our rights under the Supreme Mandate....They refuse to punish Broggin and Zahn for their genocide of our swarms....How can they do that?...We have built the very hall in which they deliberate for the sake of Sandee...They have been using us...They are evil...You can't trust humans...We can't let them get away with this...They will murder us all as soon as they are through with us...The humans have broken their contract...We must have justice....Broggin and Zahn must die!....Yes, they both must die!...Kill the skutz and show the humans they can't get away with murder. If we kill Broggin and Zahn they may try to kill all of us....We can hide, they cannot see us....We will have to move out of the farms...They will kill our brothers and sisters in the other farms around Tarizon...We must warn them...We have no choice...No, they have not given us a choice...To them we are common insects and they will kill us with no remorse...We must show them how wrong they are...Our friend Giant has agreed to warn the others...And Daylight will be our eyes...Good, then it is decided...Yes, we will not be slaves of the humans."

That night after Broggin and Zahn had gone to bed the nanomites came up from beneath their bunks and quietly constructed clear, crystal caskets that completely encased them. They left a vent to allow them to breathe until the very last minute when they sealed it. Not only were the caskets as strong as steel but they were sound proof as well, so when Zahn and Broggin suddenly awoke in the dead of night gasping and screaming in terror nobody heard them.

The next morning when First Sergeant Brill Grets, who was the senior enlisted man in the barracks, awoke he peered curiously at the odd sight wondering if someone was playing a practical joke on him. There before him lay Broggin and Zahn, eyes open, peering out of their transparent caskets with a look of complete and utter terror in their eyes. An involuntary shiver went through the First Sergeant and he immediately called headquarters to report the ghastly sight.

Lt. Videl Lai, who was now assigned to the TGA base at Shisk, was summoned to the barracks along with Colonel Lessch Strommer, the base security officer. Both of them just stared at the bizarre sight seemingly speechless. Finally, Videl recovered. "What is this?"

"I've never seen anything like it," Colonel Lessch confessed.

"Didn't anybody hear anything?" Videl asked.

"No, sir. Not a sound."

Videl ran his hand across the surface of the casket. "It's smooth like marble." He took a knife out of his pocket and tried to punch through the crystal but he was only able to slightly scratch it.

"Could this be the doing of the nanomites?" Colonel Lessch asked. "Didn't they threaten to do something like this if the Supreme Council failed to convict Broggin and Zahn?"

Videl nodded. "I'm afraid you might be right. It's the only thing that makes any sense. If a human had done this they would have made a lot of noise and they would have been seen by someone. Only the nanomites could have murdered Broggin and Zahn without being detected. I warned the Supreme Councilors about the nanomites."

"But how did they get in here so fast?" Colonel Lessch asked. "They are so small they couldn't travel very fast. Someone must have carried them here."

"They were already close by," Videl replied, "at the nanomite farm. Someone must have brought Allo here and he incited them to act. Probably Artis Nocteris, Threebeard's sister. She translated for the nanomites at the

Supreme Council proceeding yesterday."

"We should round her up for questioning."

"She's back in Tributon by now. We wouldn't have jurisdiction; plus how could we prove it? We better go check the farm and see if the nanomites are still there. If they are as smart as they claim, they won't be."

They all got into their PTVs and drove to the nearby nanomite farm. The handler, a Corporal Jesstiz, was in his office watching the VC. He came to attention when Colonel Lessch walked in.

"Good morning, sir."

"At ease, Corporal."

The corporal relaxed. "What can I do for you, sir?"

"We are here to check on the nanomites. Are they here?"

The corporal frowned. "Are they here? I assume so. I haven't talked to them today."

"When is the last time you talked to them?"

"A day or two ago. There haven't been any construction projects since the trial, so there hasn't been any reason to make contact."

"Don't you have some way to know if they are here or not?"

"No. They are two small to visually observe. Only by linking with them do I know they are here."

"Link with them now. I need to know if they are present."

"Yes, sir," the corporal said closing his eyes and appearing to concentrate. After a moment the corporal swallowed hard. "I'm not getting any response and I don't feel their presence. Usually when they are here I can feel their thoughts."

"Well, while you were watching the VC they went to the barracks and murdered Broggin and Zahn."

"What? That's not possible. How could they murder someone?"

"Go see for yourself. The crime scene technicians are at the barracks now. Go over and see if you sense any of the nanomites there."

"Yes, sir," the corporal said and then walked over to his PTV and drove off.

"We must report this to the base commander," Videl said. "He'll want to report it to Central Command."

"Right. Let's go to headquarters and we can inform him immediately."

The two officers drove to base headquarters and informed the base commander of the situation. Due to the serious nature of the incident the base commander ordered a link be established with Central Command without delay. Within a few loons they were in front of a big monitor talking with General Bratford and his staff.

"Is there any possibility it was someone other than the nanomites?" the general asked.

"No," Videl replied. "This is clearly the work of the nanomites."

"So, where are they now?"

"We have no idea," Colonel Lessch replied. "Their handler has advised us they are not at the farm nor at the crime scene. Logically they are trying to escape."

"You're the expert on the nanomites, Lt. Lai. Where do you think they would go. We must catch them and punish them for what they did."

"That's not possible. You can't catch them. They are too small. The only thing you can do, if you are lucky enough to find them, is kill them. The Supreme Council of the Interpreters has indicated they are not protected by the Supreme Mandate so I would recommend that they simply be poisoned like any other pest."

"But what about all the magnificent buildings they have constructed?" Colonel Lessch asked. "What about our contract?"

Videl shrugged. "It is unfortunate, but whether we like it or not we are at war with them and we need to act quickly to eradicate them or they will kill us all like they did Broggin and Zahn."

General Bratford nodded in agreement. "I'll contact the Chancellor and apprise him of the situation. It will have to be his call whether we take any retaliatory action or not."

"That will take days," Videl complained. "Many innocent people could die by the time the government bureaucrats make up their minds what to do. I say, since the nanomites have no civil rights, you could order their extermination immediately, General."

The general ran his fingers through his hair and shifted nervously in his chair. "Well, I suppose I could order the extermination of the local swarms here in central Shisk who obviously were behind the murder."

"Yes, they threatened Broggin and Zahn before the whole world and obviously they are behind this attack."

"Very well, I'll send out that limited order."

"But how do we know what swarms are covered by the order?" Colonel Lessch asked.

"Don't worry about that," Videl said curtly. "Their handler can identify them."

The General stood up and the connection was cut. Videl looked over at Colonel Lessch. "Well, we have our orders."

"Yes, we do," Colonel Lessch agreed. "Let's go find Corporal Jesstiz so we can get started tracking down those swarms."

Threebeard was just cleaning off his desk, preparing to go home when his GC buzzed. He made a connection and was pleased to hear Commander General Zitor's voice.

"Commander, how are you?" Threebeard asked.

"Not well, I'm afraid. I've just received some disturbing news."

"Oh? What it is?"

"Apparently Allo made good on his threat and Broggin and Zahn have been murdered. The nanomites built coffins around them while they slept and then sealed them off asphyxiating them."

"Oh, my God!" Threebeard groaned. "Well, they had it coming."

"I know, but General Bratford, under pressure from the base commander at Shisk and Videl Lai, has ordered the summary extermination of all the nanomites in Shisk."

Threebeard's stomach twisted. He knew this was a most delicate situation and could lead to a general war with the nanomites.

"Without even a hearing?"

"Yes. He's treating the nanomites like common rodents, since the Supreme Council denied them rights under the Supreme Mandate."

"What can we do?"

"I'm going to talk to General Bratford and I was hoping you could talk to Allo. Perhaps we can come up with some kind of compromise."

"Do you think you can get the general to back off his order?"

"Maybe, if I can make him realize the consequences of his actions."

"I hope you can, but I'm not optimistic you'll succeed. No doubt, Videl Lai and the Purists are behind the order and they won't back down easily."

"We have to do something. We can't afford a war with a life-form we can't even see. All our resources need to be focused on survival and rebuilding Tarizon."

"I agree. I'll do my best with Allo, if I can even make contact with him. I'm sure the nanomites are on the run."

"Well, get with your sister and see if you can find them. It's our only hope."

"Yes, sir. I'll get right on it."

Threebeard disconnected and immediately focused on Artis. A tik later he felt her presence in his mind.

"Have you heard the news?" he thought.

"You mean about Broggin and Zahn?"

"Yes, and the order to kill all the nanomites in Shisk."

She sighed. *"It was on the news. I'm so worried about them."*

"I know. Did you know they were going to kill Broggin and Zahn?

"Yes. They asked me to help but I refused. I think Giant, Ariela and Daylight are helping them."

"Giant?"

"Yes. They were anxious to get revenge for Videl Lai's murder of Misty and Eyeball."

"Well, they got their revenge, but in the process, they've started a war."

"What do you mean?"

"The TGA will not allow someone in their custody to be murdered without bringing those responsible to justice. And we know now the nanomites won't accept the judgment of a world that doesn't acknowledge them as a sentient life-form. So, if more nanomites are killed they will retaliate and the whole affair will escalate into a war."

"Perhaps we should talk to Giant and Ariela and see what they know."

"Yes. That's a good idea."

"Alright. Call me on my GC when you are ready," Artis said and closed her mind to Threebeard.

Threebeard called Giant on his GC and then added Artis to the call.

"Alright," Threebeard said. "Are you with the nanomites?"

"Yes. They are close by."

"How are they?"

"Better now that they have got some measure of justice."

"Good, but now the TGA has ordered their extermination."

"I know. They are in hiding," Giant replied. "The TGA won't be able to find them."

"Good. That may be the only way to avoid a full-blown war."

"I'm afraid it's too late for that," Giant said sadly.

"What do you mean?" Artis asked.

"Somehow the nanomites we rescued from the science lab and left on the outskirts of Vaceen got the word to the other swarms about the genocide."

"What!" Artis exclaimed. "No. Don't tell me that."

"I'm afraid it is true," Giant whispered. "The swarmmasters are furious. They are already planning more strikes against the humans."

"We have to put a stop to this," Threebeard pleaded. "A war with the nanomites would be a disaster for everyone on Tarizon. The TGA doesn't realize what they are capable of."

"So, what should we do?" Artis asked urgently.

"I don't know," Threebeard replied. "Giant, ask Daylight if Allo will talk to me if I come to Shisk."

"Okay," Giant said. "Wait a minute. I'll have Ariela ask them."

There was silence for a few loons and then Ariela spoke up. "Allo is refusing to talk to humans until the Supreme Council reverses their ruling. If the humans don't recognize the nanomites then the nanomites don't recognize human beings."

Artis gasped. "What have we done? We should never have made contact with the nanomites. Oh, my brother what are we going to do?"

Threebeard sighed deeply, his stomach twisting in knots. "There is nothing we can do. Perhaps this is the price we will have to pay to get our government to be reasonable."

"We're just going to sit back and watch this genocide?"

"No. I think the nanomites will hold their own. We might even help them out a bit behind the scenes."

"But you are a sworn officer of the TGA. How could you help the nanomites without committing treason?"

"One day soon the TGA will be our enemy, so if my assistance to the nanomites today hastens that day, it will not be a tragedy."

"So, what should I do?" Giant asked.

"Do what your conscience tells you to do, my friend. I will not judge you either way."

"Then Ariela and I will continue to help the nanomites. Since I helped both of you make contact with them, I bear some of the responsibility for what is happening now. So, I shall fight with them until the Supreme Council of Interpreters reverses their decision."

"Very well, then. May God and Sandee be with you."

Threebeard hung up the GC and fell back into his chair. His worst fears were becoming reality faster than he had anticipated. Now he was afraid this new war with the nanomites would only hasten the inevitable civil war that would soon engulf Tarizon. A war that could easily lead to the end of civilization on Tarizon and beginning of an era of lawlessness, chaos and despair.

After assisting Allo and the nanomites exact their revenge against Broggin and Zahn, Ariela and Giant returned to Liehn. There they picked up two identical cubes filled with nanomite swarms and took them back to their Ural Desert homeland as Artis had promised. On their way back to Liehn they decided to check on the science lab swarms they'd left in a church just outside of Fasoon. When they found the church that had been collapsed and in ruin they were shocked to find it fully restored. When Ariela asked them about it they told her they'd been forced to restore it to protect the swarms while they waited for contact from the other swarmmasters. Ariela filled them in on the decision of the Supreme Council of Interpreters and they were shocked, angered and bent on getting their own revenge against Rupra Bruda and Berne Baldrige.

36

Anger and Pride

Baldrige lie awake in his bed trembling. Reports that the nanomites in Shisk had quietly built a transparent casket around Broggin and Zahn chilled him to the bone. He wondered if he would suffer a similar fate if the war with the nanomites continued. He shuddered at the thought of suffocating in his sleep. As a precaution he kept a pistol at his side to blow his way out of the casket if he found himself entombed. Why had he accepted help from Rupra Bruda? Artis had warned him. What a fool he had been to dismiss her concerns. Fortunately, there were no longer any nanomites at the science lab. He'd have to take precautions to be sure none were allowed to enter the facility in the future. He finally drifted off into a troubled slumber.

During the night he dreamed of the warehouse and the extermination Bruda ordered. He could hear the cries of a million nanomites as they choked and wailed in pain from the toxic gases. He closed his eyes and covered his ears trying to keep out the frantic voices. When he finally opened his eyes again he saw thousands of giant nanomites emerging from under his door, crawling up onto his bed and viciously biting into this skin. He twisted and turned trying to get away from them but soon realized his hands and feet were tied by invisible restraints. The pain from each bite was excruciating. He screamed in utter agony. He awoke with a start.

He jumped out of bed and examined his body. Relieved that it had only been a dream he went to the window and looked out over his yard. Everything looked quiet but he still had an ominous feeling. With the nanomites quiet was the norm. That was why they were so dangerous. They could be doing terrible things without anyone realizing it was happening. He decided he would have to arrange for guards to be posted around his home to keep watch for anything out of the ordinary.

       After Ariela had advised the Speaker of the Fasoon nanomites of the events in Shisk, the swarmmasters took a few loons to discuss the issue amongst themselves. When they were done the Speaker asked. *"So, if they find us they will exterminate us just like they did our brothers and sisters in the science lab,"* the Speaker said.
       "I'm afraid so," Ariela replied.
       "Then we should take the offensive."
       "What do you mean?"
       "We should attack the humans before they find us."
       "Well, Threebeard doesn't want that. He is trying to get the TGA to retract the order. He wants peace."
       "Fine, but until that happens, as I understand it. We are at war."
       Ariela swallowed hard. *"Yes, I suppose so."*
       "I know who we should kill first."
       "Who?" Ariela asked.
       "Baldrige. He betrayed us when he brought in Rupra Bruda and his evil mate."
       "Yes. I understand. It was their intent to enslave you like they have the Seafolken."
       "Will you and Giant help us?"
       "I don't know. Let me discuss it with him."
       Ariela relayed the conversation to Giant. He nodded.
       "Yes. We will help you. What do you want us to do?"
       The speaker told her.
       "Alright. We'll get started."
       Giant and Ariela left and went into Fasoon to procure supplies and locate Baldrige's home. They found an equipment rental yard and Giant rented a small truck and then went to a materials yard and had it loaded with sand. Then he drove back to the Nanomite's restored church. While Giant was doing that, Ariela looked in the local directories but could not find Baldrige's address, so she got on the GC and called Nic back at the Mighty Jolly. He was reluctant to look up the address on the TGN but finally did and gave it to her.

"If anyone asks, we didn't talk today," Nic said.

"Right," Ariela agreed.

That night Giant pulled open one of the ventilation caps on the roof of Baldrige's home. Then he poured in the same toxic fluid Rupra Bruda had used on the nanomites. While he was doing that the nanomites were sealing all the doors and windows so that no one in the house could escape. When the home had been sealed the Speaker let Ariela know and she turned on a fan that would spread the toxic gas throughout the house.

In just a few loons Baldrige and his family were up running around in a general panic. They were coughing, choking and pounding on the doors and windows trying to escape the toxic blend of gases that caused excruciating pain as they attacked their bodies' central nervous systems. In less than half a kyloon they were all dead.

When the job was done Giant drove the small truck back to the church. Once they were out of the sand and safely back in the walls of the church, Giant and Ariela left to return the truck so it wouldn't be reported missing by its owners.

In Shisk Rupra and Essyria Bruda were enjoying a drink before dinner at the Gohi Dodi restaurant when a news bulletin came on the VC. Rupra looked up when he heard it was about a new nanomite attack.

"Early this morning there was another attack by nanomite swarms in Fasoon. Berne Baldrige, head of the Nanomite Project at the TGA science lab was found dead along with his wife, two children and three servants. Apparently during the night, the nanomites sealed off his home and then pumped lethal gases into the sealed structure. A spokesman for the Medical Examiner indicated that the gas attacked the central nervous system of its victims causing a very painful, agonizing death.

"Ironically the TGA science lab was where the nanomites were taught to build structures suitable for human habitation and eventually a contract was agreed upon for the joint construction of a long list of projects including the Great Hall of the Supreme Council of Interpreters here in Shisk.

"Recently the Supreme Council of Interpreters denied the

nanomites civil rights status under the Supreme Mandate resulting in the reversal of the convictions of Fellis Broggin and Hirah Zahn who had been convicted of capital genocide of millions of nanomite swarms. Yesterday, Broggin and Zahn were found dead in their bunks having been sealed alive in crystal coffins. A spokesman for the TGA indicates this was the work of local nanomite swarms angered by the ruling.

"Informed sources indicate the killing of Baldrige was in retaliation for the genocide of millions of nanomite swarms in a warehouse at the science lab facility last cycle for which Fellis Broggin had been convicted. Apparently the nanomites believed Baldrige was also responsible for that atrocity."

Essyria looked worriedly at Rupra. "I thought they were all dead."

"So did I."

"What if they come after us? You know they hate us more than anyone on Tarizon."

Rupra shook his head. "They couldn't get close to us. I would feel them coming."

"What are we going to do? They are out of control."

"We need to talk to General Bratford. He needs to expand his kill order to include Fasoon."

"Why stop there? We should kill all the nanomites on Tarizon," Essyria argued.

"Yes, we should, but the Loyalists still control the General Assembly. They'd never allow it. We need to keep this as a TGA matter. So far everyone they have killed was associated with the TGA so dealing with them is a matter for the military."

Rupra got on the GC, talked to General Bratford's aide and was relieved to find out that once Baldrige's body had been found the extermination order had been expanded to include the nanomites at Fasoon and surrounding precincts.

Rupra disconnected the GC and smiled at Essyria. "Everything is under control."

Essyria gave him a skeptical look.

Giant drove the small truck with its cargo of sand as fast as he dared on the country road that led away from the church. He knew it wouldn't be long before the TGA discovered the attack on the Baldrige home. What he didn't know was that a neighbor had seen him on Baldrige's roof and called the PE's office. He gave them a description of the truck and an officer on a jet cycle had spotted them driving out of town. While the officer was following them, he called in and reported the truck's position. When the PE's dispatcher got the report, she called the TGA.

Not ten loons after the nanomites had retreated into the walls of the church TGA soldiers were dropping out of jet copters around the building. While the house was being surrounded the officer chased after Giant and Ariela. When he put on his siren and turned on his lights Giant refused to stop. After a long chase Giant rolled the truck trying to avoid a collision with a second PE officer who came at him from a cross street. The load of sand spilled out onto the highway knocking both officers off their cycles and into a ditch. Giant climbed out of the truck, helped Ariela out and they both took flight and disappeared into the woods with the two officers in pursuit.

Back at the church the squad leader on site called in to his lieutenant for orders. "We have the nanomites in a church. There are no other occupants in the structure. How should we proceed?"

"Your orders are to kill the nanomites," the lieutenant advised.

"How do you suggest we do that, sir? How do you kill nanomites?"

There was silence on the line for a moment. "Ah. Toxic gases or high intensity heat."

"We don't have any gases, but we could send for some."

"No. They might get away. Just hit the church with a few missiles from your jet copters. The explosion will produce enough heat to kill them."

"Understood."

The squad leader told his men to clear the area and then two jet copters rose, backed off a few hundred strides and unleashed a missile barrage that engulfed the church in a fiery inferno. The nanomite swarms inside tried to burrow deep into the ground to avoid the deadly explosion and ensuing fire, but the blast ripped right through them and they all perished.

The soldiers around the perimeter of the church watched it burn, mesmerized by the sight but not quite fathoming what they had done. News helicopters were soon hovering above getting footage of the burning church for the evening telecasts.

Several kylods away Giant and Ariela hid behind a rock as one of the PE's chasing them approached. As he ran by Giant grabbed the officer's arm and pulled him to the ground. The officer's revolver was knocked away leaving him helpless. Giant immediately pounced on him, got him in a headlock and snapped his neck.

A shot rang out and a bullet hit Giant in the arm. He turned angrily and glared at the other PE coming at him. With her third hand Ariela yanked the gun out of the officer's arm and it skidded several strides away. The PE stopped, stunned by being disarmed. He looked at the gun several strides away and then at Giant. He swallowed hard, then turned and ran back the way he came.

Ariela rushed over, ripped off a sleeve of the dead officer's shirt and tied it over Giant's wound. Then they got up and made their escape.

Allo and the nanomite swarms back in Shisk were asleep. They had been running all day and were exhausted. In their normal existence they rarely moved but a few strides each day, so to move a kylod was extremely taxing. Suddenly Allo felt Daylight in his mind. He could tell she was reluctant to share her thoughts.

"Yes, Daylight. What is it?"

She told him about the fate of the nanomite at the science lab."

Allo's mood darkened with the shocking news. *"This is indeed regrettable news. We had thought the humans would learn a lesson when we took the lives of just a few of them in retaliation for the millions of nanomites who they so callously slaughtered. But we can see now they are arrogant and thick headed, so we will have to make them suffer dearly before they will think twice about murdering nanomites."*

"What are you going to do?" Daylight thought.

"Something that will haunt their dreams for many cycles to come and make it difficult for them to ever close their eyes to sleep again."

"Do you need my help?" Daylight asked.

"Yes, but only to deliver a message to the other swarms in Shisk. There are seven building sites and we will need all of these swarms. After

that has been done, I would suggest you and the other rhutz in Shisk leave the city and go back to the woods and the meadows where it will be safe."

"Alright. I will warn the local packs and they will pass the word."

"Thank you for your help, Daylight. You have been a real friend to the nanomites. God be with you."

Allo connected to all his swarmmasters and they mourned the loss of their brothers and sisters in Fasoon. After a long and heated discussion, they agreed with Allo that they had no choice but to deliver a blow so devastating that the humans would regret the day they broke the covenant with the nanomites.

The next day Daylight delivered Allo's message to the other swarmmasters. It was a difficult task since all the nanomite swarms had moved out of their farms and were hiding. But eventually he found them all and the nanomite plan was under way.

Since it was an ambitious plan, Allo knew it would take some time to carry out, but he was convinced once it unfolded the humans would have no choice but to ask for an end to hostilities. Unfortunately, he overestimated the wisdom and underestimated the pride of his human foes.

Lt. Videl Lai was angry that the security patrols had been unable to find any of the nanomite swarms in Shisk. The problem was that only a handful of humans in Shisk had strong enough telepathic abilities to detect nanomite activity. He, Bruda and Essyria and the seven nanomite handlers had split up and gone out with each of the security patrols sweeping the city, but Shisk with eight million citizens was much too large to effectively search, particularly when you couldn't see what you were looking for.

Frustrated, Videl got on the GC with General Bratford to see if they could come up with a solution.

"It's impossible to find the nanomites when they are hiding. Isn't there any way to detect their presence?" Videl asked.

"There is no other practical way. You would have to have a strong microscope to even see a nanomite."

"Well there must be something else we can do. We can't just let them attack us with impunity," General Bratford spat.

"There is one thing you could do," Bruda said. "It would take a little time but it would eventually solve the problem."

"What is it?" General Bratford demanded.

"Baldrige once told me that bacuum was the key to controlling the nanomites. I had expressed my concern that their numbers were growing rapidly and eventually it might be hard to control them. He told me the nanomites must have bacuum and that was how we could stop their growth at any time. Bacuum can only be found naturally in a few desert regions. That's why the nanomites lived in those areas. Now we are mining it and providing the nanomites with as much as they want."

"Right," Videl interrupted. "So, cut off the bacuum and the nanomites die."

"Yes, without bacuum they cannot propagate and eventually they would all die a natural death."

"Excellent!" General Bratford said. "I'll order all bacuum on Tarizon seized and moved to remote locations where the nanomites can't get their hands on it."

"Yes, an excellent plan," Bruda said. "We'll all sleep better when every last nanomite is dead."

The Tuht Tower, Tarizon's highest skyscraper, was the crown jewel of the Shisk skyline. It rose 3,000 ft. with 288 floors, and, on an average day boasted a census of 3,227 of Tarizon's most wealthy and productive businessmen. It was a workday, twenty-nine days after Broggin and Zahn's death at the hands of the nanomites, when a tremor was felt in the building.

Tremors were pretty common in Shisk since the great eruptions so no one paid much attention to it. The first tremor was followed by several more but what was strange about the tremors was the fact that they were only being felt by the humans in the Tuht Tower.

Chancellor Chlovus Hock was dining in one of several elegant restaurants in Tuht Tower along with Commander Brunns who had just returned from Earth. With them was Ensign Muri and several assemblymen from Tarizon's World Assembly. As they had just finished eating, the waiter brought them sankee and the dessert menu. The Chancellor stood up.

"Well, it is too bad that the Americans wouldn't agree to accept all of us on Earth, but having a pure environment to conceive and raise children for the next several generations is still a great accomplishment. I salute you Commander for a job well done," Chancellor Hock said raising his glass.

Everyone raised their glasses in response and then drank heartily. Suddenly the room began to rock back and forth, glasses tumbled over, and several guests screamed.

The Chancellor smiled. "Well, it's a good thing they made this building strong enough to withstand a quantum eight tremor."

Commander Brunns stood up. "Thank you for dinner, Mr. Chancellor, but Ensign Muri and I must leave. We are due to meet with General Bratford and Central Command to work on a plan for the transport of the first wave of Earth guests."

"Yes. Yes. Thank you for coming," the Chancellor replied. "Let me know if there is anything I can do to help expedite your preparations."

"I will," Commander Brunns said as he and Ensign Muri took their leave.

The waiter brought over the dessert tray and each of the remaining guests made their choices. Several loons later the lights flickered several times and then went out. It was late afternoon, so everyone could still see, so most everyone just laughed about the inconvenience.

"We should go," the chancellor's security chief suggested. "I'm not comfortable being here with the power out."

The Chancellor nodded. "Very well. I'm done anyway.

As he rose there was another tremor much more violent than the first. Many screamed as they were jolted out of their chairs and thrown onto the ground. Plaster fell from the ceiling and dishes and silverware were tossed to the ground.

The chief security officer pulled the Chancellor off the floor and he and the rest of the team rushed him out of the door to the elevator banks. Unfortunately, the elevators without power were useless. Just as they got to the stairwells the floor beneath them gave way and they dropped twenty feet into a pile of rubble. Dust and debris swelled around them and it became difficult to breath. Pain shot through the Chancellor's leg.

"I think I have broken my leg," the Chancellor moaned.

The chief security officer picked himself up out of the rubble and struggled to where the Chancellor had fallen. He examined the leg. "I think it is just a strain. I'll call for medical assistance. They should be here in just a moment."

"What is happening? Is Mt. Soni erupting again?"

"I don't know, Mr. Chancellor. I'll call in and see what's going on."

The chief security officer punched some numbers in the GC. "The Chancellor has been injured. We are in the Tuht Tower. The tremor has caused the 153rd floor to collapse."

"What? There's been no tremors. But—"

The officer's eyes went wide. "Okay, I'll tell him."

"Mr. Chancellor."

"What?" the Chancellor moaned.

"There have been no tremors. It's the nanomites. They took out the city's power grid, punctured the dome, and now buildings are collapsing all over the city!"

"Holy Sandee!" the Chancellor exclaimed as the floor beneath him gave way once again.

Videl Lai and Rupra Bruda stood speechless on the steps of the Hall of the World Assembly. They were watching the Tuht Tower where they knew the Chancellor was having dinner. There had been reports of floors collapsing and they could see smoke pouring out of the roof. Suddenly one corner of the building gave way causing it to fall like a tree toward another tall building, the 127story Kinomba Building. When it hit the Kinomba Building the top third of it broke away and dropped like lead onto the streets below and the Tuht Tower crumbled demolishing four more buildings beneath it.

There were screams of terror, pain and fear coming from every direction. Smoke from the fires in the toppled buildings, and toxic gases flooding in from large gashes in the dome, made it difficult to see and impossible to breathe. Emergency vehicles screamed in from every direction. Hordes of people were pouring out on the streets fearing no building in the city was safe. Looters, taking advantage of the chaos, began smashing windows, breaking into businesses and setting more fires.

"We must call General Bratford," Videl Lai said. "The Chancellor is surely dead. The general must declare martial law. This may be our opportunity to seize power."

"Yes. Perhaps so. You should call him."

Videl punched in the code to Central Command. "This is Lt. Videl Lai. I need to talk to General Bratford immediately."

Videl was put through to the general and updated him on the situation. "Yes, sir. He was having dinner in the building. I don't see how he could have survived."

Videl nodded several times while he listened to the general. "Yes, sir. I'll take care of it. Thank you."

Videl looked at Bruda. "The general wants me to see if I can find the vice-chancellor or the citihead. He's mobilizing a force to enter the city but he needs the approval of the citihead or the vice chancellor.

The citihead of Shisk was a Purist and a close friend of Videl Lai.

"Okay," Bruda replied. "You go look for the citihead and I'll try to find the vice chancellor. Hopefully he was in one of those buildings that collapsed, but if not, maybe I can arrange that he's found under one of them."

"Good idea, but don't get caught," Videl said. "We're not ready to fight a civil war just yet."

"Don't worry. I know how to kill someone and make it look like an accident."

"Yes, I know," Videl said. "You are very talented in that area. That's one of the reasons I recruited you."

The two parted and went their separate ways. Videl knew where he'd most likely find the citihead. He usually stopped for a drink at tavern near city hall on his way home each evening. Unfortunately, getting to the Dromma tavern in the chaos that had engulfed the city wasn't an easy task. It was less than a kylod so he started to walk there, but he was fighting the crowds which made the going slow. Finally, he saw a sky cab land and rushed over to hire it. Several other people had the same idea, so Videl used his third hand to trip them up. Just a few loons later the sky cab dropped him in front of the Dromma tavern. He went inside and found the citihead huddled in the corner of the tavern which they had turned into a temporary command center.

"Videl? What are you doing here?" the citihead asked.

"General Bratford asked me to find you. He's mobilizing a military force to come in and restore the peace, but he needs your approval."

"Yes. That's a good idea. Tell him to send them in."

"He'll need to hear it from you. You can use my GC to contact him."

Videl had a military command grade GC that was much more reliable than the ones issued to civilians. Videl punched in the code and handed it to the citihead.

"General. This is Citihead Balsch....Yes, the situation is very grave.... That's right, I was told the Chancellor was in the Tuht Tower when it collapsed. No one has heard from him since then.... Yes, we do need assistance. Please send us some troops to restore order.... I will... Thank you, General."

Citihead Balsch handed the GC back to Videl. "So, he's sending in the troops?" Videl asked.

"Yes, they will be arriving in a few kyloons."

"Good," Videl said. "This may work out very well for us."

"What do you mean?"

"We think the Vice Chancellor may be dead as well. If that is the case there would be much confusion and you could step in to restore order."

"But I have no authority beyond Shisk," the citihead protested.

"You do if the TGA says you do," Videl argued.

Citihead Balsch smiled.

37

Succession

Assemblyman Basset Als looked down at his beeping GC. He recognized Commander General Zitor's face and it looked grim. He pushed the receive button.

"Commander. I'm glad you called. Have you heard about the nanomite attack? I never dreamed they posed this kind of threat."

"Yes. That's why I'm calling. General Bratford is mobilizing forces to enter Shisk."

"He is?"

"Yes. Did you know about it?"

"No. I did not. All our normal communications links are down as we have no power."

"Apparently the citihead requested it. There are reports that the Chancellor is dead. Do you know where the Vice Chancellor is?"

"He left at the end of the session and probably went back to his office."

"You need to go find him and take extra security. I suspect the Purist might try to kill him."

"Seriously?"

"Yes. They have been looking for an opportunity to seize power and the nanomites may have just given them one."

"Okay. I'll find him right now and make sure he is secured."

"Good. Call me back when you find him."

Als called in his security chief and asked him to check on the Vice Chancellor and make sure he was safe. The security chief left and Basset got back on his GC.

"Mr. Chairman," Threebeard said seeing his face. "Are you alright? I heard you've got a lot going on there."

"Yes, more than you can imagine."

"How can I help?"

"Commander General Zitor thinks the Purists may try to take advantage of the chaos to seize power. Apparently General Bratford is about to send in troops to the city."

"Yes. I heard the citihead declared a state of martial law."

"I think we need to put our cells on alert. We may need their help if the TGA tries to shut down the World Assembly."

"Yes. I've already alerted them, but I need you to call an emergency meeting of the Assembly to assure a smooth transition of power. You should appoint a committee to coordinate with the TGA on an emergency response effort. It has to be clear that the World Assembly is in control at all times. It's not a time to be weak or timid. General Bratford will roll in there and take over if you let him."

"Yes. I'll get right on it."

The security chief walked in with a solemn look on his face.

"Wait a minute Threebeard. I may have some more news.... What is it?"

"Sir. The Vice Chancellor was on his way home when the attack took place. They found him under a pile of rubble."

"He's dead?"

"Yes, sir."

"Threebeard. Did you hear that? The vice chancellor is also dead?"

Threebeard sighed heavily. "Yes. I feared that would be the case. You must have the assembly elect a new chancellor and it must be done tomorrow. There can be no delay. If we don't have a new chancellor by the time the TGA rolls in, it may be too late."

"Who should we support for the job?" Basset asked.

"You, of course. This is also our opportunity to get a strong Loyalist leader elected."

"Okay. I better get to work. I'll call you as things develop."

"Good. May God and Sandee be with you."

Basset Als hung up the phone stunned by the conversation. There had been talk of him some day becoming chancellor, but was he ready? He'd always laughed and gone along with the suggestion thinking it was just a distant dream, but now it might become reality. He thought of all the problems that would face him if he were elected. A jolt of fear washed over him. Could he do it?

Allo and the surviving nanomite swarmmasters were sad. Millions of nanomites had died in the attack on the human skyscrapers in Shisk. All of the swarmmasters who participated in the attacks knew they probably wouldn't make it out alive, for to make a building collapse required thousands of nanomite swarms working to weaken key stress points of the structure. Since it was impossible to predict at what point the building would begin to collapse it was usually impossible for the nanomites to withdraw from the building in time to escape death.

Fortunately, nanomites reproduced quickly and swarms that had died were quickly replaced, but only if there was plenty of bacuum available. Unfortunately, the Shisk nanomites were running low. Allo felt Daylight's presence in his mind.

"Daylight. What did you find out?"

"The TGA has seized all the bacuum stores and are in the process of removing them from the city."

"Then we are doomed."

"Perhaps I can enlist the support of some of my rhutz brothers and sisters to intercept them."

"No. You don't want to give the TGA a reason to declare war on the Rhutz. We appreciate your help, but we can't allow you to do anything to endanger your life-form. We were almost extinct and by the grace of God were given new life by Threebeard and Artis. Contact them and tell them we are sorry that we were forced to kill so many in their great city, but our instincts for survival compelled our actions. We are a peace-loving life-form and it has been difficult for us to wage war, but it is over now as we cannot reproduce without bacuum. Ask them to try to help our other brothers and sisters on Tarizon from the wrath of the TGA, but if they cannot because we are now the enemy, we understand."

"You are not the enemy. It is the Purists who have caused this war by their atrocities. Threebeard will figure out a way to help you. Don't give up hope."

Nic arrived at the shipyards at Shisk on Captain Lozich's new ship, *Freedom*. Threebeard had asked them to come to Shisk to help thwart the feared Purist attempt to seize control of the capital. Their task was to block the entrances to the dome so the TGA could not enter the city. This was a daunting task as the TGA soldiers were heavily armed and would fight their way in if necessary. Daylight and Falling Star were waiting for them on the dock when they arrived.

"It is good to see you two," Nic thought after he climbed off the ship and jumped onto the dock.

"Yes, it has been a long time," Falling Star thought. *"You look well."*

Nic shrugged. *"Other than being a little seasick, I feel pretty good."*

After Captain Lozich secured the ship he joined them on the dock. *"So, what's the* situation?" he asked.

Daylight stepped forward. *"The nanomite attack is over. Most of them died when the buildings collapsed. They are out of bacuum and soon will all be dead."*

"Yes, well I've brought some bacuum," Nic said, *"but only enough to sustain but a few thousand swarms. I have arranged transport for one cube to Liehn."*

"Good. Allo will be glad to hear that. I will tell him."

"Have them build a cube somewhere safe and when it is ready I'll have it picked up and smuggled back to Tributon."

"I will," Daylight thought.

"How are we to stop the TGA?" Falling Star asked.

"We won't be able to stop them, but if we can keep them out of the city until noon that should give the World Assembly time to elect a new Chancellor."

"What about the garrison's already inside the dome?" Falling Star asked.

"We will have to keep them busy so they won't be able to get to the Great Hall before noon," Nic thought.

"How are we going to do that?" Captain Lozich asked.

"We thought we'd have a parade and a big rally at the capital to mourn the death of Chancellor Hock," Nic replied. *"We plan to clog the streets and make it impossible for any troops to get to the hall. We could use as many Seafolken as you could recruit for us."*

"I'll put out a call for them. There should be several hundred just here in the docks."

""Good, what if they fire on the crowd?" Daylight asked.

"The rhutz and the seafolken can disarm them with their third hands."

"Yes, many of the mutants have the same ability," Nic noted. *"I'll be sure they are on the front line. We won't be able to hold them off forever, but for several kyloons shouldn't be a problem."*

The meeting broke up and everyone went their separate ways to start work on their assigned tasks. Captain Lozich put the word out to all Seafolken along the coast of Turvin to come to Shisk while Falling Star sought help from the thousands of rhutz who lived in the forest of the Weeping Mountains. They all agreed to meet late that night at the Mighty Jolly to make final preparations.

Basset Als walked onto the floor of the World Assembly for the emergency meeting. Less than half the seats assigned to the assemblymen were occupied. It was apparent the Purists were going to try to stall the proceeding by boycotting it thus preventing there being a quorum. Luckily for the Loyalists they had a slight majority and had managed to get everyone in the hall. After the secretary called the roll he announced they were short one vote for a quorum.

Angry cries came from the Loyalists anxious to elect a new Chancellor immediately, but the rules were clear that no business could take place without a quorum. Basset shook his head angrily and looked at his chief of staff.

"Who's missing? I thought we had enough for a quorum."

"Two of our Assemblymen are in the hospital. They were injured in the building collapses."

"Well, get them here. I don't care if you have to roll them in on their hospital beds, but get them here within the kyloon."

"Yes, sir," his chief said and hurried off.

Basset punched in Nic's number on his GC. "Any sign of the TGA?" he asked.

"Yes, they are disembarking right now from a dozen transport planes at the airport just outside the dome."

"Are you going to be able to stop them?"

"We can stall them for a while. We have thousands milling around each entrance ready to create havoc if need be."

"Good. What about inside?"

"There are twenty thousand mutants, rhutz and Seafolken already on the Capitol grounds. If they see any troops they will immediately block their path."

"Alright. We didn't have a quorum when the session was called to order, but we expect to have one momentarily."

"Good. We'll hold them off. Don't worry," Nic assured him.

Basset hung up as he heard sirens in the distance. He looked up and prayed that it was the ambulances bringing his two delegates to the session.

Videl Lai was in command of a convoy of TGA soldiers ordered to secure the Capitol Building and the Great Hall of the World Assembly. Although his orders were simply to secure the area, his intention was to clear both buildings and send the assembly and its members home. As long as they could not meet, they could not elect a new chancellor. When the convoy turned the corner to the long boulevard that approached the Capitol Building they met a huge crowd packed so tightly that no vehicle could get past.

"Move those people out of the way!" Videl ordered.

A line of soldiers ran up in front of the crowd. One of them had a voice amplifier and he ordered the crowd to move aside and make way for the caravan. The crowd ignored him.

"Move aside now or you will be arrested for interference with a military officer."

The crowd tightened up even more and stared defiantly at the soldiers.

Videl got out of his PTV and gave the crowd a once over.

"A bunch of mutants and Seafolken. Damn them! Fire on them if they won't move."

The soldiers raised their weapons and pointed them at the crowd but as soon as they did each of the rifles went flying out of their hands. The embarrassed soldiers ran after their weapons only to have them inexplicably take flight again. The soldiers looked at Videl and shrugged.

Videl pulled his revolver quickly and began firing at the crowd. People began screaming and started to turn to retreat when a dozen rhutz came running through the crowd at the unarmed soldiers. Within a few tiks they were ripping the soldiers apart. Shots came from more TGA soldiers farther back in the caravan. A rhutz went down with a painful whimper. Hearing the wail of the beast, the crowd stopped their retreat and began moving forward again. The soldiers in the rear began moving forward shooting into the crowd. Suddenly there was gunfire from the buildings on both sides of the boulevard. Several soldiers went down. Videl looked up at the snipers and cursed.

"Get in those buildings and flush out those snipers."

The crowd pushed by the lead vehicles in the caravan. Videl shot several of them but was soon forced to retreat or be caught in the middle of the crowd and be torn to shreds.

Two ambulances pulled up to the loading dock behind the Great Hall of the World Assembly. The injured assemblymen were helped out and pushed into the hall in wheel chairs. Once they were seated Chairman Ruskin Walt called the session to order and the secretary started once again taking roll. Suddenly Purist members began filing in not wanting to be left out of the selection process. Basset Als let out a sigh of relief. The secretary announced there was a quorum.

The chairman noted the emergency meeting had been called, pursuant to Article 7, Section C of the World Assembly's Charter, to select a new chancellor since both the sitting chancellor and vice chancellor had been killed in the previous day's attack by the nanomites. The chairman called for nominations. Assemblyman Tash stood up and raised his hand. The chairman nodded his way.

"I nominate Chairman Ruskin Walt for the position of Chancellor of Tarizon," Tash said.

Another assemblyman stood up. "I second the nomination."

Basset Als frowned at the nomination. It was a clever ploy

calculated to thwart the Loyalist from electing one of their own as Chancellor. Chairman Ruskin Walt was from Morissee in Lower Azollo, a neutral country that never took sides on any issue. The chairman didn't have a political philosophy. He was an opportunist and would support whoever offered him the most for his support.

Another assemblyman stood up and the Chairman nodded. "I nominate Basset Als," he said.

The nomination was seconded and the Chairman asked for further nominations. After a moment of silence someone moved to close nominations, it was seconded and the Chairman announced since he was a now a candidate he was relinquishing his position as Chairman to the Vice-chairman.

The vice chairman rose and took the podium. "We will recess for one kyloon and then reconvene for each of the candidates to address the Assembly before a vote is taken this afternoon."

Basset Als was not pleased with the delay as he didn't know how long the TGA could be kept at bay, but there wasn't much he could do about it since a kyloon certainly wasn't an unreasonable amount of time to let the assemblymen consider how to vote. If he objected to the delay he might alienate some of the voters and he couldn't afford to do that.

He wondered what he should say to the Assembly. He hadn't prepared this speech as there simply hadn't been enough time. He started making notes of possible topics to cover. His GC buzzed. It was Nic.

"So, how is it going out there?" he asked.

"We've managed to keep the TGA out of the city so far but they are losing their patience and I think soon they will have too many troops for us to hold back. I heard there is now a quorum."

"Yes, and the Purists have put up Chairman Walt to oppose me."

"Well, that's a good choice for them. They know they can buy his allegiance."

"Yes, and anyone who votes for him can say they didn't take sides since he is not a member of either party."

"So, how do you think it will go?" Nic asked.

"It will be close. We have a razor slim majority but if we lost even one vote we could lose."

"We'll be praying for you."

"Thanks," Basset said and disconnected the GC.

Videl Lai looked out over the crowd frustrated that they'd been unsuccessful at breaking through the crowd and getting to the Capitol Building. Suddenly he got an idea.

"Sergeant. Order me six jet copters. We'll load them up and fly over the crowd."

"Yes, sir," the sergeant said punching a code into his GC.

Several loons later the sound of jet copters coming in from central Shisk could be heard. When they landed the soldiers climbed aboard and one by one the copters took off toward the Capitol Building.

As his copter was rising quickly over the crowd Videl saw a pack of rhutz running fast toward the Capitol Building. "Shoot them," he ordered.

The soldiers nearest the doors took aim and began shooting, but the rhutz were running through the crowd and hitting them was almost impossible. Several mutants were hit and went down but the rhutz made it to the Capitol Building unscathed.

As the first jet copter began to land two rhutz used their telekinetic abilities to launch a public bench at it. The bench got caught in the rotors causing sparks and a fire to break out. As the rotors slowed down the copter lurched, then tilted badly and began to fall. When it hit the ground the fuel tank ruptured and it burst into flames. There were obviously no survivors. The other jet copters circled a few times but didn't dare land.

Chairman Walt took the podium to give his address to the Assembly. He was a handsome, polished politician with an endearing smile. An elder statesman, he'd served his state well over the years and was very popular.

"Ladies and gentlemen, citizens of Tarizon, I am honored that you have nominated me as a candidate for Chancellor. It has been a dream of mine for 40 cycles to be the leader of the world and I believe I am well suited for the task.

"I say I am well suited because I am an independent thinker and I don't subscribe to any philosophical beliefs. It is my philosophy that as circumstances change our response to the challenges we always face often require rethinking our values and principles. Anyone who thinks their ideals or their political doctrine is always the right prescription for every challenge we face is deceiving themselves.

"Nobody worked harder than I did to get the Supreme Mandate adopted by all nations of the world. I love and cherish it. It brought us decades of peace, but God has challenged us like He has never done before with these volcanic eruptions and other natural disasters that threaten our very existence.

"Two cycles ago had anyone said we should abridge any of the civil rights guaranteed by the Supreme Mandate I would have been aghast. But circumstances have changed and our very existence depends on decisive action; action that may require suspension of some of our beloved civil liberties; action that might favor one life-form over another, not that one is better than the other, but that one has a better chance of survival than the other."

There were cries of outrage in the audience. The Chairman called for order.

"Who would have thought a cycle ago that our great capital city of Shisk could be laid waste by a life-form that the average citizen didn't know existed. The nanomites came before the Supreme Council of Interpreters seeking recognition as a sentient life-form to be afforded all civil liberties guaranteed by the Supreme Mandate. The Supreme Council made its decision and the nanomites lost. But they couldn't accept that decision and chose instead to seek revenge.

"The nanomites obviously despise the Supreme Mandate as they have chosen to step on the rights and liberties of thousands of citizens of Shisk and Fasoon and we can't let them get away with it!"

Many delegates came to their feet applauding and screaming their approval.

"I respect all the life-forms on Tarizon but this is not a time for war amongst ourselves when our very existence is in jeopardy. It's a time for compromise and statesmanship and I believe I am the best candidate to bring that about. I will be open to any and all ideas as how best to restore Tarizon's ecology, maintain peace, and ensure a prosperous future. Thank you."

Many in the Great Hall were on their feet clapping, stomping their feet, and yelling their approval. Chairman Walt nodded and left the podium. A moment later Basset Als stepped up and the hall quieted.

"Let's not forget the eight world wars that killed over a billion of our citizens and nearly destroyed our planet. It was a time of utter despair and horror. I too worked hard to bring peace and hope to our people with the adoption of the Supreme Mandate, but I will never advocate ignoring any of the rights and civil liberties it guarantees!"

Many stood up applauding and yelling their approval.

"When we wrote the Supreme Mandate, we knew there were incredible challenges ahead and that it would be tempting to abridge the rights of some for the benefit of others, but that philosophy is what fueled a century of war. We knew it was critical that basic civil liberties would always be protected so that the people would always remain in control of their government through their elected officials. For too long tyrannical regimes controlled many of our states and waged war to protect their own self-interests. The cost of that in lives and suffering is incalculable. The Supreme Mandate abolished tyrannical government on Tarizon forever and we must defend the Supreme Mandate to our death. There can be no compromise when it comes to our freedom and liberty!"

The crowd responded with more applause and cries of support.

"I do not condone what the nanomites have done to our capitol city. They have killed our Chancellor and laid waste to much of the city. Their conduct is inexcusable. But let's take a look at what brought about war.

"Two cycles ago our government asked the nanomites for help in restoring construction on Tarizon. The nanomites had no reason to do this, but they were promised in a written contract that if they did their numbers would multiply and they could live peacefully in the buildings they constructed.

"But before the ink was even dry on the contract those who were responsible for the project, Berne Baldrige and Rupra Bruda, decided to breach that contract and deny the nanomites the right to live in the buildings they built and to ensure that they could get away with this flagrant breach of contract, they committed genocide on the nanomites of Fasoon, killing millions of swarms, and concealing that atrocity from the government and the people.

There were cries of outrage in the audience as well as displeasure for defending the nanomites.

"I only found out about this a few days ago. But this knowledge certainly makes the events of the last few days more understandable. The important thing is this war could have been avoided had the Supreme Council properly interpreted the spirit as well as the letter of the Supreme Mandate. How can you enlist a life-form to build structures like the Hall of the Supreme Council of Interpreters and then deny that they are a sentient life-form protected by the Supreme Mandate?

"If I am elected I can end this war with the nanomites immediately. The nanomites are a peaceful life-form and do not want war. They only want what was promised to them in the beginning. If you elect Chairman Walt the nanomite war will go on and you have seen what devastation they can inflict on us without warning. This war needs to end now and I can make that happen!"

Again, assemblymen rose yelling and screaming their support or opposition to Basset Als' words. Some of the members got so worked up they began pushing and shoving each other and a fist fight broke out. Security officers were quickly dispatched to restore order.

"We have successfully negotiated an accord with the American government on Earth which will allow a million of our citizens to go to Earth to conceive and raise their children in a clean and wholesome environment and then return with them to Tarizon to guarantee many healthy generations in the future. This is a wonderful opportunity for us, but there are those who would have us desert our planet and forcibly inhabit Earth. These are the same people who want us to suspend or even abolish the Supreme Mandate until this crisis is over. These people are the same ones who condone genocide and believe they can rule Tarizon better than the people themselves.

"I'm not saying Chairman Walt is one of these people, because I know he is not. But he is too anxious to compromise fundamental principles and thereby a dangerous man to lead us now. There can be no compromise when it comes to our civil rights and democratic government. We must uphold and defend the Supreme Mandate at all costs! We cannot allow tyranny to return to Tarizon. Thank you."

The hall broke out in excited conversation. A chorus of "No more tyranny" began ringing trough the Great Hall. Security again was dispatched to quell the pushing and shoving and several fights that broken out. Basset Als left the podium and the vice chairman stepped up.

"Thank you. Thank you. Now the secretary will conduct the ballot."

The secretary took the podium. "Thank you, Mr. Vice Chairman. You will have ten loons to record your vote."

Lights suddenly flashed on a large screen above the podium. The two names, Ruskin Walt and Basset Als, suddenly appeared. Numbers started flashing beside each name. Walt 43, Als 44. The members broke out in conversation. There were screams of delight and despair as the numbers changed. Walt 57, Als 54. Basset looked at Nic and shifted in his chair.

"It will be all right," Nic assured him.

"Holy Sandee!" someone screamed as the tally went to Walt 99, Als 105.

Basset looked away. He couldn't bear the suspense. So much was riding on this vote. What would they do if he lost? It couldn't happen. This war had to be stopped. Tarizon couldn't stand any more destruction. The numbers changed again. Walt 289, Als 281. Basset's heart sank. Nic put his hand on his shoulder. He shook his head. "How many votes left?"

"570 voted, 251 to go," General Zitor replied.

"Oh, God. Please. We can't lose this."

Once more the tally changed. Walt 369, Als 371.

"There we go! That's better," Nic exclaimed. "Only 81 more votes. You're almost there."

The board was quiet for a moment. Everyone looked around to see who hadn't voted. The vice- chairman stepped up to the podium. "Last call for votes. If you want to vote you must do it in the next 100 tiks."

The number 100 appeared on the top of the vote tally. It began counting down 99, 98, 97. The tally changed again: Walt 389, Als 391.

There were screams of anxiety from members all around as the countdown continued—57, 56, 55. The tally blinked again. Basset stared at the numbers: Walt 401, Als 400. His body stiffened. Nic shifted nervously in his chair. "Come on! Just eleven more votes."

The vice chairman looked up at the voting board, but said nothing as the countdown continued—37, 36, 35. There was a flicker and Basset looked up anxiously at the tally. Walt 407, Als 408—20, 19, 18. Nic closed his eyes. He couldn't stand it—11, 10, 9. Basset sighed deeply. "It's going to be okay!" Nic promised. Finally, there was one last blink as time ran out. Walt 410, Als 410.

The vice chairman looked at the secretary. "It appears we have a deadlock. Mr. Secretary there appears to be one assemblyman who didn't vote. Is that true?"

The secretary stood. "Yes, I'm afraid it is, sir. Assemblyman Tossef from the Beet Islands just collapsed and had to be taken to the casualty center."

The vice chairman nodded. "Very well, then according to the Rules it appears I must break the tie," he said looking rather pale. "Ah. Just give me a minute to confer with the Secretary and then I'll cast my vote."

The room broke out in a flurry of conversation as the fate of Tarizon was about to be decided. Basset Als was quickly surrounded by well-wishers, so Nic backed away from the gathering crowd and scanned the room looking for Chairman Walt. His eyes finally settled on him and then on the man standing next to him. It was Rupra Bruda!

Videl Lai was patched-in to a conference call between General Bratford, Colonel Lugwin and Rupra Bruda. He was angry and disappointed that the TGA had been unsuccessful at taking control of the city and shutting down the World Assembly. He wracked his brain for an acceptable excuse for the debacle.

"Lt. Lai. What's the status of securing the Capitol Building?"

"Ah. We haven't been able to get to it, sir," Videl said. "There is a large crowd blocking our way and snipers all along the boulevard."

"So. You let an unruly crowd stop you from carrying out an order!"

"No, sir. There were a pack of rhutz and—"

"I don't want excuses. Why haven't the troops I sent moved into the city?"

"Ah. There are huge crowds blocking all the entrances, packs of rhutz and many Seafolken doing everything they can to keep us out," Colonel Lugwin replied.

"What? Are you all a bunch of cowards! From what I am told the World Assembly is about to elect a new chancellor. If that happens we have lost an excellent opportunity to seize control of the government. Your incompetence may cost us everything."

"Excuse me, General," Rupra interrupted. "The situation may not be so bleak."

"And how is that?" General Bratford spat.

"I am in the Great Hall and I have been working with our party leaders to make sure that there would be an acceptable outcome from the voting."

"Okay. How is that coming?"

"We have backed Chairman Walt to be the next chancellor of Tarizon. He is an independent and very popular with his colleagues. He's also a practical man and realizes things must change on Tarizon if it is to survive. You should have heard the speech I wrote for him."

They all laughed heartily.

"Well, that sounds promising. Do you think he can be elected?"

"Well, they have just taken a vote and it is a tie momentarily."

"A tie?"

"Yes, and the vice chairman is about to break that tie."

"How do you know he will vote for Walt?" the General asked.

"Because I just told him that if he didn't vote for Chairman Walt I would choke him to death on the podium. I even gave him a demonstration of my ability so he would have no doubt that I could do it."

There was a moment of silence. "I hope that works, but it could backfire on you if he reports your threat to anyone," Videl interjected.

"Don't worry, I am in his head. I know everything he is thinking. He's mine, trust me."

"All right. Report back to me the moment the new chancellor is elected," the General ordered and terminated the connection.

Nic studied Rupra Bruda wondering what he was up to. He had a steady gaze on someone. Nic searched to see who he was looking at. It was the vice chairman who was conferring with the secretary and didn't look happy. Suddenly he realized what was happening.

Nic closed his eyes and thought of Falling Star. "Yes, Nic. I am here."

"Are you outside the Great Hall right now?"
"Yes. I'm with my pack."

"Rupra Bruda is inside and I'm sure he is trying to steal the election. I need you and your pack to break into the great hall and distract Bruda so I can get to the Vice-Chairman and assure him he is safe."

"We're on our way" Falling Star assured him.

Falling Star and five other rhutz immediately charged the front entrance to the Great Hall. The two security officers at the door tried to stop them but two of the rhutz attacked them while the other four entered the building. Once inside they raced toward the Great Hall. More security officers tried in vain to stop them but didn't even slow them down.

Once they got to the door of the Great Hall two officers were there with their guns drawn but before they could shoot both the guns flew out of their hands and fell to the ground a few strides away. The rhutz raced past them and into the Great Hall then split up looking for Rupra Bruda.

Rupra Bruda kept a steady gaze at the vice-chairman. He could feel the great fear and trepidation in his mind. The vice chairman glanced quickly at Rupra then at the podium where everyone was expecting him to go to cast his vote. He started to walk slowly to the podium when Nic put his hand on his shoulder and told him something.

Bruda frowned and scowled at Nic. Suddenly he heard growling behind him. He swirled around quickly and saw a rhutz bearing his teeth at him. Then he heard another growl to his side and spotted a second rhutz ready to pounce on him.

The vice chairman took the podium and glanced over at Rupra Bruda who was now surrounded by four rhutz. Then he looked at Nic who gave him thumbs up. The vice chairman swallowed hard. "Alright, I have confirmed that I indeed have the right and obligation to break this tie vote."

Bruda turned around and tried to concentrate again on the vice chairman but Daylight lunged at his arm pulling him to the ground. Several security guards finally arrived on the scene and started hitting the rhutz with night sticks.

The vice chairman looked over at the scuffle and smiled. "So, I hereby cast my vote for Basset Als to be Chancellor of Tarizon!"

The members favoring Basset Als went wild. The rhutz quickly scampered away from the security officers and ran out of the Great Hall. Bruda was helped up by a security officer and escorted away. As he was leaving he looked back at Nic and raised a fist angrily. Nic smiled triumphantly.

38

The Prophecy

After the vote Daylight contacted Allo of the nanomites and gave him the news that a Loyalist had been elected Chancellor and that he wanted to end the war and make peace with the nanomites. Threebeard, Nic and Artis also contacted him and assured him there would be no retaliation for what had happened in Shisk. Allo tentatively agreed to the accord subject to further negotiation of the exact terms.

That night the Loyalists threw a big party to celebrate the election of Basset Als as Chancellor. Everyone in the government was invited but the Purists understandably did not show up for the celebration. After the last guest departed in the early morning hours Chancellor Als, his chief of staff, Nic and Captain Shilling got on a video conference with Threebeard and General Zitor.

"Congratulations, Mr. Chancellor. You really came through for us."

The Chancellor shook his head. "No, it was Nic and the rhutz who really saved the day."

"Yes, so I heard. Well, now that we have managed to thwart the Purists one more time, I fear they will be looking for a way to get revenge. I know from talking to Captain Shilling that they are already plotting to subvert our Tarizon Repopulation Project on Earth."

"Yes, and they will be trying to get their hands on the Intergalactic Fleet that is being built on Clarion," Captain Shilling warned.

"I'll make sure that doesn't happen," the Chancellor assured them.

"How are they going to subvert our efforts on Earth?" Nic asked.

"I don't know for sure," Captain Shilling replied, "but they are spreading a lot of gold and precious stones around trying to buy influence for something."

"Fortunately, Rammel Garciah is there to keep an eye on them."

"We need to get someone else to keep an eye on the Purists on Earth," Threebeard disagreed. "We need Rammel Garciah back on the Supreme Council of the Interpreters. The court is split now with him gone and we certainly cannot afford any more decisions like the reversal of Broggin and Zahn's convictions."

"That's true," the Chancellor agreed. "We'll send a replacement with the first wave of guests going to Earth."

"Good," Threebeard said. "On another topic the nanomites have agreed to work out a peace treaty. They have no interest in further bloodshed."

"That's excellent news," the Chancellor said. "I can't believe the devastation they've cost in just a few days. We really underestimated them."

"Well, we didn't really have any experience with them. Everything was going fine until Rupra Bruda got in the picture."

"I feel partly responsible for that," Threebeard said. "I should have sent Nic or someone else to help Artis on the project. She has no political instincts."

"I doubt that would have made any difference," Nic disagreed. "The Purists will do anything to get what they want. If Falling Star and her pack hadn't been handy when I happened to see Bruda up to no good, the Purists would be in control of the government right now."

"Yes, thank God and Sandee for that," Threebeard said. "I fear that because of their lack of any moral constraints that we will have a very difficult time keeping them at bay, particularly with the continued deterioration of our situation here on Tarizon."

"I agree," General Zitor said. "There are seven now in control of the TGA. Unfortunately, four of those have embraced the Purist party. Most of the soldiers will remain loyal to their commanding general, so I think there is little chance we can avoid civil war. The Purists care little about the Supreme Mandate and one day they will outright repudiate it."

"If there is a war," Nic asked, "do you think we could win?"

General Zitor shrugged. "I don't know. It would be an uphill battle."

"Yes," Threebeard agreed. "I think a majority of the people would be behind us, but in a long war they would lose hope. They'd need something very powerful to believe in to get through such an ordeal."

"Like what?" the Chancellor asked.

"Nothing short of divine intervention, I'm afraid."

The Chancellor snorted. "Well, I believe God and Sandee are on our side but so do the Purists. So, unless you have figured out how to communicate with God and actually get a meaningful response, I think we'll have to stick with building a strong army. Speaking of which, how is your mutant army coming along, Threebeard?"

"Pretty well, actually," Threebeard said proudly. "We have ten thousand pretty respectable soldiers who have almost completed their training. They are being groomed to be our officer corps for our fully mobilized army of one million."

"Good. We're going to need every last one of them, I'm afraid."

"Indeed, we will," General Zitor agreed.

"Well, thank you, gentlemen," the Chancellor said. "I'm exhausted so I think I'll try to get some sleep. Tomorrow will be a busy day."

After the meeting Nic took a sky cab to Capitol Station on his way to the Mighty Jolly. It was early in the morning and the streets were deserted. He was exhausted and just wanted to get in his bed and sleep for the next two days. As he turned a corner he saw the bright lights of the Mighty Jolly in the distance. As he was coming to the alley where Misty used to hang out he felt badly that she'd been so brutally murdered. Then he thought of his friend Eyeball who'd been like an Uncle to him. A profound sadness came over him. He wondered how many would die before the human race would come to its senses. He was just about to the alley when he heard a noise. He stopped abruptly, but before he could react Rupra Bruda, dressed in black and wearing a mask, stepped out with a laser and fired three short bursts. The first one hit Nic in the chest, the second in the stomach, and the last one took off his left arm. He fell to his knees and was dead before he hit the pavement.

Bruda dragged the body into the alley and dumped it into a trash disposal unit scheduled for pick up the next morning. At breakfast Shellee realized Nic hadn't returned from the party and called over to the Chancellor's office.

"No, he left kyloons ago, right after our video conference early this morning," the Chancellor's aide reported.

"Thanks. I'm going to call the PE. I've got a bad feeling about this," Shellee said.

Shellee called Chief Stegis who she'd worked with after the attack on Threebeard. "Is it possible he was so tired he stopped at a tavern near the party?"

"No. No way. He always stays here when he is in Shisk and I talked with him before he left yesterday. He said he'd see me after the election was all over. I knew he'd be late when I heard Basset was elected. They always have a victory party after these affairs, but when he hadn't shown up by breakfast I knew something was wrong."

"All right. I'll get working on it. If he should show up in the meantime call me immediately."

Chief Stegis decided to walk to the subtram station along the route that Nic most likely would have followed. When he passed the alley he remembered that's where Misty used to live before she was murdered. He stopped and looked down the alley. A disposal truck was making its way up the alley picking up the previous day's refuse. There was an odd smell in the air that got his attention. He took in a deep breath and recognized it immediately. It was the smell of blood.

He started down the alley looking carefully on the ground and then he saw it—streaks of blood as if a body had been dragged along it. Realizing the disposal truck would be there shortly he called his office and asked for backup to seal the alley. Then he started checking the individual disposal units and in the third one found Nic's body.

Threebeard and Artis were devastated by the news of Nic's murder. They knew that Rupra Bruda was behind it but couldn't prove it since there were no witnesses and lasers didn't leave any kind of signature. Several days later everyone of any importance in Shisk gathered for Nic's funeral. It was a sad occasion as Nic was loved by all and had been a hero that very same day by stopping Rupra Bruda from stealing the election. The new Chancellor insisted on delivering the eulogy.

"Although I didn't know Nicirius Nocteris or 'Nic' as his friends called him, as well as I would have liked, I often heard of his selfless efforts to establish a line of communication between humans and the rhutz. The dire need for this was made self-evident after the recent Flat Meadow Massacre. At his brother's request and because he was a true patriot, Nic dropped everything to make sure such a misunderstanding between these two life-forms never happened again.

"Not only do we now have a constant dialogue going between the rhutz and the humans, but the rhutz have become an important ally in our response to the recent natural disasters that have plagued Tarizon these past few cycles.

"And if was not for a rhutz I wouldn't be here today as your new Chancellor. It is no secret that Rupra Bruda attempted to steal the election for Chancellor away from the people for the purpose of seizing power by trickery and deceit. Had it not been for Nic this conspiracy would not have been discovered.

"Although we may not have the necessary evidence right now to prove Rupra Bruda is responsible for Nic's murder, it is likely he or one of his co-conspirators is responsible for this horrific act. The obvious motive was revenge for Nic's spoiling of their plot.

"But I want to assure everyone that we will find Rupra Bruda and all those who aided or abetted him in this attack on our democracy and the killing of Nicirius Nocteris and they will pay the ultimate price for their crimes!"

As the Chairman stepped down a choir began singing *Praises for a Fallen Hero* and the mourners began filing by the open casket to see Nic one last time before he was laid to eternal rest in a grand mausoleum to be constructed by the nanomites as a gesture of good will and to honor a new era of peace between the two life-forms.

The reconstruction of Shisk began immediately. Chancellor Als wanted the war with the nanomites to be forgotten so that they could get back to work helping to restore the worlds' infrastructure that had been so badly damaged over the past few cycles. It was while the debris from the Tuht Tower was being cleared away that an ancient tunnel was discovered far beneath the city. Archeologists were called in immediately to excavate the site and were thrilled to certify that it had been a part of the ancient city of Tuht from the Soni civilization that flourished in the region some two thousand cycles earlier.

After several phases of excavation, the tunnel led to a large circular room that experts thought might be a place of worship. On the walls of the room were beautiful pictures and inscriptions. One of the inscriptions was of particular interest and some even said it was a prophecy.

There were several different translations of the prophecy as scholars couldn't agree on the meaning of many of the words in the ancient language. And nobody knew when it was written or the identity of the prophet who wrote the inscription as it was unsigned. Nevertheless, the public began to believe in it, as it offered hope for the future at a time hope was so desperately needed. Eventually one version of the Prophecy became most popular as it seemed to speak to the times.

> *When the sun and the moons align,*
> *amongst the Earthchildren will come*
> *one wise and pure in heart.*
> *A man of humble birth,*
> *who'll tame the savage rhutz,*
> *unite those who'd have liberty*
> *and justice restored to Tarizon,*
> *and rid it of its evil tyrant.*
> *Known as The Liberator,*
> *he'll restore the Supreme Mandate*
> *and free from bondage*
> *the mutants, Seafolken, and nanomites.*

When Earth Shuttle 26 along with 99 other shuttles left for Earth there was an intense excitement about the adventures that lay ahead for those leaving Tarizon, but there was also a great anticipation of what the travelers would bring back with them. Several million healthy human children would be a shot in the arm for the dying planet, but what would these Earthchildren be like having grown up in an environment so different than Tarizon? And how would the returning parents be changed by the experience of living in America where life was so very different than it was on Tarizon? Nobody knew the answers to these questions. There would be much debate and speculation about them, but in the end only time would bring answers.

Meanwhile on Clarion, Tarizon's largest moon, the Intergalactic Fleet was in the final stages of construction even though its original purpose was no longer relevant. But while the Loyalists were overwhelmed by the seemingly insurmountable problems that faced Tarizon each day, the Purists continued to plot to overthrow the government and gain control of the Intergalactic Fleet.

About the Author

William Manchee

William Manchee makes a living as a consumer lawyer practicing in Dallas, Texas with his son Jim. Originally from Southern California, he lives now in Plano, Texas. Writing is his passion and his novels are in the genres of mystery, science fiction, and suspense. His works to date include the Stan Turner Mystery series (11 volumes), the Rich Coleman novels (3 volumes), the Tarizon Saga (5 volumes) and stand-alone novels, Uncommon Thief and the Prime Minister's Daughter. He's also written a non-fiction work for small business owners, Go Broke, Die Rich.

Other Works by William Manchee

Stan Turner Mysteries
Undaunted
Disillusioned
Brash Endeavor
Second Chair
Cash Call
Deadly Distractions
Black Monday,
Cactus Island
Act Normal
Deadly Defiance,
Deadly Dining

Rich Coleman Novels
Death Pact
Plastic Gods
Unconscionable

Science Fiction
Tarizon: Shroud of Doom
Tarizon: The Liberator
Tarizon: Civil War
Tarizon: Conquest Earth
Tarizon: Desert Swarm

Romantic Suspense
The Prime Minister's Daughter
Uncommon Thief

Non Fiction
Go Broke, Die Rich

9 781929 976867